Snug Harbor Tavern

Jacob,

A real patriot.

Bill Shinn 2011

Snug Harbor Tavern

Shaggin' for a Shillin'

WILLIAM E. JOHNSON

To order additional copies of this book, contact:
Xlibris Corporation
1-888-795-4274
www.Xlibris.com
Orders@Xlibris.com
37140

Dedication

To James and Helen Johnson, parents who set no boundaries.

ACKNOWLEDGMENTS

Jeanne for her encouragement, editing and declaring war on my errant punctuation. Carol for her constant demand for more.

Elizabeth Collopy, wherever she is. English teacher, extraordinaire, who gave me a real appreciation for the written word.

Charles River

Charlestown Ferry

Copp's Burying Ground

Old North Church

Salutation Tavern

Revere House

Mill Pond

Old State House

Hancock Wharf

Snug Harbor Tavern

Boston Harbor

Old Granary Burying Ground

Green Dragon Tavern

Faneuil Hall

Hancock Mansion

Long Wharf

British Coffee House

Common

Bunch of Grapes

Edes's Printing Shoppe

Griffin's Wharf

Sam Adams House

Boston Neck

Boston
1768

PROLOGUE

March 22, 1765
London, England

T HE CLATTER OF heavy hooves on the frozen cobblestones shattered the quiet dawn of the city. A royal blue carriage bearing the crest of the prime minister of Great Britain rumbled through the fog-shrouded London streets, making its way to Buckingham Palace. When the four black steeds, their nostrils belching steam in the frigid air, stopped at the main entrance, a liveried footman opened the carriage door. Out stepped Prime Minister George Grenville, flawlessly decorated in elite attire, though his wrinkled brow exposed his disheveled mind. With nary a nod to the servant, he rushed to the door emblazoned with the royal seal. Each long stride was taken with determination. Another servant in red silk livery escorted him down the main hallway and up the stairs to the king's private chambers. The king's secretary, seated at a small table, arose and bowed courteously.

"Good morning, my lord. This is a bit of a surprise. How may I help you?" he asked subserviently.

"It is imperative that I see the king at once. In fact, he should be expecting me," Grenville replied impatiently, his tone smothered with condescension.

Trying to conceal a look of disdain, the reedy secretary excused himself. "I shall be back momentarily. Please be seated, your lordship."

Grenville, made to wait as usual, paced the anteroom, scanning the sheaf of documents he clutched in his sweaty hands. It wasn't much more than a few minutes later when the secretary returned and escorted him into a larger reception room. Here he was again left alone with only the company of a single gold gilt chair upholstered in red velvet, situated on a dais. A small table was positioned in front of the lone chair. Again, Grenville found himself pacing, lost in his thoughts. Twenty minutes later, a rear door opened; and George III, king of Great Britain, clad in a blue brocade riding habit, marched briskly across the room to the chair and seated himself without a word. The two men stared at each other in awkward silence until King George finally addressed his visitor.

"Well, my lord prime minister, what could be so pressing that I must delay my morning ride with Lord Bute?" He rapped his riding crop hastily against his glistening boots, awaiting a reply.

Lord Grenville cleared his throat as he shifted his weight from one foot to the other. "Please forgive the intrusion, Your Majesty, but I need your signature on these documents as soon as possible."

Lightly sipping from his glass of claret, King George licked the droplets from his bulbous lips. His bulging gray eyes absorbed Grenville's obvious discomfort. He disliked George Grenville, finding him small-minded, grim, and quite long-winded. To spite him, he had intentionally ordered the room cleared of all furnishings, save those for his personal use. King George refused to allow any comfort to this nuisance of a man.

"Do proceed, Lord Grenville. I have a busy schedule today," commanded the king, as his eyes wandered to the window.

"As you know, Your Majesty, with pressure from the banks and merchants, we have been forced to reconsider our stance on the Stamp Act. Hence, the Parliament has repealed this tax upon the American colonies, and it merely requires your signature to complete the documentation." Wiping the moisture from his hands onto his leg, he placed the documents on the table.

The king pursed his lips. "Just a year ago, you told me of our being mired in debt to the tune of more than £129,000,000, due to the Seven Years' War with France. Further, you told me it was time for the colonies to pay their fair share of what they called the French and Indian War by imposing this stamp tax. It would require that all legal documents, writs, and bills of sale must bear the official seal of the Crown; said stamped documents would be purchased for a fee." Each word resounded against the bare walls as his momentum gained.

"Now you suggest that I ratify a repeal of that very same tax that would erase part of our financial burden. This wavering does not appeal to me one damned bit, my lord prime minister; not one damned bit!" The table shook beneath the impact of his pounding fist as his final words exploded in the air, leaving a cloud of discomfort in the room.

Grenville, taking a step back, responded meekly, "This has been debated at length in Parliament, Your Majesty. The rioting in the streets of the major cities in America has been most alarming."

"We have an army over there, for god's sake! Let them take the rascals in hand."

"Riots are one thing, Your Majesty. But the real problem was the refusal to use the required stamps; it has stopped all courts, trade, and commerce. The London merchants are losing trade and profits, forcing many into bankruptcy. We have no choice at this time, lest we have rioting in the streets of London as well," Grenville pleaded.

The king's hard glare suddenly morphed into a sardonic grin. "The key words are 'at this time,' Lord Grenville." Taking up a quill pen, George III signed the document repealing the Stamp Act. Pausing to regain his thoughts, he continued.

"Now, my lord, I still need funding for the expansion of Buckingham Palace; don't shirk your duty to the Crown. And, furthermore, I expect my Parliament to get creative in clearing up these finances. My American colonists love me, I'm sure. They will bear any tax burden I impose, if the imposition is done properly. My American subjects will simply acquiesce, as little sheep. Don't forget that they have seen the supreme might of the British army on their own soil. In fact, they fought at our side. We have no reason to worry ourselves about this taxing trivia."

"Their cry was No Taxation Without Representation, Your Majesty. It seemed to be a battle cry of sorts," argued Grenville, as he folded the signed documents.

"Who would say such a thing? It's an affront to the Parliament and the Crown, for god's sake," grumbled the king.

"Our agents from the colony of Massachusetts and Governor Bernard tell us of a radical named Sam Adams. He seems to enjoy stirring up the masses in that particular colony."

Rising from his chair, King George downed the last of his claret and swiftly waved Grenville away. "Keep us advised of this Massachusetts situation. Now I'm off for my morning ride. This paperwork is most tiring."

ΩΩΩ

Meanwhile, the heavy mix of sleet and snow blistered the small windows in the cramped, dingy upstairs room of a small house near the waterfront in Boston, Massachusetts. Sam Adams, clad in his threadbare nightshirt, struggled to control the quill pen in his palsied hand. His eyes strained in the dim candlelight as he composed his latest editorial for the *Boston Gazette*. He knew it was risqué attacking the tyranny of the Crown and Parliament, but it was a worthy cause. Freedom could only be obtained by shedding the shackles of England and declaring independence. His objective was to, first, oust Governor Bernard and get all of Boston and Massachusetts behind his just cause of renouncing this "taxation without representation." The rest of the colonies would soon follow; he was sure of it. His quill scratched deliberately and rapidly across the paper under the pen name of Publicus. Sam realized that his enemies were powerful and his friends were few, but the rights of man were on his side.

ΩΩΩ

CHAPTER 1

Boston, Massachusetts
May 15, 1766

ZEKE TEEZLE TUCKED his bony neck deep into his collar against the wind-driven rain. Creeping along the dark of the Boston waterfront and trying to maintain his balance on the slippery rounded cobblestones, his eyes adjusted to the blackness that enveloped him. The wind whistling through the rigging and the jutting bowsprits presented an alien environment for him. He was much more accustomed to the cozy confines of his small candle shop farther from the waterfront on Milk Street. It was three hours past sunset, and in the darkness, he was very careful to keep to the shadows of the alleyways to conceal his passage.

He hadn't told anyone what had happened. Based on the mere information he was given, there really wasn't much to tell at the present time. But this evening, he hoped to find answers to the questions that tormented him throughout the day. For, earlier that afternoon, his typical routine was interrupted by a torn piece of paper. The mysterious note he found on the counter of his candle shop read simply,

> *15 May 1766*
> *Teezle. Urgent!*
> *Snug Harbor Tavern. Three hours after sunset. Ask for Charity.*
> *The enclosed shilling is for the one behind the bar.*
> *Tell no one about this. Your life is in the balance. Be there!*

Ω

Teezle, sweating profusely at the collar, glanced furtively up and down Fish Street for signs of being followed. Assured he was alone, he rushed across the muddy street to the candlelit windows of the Snug Harbor Tavern. As he entered, he found the taproom filled with sailors, tradesmen, and merchants exchanging gossip and arguing over their pints of rum or ale while the doxies of the waterfront plied their trade. Pipe smoke wafted to the ceiling while the candlelight and fireplace created friendly shadows dancing throughout the warm glow of the tavern. The mixed odors of pine tar, clam chowder, cheap perfume, sweat, spilled rum, and ale assaulted his nostrils.

In the corner, an off-key chorus of bawdy song pounded his ears:

> *The groom was a man named Loren*
> > *Who found that his bride was borin';*
> *She went to sleep,*
> *And he made a leap,*
> > *To the Snug Harbor for whorin'.*

The laughter and gaiety was contagious in the Snug Harbor Tavern. The strumpets made certain the patrons enjoyed themselves – for a shilling.

He needled his skinny frame through the crowd to the bar, which was chest high for a man of his stature. Everyone knew that you couldn't order a drink in the taproom unless you could see over the bar; this kept youngsters from drinking before their time. Carved into the ceiling beam behind the bar, he read,

It's Your Life: Live It; Love It; Critics Be Damned!

Amos the barman, a massive hulk of a black man with a barrel chest and well-muscled arms asked, "Would you care for a pint, sir?"

Teezle leaned closer and, nearly spitting through his five yellow-stained teeth, said quietly, "Actually, I'm looking for Charity." Amos gave a hearty baritone laugh. "Now ain't we all? You won't find any Charity here," he responded for the enjoyment of anyone within earshot.

"But I have the shilling," whispered Teezle, with urgency in his voice and holding the coin tightly pinched between his boney fingers, as he glanced around fearing the attention the barman had attracted.

Suddenly, Amos received a jab in the ribs. He looked down to find Amanda Griffith glaring at him. "You didn't have to hammer me ribs, Ms. Amanda," he said, grimacing. Her stern topaz blue eyes suddenly softened, as she smiled. "I'll take care of this, Amos," she said, pushing his heavy body aside. She now turned her twisted smiling curiosity in Teezle's direction.

Amanda Griffith was not a beautiful woman, but nature had endowed her with an ample bosom and a keen sense for business. Her seafaring husband had gone to sea and never returned. As a widow with no children, she initially sublet a few rooms of her rented harborside home to boarders in order to survive. Her reputation for serving the finest New England clam chowder and fresh bread brought more sailors to the dinner table. One winter evening, an old salt, just in from the Indies, noted that it was good to berth in a snug harbor again. That evening, the Snug Harbor Tavern was born, as rum, punch, beer, and ale were added to the menu.

Amanda, ensuring that her cleavage jutted well above her bodice, accenting her narrow waist, gazed into Teezle's eyes, as if she could see his soul. "What was it you were asking for, luv," she asked. "And what was that about a shillin'?"

Teezle, taking off his tricorn hat, was uneasy in this company and, using all the bravado he could muster, said in his all-too-squeaky voice, "I was told to ask for Charity and give this shilling for you behind the bar." Amanda gave him a knowing look and, snapping the shilling from his trembling hand, said in her husky voice, "We have many girls on the slate this evening, but I haven't seen Charity. But you just might find her in her room on the second floor; that's room D. Leaning closer, she added, "Are you sure you wouldn't like a pint of rum and perhaps a little tumble?"

Shaking his head nervously, Teezle hastily rushed to the back of the taproom. He paused to read what was painted in red above the stairway:

Shaggin' for a Shillin'

Wiping his nose on his sleeve, he retreated up the creaky stairs to the appointed rendezvous. From a distant corner table, one of the girls observed the passing of the coin and nervously shifted her gaze to the stairway.

As Teezle ascended the stairs, Amanda looked at Amos. "I wonder what that little runt is up to. He doesn't really fit the rigging of our normal drunk and horny sailor, does he, Amos?"

Looking at the stairs as he poured a tankard of ale, "It don't take a genius to spot a goat in a flock of sheep. Now he might not be a goat, but I've learned to judge white folks by their eyes, and those little beady eyes of that fella spells trouble to me, Ms. Amanda."

Upstairs, Teezle came to a dead stop before the door of room D at the end of a darkened hallway. For a moment, his mind flirted with the idea of running back to the safety of his shop; however, his simple curiosity and sense of false bravado forced his shaking hand to rap on the door. From the other side of the door, a deep, raspy voice said, "Enter!"

He found a rather fat man of average height opening the window slightly at the rear of the dingy room. "I must dissipate these mixed olfactory blessings of mildew and cheap French eau de cologne," the stranger said condescendingly, as he remained facing the window and the harbor beyond. The dim light of a small flickering candle created dancing shadows on the walls.

Who was this portly fellow, and what did he want? Teezle wondered to himself. He mustered a meek perfunctory cough to announce his presence.

The fat man grimaced at the thought of face-to-face encounters in these tawdry surroundings, hoping he wouldn't be recognized. And he realized his disguise of an ill-fitting, tattered blue seafaring jacket and fop hat did little to conceal his sense of culture and disdain for the fleet rabble. Nevertheless, he felt these rags would bring less attention to him on this occasion.

He was certainly no stranger to the waterfront because business sometimes required his coming here; however, on those public occasions, he dressed in high fashion, more in line with his profession. But this night, a low profile was required because his profession had little to do with the nasty business at hand.

He had arrived early by the back stairway, with arrangements having been made by his apprentice. The room served as both home and business to a strumpet named Charity, who conveniently made herself scarce for a mere shilling. He stared at the vast expanse of Boston Harbor, but his focus was on Hancock's Wharf.

As he turned from the window, he did his best to conceal his surprise at the sight of Teezle standing there. He recovered his composure with a fabricated cough and, with a tone of authority, said, "I did not expect you here personally, Mr. Teezle. Did our girl not give you instructions at the bar?"

"What girl? What instructions? A lady took the shilling, but there weren't no instructions, sire," muttered Teezle.

The fat man grimaced to himself, realizing that somehow the wrong person had been working behind the bar. He hardened his gaze, as Teezle remained timidly standing by the door, shifting his weight awkwardly from one foot to the other.

Teezle couldn't see the fat man's face, which was concealed by the fop hat and dancing shadows of the flickering solitary candle. But he noticed the silver buckles on his shoes and a gold signet ring on his right hand; these did not go with a tattered mariner's garb. He stepped forward to get a closer look.

His forward motion was halted, as the portly stranger raised his voice, "Stay where you are, Mr. Teezle. You needn't come closer; it will be better for you. Trust me on this. However, more to the point, we know about you; and you have been selected."

"Selected for what, your lordship?" asked Teezle, his hands trembling.

The fat man smiled to himself, enjoying the discomfort he was imposing on Teezle. "We have learned of your loyalty to King George. Unfortunately for you, so have the Sons of Liberty. There are those who call you 'Teezle the Tory.' If you continue voicing your opinion, things shall become difficult for you," he said, looking for a response.

Teezle, fiddling with his tattered tricorn hat and mustering a bit of courage, spoke up, "I don't take back my words. You high Sons of Liberty will suffer when the king sends his army. I know that for certain, I do!"

The fat man laughed aloud. "Relax, Mr. Teezle. I'm . . . er, we are on your side. Or, I should say, that you are on our side. However, we must be smart. Will you work with us?"

"Who is 'us'?" asked Teezle.

"Who we are is not important. The fact that you can be trusted and well paid for a service is the issue tonight."

At the sound of being well paid, Teezle's curiosity for details ebbed, and he pretended to understand. "I'm a candlemaker. What could you need of me?" he asked.

"The first thing you must do is keep quiet about your loyalty to the Crown. In fact, you must begin to speak of your love of liberty in order to earn the trust of your fellow tradesmen, like Paul Revere."

"You mean the silversmith? The fellow who lives just around the corner?" he asked. "Why, he's almost as bad as Sam Adams and not to be trifled with."

"Exactly," said the fat man, raising his finger to accentuate the point. "You are a very smart man, Mr. Teezle. But we must learn more about these men, about Hancock, and about Adams and Otis . . . from someone we can trust. That someone is you . . . a man of the Crown."

Teezle smiled. He was now recognized as a "man of the Crown." Suddenly, his short skinny frame felt taller and stronger. Recognizing this, the fat man added, "It would be wise for you to also use an apprentice as your eyes so as not to draw too much attention to yourself."

"Aye," said Teezle. "Emmet Glunt is my apprentice."

"I've seen him before. Are you certain we can trust that chubby bastard to keep his mouth shut if he gets caught?" he asked sharply, trying to remain in the shadows cast by the dim candlelight. "I know you can be trusted, but I know nothing of this Glunt."

Teezle was suddenly concerned about his tawdry country homespun attire and the trust it inspired. He tried to seem confident, as he nervously picked wax from his fingernails. Seldom in the company of the landed gentry, he responded, "Glunt has been my apprentice for many years, and he follows orders to the letter." However, that little voice in the back of his mind prayed that Glunt could keep his mouth shut and stay clear of trouble for a change. He continued, "I could use him to spy on the other apprentices. But what exactly do you need to know, sire?"

"The greatest concern is their hiding weapons for an insurrection. Do they have muskets, cannon, powder? How much and where? These are the things we need to know. You must keep your eyes and ears open. We also know that Hancock is a smuggler. We need to know who is helping him, when his smuggled goods are expected and his shipping schedule. Do you understand me?" queried the fat man, raising his voice, as though he was lecturing a slow student of the obvious. Teezle began to quiver at the thought of weapons and spying on the squire.

At the clamor of a sudden rap on the door, the fat man growled, "What is it?"

A female voice responded meekly from the hallway, "Your note, sire; I have it here in my hand."

"Slide it under the door," he said sternly. "I'll talk to you later about this."

A note sealed with wax, bearing the "Ω" impression, appeared under the door. "Pick that up, Teezle; it's for you," ordered the stranger.

The strange fat man, adjusting his fop hat to ensure that it half covered his face, said, "We must know what the Sons of Liberty are about, Mr. Teezle. This will be the last time we meet, for secrecy's sake. Hereafter, all your orders will come through others. Besides, I'm not comfortable meeting in this place."

Teezle asked, "How will I know this contact comes from you? And just who are you, sire?"

The stranger smiled. "Just don't you worry who I am; it is best that you don't. Be satisfied that you will be well paid for any information you provide. As for those who contact you, they will have messages sealed in wax with the same signet mark, the sign of the Omega, like the one on that note. The messengers will ask if you have been to Concord; you will reply "Not today!" You will seldom see the same courier because secrecy is paramount in our organization. Do you understand?"

Nodding in agreement, Teezle asked quizzically, "What is the 'Omega,' sire?"

"Don't you concern yourself with the Omega; to you, it is simply a signature and assurance of your security," snapped the rotund stranger, still in the shadows.

"As your lordship wishes! My wife would be quite upset if she knew I was visiting the Snug Harbor Tavern. I pray we can meet elsewhere," said Teezle.

The fat man, glaring at Teezle from under the brim of his hat, said curtly, "I told you we will not meet again. But come to think of it, the Snug Harbor Tavern is the perfect place to pass information. It is always noisy and crowded; meetings are hardly noticed by anyone. If you have a message for me, leave it here with Charity. She will get it to me somehow. Just make sure there are no mistakes. That sealed note in your hand is to remind you of your orders, with a golden guinea inside for your trouble. Stop in the taproom for a pint before you walk out the front door and put a satisfied look on your face. Remember, I was never here, and you came here for the common shagging with Charity," said the stranger.

Teezle ripped open the note and grasped the enclosed golden guinea. At the same time, the fat man stepped to the door, pausing long enough to notice a small pile of wax shavings on the floor where Teezle had stood. Teezle had been nervously slaking candle wax from under his fingernails the entire time. Shaking his head in disgust, the portly stranger rushed out the door and disappeared down the back stairway.

With a puzzled look on his face, Teezle tucked the note into this shirt. He gripped the golden coin tightly in his fist and crept back downstairs to the taproom, where the reverie continued. Amanda Griffith, ever vigilant of those who ventured upstairs, watched Zeke Teezle wander meekly toward the bar. "Have you decided to join us for a tankard or a tumble? Now that you have finished with Charity, perhaps you'd like a little romp with Purity, Chastity, or Faith. It seems that Hope is already occupied." She nodded toward a large-buxom lass, sitting on the lap of an old balding sailor, as they continued their off-key chorus of ribald songs.

Teezle, glancing furtively around the taproom and wanting to follow the fat man's orders, stammered, "Perhaps a pint wouldn't hurt, would it?"

Amanda watched as Teezle nervously sipped his ale while she occasionally glanced around the room. She nodded to one of the girls to make her move. At that, Chastity, exposing her ample cleavage, brushed up to Teezle at the bar. "Buy a girl a pint, would you, you handsome man?" she asked. Teezle, unaccustomed to such behavior, hugged his tankard to his puny chest, saying, "But I'm a married man."

Chastity responded, "Come on, luv, I'm not asking you to walk me down the aisle. But how can you refuse the warmth of a pint of flip to a poor girl on a rainy night?" Teezle shuffled his feet, as if preparing to leave, but then he remembered the golden guinea the fat stranger gave him. Besides, he thought, what could be the harm in having a pint with a lady. "A pint for the lady," ordered Teezle with newfound bravado, as he puffed up his otherwise sunken chest. Amanda poured one for Chastity and another for Teezle.

After Zeke was well into his second pint, Amanda casually asked, "How was his lordship?" Her deep blue eyes seemed to penetrate his skull.

"Just fine," retorted Teezle, without thinking. Immediately regretting his lapse of discretion, he continued, "Er . . . I don't know what you are speaking of. As I said, I was looking for someone, and I found him . . . er, her . . . in room D, as you said I would." At that, he guzzled his pint of ale, scampered to the door, and rushed out into the driving rain.

Amanda had merely suspected that the meeting upstairs with "Charity" was a different kind of rendezvous because Charity had left with a sailor hours ago. Now she knew for sure. But she wondered, *Who it could be? And why Teezle the Tory?* She made a mental note to watch Charity more carefully.

Amos, carrying a keg behind her, was laughing. "That skinny fella sure left in a hurry. He wasn't up in the crib for very long, was he? I swear, some men folks is like rabbits!"

Still in deep thought, Amanda smiled. "You don't miss much, Amos. Men around here usually have one of three things on their minds: the Thirsties, the Hungries, or the Hornies. If I see him without an erection, I give him ale and bread. That skinny fella wasn't thirsty, hungry, or horny; he didn't fit. Where's Imp?" she asked Amos, as he tapped the fresh keg.

Amos shrugged. "I don't know where that little rascal is."

"When you see him, tell him I have a message for him to deliver," she said, as she left the bar heading for the stairs. "If you need me, I'll be in my room."

ΩΩΩ

CHAPTER 2

May 16, 1766

THE FOG HAD already burned off by midmorning; and Emmet Glunt cursed the sun, the heat, and especially his master Zeke Teezle. He had hefted his pudgy frame atop a barrel of fish located midway up the length of Hancock's Wharf. His beady black eyes, seated deep in his chubby face, peered from under his dirty brown tricorn hat, as he made mental note of the waterfront hustle and bustle. His attention was drawn to a small crowd at the entry to the wharf.

In the midst of the crowd, John Hancock strutted down the length of Hancock's Wharf, smiling at the expanse of his domain. It was humid with the threat of rain again in the salt air.

Hancock was not a large man, standing a mere five feet four inches, but few seldom considered his stature when, at age twenty-nine, he was the wealthiest merchant in Massachusetts Bay colony. It was his policy to greet each of his merchant ships upon arrival. Wearing a burgundy-colored velvet coat neatly accented with gold buttons and trim, he was dockside to greet the captain and crew of the Brig *Harrison*, one of four merchant vessels he owned. His attire, accented by his gold-knobbed mahogany walking stick, certainly set him apart from those who wore sweat-stained homespun, as they toiled with sails, cargo nets, and barrels.

It was an hour before noon, May 16, 1766, when the *Harrison* settled into her berth at Hancock's Wharf in Boston; she was six weeks and two days out of London, England. Hancock waited patiently, bantering with his clerks.

Meanwhile Sam Adams, dressed in the only well-worn red suit he owned, paced at his side in a high state of agitation. His stockings were gray as his hair, but no one could deny the burning spark of life in his gray eyes. Adams, at age forty-three, was not a patient man; however, he was in his element with the out of work sailors, ropemakers, and the salty dogs of the wharf. Years ago, he had lost his job as a tax collector because he was reluctant to pursue those unable to pay. This reputation endeared him to the dregs of society and the fleet rabble, as he called them in private-cultured company. Pounding his walking stick, he muttered, "What's holding things up, John? Can't we simply jump aboard? After all, it's your boat, isn't it?"

Hancock chuckled, "Take it easy, Sam. There are proprieties to observe with sea captains, in case you didn't know. And, by the way, it's a ship, not a boat."

"Boat! Ship! Who cares?" mumbled Adams.

Emmet Glunt jumped behind the fish barrel to conceal himself, as ordered by Teezle. To the casual observer, he was simply idling the day away, watching the sailors mend sails and repair rigging on Hancock's Wharf. Actually, Emmet was a nine-year-old apprentice chandler to Zeke Teezle, and he normally worked with tallow in the candle shop. Today, however, he was ordered to simply sit on Hancock's Wharf and watch, without being noticed. Mr. Teezle had said, "If you see any strange activity with John Hancock, report it to me immediately. Watch for cannon and powder. And don't be seen or get caught. Do your job well, and there's a shilling in it for you."

As he pondered the shilling he would receive, he keenly watched Hancock's arrival in the company of Sam Adams, who had made his reputation as a failed tax collector in Boston – and as a troublemaker. With his focus on Hancock, he disregarded the well-orchestrated chaos on Hancock's Wharf. He didn't realize that Imp Smythe, just approaching Hancock's Wharf, had caught sight of him.

Imp, a short, wiry, unkempt, and unwashed wharf urchin was a well-known favorite on the waterfront, and he "knew the ropes," as the sailors said. He didn't like Emmet Glunt and knew he didn't work near the wharf. *Glunt didn't belong here, in* his *part of Boston,* he thought to himself.

Imp's mother had died when she bore him eight years ago. His father, a sailor named Smythe, went to sea a few days later, leaving his newborn son in the care of the widow Amanda Griffith, who operated the Snug Harbor Tavern. The day he set sail, Smythe told Amanda, "I be thankin' ye for carin' for the little imp. I promise I'll be back in three months."

Amanda, looking sadly at the infant, said, "I'll care for the child until you return, but no longer. What did you name the boy?"

Smythe held his infant son high in the air saying, "I don't know much about names. Why don't you name the little imp?" With that, he rushed out the door. It was the last anyone ever saw of Smythe in Boston. Many speculated that either the ship sank or he simply abandoned his life in Boston for the adventures of the West Indies. Remembering Smythe's last words to her, Amanda started calling the little boy "Imp." And so did the Boston doxies who helped raise him at the Snug Harbor Tavern.

Now at age eight, he slept on a cot in a small back storeroom of the Snug Harbor Tavern, which he shared with Amos, the barman. He survived by running errands for merchants, tavern keepers, and ladies of pleasure on the waterfront. Behind his back, he became known as Imp the Pimp to the multitude of apprentices in Boston.

Imp, as he neared the Brig *Harrison*, rubbed the scar on the side of his neck, which reminded him of the score yet to be settled with Emmet Glunt. Imp first met Glunt a year earlier, when he accompanied one of the Snug Harbor strumpets named Charity to Teezle's Candle Shop. Glunt, ogling the pretty young doxy from behind the counter with his shifty eyes, rudely yelled, "How many pence for a tumble, whore?"

A heavy silence filled the candle shop. Prostitution was quite common in Boston, but polite society provided a quiet acquiescence of the profession. Imp, his hands on his hips, said angrily, "What is that you said?"

Glunt grinned boldly. "Well, if it ain't Imp the Pimp. I asked the damned whore how – "

Suddenly, little Imp leaped across the counter, pounding Glunt in the face. Glunt, being a bit heavier, pushed Imp aside and tossed a ladle of hot candle wax at his assailant's face. Imp quickly feinted to his right to avoid the spill, but some wax severely burned the left side of his neck. The massive hands of Amos, the Snug Harbor barman, grabbed both boys, "I suggest you two stop it afore someone really gets hurt."

Zeke Teezle, rushing from the back room, yelled, "Glunt, get back to work. What is going on here?" Upon learning of Glunt's insult, Teezle apologized, looking up at the hulking Amos, "I'll set the boy straight; that I promise. But you keep that little ruffian on a leash."

The hot wax had left a burn scar as a constant reminder of the evil within Emmet Glunt; he couldn't be trusted.

Earlier that morning, Amanda told Imp to deliver a message for Mr. Hancock, which he held tightly in his hand. He tried to concentrate on his mission, but he had an uneasy feeling about Glunt idling on that stack of sails, when he should be making candles. He didn't fit into the picture, and he certainly didn't belong on the wharf. The Sons of Liberty taught him to look for things that didn't fit. He might be little, but he had his wits and a keen eye.

Soon the *Harrison* was secured to the dock, with the gangplank lowered. Captain Shubael Coffin called from the quarterdeck, "Good day, Mr. Hancock. Please come aboard." At that same moment, Imp yelled, "Mr. Hancock, I have a message from – " But he was too late. Hancock had hastily crossed the gangplank and was lost in the din of activity on the deck.

"Good day to you, Captain Coffin, and welcome home," John Hancock said, with a casual salute. "I trust the voyage was without incident with fair winds."

"Aye, Mr. Hancock, and be assured, we didn't lose one bottle of your cherished Madeira wine. Come into my cabin so that we can hear one another; the noise on deck is deafening." The captain doffed his tricorn hat.

Once inside the quiet of the captain's cabin, Hancock eased himself into a chair while Adams, obviously tired of the formalities and niceties, hurriedly asked,

"What news from London, Captain? Is there anything new from Parliament or King George?"

Captain Coffin, accustomed to storms at sea, was not to be baited by the agitation of a landlocked prima donna. "Calm down, Mr. Adams," he said, as he casually sat down in his captain's chair. He slowly and deliberately searched through a stack of charts and bills of lading, until he found the document he was looking for. "Ah, here it is the March 18 copy of the *London Gazette*. You will be happy to note that His Majesty King George, meeting in the House of Peers, has repealed the Stamp Act."

"Well," said Hancock, looking at Adams and smugly leaning back in his chair, "It seems that all our clamor and noise was heard after all, Sam. Our problems with Parliament, Lord Grenville, and King George are over; and we can now get back to business as usual."

"I wonder," replied Adams, as he hurriedly scanned through the paper. "It's true. The Stamp Act has been repealed. But it is not like King George to submit so easily, John. I doubt he will accept having his nose tweaked for long. And I still think we should have readied ourselves for armed conflict; in fact, it might still come. Nonetheless, let's meet with the others at the *Boston Gazette* on Queen Street. Benjamin Edes and John Gill must print this glorious news of our triumph in the next edition."

"Tonight then; at sunset," said Hancock, as Adams rushed from the captain's cabin. Hancock turned his attention to the ship's master adding, "You must forgive Mr. Adams, Captain. Somehow, he has deluded himself into thinking we should prepare for armed conflict and cache cannon and powder around the colony. Your good news has certainly taken the wind out of that argument." Gazing around the cramped quarters, he added, "Now let's get ashore, Captain Coffin. The crew can unload the cargo and the purser can take inventory while we wash down our lunch with a glass of Madeira or a pint of rum, if you prefer."

At the edge of the dock, Hancock noticed the rather shabby, barefoot young boy, pacing the length of the ship. "Mr. Hancock, sir. I have a message for you," Imp yelled, with a sense of urgency in his voice. He approached the ship with his hand containing the note outstretched. Suddenly, a slippery hand ripped part of the note from his grasp and a heavy blow to his back knocked him into the cool waters of the harbor.

It was not uncommon for someone to fall into the harbor or for that matter, for anyone to be running the length of the wharf, so no one pursued the thief with the note. Captain Coffin and Hancock helped a sodden Imp from the water. Immediately Imp said, "I gotta talk to – "

Captain Coffin interjected, "Is this wharf rat bothering you, Mr. Hancock? I'll have one of the men take care of this."

"It's quite all right, Captain. Imp here is quite a fixture here on the wharf. And he delivers the *Boston Gazette* for our best printers, Edes & Gill," replied Hancock, smiling. Turning to the small boy, he continued, "Now tell me what's on your mind today, Imp."

Imp hurriedly explained to Hancock that someone at the Snug Harbor Tavern had a message for him. He felt it smart not to say who sent the message in the company of Captain Coffin.

"Perhaps we should stop at the Snug Harbor Tavern," said Hancock to Coffin. "It is a fine grog shop, Captain." His casual attitude belied his concern. Hancock had rented out the building, now known as the Snug Harbor Tavern, to Amanda Griffith when she lost her husband. Amanda had proven herself to be a wise investment – in more ways than one.

As they made their way down the wharf, Imp adopted the same strut in his stride as that of Hancock. It seemed that all who knew him on the wharf had their eyes glued to the company he was now keeping. Imp reflected that Amanda always said, "A man is judged by the company he keeps." *She was right,* he thought, as he puffed up his chest.

ΩΩΩ

Rivulets of sweat channeled into the crevices of his face, as he skimmed the yellow grease from the tallow kettle. Oblivious to the steaming stench which pervaded the back room, Zeke Teezle mopped his brow with his sleeve as he turned his attention to the array of wick strands he had cut earlier. He turned slowly at the sound of the rear door creaking. Emmet Glunt periscoped his head into the kettle room, which housed barrels of tallow, as if he was a thief. Teezle glared, "Git your fat ass in here, Glunt. What do you think you are doing sneaking around? And just where exactly have you been while I work my fingers to the bloody nub?"

Despite Teezle's tirade, Glunt strutted in with a grin on his face. With great pride and without a word, he handed the note he had snatched earlier on the wharf. Teezle grabbed the scrap of paper and scanned it while asking rhetorically, "What's this?"

His face became ashen as he read,

"about a strange visitor last night. Griffith"

Without looking up from the scrap of paper, he asked quietly, "Where's the rest of this, Glunt? And where did you get it?"

"I was on Hancock's wharf, like you ordered, and I snatched it from a wharf rat named Imp. He was handing it to Hancock himself. You said to get what information I could, and I figured you could use it. Sorry to see it tore itself when I grabbed it." Leaning forward, he asked, "What's it say, Mr. Teezle?"

"You don't worry yourself about what it says," muttered Teezle.

"You said I could have a shillin' for findin' stuff down there, Mr. Teezle," said Glunt, as he shuffled his feet.

Shaking his fist, Teezle howled, "You get nothing for this measly scrap of paper. It tells me nothing. Now get back to that tallow kettle and skim that yellow grease. I have work to do." He slammed the door as he hustled to the front of the shop. His hand began to tremble as he read the note again. "This Griffith woman doesn't miss much," he mused. Looking back at the door, he pondered, "Can't use Glunt again. There were probably witnesses to his snatching this note. I must find a way to contact that fat man. Guess I'll spend more time at the Snug Harbor." Looking at his narrow stairway leading to the upstairs bedchambers, he chuckled aloud. "If Gerty only knew what I have to do!"

ΩΩΩ

Amanda had been watching from the second floor of the Snug Harbor, when some chubby lad shoved Imp into the harbor. Now she realized that Imp was escorting Hancock directly to her, and she was not prepared to meet with anyone. Immediately, she yelled to Amos in the taproom to greet the gentlemen and give them a quiet table.

The sweet aroma of fresh-baked bread, clam chowder, and fresh fish, mixed with the pungent odor of pine tar and unwashed sailors, greeted Hancock as he was led to a quiet table in the rear of the taproom. The idling sailors and ropemakers, sitting at their pints of rum, watched in awe as their own little Imp sat at the corner table with John Hancock, Esq. and the captain of the Brig *Harrison*.

Within moments, Amanda Griffith came down the stairs and seemed to glide to their table, dressed in her finest low cut white dress, which accented her best mobcap, a white circular cap fitted with a drawstring. She didn't miss the fact that both Hancock and Captain Coffin were visibly taken with her ample décolletage and deep cleavage, accented in white lace. Regardless of their station, men were basically the same in their lustful pursuits. *If only her ladies could keep that in mind while taking care of business,* she thought to herself.

In a second, her wandering mind returned to the urgency of the moment, when Imp said, "Amanda, I'd like you to meet Mr. Hancock and Captain Coffin. This, gentlemen, is Amanda Griffith; she owns the Snug Harbor."

"Welcome, gentlemen," said Amanda. "Amos, please bring the gentlemen whatever they desire." Captain Coffin was happy to have a pint of grog while Hancock asked for Madeira wine. A discomfited Amanda said, "I'm sorry, Mr. Hancock, but Madeira is very hard to come by, as you probably know."

Hancock gave her a knowing glance, well aware that Madeira wine was most often smuggled into Boston Harbor. "If I may be so bold," he said, "it would be my pleasure to provide a case for you, in the event that I may visit sometime in the future, Mrs. Griffith." Amanda returned his gaze with her best coquettish smile. Their silent communication spoke volumes while Imp and Coffin sat with them, lost in their own conversation about the sights of London and the Atlantic passage.

Amanda whispered, "Could I speak to you privately, Mr. Hancock? There is something I must show you, and it won't take a moment." They excused themselves, and she led him up to room D. Once inside the room, Amanda turned abruptly, facing Hancock with her hands on her hips. After an awkward moment, her stern look melted into a broad grin as she threw her arms around his neck and pressed her heavy breasts against him saying, "Where have you been? It's been more than a week since you warmed my bed, you rascal."

"Easy Amanda!" replied Hancock uncomfortably. "The good captain will hear you."

Immediately, Amanda stood back, her arms again akimbo, a scolding pout on her face.

"Don't be like that, Amanda!" said Hancock defensively.

"Don't be like that!" mimicked Amanda. "Well, you certainly enjoy a private tumble – when you get the urges. But this public denial of our 'relationship' is driving me to lunacy."

"In time, Amanda! In due time! But you must see my side of this. I have my aunt Lydia to think of; you know that, Amanda."

"What does your precious Aunt Lydia have to do with us?" she growled, her arms folded over her bosom.

Hancock suddenly glared. "Everything I have, I owe to the benevolence of my deceased Uncle Thomas. And my aunt Lydia will make her home with me as long as she needs it. Do you understand?"

Amanda turned her back to him. "Well, if that's how you feel about us – "

"Amanda, you know you are very special to me," said Hancock, sitting on her bed and patting a space for her to sit next to him. "I simply need time to get Aunt Lydia to warm up to the idea of another woman coming into my life. Now what was that note about?" he asked in a soothing tone.

"I guess you are right. But the sands of time are flowing through the hour glass, Mr. Hancock. And I can't wait forever." Then a smile came to her face and changing the subject, she said, "Last night, Teezle the Tory met someone in this very room."

Hancock smiled. "That's why men come here, Amanda. Your plum pudding is fine, but that's not the menu that draws men to the Snug Harbor; you can trust me on that!"

"It wasn't one of the girls this time, John," said Amanda with a serious tone in her voice.

"What else could it be? And please don't tell me that two men were – "

"Hell no! Not here in the Snug Harbor! No, this was a special sort of meeting with someone more refined than we normally see around here," she said.

Hancock responded, "What has that to do with me? I have very little trade with Teezle."

Amanda shot back, "It's not Teezle, but rather the man he met."

"And who was that?" asked Hancock, his curiosity piqued.

"I'm not really certain, but he went to great trouble to be someone he is not. A common seaman does not have silver buckles on his shoes. And further, a seaman does not pay for a tumble with a lady and not take the tumble. Charity told me about a fat gentleman using her room, just before she departed for a rendezvous last night."

"That is curious. But what has that to do with me?" asked Hancock, wandering to the window.

"Purity . . . that's one of my other girls, just happened to be in the next room over last night. The bloke had the window open, and she could hear half the talking. It seems Teezle is to keep watch on you and yours, if you know my meaning."

Hancock pondered for a moment, then, for no apparent reason, he took Amanda by the hand. *Tumbling was easy,* he thought, *but sharing a common cause with a woman was different.* "I suppose I'd better arrange for you to get that case of Madeira soon. It seems we shall have much to discuss. Meanwhile, we must find a way to keep Mr. Teezle meeting more often at the Snug Harbor. Is that possible?" he asked.

Amanda laughed. "Last night, he came for Charity. With a nudge, I'm sure he can become addicted to Faith, Hope, Chastity, and Purity as well."

"A man can become addicted to those high virtues!" he asserted with a knowing grin.

Again Amanda laughed. "Let me remind you that I'm the only virtue on the menu for you at the Snug Harbor, Mr. Hancock. The others are shopping in the north end at the moment," she said. Rubbing his cheek tenderly, she added, "Why don't we . . ."

Backing off, Hancock said, "Perhaps I can return soon to continue this discussion, Amanda. Right now, there is much to be done. We have learned that the Stamp Act has been repealed."

With an exaggerated curtsy, Amanda responded sarcastically, "I look forward to our next meeting with pleasure, your lordship. No doubt we will be busy this evening, celebrating the demise of the Act." They returned to the taproom, where it seemed that Captain Coffin and Imp never missed them.

Suddenly, the booming baritone voice of Amos echoed from the doorway saying, "I don't care what you want or who you are; no strumpets are permitted in the Snug Harbor without the permission of Ms. Amanda."

"But I was told that Captain Coffin was here, and I must see him," retorted a petite, yet curvaceous young lady.

At the sound of his name, Captain Coffin rushed to the door with Amanda at his side. Amanda, annoyed at the interruption, growled, "What is the meaning of all this?" Her ire was further agitated by the stunning high-fashioned dress of azure blue silk the lady was wearing. A white ostrich feather accented her heavy mane of bright auburn hair, which cascaded over her shoulders.

Captain Coffin smiled. "It's quite all right, Mrs. Griffith. This lass was a passenger on the *Harrison.*" Turning to the petite beauty, he asked, "What can I do for you, Ms. Cross?"

"First, you can let me in off the street. It's enough that I've been cooped up on that ship with all those men. Must I now suffer the indignity of begging an audience with you from the street?" she retorted.

By this time, Hancock had arrived at the doorway and, smiling, said, "I'm sure Mrs. Griffith would permit your admittance. Captain, would you please escort the young lady to our table and offer her a refreshment of some sort."

"Of course, Mr. Hancock; this way, Ms. Cross, if you please," said Coffin, solicitously offering his arm.

Amanda, glaring at Hancock and noting his lustful look at the new arrival, exclaimed sarcastically, "I suppose you feel she deserves a glass of Madeira also!"

As they all sat down at the table, Captain Coffin introduced everyone, adding, "Let me formally introduce Ms. Angel Cross. We had the pleasure of her company in the crossing from London. I wish the accommodations had been more to your liking, Ms. Cross."

Angel, tossing her mane of auburn hair, coquettishly said, "I suppose there is always room for improvement, especially the food."

Hancock, taking note of her green eyes, said, "I'm sorry you feel that way, Ms. Cross."

"I was speaking to the captain, Mr. Hancock. This is none of your affair," she said testily.

Suddenly, Imp began to interject, "But Mr. Hancock is the owner of – " But he was interrupted by a nudge from Hancock. Amanda noted that Hancock was not one to share too much information.

Captain Coffin asked, "Exactly, what is it that you needed to see me about, Ms. Cross?"

I have a letter of introduction from Dr. Lyle Leary in London to a Dr. Benjamin Church. Where might I find this Dr. Church?"

Imp jumped to his feet, saying, "I can take you there. His place is not too far from here."

Captain Coffin added, "Where would you like your trunk delivered, Ms. Cross?"

Angel, revealing a note of doubt, seemed to stumble for an answer. Hancock came to her rescue saying, "Why don't you just leave the trunk at my warehouse on the wharf until Ms. Cross finds suitable living arrangements. Someone will be there till late this evening, since there is much to do with the *Harrison* cargo. Is that satisfactory to you, Ms. Cross?"

Angel gave him a demure look. "Thank you, Mr. Hancock. That is very kind of you." Looking at the little boy, she continued, "Imp, show me the way to Dr. Church." She paused at the door and looked back at the table. *It seems that she was underestimating this man in the fine clothing*, she thought.

Amanda sat at the table with her arms folded tightly across her breasts, unable to conceal her distaste for Angel's demure act of petulance and coquettishness.

Hancock and Coffin, oblivious to the subtleties of female fencing, finished their drinks and left immediately back to the *Harrison*. Amanda, standing at the doorway, snapped, "Amos, when the ladies return from shopping, we shall have a small meeting. And if you ever see that Angel woman around here again, let me know, especially if she is in the company of Mr. Hancock."

Amos leaned on the bar and chuckled, "That Angel woman seems to me to be a lady of some refinement, if you ask me, Ms. Amanda!"

"Well I ain't askin' you!" growled Amanda. "And furthermore, I'm willin' to bet that there is a lot of devil in that green-eyed "Angel." Now when the girls get back, call me. We should have a meeting before sunset."

Amos, wiping down the bar, asked, "Well, I never miss a good chance to shut my mouth! But what's the meeting about, Ms. Amanda?"

"It seems that we might find a way to sell more than drinking spirits and little tickles at the Snug Harbor," she said, as her gaze continued to rest on the back of John Hancock, as his visage faded into the madness of activity on the wharf. "Besides, there will be celebrating tonight, with the repeal of the Stamp Act. You'd better tap another barrel of ale," she added, turning to the bar.

She patted Amos's large scarred hands, knowing full well that those scars were the result of his acting as enforcer at the Snug Harbor. The ladies were always safe with Amos around. More than one sailor had been on the receiving end of his wrath. And besides that, he was the protector and father figure to Imp.

ΩΩΩ

CHAPTER 3

WHILE ALL THIS occurred on the wharf, Governor Francis Bernard, age fifty-six, smiled as he sat with his feet propped on his large mahogany desk in his office at the Old State House on King Street, reading the latest official dispatches from London. Lifting his eyes from the papers, he said, "Thomas, will you please stop pacing. You will wear out the rug."

Lieutenant Governor Thomas Hutchinson, at fifty-five years of age, paced with an aristocratic strut that belied his years and amplified his six foot height. His slender build, coupled with a fair, almost delicate, complexion further magnified his pomposity. Looking down his nose at the governor, he said in a haughty voice, "You may think this is the end of it, Francis, but I know these Boston radicals. This mad multitude is a totally contemptible gaggle of foreign seamen, servants, Negroes, and other persons of mean and vile conditions."

Shifting in his seat, Bernard glared at him. Having graduated from Oxford and admitted to the London bar in 1737 and having served as governor for both New Jersey and Massachusetts, he was not about to be lectured to by this colonial-bred popinjay. "You forget yourself, sir. Keep in mind that you hold your office at my pleasure. As governor of Massachusetts Bay Colony, my primary concern is to enforce the will of King George and the British Parliament. This was proving to be most difficult, and the Stamp Act had nearly caused a rebellion. Now it has been officially repealed by the king. We can now expect peace to prevail. I am sure of it."

Hutchinson smiled, saying, "My apologies, sir. No disrespect intended. It's just that since last August, I and my family have received the brunt of fire from the Boston mob, and I don't trust them one iota."

Bernard nodded and, lighting his clay pipe, said, "Yes, I am mindful that the mob destroyed your home, robbed you, and pillaged the possessions of you and your family." He blew a whirling cloud of smoke across the room, adding, "But the town has reimbursed you for your loss, Thomas. Besides, if you recall, I was forced to flee to Castle William in the harbor that same evening. Hell, I remember trembling that night, and I was behind those ten-foot thick walls of the fortress with batteries of cannon to protect me. We are of the same mind, Thomas, but we needn't aggravate the situation further."

Hutchinson added, "Don't tell me about aggravation, when the real problem is agitation; and the real agitator is Adams. I tell you, Sam Adams and his rabble cannot be trusted. You may think the repeal of the Stamp Act is the end of it, but I know better. That mob enjoyed their mischief, and not one of them was ever prosecuted or even persecuted for it."

"Thomas, I've appointed you chief justice of the superior court, and you have served as lieutenant governor since '58. With that power and influence, both administratively and in the courts, it seems that you should have brought someone to justice for all that rioting over the act," said Bernard.

"These radicals are nothing but liars and cheats. Sheriff Greenleaf told me that everyone seemed to have an alibi for everyone else. If we believed them all, it would mean that everyone in Boston was either in bed or in a tavern while my home was ransacked and nearly razed," said Hutchinson, wagging his finger in the air for emphasis. "I'm still trying to reassemble my notes on the History of Massachusetts, which were found strewn in the mud, along with all my clothing and dishes. Even the decent citizens have been cowed into temporary amnesia, fearing retribution from these radicals. I can still see my wife and children rummaging through the mud trying to salvage what they could. It was disgraceful. That's what it was – disgraceful and humiliating." He paused to straighten the lace at his cuffs.

Suddenly, there was a rapping at the door. "Enter," commanded Bernard, without taking his eyes from his irate lieutenant governor.

He glanced at the door and upon seeing Hubert Slank, his secretary and aide, Bernard growled, "I told you that I wasn't to be disturbed, Slank."

Slank took great pride in his status as a "gentleman's gentleman," and he knew how to make his employers feel superior. He reduced his normal erect military bearing, learned from his father who had been a sergeant major in the King's Own, and stooped slightly. Meekly, Slank slinked into the office saying, "If you will excuse the interruption, sir. But a strumpet of obvious ill repute just left this note for the governor."

Bernard took the note from Slank's long bony fingers asking, "Did she say anything?"

"No," said Slank, "only she added that the fat man said it was important."

Scanning the note, Bernard said, "That will be all for now, Slank. You may go about your business. I will be out for the remainder of the day." Slank, making mental note of all who were present, shuffled out the door. He then resumed his normal bearing and gait, taking pride in knowing he was as well attired as anyone in that room. It was one of the privileges a gentleman's gentleman enjoyed.

When they were alone, Bernard arose and patted Hutchinson on the shoulder saying, "I'm certain that all this trouble is behind us now, Thomas. Our corpulent friend tells me that he has recruited a new spy to keep an eye on Adams and his rich young friend Hancock."

Adjusting the lace at his cuff again, Hutchinson asked, "We have a few merchants watching already. Who is this new one?"

Bernard laughed. "Would you believe it is Teezle, the chandler? He is the first tradesman the fat man felt he could trust. By god, he can fit right in with Revere and the Sons of Liberty."

"I swear by heaven itself that those are the very men who razed my home," said Hutchinson angrily. "Finally, we have someone to watch them on their level."

Bernard, donning a fine blue brocade coat, said, "Temper yourself, Thomas! We must never let the radicals know our real thoughts. Let us go out among the fleet rabble to show them we share in the joy of the Stamp Act repeal. Join me for a glass of Madeira at the British Coffee House on King Street, where we can be seen by all."

ΩΩΩ

It was early evening, near six o'clock, and the fat man sat alone at a rear table of the Salutation Tavern in north Boston near the Old North Church. He sipped his ale slowly from his chubby right fist while his left hand nervously rapped a tempo on the tabletop. He glanced frequently at the door – waiting, as he pretended to read the latest issue of the *Boston Gazette*. Stale pipe smoke filled the taproom, and there were patrons enough to create a din of noise, as the workday was coming to an end.

A lanky, stoop-shouldered old sailor wearing a dirty red stocking cap entered and casually shuffled his way to the far end of the bar. He paused to gaze about the room, noting the presence of the fat man. He gave a subtle nod and turned to the bartender saying, "A tankard of ale, my good man, if you please." When he turned again to face the open hearth, he noticed that the fat man had departed by the rear door. He smiled to himself and shuffled to the seat previously occupied by the fat man, where he found the newspaper on the dirty floor next to the chair leg. He casually opened the paper and began leafing through the pages.

Turning to page four, he found a folded note with a wax seal imprinted with "Ω" He stashed the note, unopened, into his shirt, quickly downed his ale, and shuffled slowly out the front door. Within fifteen minutes, he was alone in the candlelit office of his employer. He broke the wax seal with his bony fingers, and spreading the folds flat, he read slowly:

> *It seems our girl Charity has become greedy – too greedy for her own good. She stopped by my office today, demanding more money. When I asked what the money was for, she said that her silence has a price.*

We cannot afford to have disloyalty in Omega, and she must be silenced. I trust you can handle this. If done properly, it will send a strong message to all the others in our network. Charity must be silenced – immediately!

Ω

The old sailor picked up a quill pen and scrawled at the bottom of the note.

It shall be done – tonight, after sunset.

He left the note in his employer's top drawer and, exiting out the back door, headed for the wharf and the Snug Harbor Tavern.

ΩΩΩ

At nine o'clock that same evening, Sam Adams, seated at the head of the long table in one of the upper rooms of the Green Dragon Tavern, gave a sardonic grin as he peered through the smoke-filled air at the small group of men better known as the Caucus Club. It was owned and operated by the St. Andrews Lodge of Freemasons; hence, considered safe from prying Tory eyes. Many of his friends were lodge members, and their penchant for secrecy was legendary. He relished his position among these men, as the only remnant of significance he could provide to the memory of his father. Sipping his ale, he reflected on how far he had come.

The senior Sam Adams had been a deacon, successful owner of a brewery and civic leader years ago. In order to cope with the government ban on printing currency, he had invested in a joint-stock banking company, issuing script as a promissory note. The British Parliament eventually had declared the venture illegal and the issued script worthless. Suddenly, all investors were financially ruined, leaving the brewery as the sole support of the family. After many years he recovered, enabling his son Sam to attend Harvard College.

Continuing his ruminations, Sam reflected that every business venture he had delved into fell into ruin, for one reason or another. Sometimes he just trusted the wrong people. His problems as a tax collector were still to be resolved in the courts. Now that his father was gone, he maintained a small interest in the brewery, providing small support for his wife and two surviving children. He shook his head at the thought of his three infant children who had been lost to fevers and such. It seems that his skill as an orator and writer made him a natural politician; his disdain for government tyranny and pomposity made him a natural propagandist.

Recovering from his private thoughts, Adams rubbed his hands together to steady his shaking from the palsy and said, "Gentlemen, I'm glad you could all make it this evening. We have much to plan for the official celebration of the Stamp Act repeal. The festivities should commence on Monday, leaving us time for planning and the Sabbath."

Paul Revere, the unofficial leader of the Sons of Liberty, chortled, "It seems to me that much of the town is already celebrating, Sam." Revere, though not as well educated or wealthy as the others, was universally accepted in every Boston meeting, caucus, and club. He was acknowledged to be the best silversmith and goldsmith in the entire town. Average in stature, he was surprisingly well muscled, and certainly, the best horseman in this gathering of civic leaders.

James Otis sat at the far end of the table, puffing on his clay pipe, as he scanned the room with his keen, shifty, beady eyes. He was rather plump, with a round face and short neck. This porcine appearance belied the sharp mind of the most accomplished barrister in the colony. His claim to fame was his successful defense of the colony against Parliament's Writs of Assistance in 1761. The Crown had given customs officials an open warrant to inspect, not only a ship's cargo, but also the owner's warehouses and homes at will. Otis had argued that every man lived in a state of nature and that every man was his own sovereign, subject to laws engraved on his heart and revealed to him by his Maker. No other creature on earth could legitimately challenge a man's right to his life, his liberty, and his property. The Writs of Assistance represented destructive and arbitrary use of power. As a result, from now on, in his opinion, every action from Parliament and the king's ministers had to be weighed carefully to see what motive lay behind it. With this in mind, he raised his ample girth slowly and said in his best barrister's voice, "I'm sure that is true, Paul. But we must do something more formal and grandiose."

Dr. Joseph Warren, sitting at the far end of the table directly opposite Sam Adams, carefully eyed each man at the table. He sat in a relaxed manner, his elbows on the arms of the chair while his fingers formed a tent before his eyes. All knew he was the resident physician to hundreds of wigmakers, ropemakers, sailors, bartenders, strumpets, and even slaves. In addition to the common folk, he also cared for most men at the table and surprisingly many prominent leaders of the colony, including Lieutenant Governor Hutchinson. Hence, he was quite popular with both the lower classes and the better educated wealthy citizens.

Placing his hands around a tankard of ale, Warren said in an almost too casual tone, "Let me remind you, gentlemen, this repeal of the Stamp Act is merely a ruse of Parliament and the Crown. Governor Bernard still has us under his thumb with his control all of the General Court, to say nothing of his dastardly patronage. He has, at my last count, appointed six justices of the peace, fifteen judges, four probate registrars, and three sheriffs. With that kind of support, how can we ever overcome his influence? And now, you have the temerity to rest and acquiesce and suggest we have a party. I am certain that if we do not start gathering arms and powder, we will regret the neglect. Are we not convinced that Governor Bernard and his henchman will eventually call the king's troops to Boston, just as he has nibbled at our rights as Englishmen?" Rising from his chair, he added with a tone of disgust, "Sadly, the poor people of Boston are not aware of this danger. I was doctoring a few tavern maids today, and they tell me that Boston is about to erupt, especially among the unemployed wretches. Extra barrels of rum have been tapped already in most taverns and inns."

Adams grinned. "Let me echo that sentiment. We dare not become complacent. As I said before, I'm convinced that Governor Bernard had his greasy hands in this Stamp Act idea, as he did on the Writs of Assistance years ago. And our focus should be to oust him from office; I'm sick of his personal stamp of nepotism throughout the colony."

Just then the door opened unexpectedly. Adams, without looking up, immediately shouted, "I told you never to enter without knocking." Upon seeing John Hancock at the doorway, his tart demeanor turned to pure honey. "Good evening, John; it's about time you showed up. Who's that with you in the shadows?" he asked, smiling broadly.

Hancock, waving his hand before him to clear the pipe smoke from his face, said, "Someone had better open a window; I can't breathe with all this smoke. And look who I found down below; it's Dr. Church."

Dr. Benjamin Church, greeting everyone with a wave, immediately sidled his ample girth over to his colleague Dr. Warren. "Joseph," he asked, "how busy have you been with your medical practice on the north side of town? I seem to spend most of my time treating an alarming rash of the pox and some new cases of whooping cough on the south side." Nudging Warren in confidence, he asked, "What is Sam's tirade about this time?"

Warren responded, "He's haranguing the existence of Governor Bernard; that's all. As for business, it's nothing extraordinary! Today, I had a visit from a strumpet with consumption. I told her to spend more time in the country. Actually, she had a case of the French disease, but I didn't have the heart to hurt her feelings. God only knows what those sailors deliver along with their cargo from across the sea." In a whisper, he added, "Actually, Ben, I don't know what to say to our friend Revere sitting over there. Another one of his daughters has a fever, and he's already lost one last year with the same illness. That one was little more than a year old. Now little Frances, born this February, has the same thing."

Dr. Church frowned and with a note of sadness in his squinting beady eyes said, "I'm amazed that his wife keeps getting pregnant. Maybe you could help him with mucilage to harness his potency."

Warren responded, "I make it a policy not to recommend such remedies, unless requested. It seems to me that Mrs. Revere is quite content to populate this colony as best she can. Actually, as you well know, many ladies in Boston are of the same mind. Hell, now that I think about it, Governor Bernard himself is the proud father of nine children."

"Perhaps you are right, with the possible exception of the doxies and strumpets of the waterfront. When one of those poor dregs becomes pregnant, there is pure hell to pay," Church added knowingly. "Speaking of ladies," yelled Church to all assembled who had been caught up in their own private discussions, "today I received a young lady, just arrived from London. It seems she was a ward to Dr. Lyle Leary, one of my instructors at medical school. She comes from good family, but her father recently died of a stroke, and sadly, she had lost her mother at childbirth. The young lady, her name is Angel Cross, was left alone in London. Dr. Leary thought it best for her to get a fresh start in the new world. With what little money she could salvage from the family fortune after the debtors finished picking it clean like a flock of vultures, she has been sent into my care to get her started."

Hancock added with a smile, "I met the lady today, Dr. Church. She came in on my ship, the *Harrison*. She seems to be a fine young lady. What will she do here in Boston?"

Church said, "I'm not sure. She can stay at my place for a short time, but my wife would forbid a prolonged stay. Ms. Cross is educated, and she claims to be trained as a seamstress. I'll see if I can get her a position in one of the dress shops."

Adams grunted, "Enough of this about a London tart. Let's get to business. I'm convinced that the governor is behind all this chicanery from Parliament. If we could only get our hands on his official correspondence with those Lords of deception, we could get him removed. I'm positive we could control Hutchinson; after all, he was born here, wasn't he?"

Dr. Church interrupted, "You and your conspiracy theories, Sam. Forget it! Now about this lady from London! And let me inform you that this is the real business we are about. You haven't seen this woman yet, but she looks like an angel and carries herself like a queen. I have a feeling she would be useful to our cause. We all know that the Tories are always trying to learn of our plans. And I think with a little prodding, these same Tories, who are mired in their blind obedience and acquiescence to the Crown, would be captured by the charms of our Ms. Cross."

Revere bluntly asked, "But can she be trusted?"

Church smirked, "She will owe her life and well-being to my care and guidance. She will do as I direct. Trust me on this, and I will handle the whole thing." Hancock, not saying anything, wondered to himself if Angel Cross could really be "controlled," as Dr. Church said.

Revere retorted, "Please forgive my doubts. Obviously, Doctor, you are a man of extraordinary influence. And I suppose she can be trusted to obey your orders."

Sam Adams smirked, "Careful, Ben! If you get to thinking you are a man of influence, just try ordering someone else's dog around." All at the table laughed.

Dr. Church bristled, "She will follow my orders. Trust me!"

James Otis added, "Why are we wasting time discussing about this London lass? On with the celebration plans; we should have fireworks for sure. The children love and adore fireworks; in fact, so do I."

Adams added, "And a formal ceremony on Monday at the liberty tree." Looking at Hancock specifically, he continued, "John, you should make a speech. Otis and I will help write the remarks for you. And, Paul, we need you to be certain the high Sons of Liberty are all there."

Revere noted, "I'll get Mackintosh, and the gangs together and send messengers to Cambridge and Charlestown. Let's keep the children and slaves off the streets and let no bonfires be set, unless we set them. In fact, I believe Mackintosh is down below in the taproom."

Sam Adams scratched his head with his trembling hand saying, "We should have a talk with Mackintosh before he goes off half-cocked with that gang, Paul. Let's do that first thing. And we should have Mr. Otis here at that meeting." Rubbing his chin, he added, looking at Hancock, "And wouldn't it be a fine gesture if all the bills were paid for those in debtor's prison, and we could empty the jails." Suddenly, all eyes came to rest on John Hancock, picking lint from his coat. "All right," said Hancock, after a long pause, "I'll take up a collection from the Merchant's Club and get the poor folks out of jail. And I suppose I should get a few barrels of Madeira ready for the gala."

Adams, though stoic on the outside, smiled to himself on the inside. "*That young man's fortune will soon be dedicated to our struggle*," he thought to himself.

Again, a pounding on the door interrupted the discussion. A young serving wench entered saying with urgency in her voice, "I have a note for Mr. Hancock."

Hancock, upon reading the short note, said, "Gentlemen, I think our plans are nearly concluded, and I must take care of a bit of personal business. You will, of course, excuse me." At that he picked up his gold-trimmed tricorn hat and, adjusting the lace at his sleeves, stepped into the hallway. To the young girl, he asked, "Where is the boy who delivered this?"

"He waits outside at the door," she responded, unconsciously straightening her mobcap.

Hancock rushed down the stairs and out the door. Catherine Kerr, who tended the bar, noted that the squire wasn't usually in a hurry like that. She stared vacantly at the stairway, wondering who else was up there.

Outside, Hancock glanced again at the note and found young Imp pacing in the shadows created by the light from the windows. "Tell me exactly what happened, Imp," he said firmly, holding him by the shoulders.

Imp was shaking. "Amanda told me to get to you as fast as my legs could carry me," he said. "One of the tars from the *Harrison* found her floating face down, just off Hancock's Wharf. That's why Amanda figured you should know first."

"Who was floating off my wharf?" Hancock asked urgently.

"It was sweet Charity," Imp said, with tears in his eyes. *It was embarrassing*, he thought, *to be crying in front of John Hancock of all people.* He so wanted to impress the squire.

"Who is Charity?" Hancock asked.

"She's one of the doxies at the Snug Harbor," Imp said, still blubbering and wiping his eyes and nose on his dirty sleeve.

"That's terrible, but you should tell Sheriff Greenleaf first. It is sad to say, but an accidental drowning is not unusual on the docks," said Hancock. "Besides," he added, "why should I be concerned about a doxy at the Snug Harbor?"

Imp, showing frustration added, "Amanda said that you were in Charity's room earlier this afternoon, and you should know that Charity did not just fall in the harbor and drown. Her face was beaten, and her head bashed in. She was my friend. Who could do such a thing to a frail little maid like that?"

Hancock, pausing to gather his thoughts, said, "I want you to go find Captain Coffin. Tell him that I need him to go to the Snug Harbor and get the particulars about this and report to me first thing in the morning at my home on Beacon Street. After Captain Coffin leaves, you will alert Sheriff Greenleaf. Do not tell him that I am aware of anything. Do you understand, Imp? You have not seen me tonight."

Imp nodded his understanding, although he wondered why. "But I was told to fetch you to the Snug Harbor."

"Just tell Mrs. Griffith that it isn't wise for me to be there at this moment. I will see her soon," he said. "If she has another message, she can leave it with Captain Coffin."

Imp ran off into the darkness back to the wharf. Hancock, looking up at the candlelight flickering from the windows of the Green Dragon Tavern, decided it was best to wander home. This game was becoming more trying. *I had hoped that peace and business would return to normal with the Stamp Act repeal,* he thought. *Now this mess with a doxy; I just wonder!* He turned right down Hanover Street, headed for Beacon Hill and the comfort of his mansion and Aunt Lydia. His mind wandered to Amanda's bosom; and he smiled, musing, *Sex is like air; it's not important unless you aren't getting any.*

He was not aware of the beady pair of eyes watching his every move. The spy elected to follow Imp, knowing full well where Hancock was headed. His furrowed brow showed concern that he couldn't hear what had been said, but he knew that if Imp was headed to the Snug Harbor Tavern; he might catch a bit of news. A small pile of candle wax remained on the ground, where he had hidden in the shadows.

ΩΩΩ

Watching Hancock and the others leave, Sam Adams paused at the bottom of the stairway, gazing through the smoke of the Green Dragon taproom. Standing at his side, Jim Otis said, "I can't see a goddamned thing through all this smoke, Sam." Adams grimaced, "No reason to swear, Jim. Let's be mindful of God's blessings and not his damning. Now where is Mackintosh, Paul?"

"Follow me," said Revere. "He's over here by the hearth."

Mackintosh was a large man, taller than anyone in the taproom, and he arose to his full height as the three men approached. "Please be seated," he said cordially in his gruff voice. "Paul said you might be needin' to talk with me."

As the four men huddled together at the table, Adams leaned forward taking charge of the meeting. "Now, Mac, we think it should be clear to you by now that the Stamp Act has been repealed. Do you and your men understand what this means?"

"Certainly do, Mr. Adams. Means me and my boys scared the hell out the damned commissioners and all them royal officeholders," chortled Mackintosh.

Sam gave a grim smile. "You are quite right, Mac. But now we have to temper our Sons of Liberty. Do you get my drift?"

"Hell, we got the bastards on the run, Mr. Adams. Why stop now?" said Mackintosh in a pleading tone.

Shaking his head impatiently, Jim Otis answered, "Let me explain the law to you, Mr. Mackintosh. Ever since you, as leader of the Southside gang, and Mr. Swift, leader of the Northside gang, have made peace, things have been quiet as we need, with certain exceptions."

"You have that right, Mr. Otis. We sure took care of Mr. Hutchinson, didn't we? His house hasn't been the same since."

Nodding with a grim smile, Revere said, "That sort of thing has to stop, Mac. Mr. Adams here made certain you were appointed sealer of leather these past few years, and that works well with your shoemaking, does it not?"

"Sure does. Ain't no leather used without my seal of approval. I'm doin' a good job, ain't I?" asked Mackintosh defensively.

Patting his gnarly fist, Adams said, "You certainly are, Mac. And we are proud of you, and we intend to make sure the Assembly keeps you in that job."

Otis interrupted, "Now we have to work smart, Mac. Let me explain the law a bit."

"Keep in mind, Mac. Mr. Otis here is the best legal brain we have here in Boston. He knows his stuff," interjected Revere.

Otis, shaking his head continued, "Thank you, Paul. Now, back to the law; what you did with Mr. Hutchinson was totally against the law, technically. If Sheriff Greenleaf had been there, we would have trouble defending you."

"The sheriff is good for nothin'," said Mackintosh, with justified bravado. "He and his ilk are good for servin' summons and writs. Otherwise, he controls nothin', and he would never try to control my gang, er . . . the Sons of Liberty."

"Quite right!" continued Otis, impatiently. "Now to the law, have you heard of the Riot Act."

Standing abruptly, Mackintosh roared across the room, "Let's have a serving wench over here; me and my friends are dry as the bones of a dead man, for Christ's sake."

"Sit down," muttered Adams, impatiently. "We can drink anytime, but this is important Mac."

Otis tapped the table. "If the sheriff and his men ever face twelve armed men or fifty men armed or not, he can call on the crowd, in the king's name, to disperse. By reading this proclamation of a riot act, the crowd must leave within an hour."

"What kind of law is that?" grumbled Mackintosh. "I have my rights to meet and gather whenever I like. I'm an Englishman, by god!"

"Let Mr. Otis continue," grumbled Revere. "Don't be a hardhead."

"Now anyone failing to do as ordered by the sheriff could be liable to forfeiture of all his land and goods, plus flogging, plus a year in prison. Do you understand me, Mac?" asked Otis with finality.

"Let me get this right. We lose land, goods, get flogged and go to prison, if we don't disperse when the sheriff says."

"That's correct," said Otis.

"That's bullshit!" said Mackintosh.

"That's the law, damn it!" exclaimed Adams. "Now listen to me, Mac," he continued, wagging his trembling finger. "We've come too far together to mess this up. The Stamp Act is repealed. We will celebrate and the Sons of Liberty will temper their need to break things, unless they are ordered to do so. Do you understand me?"

A round of tankards was delivered to a quiet table, as Mackintosh digested the news. Once the serving wench had left, Mackintosh said quietly, "All right, Mr. Adams. I get the picture. Me and the boys will keep things quiet. And we take action, but only when you and Paul say so."

"That's right. We will give the sheriff no legal reason to do anything. We will be perfect citizens in the eyes of the law," said Adams triumphantly. "All your orders will come through Mr. Revere. For now, let's all enjoy the repeal and celebrate."

"There's no law against celebrating, is there?" said Mackintosh loudly for the whole taproom to hear. Everyone at the table beamed at the new understanding.

ΩΩΩ

As Hancock passed through the door of his mansion on Beacon Hill, he was surprised to find the faint glow of candlelight from his library. Upon entering, he found his Aunt Lydia had nodded off to sleep in a large easy chair, her hand clutching a small note. He crossed noisily to a sideboard to pour a tumbler of Madeira, hoping to slowly arouse her from her slumber.

"John," she said in a groggy voice. "Where have you been? I've been waiting to speak with you."

"Merely a business meeting with a few merchants, Aunt Lydia," he responded casually.

"As long as you aren't keeping company with Sam Adams and those other rascals," she said, her lips pursed tightly.

"Now why would I have anything in common with Adams and his crowd? Meeting with him wouldn't add a farthing to my coffers," he said smiling. "Now what do you have in your hand there?"

"I received a letter from Elizabeth Quincy, Judge Quincy's wife, and she tells me that her youngest daughter, Dorothy, shall be visiting Boston sometime soon. Isn't that exciting, John?"

"What does Judge Quincy's daughter have to do with us?" asked John, sipping his wine.

"It is only proper," said Lydia, "that we provide lodging during her visit. She is a proper girl and should be introduced to the best families. Besides, she will be excellent company for me."

Hancock smiled. "Do what you like Aunt Lydia. The companionship will do you good. Just be certain to make no plans for me. And that includes your matchmaking; I have no time for the formalities of romance, and you know it."

"I would never consider such a thing, John. But she is from the proper family, and you must think about these things. You are not getting younger, you know. I shall invite the young girl to join us in our home for as long as she likes," said Lydia, again pursing her lips and raising her chin defiantly. "And I expect you to spend some time with her." She then rushed up the stairs, leaving little time for John to respond. She enjoyed getting in the last word in these discussions with her nephew.

Looking at the vacant stairway, Hancock sat at his small secretary desk, making notes about the coming celebration. He then sat back, his hands behind his neck, pondering the situation of the dead strumpet. It was troubling to both the Snug Harbor Tavern and his wharf. As for Amanda, he downed his wine at the thought of her. How would he respond to another woman, besides Aunt Lydia, living under his roof? Shaking his head to clear the tangle of thoughts, he glared at the empty wineglass and ascended the stairway to his bed chamber. He would deal with Amanda when the time came.

As he climbed into bed, Hancock again reflected on his very good fortune. As all of Boston well knew, his grandfather had been known as the bishop of Lexington and reputed to be the best preacher in the region. His father, for whom he was named, became the reverend in Braintree, Massachusetts. Sadly, his father died early in May 1744. John Hancock was seven years old at the time; and his mother, with three small children to raise, did not know exactly where to turn. The bishop of Lexington came to the family's rescue, taking them all in to live at the manse in Lexington.

Observing the crowded conditions at the manse and lacking any children of his own, John's uncle Thomas chose young John to join him and his wife, Lydia, at their mansion on Beacon Hill in Boston. Immediately, young John was treated as a merchant prince. He was privileged to attend the finest schools available, including Harvard College. Uncle Thomas taught him through hands-on experience about the ways and means of conducting business in colonial America. This included both the legal and illegal ways of achieving success. Smuggling was a major course of study, which included paying off the proper authorities, who learned to look the other way when certain goods came ashore. Taxes and duties were seldom paid; it was almost a family tradition.

John Hancock's reflective smile faded, as he recalled the terrible day in August 1764, when his uncle Thomas died of apoplexy. It was bittersweet to lose both his mentor and his benefactor. He inherited his uncle's entire business, known as the House of Hancock. Aunt Lydia had been well provided for, and all of Boston knew that she would live in the mansion on Beacon Hill, until the day she died.

Hancock dozed off to sleep with a smile on his face, knowing that he had the tools and the knowledge to cope with any challenge the Crown or Parliament placed in his way. If only Parliament would stay out of his business and halt their meddling taxation, he would be content to work with Governor Bernard. On the other hand, both Sam Adams and Dr. Warren had his full support, if the situation continued to deteriorate. He made a mental note to set aside a small amount of funding for the Sons of Liberty in order to keep his options open. As for Amanda and the Snug Harbor Tavern, he would find some way to keep a close eye on that operation. It all depended on what Governor Bernard and Parliament would do next. Hancock slept well.

ΩΩΩ

CHAPTER 4

Monday, May 17, 1766

AT 1:00 AM Monday, John Hancock was awakened from his slumber by the incessant pealing of church bells. At first, he thought it was a fire alarm, which was certainly possible. Equally incessant pounding at his front door awakened the entire household. Standing in his nightshirt, he found Sam Adams and Paul Revere standing at his doorstep, beaming in jubilation.

"Get up, John," shouted Adams, as he barged into the foyer. "Now is not the time for slumber. The whole town is awake, and it is time to celebrate."

Revere added, "Both the Northside and Southside gangs are in the streets. The Sons of Liberty couldn't contain themselves any longer. It was both improper and illegal to celebrate on the Sabbath, but it is now time for the official festivities to begin." Every church bell in the town started to ring, mixing with the blare of bands, the pounding of drums, and the discharge of muskets.

"Isn't it a bit early to start all this?" objected Hancock, pointing at a clock on the mantle.

Adams, using his lecture tone of voice on his political protégé, said, "The people have been waiting for this moment, and it is time for Bernard and Hutchinson to learn of the people's passion and hatred of illegal taxation."

"Is it *their* passion or *our* passion?" queried Hancock, with a sarcastic grin.

"It makes no difference. Get dressed. Do you have the funds to pay what the inmates owe at the debtors' prison?" reminded Adams. Hancock nodded his head, as he rushed up the stairs to get out of his night clothes.

By daybreak, the debtors' prison had been emptied, and every public building and home had been decorated with flags.

ΩΩΩ

That afternoon, Governor Bernard, again meeting with Lieutenant Governor Hutchinson and other Crown officers at the Old State House, said, "I tell you, this is the best news ever received in the colonies. Just look at the joy in the streets, gentlemen. Let us drink a toast to His Majesty King George. Hereafter, this shall be known as Repeal Day, the day that peace returns to the streets of Boston."

Hutchinson raised his lead crystal tumbler and responded, "Here's to King George. And I pray you are right about peace in the streets. I remind you all, however, that Adams and that rabble cannot be trusted and bear watching." His gaze rested on Andrew Oliver, his brother-in-law. Oliver had resigned his commission as stamp master, after he was hanged in effigy at Boston's Liberty Tree.

Oliver said, "I'm afraid Thomas is right. I was lucky to escape with my life, and my family is still fearful of the Sons of Liberty. In fact, they tremble at the name."

Sheriff Greenleaf lifted his heavy bulk, saying, "I have only eight deputies, and it is impossible to control a riotous mob. They feel they have the right to interpret the law as they see fit."

Hutchinson added, looking directly at Bernard, "He's right. This fleet rabble scoffs at the sheriff's authority and disputes the courts at every turn. I tell you now is the time to quarter the king's troops in this town and regain control!"

Oliver added, "He's right! Perhaps a British bayonet will make them understand the power of the Crown."

Governor Bernard looked at them all quizzically, "Gentlemen, I realize that the past year has been very trying for us all. But let us remind the people that we have been on their side. We should try to convince them that it was *our* influence that got the Stamp Act repealed. They are unwashed, unlearned, and easily led; we can convince them of anything we want. Now is not the time for Crown troops to be patrolling the streets of Boston. We have gained a cheap peace; let us try to keep it. To that end, I have a plan."

At that, Hutchinson glanced quizzically at Oliver and Sheriff Greenleaf. "What sort of plan?" he asked.

"I will personally speak with John Hancock. Our mutual friend informs me that his business has suffered. His supporting Sam Adams's radicals may have tapped his resources, and he may be ripe for a move to our side," said Bernard.

Hutchinson smiled, rubbing his chin in thought. "Yes. But remember to play upon his vanity. He's a pompous ass, dressed in all that silken brocade. If we can get Hancock's purse away from Adams and on the side of the Tories, we will prevail without the use of bayonets." As he straightened the lace at his sleeves, he added, "With him in the fold and the continued effectiveness of our spy network, we should have Adams and his mob where we want them . . . in the palm of our hand."

Bernard added, "Yes. It will cost us a few more golden guineas with our new spy in the fold, but it should be worth it."

Oliver immediately asked, "What new spy?"

Hutchinson jumped in saying, "At this time, it is best that you not know, Andrew. The fewer involved, the better for us all."

Sheriff Greenleaf, belching loudly, patted his ample belly and responded in a huff, "Perhaps our new spies can help me with the recent death down at the wharf. It seems that a strumpet from the Snug Harbor Tavern was badly beaten and fed to the fishes. No one seems to know who treated her so badly, but her skull was mostly crushed. It was no accident, and the water didn't kill her."

Hutchinson said, "It's a pity. But what is the loss of another doxy of the wharf to do with us? Besides, nothing good ever came from the Snug Harbor Tavern." He glanced knowingly at Andrew Oliver as he added, "It would be best if we joined the gaiety this evening to spread the word that WE coaxed the Crown to repeal the Stamp Act. How does that sound?"

ΩΩΩ

Later that evening, the Sons of Liberty created the greatest illumination ever seen in New England. The centerpiece was a pyramid of two hundred eighty lamps, stacked four stories high, while every child in Boston gasped at the splendor of the fireworks display on Boston Common. Not to be outdone, Hancock offered his own pyrotechnics on the front lawn of his mansion, which overlooked the Common, below the crest of Beacon Street. He had pipes of Madeira placed there for the enjoyment of the populace while he held an open house for the gentry.

While the Sons of Liberty and the rest of the town celebrated on the Common, John Hancock and twenty-nine gentlemen gathered at 8:00 PM at the Bunch of Grapes to enjoy a banquet. More than fifteen toasts were offered, not the least was to His Majesty's continued good health.

Sullenly, Sam Adams observed the gathering, noting the attendance of a few Tories. As the gentry, dressed in their finest silks and brocades, fed their faces on roast duck, baked hams, venison, turtle, salmon, yams, fresh-baked bread, and plum pudding, Adams slowly sipped a bit of rum. He seldom drank, and many felt it was due to his observance of religious temperance. Actually, Sam felt he needed to keep a clear head about himself.

In the depths of his soul, Sam Adams knew that the ultimate aim of Massachusetts and all American colonies should be independence. He pondered this secret belief, which was founded in the repeated efforts of the British Parliament to bleed the American colonies with more taxes. He knew that since 1763, when King George III replaced William Pitt with George Grenville as prime minister to the Crown, the demands on America had increased. The Seven Years' War, known as the French and Indian War in the colonies, had swelled England's national debt to one hundred thirty million pounds. Grenville seemed destined to raise taxes because a British garrison of at least ten thousand men would be needed in the American colonies to defend the Crown's interests.

His quiet reflections were interrupted by Dr. Benjamin Church, who had noticed Adam's solitude. Church interrupted, a decanter of Madeira in hand saying, "Sam, what are you doing in this corner alone? Let me refill your tankard in a toast to His Majesty's health and the death of the Stamp Act."

Immediately, Church regretted the intrusion. Adam's eyes seemed piercing, as he responded, "Benjamin, I don't feel like drinking to King George, but I will drink to the death of taxes. But I assure you, this is not the end of the contest. Lord Grenville first introduced the Sugar Act in 1764, which reduced the tax on molasses from six pence to three pence per gallon. However, new tax collectors and customs inspectors arrived to ensure that the taxes would be collected, and our rampant smuggling was eliminated. I'm sure you are aware that there were more than sixty rum distilleries in Massachusetts at the time, creating a great demand for molasses. One of those distilleries has been in my own family for decades. We need the molasses, and fortunately, the customs agents fear us. But I feel that Grenville and King George will not sit idly by and let us dictate Crown policy. Time will prove me right, as I await their next move."

Church shifted his large bulk, smiling. "Hancock, come over here. It seems that our friend Sam doesn't trust the king, who so very kindly repealed the Stamp Act."

Hancock, adjusting lace sleeves smiled, saying, "Sam, let us get back to business as usual. The king has conceded to our wishes, and that is the end of it."

Acquiescing, Sam said, "Perhaps you are right." As they rejoined the merriment, Sam Adams didn't believe his comment for a moment.

ΩΩΩ

It was near midnight when Amanda Griffith sat at the end of the Snug Harbor taproom bar, watching the sailors, tradesmen, and dockworkers wallow in their collective revelry. Amos wandered to the end of the bar saying, "It hasn't been this busy since last Guy Fawkes Day, when the Northside and Southside gangs lit up the streets in celebration."

In the corner of the taproom, the sailors again were off-key in their bawdy songs, as Purity and Chastity harmonized in their reedy soprano voices:

You might find yourself stumble,
You might let yourself grumble,
But you won't regret.
And you won't forget.
Your finest Snug Harbor tumble.

Amanda smiled. "I guess you're right. But I still feel it's indecent, considering that sweet Charity is hardly cold in her grave while we celebrate. Just look at us. The girls are hustling these sailors like Charity was never here. In fact, Faith wants the poor girl's room, and I haven't cleaned it out as yet."

Amos looked sadly at Amanda. "I didn't realize you cared that much."

Amanda said, "I don't. But even if I did, I'm telling you not to notice. Tomorrow, you and I will clean out Charity's room. I'll use what money we find to pay for the burial and split the clothes and perfume among the girls. She didn't have any family besides Faith, Hope, Chastity, Purity, and us."

From behind the bar, Amos's sad eyes spoke volumes about their lonely state of affairs. "At least, she had us. Some don't have even that much. We shouldn't judge folks by their relatives, and we is relatives," he said quietly. Then he wiped his misted eyes on his dirty sleeve, and in a phlegmatic voice, he said, "Guess I'll get back to work, and you don't worry none about Charity; she's in a better place."

Amanda smiled. "Yeah! I suppose we should all get back to work." She was about to bury a sailor's face into her cleavage when the door slammed open, and Angel Cross ran into the taproom, her auburn hair a mess, and the sleeve of her dress torn away. A heavy quiet pervaded the taproom; then, just as suddenly, heavy laughter returned.

Angel, obviously traumatized in her tattered state, looked around in bewilderment at the crude gathering, wondering what to do next. She began to cry, as she brushed her disheveled auburn hair from her face.

Amanda grabbed her by the arm and guided her back outside. "What are you trying to do in my place?" she asked tersely, in a near growl. Then, standing back, appraising the girl, she said, "Or maybe I should ask, what in hell has happened to you, your ladyship?" she said sarcastically, her hands on her hips.

Through blubbering lips, Angel mumbled, "I didn't know where to go. It was Dr. Church. He came home drunk and came to my room instead of his own. Before I knew he was there, he had his hands all over me. I tried to fight him off, and he tore my sleeve. Then the door opened, and a startled and embarrassed Mrs. Church accused me of luring and enticing her poor husband. She ordered me out of the house."

"What did Dr. Church say?" asked Amanda, as she visualized an angry Mrs. Church catching her spouse with his breeches undone.

"There was so much screaming at the time, I didn't care what he said. I just wanted to get away from there. It was terrible." Angel continued to sob, tears flowing down her cheeks.

Amanda, gathering her wits, realized that a waterfront crowd was gathering, half of them staggering drunk. "Go about your business!" she growled. "Didn't you ever see a girl who fell and hurt herself?" she added to everyone within earshot. In a more soothing voice, she said, "Let's get you off the street and cleaned up a bit. What you really need is a stiff tankard of rum to settle you, my dear. Let's go around to the back. This is no time for questions from nosy people in the taproom."

A few minutes later, Angel Cross found herself staring out the window at the Brig *Harrison*, lost in thought, when the door to room D opened, and Amanda entered with a tray containing two mugs. "I had second thoughts about the rum and brought some tea for you instead," said Amanda. "Just sit yourself here on the edge of the bed."

"I don't know what to do," said Angel, more composed now. "All I have are the torn clothes on my back. Everything I have is with Dr. Church."

Amanda, rifling through the closet, said, "Right now, you can stay here. This room has just become vacant, and the last tenant left a few things." Rummaging through the chest of drawers, she found a nightgown. "It might be a little more revealing than you are accustomed, but it is better than your torn dress. Get out of that thing, wash yourself in the basin there, and get some sleep. We can talk about what to do in the morning," Amanda ordered, as she closed the door behind her.

Faith, Hope, Chastity, and Purity were still working the taproom as Amanda descended the back stairs. Ambling over to the bar, she called to Amos, "Where's Imp?"

"I suppose he's sleeping in the back. He was up at the Common all day celebrating the good news and the fireworks. It's my guess that his friends slipped him a few tankards of ale," said Amos.

Amanda smiled. "Our little Imp is running with a tough crowd. We must keep an eye on him, Amos."

Amos grinned while wiping down the bar. "The problem is that when you wallow with pigs, you gotta expect to get dirty some. But don't worry," he said, "there are many caring eyes on him, and he doesn't know it."

"Just the same, he is my responsibility, and sometimes I get so wrapped up in this business, I forget about him," she said. "I must see him before he runs out in the morning. There is work for him to do." Amos nodded that he'd take care of it.

ΩΩΩ

CHAPTER 5

Tuesday, May 18, 1766

THE SUN WAS streaming through the windows of the Snug Harbor Tavern at midmorning when Amanda found Imp sitting at a corner table in the taproom. He was wearing his nightshirt and holding his aching head, as he sipped a mug of cider and ate a breakfast of dark bread slathered with butter. Amanda, wearing only a robe that barely concealed her ample bosom, sat down heavily, realizing she had enjoyed only a few hours of sleep. Imp grinned, saying, "Your eyes are red."

Amanda grinned back, saying, "You should see them from my side. Anyway, don't be a smartass. I want you to find Mr. Hancock today. Tell him he should come again to the Snug Harbor as soon as possible. There is a touchy situation beyond our control, and we need his help."

Imp frowned, asking, "What's wrong?"

"You ask too many questions. Just finish your breakfast and find Mr. Hancock. And keep quiet around here this morning; the ladies had a busy night and earned the right to sleep late."

Imp scurried to the back storeroom to get into his street clothes while Amanda opened the front door and opened the windows. The salt air was a welcome replacement to the pungent odor of spilled ale, cider, and rum. She made a mental note to have Amos mop the place.

She began to organize her thoughts as she gazed out at Hancock's Wharf. Sheriff Greenleaf had promised to stop by at noon today to investigate the death of Charity, and she had to speak with Mr. Hancock about Angel Cross. She had some ideas about her situation, but she needed Hancock to set them in motion. Her eyes came to rest on the Brig *Harrison*. Ever since that ship had put into port, her life had become complicated. *How would this all end?* she wondered.

ΩΩΩ

It was an hour past noon before Imp found Hancock at the British Coffee House on King Street. At a table near the window, Hancock was having tea with Governor Bernard and Lieutenant Governor Hutchinson; Imp wasn't sure what to do. He couldn't interfere with this meeting of the gentry, but Amanda said it was important, and Imp always did his work well. He knew there was trouble brewing because he saw the sheriff stop by the Snug Harbor a bit earlier. He decided it was best to wait until the squire was alone.

The Bunch of Grapes Tavern was located just across the street from the British Coffee House, and Imp decided to seek refuge from the sweet music of street vendors hawking lobster and fish with their incessant bell ringing. He entered the Bunch of Grapes taproom like he owned it, and immediately, Big Bessie Clump lifted him and hugged him to her fleshy breasts, mugging him with kisses. "Where have you been hiding, Imp?" she asked, putting him down.

"I ain't been hidin'," he said. "I just been real busy." *Why,* he wondered, *does this woman slobber all over me like that?* as he wiped his face on his sleeve.

Big Bessie smiled. "I know you live at the Snug Harbor, but you can still come to visit more often than you do. In fact, you can tell Amanda that we should talk sometime soon. I have an idea that could help both our houses." Most townspeople knew that Big Bessie Clump had the largest stable of strumpets in town because she was located right at the entrance to Long Wharf, which was the busiest in Boston. The sailors referred to a tumble with her as getting "clumped," and most of her trade was with the radical element of society. No decent Tory or merchant would be caught dead in the friendly confines of the Bunch of Grapes.

Imp wandered to the taproom bar and said, "I'll have a tankard of ale."

Big Bessie interrupted, telling the barman, "Give him a mug of cider. You know very well, Imp, that you can't have drinking spirits, until you can see over the bar."

"Don't worry, Imp. You won't be short forever," said the barman, laughing as he went about his business.

Imp barely heard him, as he peered out the window. He noticed Dr. Benjamin Church enter the British Coffee House, seating himself with Hancock and the others, and speaking animatedly with his hands waving. The meeting immediately adjourned, with Bernard and Hutchinson turning up King Street toward the Old State House, while Hancock and Church headed toward the waterfront.

Imp downed his cider and, yelling a thank you over his shoulder, he ran down the cobblestone street to catch up with the squire. Catching up with them at Faneuil Hall near the Town Dock, Imp said, "Beg pardon, Mr. Hancock, but Amanda, er, . . . Ms. Griffith needs to see you today. She needs your help."

Dr. Church, looking with disdain at the interruption by this street urchin, said, "Go away, lad. Can't you see the squire and I are busy?"

Hancock smiled and with exaggerated politeness asked, "What is this about, Master Smythe?"

Imp, feeling puffed by the formal address, said, "She don't tell me nuthin', but that she needs to see you today."

"Tell Amanda I'll stop by after I finish my business with Dr. Church." With that, they continued on toward his offices on Hancock's Wharf. Imp, feeling his task completed, headed past Faneuil Hall to Queen Street, where the printers Edes & Gill would have the latest edition of the *Boston Gazette* for him to deliver on the North end of town.

ΩΩΩ

That same afternoon, Zeke Teezle sat in the upper room of his shop gazing out the open window, which overlooked Milk Street. The heat from the vats of candle wax was stifling, and the open window offered little respite. He could hear a gaggle of radicals just down the street at the South Battery of Fort Hill, messing with the cannon. He grimaced at the thought, as he once again read the remnants of the note that Glunt had torn from the hand of a messenger on Hancock's Wharf a few days earlier.

The small wedge of paper read, in part, ". . . used her room, but Charity wasn't there."

Teezle then picked up Monday's issue of the *Boston Gazette*, where he scanned the small article headed, MURDER ON THE WATERFRONT. The article named the dead girl as Charity Lane. He read that there was little more to go on and that Sheriff Greenleaf was investigating. Again, Teezle shuddered. "What have I gotten myself into?" he asked himself. And now that Charity is dead and gone, he wondered how this piece of note could be passed on to the fat man.

He bustled down the stairs where he found Emmet Glunt hard at work for a change, hanging freshly layered candles to dry on the line. "Emmet, I want you to take a box of candles to sell down by the wharf," he ordered.

Glunt, wiping the sweat from his brow with his sleeve, said, "I just got back from Long Wharf and sold all we had, except for orders to be picked up here at the shop. Besides, I'm tired, and it's almost time for supper, ain't it?"

Teezle growled, "Supper will be late today. And forget about Long Wharf; go up the north end to Hancock's Wharf and ask around the shops if anyone needs candles. In fact, stop at Hancock's warehouse to see if they need anything. And keep your eyes and ears open. You know what I mean, don't you?" Glunt sauntered toward the door reluctantly. Teezle grunted abruptly, "Just a moment. On second thought, I want you to stop at the Snug Harbor Tavern first. Ask them if they need candles. And here's three pence; linger there and have a mug of cider and keep your ears open. There's something amiss with that place!"

Glunt asked, "What am I supposed to look or listen for?"

Teezle hastened him out the door saying, "Just tell me everything you see and hear, especially if someone mentions the name Charity. You understand me? I'll judge what's important. Now go!"

ΩΩΩ

John Hancock sat in the quiet of his private office on the third floor of his warehouse on Hancock's Wharf, enjoying the freshness of the ocean breeze passing through the open windows. In contrast, Dr. Benjamin Church shifted uncomfortably in his seat opposite the squire's large oak desk, which was covered with ledgers, letters and bills of lading set for his signature.

"Now Ben, tell me once again from the beginning how this all happened," he said in a calming voice.

Church, initially stammering, said hurriedly, "Well, it was despicable; that's what it was. I arrived home after the banquet at the Green Dragon Tavern last night and was about to go upstairs to my bedroom. Suddenly, that Cross woman stumbled from the rear of the house where we had made a spare bed for her. She must have been drinking some of that fine Madeira wine you gave me because she cooed at me saying that she knew I wanted her, and she was ready for it."

Hancock, shaking his head, wandered to a sideboard saying, "I think I could use a glass of Madeira right now. How about you, Doctor? You look like you could use a bit of cheer."

Church, shaking his head no continued, "With all that racket, my wife of many years, suddenly appeared at the head of the stairs in her dressing gown just in time to witness that harlot groping for my private parts. Then the screaming began. I was never so embarrassed in my life. The only way to settle my wife down was to exile that brazen hussy from the house."

"Sounds like the smart thing to do to me," responded Hancock, doing all he could to hide his amusement. "Where did that brazen hussy go, if I may ask?"

"I don't know. And that's the problem. God only knows what she will do to my good reputation. She probably stole some things from the house also. I honestly didn't know she was that type of strumpet. That's what I get for trying to help someone. Just wait till I tell my colleague in London about it," said Church, his hands fidgeting with his lace cuffs.

"Well, Ben, what can I do to help you?" asked Hancock.

"Your ship brought her here, and I need you to take back her trunk of possessions. My wife refuses to have any memory of her in her home. Maybe she will turn up somehow. But I don't care if you throw it out or sell it; just take it away for me. Otherwise, there will never be peace," Church pleaded.

Hancock smiled. "All right, Ben. Consider it done. And tell Mrs. Church to forget the whole episode." Sipping his wine, he added, "I wonder where the Cross girl went, however."

"Who cares? If she was smart, she has run inland toward Concord or Worchester. As long as she has departed from Boston, that's what's important. By the eternal, I'll have the sheriff arrest her for vagrancy; she has no means of support, you know," added Church.

Hancock downed his glass of wine and patting Dr. Church reassuringly on the back, said, "I'll send a few men to get the trunk this afternoon. It will be stored here in my warehouse, until we figure out where the girl went. If she has vanished from Boston, I'll give the goods to the poor. Is that satisfactory, Ben?"

Church smiled. "Thanks, John. I won't forget this, nor will my wife." He rumbled down the two flights of stairs, with a look of achievement on his face. As he crossed Fish Street, a young lady hailed him from a second-story window saying, "Would you care for a tumble, your lordship?" He shook his head in disgust, as he continued his journey home. The bright red sign below the young lady's window read, Snug Harbor Tavern.

ΩΩΩ

Governor Bernard sat in his office at the Old State House with a smug look on his face. "I told you that Hancock would see the reasoning of our argument, Tom," he said.

"I suppose you are right. I was surprised to hear him address the need of business as usual. He was right that the Stamp Act required official Crown stamps on every legal and business document and currency in the colonies. The added cost to him would have made life unbearable. If he went under, all of Massachusetts would suffer," added Hutchinson.

"I'll make a point to steer the Tory merchants to send him more business, and we can do the same personally. His main motivation is money and greed. Soon, he will totally forget about Sam Adams and his rabble. We will own him," noted Bernard with a self-satisfied smile.

After rapping on the office door, Hubert Slank appeared with a tray saying, "Your tea, sir. And I have the latest issue of that rag, the *Boston Gazette*, per your request."

"Thank you, Slank," said Hutchinson, scanning the paper and smiling. "You continue to do a fine job." Slank paused at the door and smiled as he left.

Hutchinson said, handing the *Gazette* to Bernard, "It seems there was a fatality down on the waterfront at Hancock's Wharf. That riffraff never fails to amaze me at their brutality."

Bernard, reading slowly, added, "It was obviously a girl of low means. What a name . . . Charity."

Hutchinson said, "Sheriff Greenleaf told me of this tragedy earlier. I'll make certain that he doesn't waste too much time on this. Obviously, the strumpet crossed the wrong sailor at the wrong time. The wages of sin is obviously . . . death!" He chuckled at his own use of scripture.

ΩΩΩ

While Purity was busy at the second-floor window of the Snug Harbor Tavern soliciting her services, Amanda was in heated conversation with Sheriff Greenleaf, seated at the rear corner table of the taproom. "What do you mean there is nothing you can do?" she asked tersely. She was still wearing her only black dress in Boston funeral tradition. "Let me tell you that me and the girls washed and dressed Charity's body in her finest, and the entire staff of the Snug Harbor Tavern attended the service at the Old North Church, where black drapes adorned every window. And as tradition dictates, we all wore heavy black gloves, which I provided. The church sexton dug the grave and rang the passing bell for us mourners, and the preacher gave a fine short sermon at the Old Granary Burying Ground. We paid for it all and, as you know, the ground space is free. Charity got as good a send-off as any other Bostonian. Now you tell me, you can't find who killed her. What's that all about? If she was a gentry's woman, you and your deputies would solve it pretty damned quick! And you know it."

"Mrs. Griffith, so far I can find no one who has seen Charity since Thursday morning last. She seemed to disappear until a sailor found her body floating near the wharf out here on Monday. But you already know that. There are no witnesses, and the last to speak to her are your own ladies on the second floor," said Greenleaf, pointing at the stairs.

"I guess that doesn't help much," Amanda admitted. "But I know for sure she had a rendezvous with one of the gentry folks last Thursday."

"Who was it?" asked the sheriff, with a poorly concealed look of concern.

"I can't say exactly because I'm told he was disguised. But he couldn't hide his breeding and polish. He was a gentleman all right," said Amanda, becoming angrier by the minute. "Why don't you ask some of the merchantmen over on the Back Bay?"

The sheriff began to laugh. "Be serious," he said impatiently. "I can't just go ask anyone at random if they saw someone with Charity. Did you see anyone new or suspicious around here last week?"

Amanda eyed him cautiously, wondering if Greenleaf really cared or could be trusted. So far, he made every excuse not to pursue the case further. She wasn't quite ready to play the "Teezle card," not at this time anyway. "No, I don't recall strangers recently," she lied. "If I think of anything or anyone, I'll let you know." Her eye caught sight of a little chubby boy wandering into the taproom and signaled Amos to take care of him.

Sheriff Greenleaf struggled to move his large bulk from the chair. "Send a messenger, if anything comes to mind, Mrs. Griffith. The death of any citizen is a great loss to us all," he added, as he shuffled to the door.

Amanda noted that he didn't bother to pay for his pint of ale, as he lumbered up Fish Street. "I'm surprised he didn't expect a free tumble with Purity, for god's sake," she said disgustedly to Amos, as she cleared the table and returned to the bar.

Amos, glancing at the empty doorway, said, "All them constables expects free pints and quarts." As he picked up a mop, he continued to mutter, "Seems to me it might best to keep all them skunks, bankers, lawyers, and constables at a distance!"

Ignoring the comment, Amanda rushed to the doorway yelling, "She may be just another dead doxy to you, but she was a sister to us here at the Snug Harbor. And she was murdered, beaten . . . it wasn't just a death. You remember that. You haven't heard the last of this." By now, she was screaming at the fading image of Greenleaf shuffling slowly up Fish Street. Her smirk indicated that the yelling made her feel better.

She turned and rushed back into the taproom, where again she found the pudgy little boy with beady little eyes standing near the bar. Amos said, "He wants to know if you be in need of some candles; he works for a chandler on the south end."

Glunt looked up at Amanda, trying to muster a sweet, innocent look, which failed miserably. Actually, he was gaping at the pendulous breast that hovered above his head. Amanda was wearing her "cleaning clothes" and was not dressed for business. She noticed his gaze and said, "You're a little young to handle these, young man."

Involuntarily, Glunt blushed saying, "My name's Emmet Glunt, and we have candles to sell. I can deliver when you need 'em . . . anytime and anyplace."

"Who is your master?" asked Amanda, calming down somewhat from the encounter with the sheriff.

"I work for Zeke Teezle. Could I have a mug of cider? I can pay for it," he said in his most innocent voice.

A glint of an idea suddenly smoldered in Amanda's eyes, as she softly muttered, "Amos, give Master Glunt here a mug of cider." To Glunt, she added, "Why don't you sit down here by the window, so we can talk about . . . candles."

While Glunt sipped his cider, he asked, "Why was the sheriff here? Is there trouble? I never get to come down by the waterfront much. I'm usually stuck in the shop with all that hot candle wax and tallow."

Amanda smiled. "No trouble. The sheriff's just a friend of ours. Tell me, how does Mr. Teezle treat a fine boy like you? It's a shame you have to mess with that hot wax and tallow, you poor dear, little boy."

Glunt responded, "Just like most folks, I guess. I'm learnin' a trade, so I can open my own shop someday." He began to nervously peel wax from under his grimy fingernails.

"Where does Mr. Teezle spend his off time? We never see him around here, and if we buy his candles, it's only fair that he drinks our ale," Amanda queried.

"Mrs. Teezle would never let Zeke, er . . . Mr. Teezle come down here," Glunt murmured, suddenly gazing at the pile of wax shavings on the table. "Sorry ma'am, but we don't get much business in this kind of place."

At that moment, Amanda peered out the window to discover John Hancock walking down the wharf toward the Snug Harbor. Immediately, she rushed to the back stairway saying hurriedly, "You tell Mr. Teezle to come visit me personally, and we can do some business together." With that said, she disappeared up the stairs.

Glunt looked a bit puzzled. *Why did she rush away so quickly?* he wondered.

Amos looked at him, saying, "Boy, your business here is finished. You best get back to your side of town. And keep in mind that sometimes you get, and sometimes you get got. Now scat!"

The mere size of Amos was enough encouragement, as he recalled their first encounter. He tossed down the remaining drops of cider and rushed out the door, running into the silk brocade breeches of the squire himself at the doorway. Hancock looked curiously at the beady eyes attached to the pudgy body. "Watch it, boy. No reason to be in such a rush," he said smiling.

Emmet Glunt said nothing but ran up Fish Street and out of sight. Hancock paused at the door for a moment, wondering where he had seen that urchin before. He decided to let it pass; there were many young apprentices running the streets of Boston these days. Why would this one standout?

Amos said joyously in his deep bass voice, "Welcome Mr. Hancock. How can I serve you, sir?"

John grinned. "Did my man deliver the case of Madeira wine?" he asked.

"Yes, sir, he did. It arrived early this morning," Amos answered, as he polished the bar.

"Then I suggest you give Mr. Hancock a glass of his private wine stock," said Amanda, suddenly appearing at Hancock's elbow. "And use our best crystal for the occasion."

Hancock smiled more broadly, noticing the red satin dress and the lace, which accented her décolletage. *She certainly knew how to promote her assets,* he thought to himself.

Amanda led him to the extreme rear table she used with Greenleaf. Hancock's not-so-subtle glance at her cleavage did not go unnoticed. *He may be rich, but down deep, he's still a male animal,* she thought to herself.

Hancock came right to the point. "Imp tells me you needed to talk to me. If it's about the Madeira, think nothing of it."

Amanda touched his arm, pulling him closer. "No," she whispered. "Thanks for the wine. But I have a situation that only someone of your station can handle. You see, that young lady Angel Cross who arrived on the *Harrison*, is now hiding in one of my upstairs rooms."

Hancock recoiled at the news. "It's no wonder she's hiding. Dr. Church tells me that she turned out to be a thief and that she made indecent advances in front of his wife."

Amanda gave him an icy stare. "Let me inform you, Mr. Hancock, that your story is pure hogwash. That poor girl came to the Snug Harbor well after midnight, with her dress torn and bruises on her inner thighs. I would question who made the 'indecent advances.'"

Hancock sat back in his chair, taking a large sip of his Madeira. *It's curious how a good rich wine helps a man think,* he reflected to himself. Looking at the stairway, he said, "May I suggest that I speak with Ms. Cross personally. It seems we do indeed have a dilemma here." Together they ascended the stairway to room D.

Upon their departure, Amos cleared and wiped the tables. With crystal glasses in hand, he passed the window table where Glunt had been sitting with his cider. Disgustedly, he wiped up a small pile of wax shavings that were left on the table.

Meanwhile, upstairs Amanda and Hancock looked at the cowering figure of Angel Cross, who sat meekly in a corner chair. Hancock, remembering the last act of bravado he had witnessed at their first meeting, said, "Mrs. Griffith tells me that you had a rough time of it with Dr. Church last night. Would you care to tell me about it?"

Angel looked pleadingly at Amanda. "It's all right," said Amanda. "You can trust Mr. Hancock."

Angel related the entire story, as she had told Amanda. "Now I don't know what to do. My trunk with sewing material and my bolts of cloth are with Dr. Church. He also has the few pounds sterling I brought from London." She began to sob, holding her head in her hands.

Shaking his head, Hancock stared out the window at his wharf and his warehouse buildings, lost in thought. He turned, looking first at Amanda, then at Angel. "Let me first say that, although Dr. Church is my friend and a man of impeccable credentials, I tend to believe your story, in preference to his version of what happened. Sadly, because of his good name, Sheriff Greenleaf would place you in jail, and Lieutenant Governor Hutchinson would convict you of theft, based on the word of Dr. Church and his wife. You don't stand a chance in the Boston courts. Again, you would find yourself in jail for quite some time."

Amanda placed her hands on her hips. "Well, if you aren't a bundle of good news!" she said sarcastically. "I had hoped you could help us. You just convicted the poor girl."

John smiled, raising his hands to defend himself from her wrath. "Hear me out," he said. "Actually, there are very few people who have even seen Angel in Boston. I would venture to say Ben Church has seen her a few moments in daylight because most of his time was spent with us regarding the Stamp Act celebrations."

Angel added, "This is true. In fact, I couldn't go to church because my trunk with proper clothing had not arrived at his house until Monday. They were out of the house most of the time. But what does that do for me?" she asked.

John said, "You have beautiful auburn, almost red hair. Now you must change the color." To Amanda, he added, "Do you have any hair coloring for this young girl? If you don't, I imagine something could be found in my warehouse."

Amanda suddenly beamed at the new idea. "You can consider this room yours for the time being, Angel. We will make your hair raven black. With a bit of makeup and a dark red lip coloring, you will become a new you."

Hancock added, "Dr. Church would never consider being seen in the Snug Harbor; so in no time at all, Angel will be forgotten. If he does happen to see you, the blackened hair should be enough to confuse him."

Amanda smiled smugly. "You will fit in perfectly here, Angel."

Angel stood up immediately. "But I'm not one to sell my – "

Amanda pursed her lips. "No girl ever starts out intending to sell their talents, dearie. You can help Amos behind the bar and serve platters of food to earn your keep for now."

Hancock added, "My men will retrieve your trunk with your personal goods, and I'll argue for the bolts of cloth. Perhaps you could make a few dresses for the girls at the Snug Harbor. If things work out, I'll bring more orders for business. But keep in mind, you must keep yourself to the tavern for a while – for your own good. Do you understand?"

Angel nodded. "It will take some getting used to, but I guess I have no choice."

"Good," said Amanda. "There's no time to waste. I'll get the hair coloring, and together we can get some clothes for you to wear. We use only first given names around here, and most have been made up to make it sound like a nunnery. Even so, the "Cross" part of your name should not be mentioned; at least, until we are sure that Dr. Church has forgotten you."

"What about a full name for me; in case, someone should ask," said Angel.

"How about Angel Black with respect to your new hair color, that is?" suggested Hancock. "I'll have Captain Coffin spread the word that you also arrived aboard the *Harrison*. He and the crew are due to sail at the end of the week, so no one will be around to dispute the story."

Hancock crossed the room to leave, paused, and turned at the doorway saying, "Incidentally, I was never in this room today, I never saw you, and you never saw me. Is that clear?" Both ladies nodded, obediently. "Your trunk will arrive shortly; be certain to destroy it, once you have removed its contents. Remember, Angel Cross does not exist in Boston; at least, as far as Dr. Church is concerned." He closed the door and left down the back stairs, hoping that he could make this story stick.

Now that they were alone, Amanda said, "Let's waste no time. I'll be right back with a basin and hair coloring. Strip down to your shift."

A short time later, Angel found herself gazing out the window at the Brig *Harrison*. Her faint reflection in the window pane showed a raven-haired woman. Gone were her bright auburn tresses. It now fully dawned on her that her new home was the Snug Harbor Tavern, and her closest friends were basically strangers . . . in a strange profession.

Amanda interrupted her quiet reflections by holding a blue satin dress up to Angel's torso saying, "Get out of that shift and slide into this little number. And here's a bodice to amplify your chest. Puff those puppies up and the sailors will never leave the Snug Harbor."

Angel objected, "But I never – "

Amanda, her hands on her hips, said, "Listen, girl, what you 'never' did doesn't matter. You now have to survive, and I'll teach you the tricks. You don't have to sleep with them, but you must let them think they can. Those gorgeous breasts of yours are now the forbidden fruit in the Snug Harbor garden of Eden."

Angel said in a surrendering tone, "I suppose you're right."

Amanda smiled to herself as she watched Angel transform herself into a marketable commodity. *This definitely had possibilities in more ways than one,* she thought to herself. "Chin up, Angel. Let's get you down to the taproom. Amos will teach you about ales and flips and such while no customers are here." As Amanda followed her down the hallway, she again began to think of a new way to handle Teezle. *Angel could definitely be useful; that sweet innocence was a rarity on the waterfront,* she mused.

ΩΩΩ

Amos had washed the mugs and tankards in a huge country dishpan and was now drying and hanging them on hooks above the bar. Chastity, Purity, Faith, and Hope were sitting at a table, sharing a late lunch of white fish, broiled lobster, bread, and Indian pudding, washed down with mugs of cider. It would probably be their last formal meal of the day because the evening crowd would arrive in a few hours, and they would be busy entertaining.

From the rear of the taproom, Amanda stopped at the foot of the stairs to see who was present. With no strangers in sight, she said loudly, "Gather round the bar folks. I want to introduce you to a new member of the family." She and Angel marched over to the bar. Amos dropped a pewter mug at the sight of the new arrival.

Amanda smiled to herself at the reaction. The girls rose from their nearly finished lunch and each, in her own way, appraised the raven-haired woman. Amanda said, "Let me introduce you to Angel. She arrived on the Brig *Harrison,* and her promised employment is no longer available; I've agreed to take her on here at the Snug Harbor."

Purity stepped forward, fingering the blue satin dress. "I recognize this; it belonged to Charity. What gives this trollop the right to wear her clothes? Hell, the girl's body isn't even cold yet."

Angel recoiled, but Amanda abruptly interjected, stepping between her and Purity, "What she wears is my business. And what was left behind in the Snug Harbor is my business. Do you have any questions about that?" After an overlong silence, she added, "I didn't think so. Now you girls can just relax because Angel here will not compete for your common trade; that is, she won't be shaggin' for a shillin'. She will simply work behind the bar with Amos."

Chastity asked, "What about Charity's belongings? Who gets them?"

Amanda answered, "A few things will go to Angel, but most of her finery and perfumes, you ladies can divide between you. Angel will get room D, and it won't be used for tumbling. I'll leave it to you to figure who gets the trade of Charity's regular sinners."

Realizing that Angel was no threat to their profits, the girls collectively gathered round her in a full welcome to the family, if not to the sisterhood of strumpets. Amanda smiled triumphantly. This was working out as she had planned.

Suddenly Imp appeared at the front door, after delivering the *Boston Gazette*. This was Angel's first test, Amanda thought to herself. If Imp doesn't recognize Angel, no one will, because he was closest to her on the day the *Harrison* docked.

Imp stopped in the doorway, as everyone in the taproom turned to gaze at him. He immediately took note of the new lady in blue satin. He couldn't keep his eyes off the long black hair that draped caressingly over her breasts, which were perched above the bodice. Amanda smiled, suddenly realizing that little Imp had all the makings of a future patron. *She and Amos should have a long talk with that little man soon,* she thought.

Faith said, "Come here, Imp. This is Angel, and she is going to be part of the Snug Harbor family."

Imp immediately looked at Amanda, who nodded her official sanction. "That's right Imp. Angel will work the bar with Amos, and she will live upstairs."

Imp walked closer and, looking up at Angel's eyes, said, "Pleased to meet you. I'm Imp, and if you need anything, these ladies will tell you that I'm the one who can get it for you." He tilted his head in a bit of puzzlement. Something was familiar, but it couldn't be. Angel had bosoms almost as large as Amanda, and he'd remember that. But there was something in those dancing green eyes that was familiar. He let it pass as that weird feeling he was starting to feel around pretty women.

Angel, feeling more at ease, said, "Thank you all for your kindness. I'll do whatever I can to help around here." Inwardly, she knew that a large hurdle had been passed.

Amanda ordered Amos to instruct Angel in handling the bar, as she gathered the girls aside. "Listen," she said to them all, "no one asks Angel any questions about her past. Is that understood? I have never asked any of you, and I expect the same with her." There was no argument. They all knew about a dark past, and some things were never discussed.

Amos said, "Come behind the bar, Angel, and I'll show you what we do here." Imp perched himself in an Indian sitting position atop the bar to watch. Most of the time, folks were telling Amos what to do, and this was new. Amos proceeded to show her how to draw ale and rum. "Down below here, in this cabinet, we have a small stock of brandy and a private supply of Madeira for Mr. Hancock," he said. "Now we have the specialty of the house called the Amos Flip. First, you fill a large pewter mug, it's actually a pitcher, full of beer; then sweeten with sugar or molasses, and we add a gill, that's about a quarter pint, of rum. Now we stir this mix with a red-hot loggerhead."

"What's a loggerhead?" asked Angel.

Amos smiled. "Imp, get that small hot poker from the fireplace," ordered Amos. Holding the blazing rod in his meaty fist, he added, "This, Angel, is a loggerhead; and it's white-hot, so be careful. You stick this in the flip, and it foams right up. Now you have a finished flip."

Clapping, Imp added, "Tell her about the Dinner Flip, Amos."

Amos said, grinning, "Sometimes the folks are hungry and thirsty, and they want a Dinner Flip. We take a quart mug two-thirds full of beer, but we add four spoonsful of my special creamy mix, made of a pint of cream, four eggs, and four spoons of sugar, add a gill of rum, and hit it with the loggerhead."

Imp gave a knowing smile, "I love that flip, but don't be tellin' Amanda."

His confession was interrupted by the sudden reverberation of Big Bessie Clump's booming, staccato voice from the doorway. "Amanda! We have to talk," she ranted, as she barged into the taproom. As she passed the bar, she added, "Amos, a Dinner Flip, if you please."

Amanda dismissed her girls and, pulling her buxom visitor aside, said smiling, "Bessie, what brings you to the Snug Harbor? It's been months." Bessie whispered in her ear. Amanda added, "Let's go up to the second deck." Bessie grabbed her mug of flip before ascending the stairs.

ΩΩΩ

Zeke Teezle sat cowering in the dusty confines of the back room of his candle shop, with his trembling hands gripping the note. A common doxy he had never seen before simply asked, "Have you been to Concord?" Remembering the fat man with the silver buckled shoes, he had automatically answered, "Not today," as instructed. With that said, she handed him the note and quickly vanished into the crowded street.

He tried to read the note through his quivering fingers. It read, in a fine hand,

Teezle,

The doxy is dead, and we need to know why you killed her. For now, you will cease all activities and harness Glunt. Enemy eyes are on you now. You will tell us about the dead doxy by leaving a note tonight three hours after sunset at the Snug Harbor Tavern. Address the note to Hope. Be casual and have a mug of rum before you leave. We will be watching.

Ω

Gertrude Teezle jiggled her ample girth into the back room as she scratched her sweaty midriff and grunted, "Zeke, what are you doing back here? There are customers out front, and I can't cook, clean, and take care of them too. And where's that lazy ass Glunt? I need water for my monthly bath." She paused abruptly and added, "Why, you're white as my pantaloons. What's wrong, Zeke?"

Teezle, quickly folding the note away into his shirt, said, "Er . . . nothing, Gerty. I was working on a candle order, and I burned myself with some wax. I have a rush order of candles to deliver tonight down on the wharf."

"I told you I didn't want you down there with all those strumpets running loose. What will the neighbors say, for god's sake? Why don't you send Glunt?" muttered Gerty, wiping sweat from her brow with the hem of her homespun dress.

Teezle arose from his corner stool and said, "Gerty, this is business. You'll have to trust me. And speaking of trust, Glunt is not to be trusted with all our business." He recalled that Glunt had told him of his meeting with Amanda earlier and the request for his personal visit. Tonight would be the perfect time to see her about candles while delivering the note at the same time. He could use Amanda as an excuse to be there, and she would never realize she was being used. *Women were so very stupid,* he thought to himself.

He rushed past Gerty to the front room. "Where is my notepad?" he snorted. "I need to write out a bill for tonight's delivery."

Gerty said, "How should I know? Besides, my stew is burning." She scurried away to the kitchen in a huff, still scratching her sweaty sides.

Emmet Glunt had been idling near the back window, listening to the entire exchange. *What was in the note,* he wondered, *to make Teezle act so strangely?* He usually withered under Dirty Gerty's nagging; something was very different. *What would happen if he followed Mr. Teezle this evening?* he wondered to himself.

ΩΩΩ

It was just after sunset, and Sam Adams sat at a corner table in the second-story offices of Edes & Gill, publishers of the *Boston Gazette*. He tried to control his shaking hand, as he put the finishing touches to his latest editorial, which he signed Vindex.

"Vindex!" exclaimed Ben Edes, gazing over his shoulder. "That's a new one. Don't you think the men of the Crown know who really writes these articles by now, Sam?"

"Whether they know or not is unimportant. The pseudonyms keep them guessing, and it keeps the people content that many fellow Bostonians feel as they do," answered Sam, without looking up from his quill.

Ben said, "All the same, with the Stamp Act dead, we really have no real complaint. Even Hancock agrees with that."

Sitting at a small table against the wall, Dr. Joseph Warren chimed in as he placed his own quill pen aside, "I guess you don't really care for my Paskalos then, do you, Ben? Here, look this over and tell me what you think."

Ben snatched the document from Warren's hand. Standing in the middle of the room, he began to shake his head negatively. "If I print this, Governor Bernard will certainly shut down the *Gazette!*" he said hesitantly.

Sam Adams stood near the window chuckling, "What did old Paskalos say this time, Ben?"

Clearing his throat, he said, "Listen to me, Sam. In the past, Dr. Warren has called Bernard a beggar and a coward, who had wantonly sacrificed the happiness of the province to his foolish passions. That was when Jim Otis was vetoed as speaker of the House, and Bernard demanded payment of damages to victims of the Stamp Act riots."

Sam nodded yet grumbled, "I recall all of that mess; so what! It was the truth, wasn't it?" At that, he winked at Dr. Warren across the room.

Ben continued, "Well, now our dear Paskalos has dipped his pen in gall. He writes, "I can no more allow this country to be harmed than to stand by and see my parents stabbed by a ruffian. You are either a liar, or you are insane. In either case, you should be removed from office." He looked up. "Are you hearing this, Sam?"

At that, Sam simply waved his shaking hand. "Continue! Continue!" he said bluntly.

"And now, sir, if you are not too angry to hear my friendly advice, I counsel you to depart from this province in as honorable manner as you can. Your duplicity in pretending that this Stamp Act repeal is due to your efforts is an affront to the intellect of your fellow citizens. I prefer to see one worthless treacherous man reduced to his native insignificance than to see thousands of innocent men hurt. You have the gall to accuse some in this province of disloyalty. I suggest you look in the mirror for disloyalty. Then be gone!"

Sam Adams began to laugh while clapping his hands. "Why, Dr. Warren, let me be the first to applaud you."

Warren smiled. "It should get the governor's attention, don't you think?"

Edes, shaking his head in submission, said, "This will probably be the end of the *Gazette,* but we'll print it. Besides, he wouldn't dare try to attack freedom of the press a second time, would he?"

Adams smiled. "He wouldn't dare!"

Dr. Warren put his arm around Edes strong shoulders. "Ben, you are the voice of the Liberty Party. Without the *Gazette*, the entire colony would be trampled by the governor and Parliament. Just let Vindex and Paskalos take the blame for this. The governor's Prerogative Party has its own publications for their propaganda. We are simply keeping them on their toes."

"If you ask me, you are actually stepping on their toes," said Ben.

Sam grunted, "I tell you we haven't heard the last of King George and his Parliament. We must remain vigilant, Ben. Print the damned editorials please."

Edes shook his head, saying, "All right, Sam. We'll print it. But most everyone feels that peace will now prevail. By the way, I was wondering where your cousin John is these days. With his lawyer training, he should be a natural to contribute to the *Gazette*."

Sam smirked, "Actually, I personally asked him to do so months ago."

Dr. Warren queried without looking up from his work, "And?"

"He said he wasn't interested in scribbling in the newspaper and that he could argue these issues without painting, pathos, rhetoric, or flourish."

Warren shook his head, "Doesn't he realize what a great delight it is to tweak the governor's nose on a weekly basis?"

"I guess it is just not his cup of tea, so to speak." Sam shrugged, in familial surrender. "That leaves the job of writing to you, me, and John Otis, when he is of a mind to do so." Adams stared out the window toward the candlelights flickering in the windows of the Old State House, just beyond the alley. "I wonder what's going on in the statehouse tonight. Lights don't normally burn this late. Something tells me we should have armed every man in the colony. I'm convinced that power-mad cretin isn't finished with his nefarious ideas."

Edes looked up, his arms akimbo, "Next, you will tell me that we need an army, Sam."

Gazing out the window, Sam muttered to himself, "When the king sends his troops, we will all regret our neglect." Picking up his papers, he turned to the printer, "But the consensus seems to be that we now take time to celebrate." Handing over the sheaf of papers, he added, "The next civic opinion of our dear Vindex, if you please, Mr. Edes."

ΩΩΩ

In the Old State House, Governor Bernard sat at his desk and placing his quill aside, sealed the envelope with wax and his official embossing stamp. Standing at the side of his desk, Hubert Slank asked, "Will that be all, sir?"

"Yes," said Bernard. "Be certain to get this on the next ship to London along with my shopping list for the wife and children. I'll be damned, if I'll continue paying the prices Hancock charges for his wares. As governor, I can get better bargains by dealing with my own factors in England. Perhaps I can get you a bauble or two, if you like Hubert."

"No, sir," responded Slank. "I could never abuse our relationship. Your lordship is already too kind to me. Now, if that is all, I must run down to the wharf to get this posted."

Upon his departure, Bernard turned to Thomas Hutchinson, who had been standing at the window, sipping brandy from his finest stemmed lead crystal glassware. "Exactly what are you gazing at, Thomas?" he asked.

"I notice that the lights of the *Boston Gazette* are still burning. Just what kind of drivel could they be printing at this hour, I wonder? Nothing but radical propaganda comes from that building," said Hutchinson.

"Relax," said Bernard. "I've just written Lord Grenville in London to tell him that our cry for troops can be cancelled and that peace has returned to the streets of Boston. His Stamp Act repeal has worked, and the radicals have retreated to their holes, like so many rats."

"I pray you are right, Governor. But where do Adams and his patriot party stand, I wonder?" quizzed Hutchinson.

Bernard smiled patronizingly, as he patted him on the back. "Who cares?" said Bernard. "We now have Hancock on our side, along with the other merchants. Adams has no money and is now powerless with nothing to complain about. Let's enjoy the peace."

ΩΩΩ

It was a few hours past sunset and pipe smoke wafted to the beamed ceiling of the taproom in the Snug Harbor Tavern. Angel stood beside Amos behind the bar and asked, "How does anyone recognize anyone in this place with all this smoke?"

Amos gave a toothy grin saying, "Amanda says that it is best this way. Some folks don't want to be even seen, let alone be recognized, in the Snug Harbor. I guess the wives sometimes just don't understand."

Outside, Zeke Teezle stood hidden in the shadows, beneath the bowsprit of a merchantman that was docked at the land end of Hancock's Wharf. Feeling secure in the darkness provided by the rigging, he mopped his sweaty brow, as he carefully watched and listened for any sign of his being followed. The note had said they would be watching, but he needed to know who it was.

His gaze finally settled on the well-lit windows of the Snug Harbor Tavern, just across Fish Street from the wharf. It was clearly evident that this was the busiest tavern on the waterfront. He patted the notes in his hip pocket; the one he received, and the one he had written to defend himself. How could they blame him for the death of some strumpet? He reflected that just a few days ago, his life was much simpler, and it all changed in that dastardly tavern. He straightened his collar and shuffled across the street, feeling that up till now, no one was trailing him.

No one took notice of his entering the taproom, as he once again edged his way to the bar. He couldn't hide his pleasure at the sight of the raven-haired barmaid's luscious cleavage, as she asked loudly over the din of the crowd, "What will you have, my good man?"

Teezle, wiping spittle from his lip, muttered, "I'll have a mug of rum. And I have something for Hope." Angel smiled knowingly, saying, "I'm sure you have something to hope for . . . er . . . for Hope."

She walked to the far end of the bar and casually remarked to Amos of another fare for Hope. Amos peered through the smoke and said, "He was here last week, asking for Charity." Angel grinned. "This is hardly a place to go begging!"

Amos, giving her a dour look, said, "Charity is our girl who got herself killed. You best go upstairs and tell Amanda about this one. I'll take care of the bar and watch this fella."

Angel noticed the small sign on the door that read Busy, but she knocked on the door to room A and heard Amanda's breathless smiling voice from within saying, "Amos, I told you, I'm not to be disturbed during business hours." A male voice joined her laughter.

"Sorry to bother you, Amanda, but Amos said there's someone you should see in the taproom who has something for Hope," said Angel urgently.

"Sit tight and I'll be down shortly. He's probably not the only sailor who has something for Hope. At this moment, someone has something for me," said Amanda, giggling. The plaintive twang of an errant bed strap told Angel to retreat back to the taproom.

Ten minutes later, Amanda stood in the hallway, waving adieu to her paramour, as he departed down the private back stairway. She glanced back into her room, noticing that the only evidence of the tryst was an empty bottle of Madeira. She patted her hair and descended the stairs to the taproom.

After a short briefing from Amos, Amanda said, "Give me a mug of cider, Amos." His eyes were full of questions. "Cider? For you?" he asked.

She nodded, adding, "I need a clear head for this one."

Amanda, puffing her bodice, wandered to the corner table Teezle had obviously selected for its solitude. She sat down heavily, pulling a chair closer to him. "It is so very good to see you again, Mr. Teezle. I told you that you would be back, and if my information is correct, you have something big for Hope," she said boldly.

"Yes . . . er, that's correct. I do have something for Hope," said Teezle, feeling his pocket for the note. *Why,* he wondered, *did this woman make him nervous?*

Amanda gazed around the smoky taproom and said, "It seems that Hope is busy getting 'something' from someone else at the moment," she chortled, smacking Teezle on the back. "What you need is another mug of rum while you wait." She waved to Amos for another round, as she noticed Teezle's furtive gaze shift to every part of the taproom, as if he was a cornered rat.

Amanda smiled when the mugs arrived. "I thank you for coming back, Mr. Teezle. We have much to talk about. And please relax, and don't worry about someone seeing you here; I'm the only one with eyes on you, luv." She was about to mention her talking with Glunt that afternoon, when Teezle grabbed her arm suddenly.

"Did you say *you* was watching me? It's you," said Teezle accusingly. "I should have known. You and that strumpet . . . well, I didn't do it." With that said, Teezle stood abruptly, spilling his rum. Glaring down at her seated at the table, he threw two envelopes at her. "Here's your note and mine. I'm finished with this whole affair," muttered Teezle. "You tell that fat man that he best not come near me." He then rushed out the door before she could respond. No one seemed to notice the slight verbal jousting, as the boisterous crowd continued in their private celebrations of life. No one bothered to take note of the lanky old sea dog, wearing a red stocking cap and sailing jacket, who shuffled out the door within seconds of Teezle's deliberate exit. If anyone had taken the time, they would have noticed the fine tooled silver buckles on his shoes.

Amanda, a bit confused, gathered the envelopes, noting that one had been opened, and the other was sealed. She stuffed them into her bodice, as she cleared the table in pretended casualness. She tried to gather her thoughts. *What was this about a 'fat man?'* she wondered. At the bar, she caught sight of Angel speaking with Hope, who had just descended the stairs. She rushed to the conversation.

"And he said he had something for you specifically," she heard Angel say to Hope. "Isn't that right, Amanda? Where is that man? I thought he was with you?" asked Angel.

Amanda smiled, saying, "He said that he couldn't wait, but he'd be back sometime soon. It seems you have a new admirer, Hope."

Hope, feeling a bit puffed, said, "I told you I could bring a few gold guineas to this place, Amanda. What was the bloke's name?"

"He didn't say," fibbed Amanda, "just another sailor who likes the set of your sails, Hope!" She turned to Angel and Amos. "You two take care of the taproom. Suddenly, I'm a bit tired, and I think I'll call it a night."

Watching her retreat up the stairs, Amos said to no one in particular, "That's strange; Amanda is usually the last one to leave the taproom. She's been working too hard lately." As he wiped down the bar, lost in thought, he continued to mumble, "Hard work don't make any sense. I gives minimum work for minimum wages; but for her, it's family business. I gotta watch that lady. There's meanness brewin' around here; I can feel it in my bones. And meanness don't just happen overnight!"

Amanda sat at her dressing table, holding her head in her hands. She had read the notes, but they made no sense to her. One note accused Teezle of a murder; and in the other, he denied it. But she wondered. *Who is it that accused him? And who is the fat man he mentioned? And what does Hope have to do with this? This afternoon, Big Bessie said something was amiss and that we girls should force the issue,* she reflected. She then glanced at the empty bottle of Madeira on the nightstand; she would need help with this, and she now knew exactly where to turn.

ΩΩΩ

Earlier, Emmet Glunt had been sitting in the shadows amid ship riggings outside the Snug Harbor Tavern, when old man Teezle burst through the door like the devil was after him. He was about to rise and follow him, when an old sailor suddenly appeared at the door, and he seemed to trail in the wake of Teezle. What made this strange was that Teezle was almost running in the direction of the candle shop, with the sailor maintaining a discreet distance but keeping pace. With his short chubby legs, it was all Glunt could do to keep up. Fortunately, there was enough foot traffic that night for no one to notice.

In a few moments, chubby Emmet Glunt was in the side alley of the Bunch of Grapes Tavern on King Street, gasping for air to catch his breath and wondering who to follow. It was clear to Glunt that Teezle was making his way home to Milk Street, but the sailor had stopped his pursuit, turning right on King Street.

Suddenly, Big Bessie Clump appeared just outside the doors of the Bunch of Grapes. "What are you doing, you fat little runt? Are you trying to sneak a peek at my girls at work? Get moving and come back when you are old enough to enjoy the goodies we have here. Now git!" she growled sternly.

Glunt, wilting under the tirade and having stopped his wheezing, ran home to the candle shop. Big Bessie, tucking her breasts into the stretched fabric of her dress and turning to reenter the tavern, noticed the flicker of candlelight in the Old State House, just up the street. *That was strange for this time of night,* she thought. But she quickly returned to her foaming flip and another tradesman looking for a tumble. "Stand by to get clumped, you hairy little devil," she cackled, barging through the doorway.

The old sailor in the red stocking cap had furtively entered the rear doorway of the Old State House, feeling that no one had spied his return or noted his disguise. His mind was racing, as he sat down. *Why did Teezle give the note to that Griffith woman? His instructions specifically said to contact Hope. The plans were going so well, until the Snug Harbor connection.* He would talk to the fat man; somehow, he must know who could be trusted in the network. *It was a shame that Charity had to go the way she did,* he mused. But she had to be silenced; there was no room in Omega for a yapping doxy. Tomorrow, he must speak with the fat man. *Now to hide these tattered ruffian clothes,* he mused.

ΩΩΩ

CHAPTER 6

THE INCESSANT POUNDING at the door of the Old State House the following morning roused Hubert Slank from his organizing Governor Bernard's correspondences to London. Angrily, he rushed to the door to find what he least expected. Standing before him stood Big Bessie Clump and Amanda Griffith. They were dressed in what they felt was their Puritan best, but it barely concealed their lack of Puritan demeanor.

Big Bessie immediately bustled across the threshold into the Old State House, with Amanda close behind. "Where's the governor?" demanded Bessie.

Slank, having been pushed aside, and regaining his official composure, stood between the two women and the narrow spiral staircase. "Do you . . . er, ladies, have an appointment with Governor Bernard?" he responded belligerently, with his arms folded across his chest. *I'll be damned,* he thought, *if I will be intimidated by these riffraff.*

Amanda responded with a growl, "We don't have an appointment, and we don't need one. We don't have much time. Now where's the governor?"

With all the pomposity he could muster, Slank retorted, "The governor sees no one without an appointment. I will be happy to take your names and see when he will be available."

Amanda looked at Big Bessie confidingly. Then to Slank, she said, "But of course. Ms. Clump and I must have forgotten our Christian manners. Would you please tell Governor Bernard or even the Lieutenant Governor that Ms. Clump and Ms. Griffith would like to have an audience at their earliest convenience? And, by the by, who are you, sir?"

Indignantly, he responded, "I am Hubert Slank, secretary to the governor. Please remain here by the door, and I shall check the governor's schedule." With that, he rushed up the spiral stairs to the governor's office.

He had no sooner cleared the stairway on the first landing than Bessie and Amanda were on his trail up the stairs at a discrete distance and as quiet as they could manage. They watched Slank enter a room to his right at the end of the hall, which would obviously overlook King Street. They rushed to the closed door, listening intently. "All I can hear is mumbling," whispered Bessie, panting from the exertion of the stairs. "It doesn't matter," said Amanda, "just wait and follow my lead."

Suddenly, the door opened with Slank exiting toward them. Amanda, holding Big Bessie's plump hand, barged past Slank, and entered the office. Both Governor Bernard and Lieutenant Governor Hutchinson turned to the door with looks of bemused anger. "What is the meaning of this?" growled Bernard.

"Thank you for taking the time to see us, Governor," said Amanda casually. "Mr. Slank said you would make yourself available to a few poor citizens of Boston." Slank, standing helplessly behind the two women, was about to interrupt, when Hutchinson raised his hand in a quieting motion and said, "Thank you, Mr. Slank. That will be all for now." Bernard looked at Hutchinson quizzically. Hutchinson gave him a surreptitious wink, as he rose from a corner chair near the window.

"Good morning, ladies," said Hutchinson casually. "Forgive us, but your abrupt entry eliminated Mr. Slank's ability to formally introduce us." Coughing into his lace kerchief, he added, "We had just sent for you. I am Thomas Hutchinson, and of course, this is Governor Bernard. How may we help you ladies?"

Taken back with the formality and politeness, Big Bessie stammered, "We know who you are! I'm Bessie Clump, and this is Ms. Griffith. We are wearing our black mourning weeds because of a murder most foul, and we want to know what the courts are going to do about it."

"A murder?" questioned Bernard, glancing at Hutchinson knowingly. "Why haven't I been told of such a thing? Who was murdered? Where and when did this happen?"

Amanda replied sternly, "Don't you read the newspapers? It happened last week, and it was one of my girls down by Hancock's Wharf. And that lousy sheriff says he can't do a thing."

Hutchinson said, "I'm sure that Sheriff Greenleaf will do all in his power to bring justice to bear. Sadly, those are his duties and not ours. I am merely a justice of the superior court, and the governor relies totally on the good sheriff. Isn't that correct, Governor Bernard?"

Bernard rose from his desk and, shaking his head somberly, said, "Mr. Hutchinson is right, ladies. It would be a violation of royal mandate for either of us to interfere with the duties of the sheriff. And I agree that Sheriff Greenleaf will do everything possible."

Hearing this, Amanda became angrier, and it was showing, but Big Bessie interrupted first, saying, "If you think that old geezer could do his duty properly, you are dreaming. Besides, when they found poor Charity, old Greenleaf said it was only a drowning of a doxy, and that was the end of it."

"A doxy?" asked Bernard. "My word!"

"Your word, indeed," said Amanda angrily. "She was a fine young girl and one of my own at the Snug Harbor Tavern. I told the sheriff that she was with one of the gentry when we saw her last. And he said that was the end of it. Now we come to you. What are you going to do? We want justice for us, ladies."

Bernard stepped closer, his hands pressed before him in a prayerful pose saying, "My dear, ladies. Let Mr. Hutchinson and I speak to the sheriff about this personally. I'm sure we can ensure that he does all that is possible. Are you certain it was a murder and not merely an accidental drowning? This happens often down on the waterfront."

"Now you sound like Sheriff Greenleaf," growled Big Bessie, "The poor girls face was beaten, mangled even! It was no accident; it was murder! Now you best do something about it. She wasn't highborn, but she loved the king. And she was a loyal English subject."

Hutchinson patted Amanda's arm soothingly, but she brushed his hand aside. "No one touches me without paying first," she said. "Er . . . I mean, forgive me, but since the loss of my husband, I find it hard to have a man get real close, if you know what I mean, sir."

Hutchinson, with a twisted grin, continued, "You must understand that these things take time, Ms. Griffith. Let the governor and I speak with the sheriff, and I am certain we will get to the bottom of this. Every subject of the Crown is precious to us all. Now, if you ladies will excuse us, there is much work to do." With that, he went to the door, and Slank entered from the hallway. "Mr. Slank will show you out. We will let you know of our progress. Please tell Mr. Slank where you can be contacted."

Amanda looked at him suspiciously. "I can be found at the Snug Harbor Tavern. and I would love to have you both over some evening." Slank escorted them down the stairs and to the door in silence. His scowl left little to be said, as they stepped into the bustle and noise of King Street and turned left toward the Bunch of Grapes.

Big Bessie, looking back over her shoulder at the Old State House, said, "Amanda, that was a mere shuffle of the cards. I doubt we can trust them. They are lying like most men do, and I am never wrong about lying men."

Amanda pondered, "Sadly, you are very correct, Bessie. They used the same exact words Sheriff Greenleaf used when he visited the tavern. If they aren't with us, they must be against us. Even if Charity wasn't born to a high station, she deserves better from the law. Let's you and me keep an eye on these government officers. Something is strange when they don't seem to care. Someone is hiding something." Big Bessie nodded in agreement and stepped into the Bunch of Grapes while Amanda continued down to the familiar confines of the Snug Harbor Tavern.

Both Bernard and Hutchinson were standing at the window of the Old State House overlooking King Street, watching their exit. "It seems that our two 'ladies' are in deep discussion about this little impromptu meeting," observed Bernard, "How stupid of them to think that two strumpets could order me around!" He stepped to the sidebar to pour a glass of claret. "Exactly what could you be thinking, Thomas, to let them ramble like that at us?"

"Forgive me, Governor. But it seems that it is best for us to let this rabble think we care. We needn't give these radicals any reason whatsoever to break the peace. I'll speak with Greenleaf, and we will find someone to convict of the crime. Perhaps one of the high Sons of Liberty; now wouldn't that be amusing on the gallows? To have one of the radicals on the gallows for the murder of a strumpet, Adams and his rabble would have nothing to say but to render apologies to the lowest of our society. We have them in our sights, I tell you. These ignorant strumpets have dealt us a fine hand to play here."

Bernard peered at him, thinking for a long moment. "Yes, do that, Tom. But I don't want to know the details. This will give me plausible deniability and protect the Crown."

Hutchinson smiled, saying, "I must visit the good sheriff," as he stepped out the door.

Just as Hutchinson left the room, Hubert Slank entered with a handful of documents. "Sire, these require your signature," he said.

Bernard picked up his quill and began to sign. "Slank," he said, "I need someone to keep an eye on the Bunch of Grapes and the Snug Harbor Tavern. Somehow, I feel that those two strumpets could bear close watching."

Slank said simply, "I'll have the old sailor take care of it, sire."

ΩΩΩ

When Zeke Teezle stumbled down his stairs to open his candle shop the next morning, he found a note that had been shoved under the front door. Ensuring that he was the only one up at that early hour, he broke the red wax seal and read,

> *Teezle,*
>
> *Never! I say never will you ever leave messages with the wrong people. You must follow orders. We are watching you. The dead doxy is still a problem; we will be in touch. Stay quiet about our business, and we will be in touch when it is safe. Destroy this note.*

Ω

Teezle lit a fire in the stove and did as ordered.

ΩΩΩ

At that same moment, John Hancock was reading two notes, the seals of which had already been broken. Wearing his house coat, he was standing in his library. Little

Imp stood before him, gazing around the vast room. "Did you really read all these books?" asked Imp in amazement.

Hancock smiled. "Yes, Imp. Many were read because it was ordered to do so by stern schoolmasters, whom I hated at the time. Perhaps you would like to borrow one."

Imp pursed his lips. "I don't have much time to read. I'm a bit of a businessman myself, you know." Changing the subject, he asked, "Is them notes worth my running up here to Beacon Hill? Ms. Griffith told me to wait for a return message or something." He shuffled his feet impatiently. His inability to read even one word was an embarrassment he chose to conceal. Somehow no one thought to send him to school. Amanda was the only one he knew well who could read and cipher.

"Ms. Griffith said that the man seemed very afraid and in a hurry?" asked Hancock, confirming what he had heard.

"Yessir," said Imp. "He said he didn't do nothin'. And he ran out the Snug Harbor like he was on fire. Leastwise, that's what Ms. Griffith said for me to tell you."

Looking sternly, Hancock said half to himself, "These notes are quite important, Imp. Tell Ms. Griffith that I thank her." He paused in thought, looking out the window at Boston Common, then added, "Tell her to do nothing. I will have others handle this when the time is right. Wait here just a moment." He rushed to his small secretary desk. Imp's curiosity was piqued at the scratching of the quill pen.

Hancock handed two notes sealed with wax bearing his signet imprint. "Take this one to Mr. Sam Adams and the other to Paul Revere. Do you know where to find them?"

Imp replied proudly, "Everyone know where Mr. Revere's silversmith shop is, and Mr. Adams can be found either at the brewery near the Green Dragon Tavern or at Edes & Gill on Queen Street. I deliver the *Boston Gazette* for them."

Hancock smiled. "Good lad! Now here's a shilling for your trouble. Now be quick about these messages, and be sure that no one sees what you are about."

After Imp left, Hancock placed Amanda's notes in a hollow book on an eye-level shelf. *Teezle will bear close watching*, he thought. This was a job for the Sons of Liberty . . . when the time was right. If he let loose the dogs too early, Teezle would probably be dead or somehow disappear. *Someone was pulling the strings of this candlemaker*, he thought. Only time would reveal exactly who.

ΩΩΩ

Shortly after sunset, Hancock entered the Green Dragon Tavern, quickly rushed through the taproom, and sprinted up the back stairway, uncharacteristically ignoring everyone present.

Catherine Kerr, working behind the well-worn bar, nudged Millie, the serving wench, saying, "The squire rather fancies himself. Can't be bothered to greet the likes of us. Curse him and all his finery."

Millie merely shrugged in her dirty mobcap. "Who cares about him? All I know is that I serves the pints and quarts and they favors me with a shillin' now and again."

"What do they talk about up there in that smoky room all evenin'?" asked Catherine.

"They's mighty secretive, they is," said Millie in a hushed tone. "When I enters, all the talks about food and drink."

"They spend a lot of time up there, and I was just wonderin'," said Catherine.

"Sometimes, when I'm waitin' outside the door, I hears 'em talking 'bout the guvna and some sons and such. But it's only food and drink when I enters," added Millie.

Meanwhile, upstairs, smoke was wafting to the ceiling from the long tapered clay pipe that was cradled in the strong grip of Paul Revere. Paul was seated near Sam Adams when Hancock arrived in a rush. *How is it,* he wondered to himself, *that Hancock always appears to be so neat and unrushed, even when he is rushed? On the other hand, Sam Adams is again pacing in his perpetual agitated state.* Paul took a long casual draw on his pipe, savoring the tobacco saying, "Mr. Hancock, I should warn you that Mr. Adams here has been pacing the floor like a butcher awaiting the arrival of a hog."

Pursing his lips, forbidding profanity to escape them, Adams grumbled accusingly, "John, you are late. Your note said to meet here at sunset."

Hancock smiled. "It seems, gentlemen, that I am being followed these days. I did my best to lose him, but I fear I am far too visible a target. For all I know, whoever it is may be in the taproom below."

Rising to his feet, Revere asked, "Who is it? I'll have this taken care of immediately. I have a few high Sons with me in the taproom, as we speak."

Adams placed his shaky hand on Revere's elbow, staying his move to the door. "Slow down, Paul! Let us think this through. Perhaps it would be wiser to learn more about this spy who is so interested in Mr. Hancock."

Looking at Hancock, he continued, "First, why did you call us here this evening, John?"

Hancock told them about the two notes left at the Snug Harbor Tavern and specifically about the actions of Zeke Teezle. "My biggest question is what or who is this 'Omega'?"

Revere's gaze followed his pipe smoke to the rafters. "Teezle the Tory, eh? His fat, dumpy wife could soon become the 'Widow Teezle' if I told a few high Sons of Liberty about this."

Again, Sam Adams raised his hand in a calming gesture. "Paul, these things must be handled delicately. We should not use a hammer to swat a fly."

Hancock, watching the exchange, added, "I see what you mean, Sam. Let's just watch Teezle and see who he contacts. He could lead us to this 'Omega.'"

Sam smiled knowingly. "No John! We will do better than that. Paul here will adopt Teezle into our fold and make him feel welcome. It is best to keep our enemies close, if possible."

Revere, rising, looked at them both incredulously, his pipe tobacco spilling to the floor. "You cannot be serious! How can we befriend a known conspirator against us? Have you lost your taste for action? I tell you Widow Teezle is sounding better to me, the more I think about it."

"We will not 'befriend' him in the true sense, Paul," said Sam smiling. "You must share with him only the most obvious information and introduce him to the already known high Sons of Liberty. In fact, it would be ideal to set him close to Mackintosh." Laughing aloud, he added, "Now that is a matched set, Teezle and Mac."

Hancock added, "Let him feel he knows everything, Paul, while telling him nothing; let him feel he knows everyone while he has met no one."

"Meanwhile, you should have a few covert eyes glued to his every move and every contact. They should report anything that seems out of the ordinary for this candlemaker," added Adams.

Paul, nodding his reluctant assent asked, "And what about this one who follows John here?"

Hancock stood and wandered to the window. "Let me handle my shadow. I am too visible to hide, and it seems he means no real harm. I will simply guide him where I desire. As for our meetings, I will always arrive last and depart first."

Adams said, "You are correct, John. Furthermore, our meeting places shall henceforth be rotated among the various taverns and shops. We will need a courier to share information between the various groups and meetings."

Hancock grinned. "I can see it in your eyes, Paul, that you have someone in mind. And it is probably someone you trust and probably a grown man, who can handle himself." He sauntered to the window as he continued, "But a grown man is too obvious. On the other hand, I have the perfect courier – that little urchin who delivered the notes to me this afternoon."

Looking at Adams and Hancock for agreement, Paul responded, "The way I see it, we have St. Andrews Masonic Lodge that meets here at the Green Dragon, the North Caucus, which meets at the Salutation Tavern by the Old North Church, and our meetings at Edes & Gill on Queen Street. Can this lad be trusted to keep his mouth shut and his ears open?"

Hancock glanced sharply, "He has already proved his worth. You have my word on it. You might as well add the Snug Harbor Tavern to your list, Paul."

Both Sam and Paul looked quite surprised. Almost in unison, they asked, "Why the Snug Harbor?"

"Simple! It is very near my warehouse; hence, convenient without my having direct contact with any of you. My shadow could never suspect a little boy of anything more than petty theft from a lobster vendor; eventually, he would become quite bored sitting on the wharf, with me out of sight. Besides, Imp – that's the lad's name who lives at the Snug Harbor Tavern – can be trusted. If either of you have something important for me, get a message to the Snug Harbor Tavern, and I will get it for sure."

Sam asked, "Who can you trust at the Snug Harbor besides this 'Imp'?"

"I will make arrangements for your messages to be directed to the proprietor Ms. Griffith; the barman, Amos, could also be trusted. They will use Imp as our main relay and conduit; he is perfect for the job."

ΩΩΩ

The sun had just set, but no one seemed to notice through the driving rain of this late October day. In her dingy upstairs room F of the Snug Harbor Tavern, Purity gazed at her reflection in the looking glass of her small dresser, lacing her bodice, and punching up her perky little breasts. She glanced over her shoulder and shivered in disgust at the sight of Sheriff Greenleaf trying to pull his holey breeches over his hairy protruding belly. He belched in the process of sucking in, as he tugged, while sitting on the edge of her small bed.

Casually, she said, "That will be a half crown, your lordship!"

Greenleaf, his powdered wig askew, coughed in midtug of his breeches. "You cannot be serious, Purity; you know that we men of the constabulary always enjoy a free tumble."

Purity turned to face him, her eyes aflame. "The days of a free tumble are past, my lord sheriff. Now where is my half crown?"

Greenleaf struggled to his feet, finally cinching his breeches, and reached for his green silk waistcoat. He began to laugh at the tiny strumpet standing before him, her arms akimbo. "Just try and collect that half crown, missy; you are hardly worth the usual shilling for the shaggin' you provide. Now hand me my boots there by the door."

Purity, with a tender pout on her face, picked up the muddy boots and stepped to the foot of the bed, as Greenleaf hunched over his belly, now tugging at his stockings. Instead of handing him his boots, she casually opened the window and shutters.

"What are you doing, you silly strumpet? You're letting in the rain. Now hand me my boots," he commanded.

Purity smiled at his command, as she tossed the boots out the window into the downpour. "My, my, my, Lord Sheriff, it seems I've dropped your boots."

Standing abruptly in his stocking feet, Greenleaf growled, "Why, you filthy doxy, I'll wring your little neck."

On reflex, Purity screamed at the top of her voice, as piercing as that of a hog slaughtering.

Below in the taproom, a table of sailors laughed. One salty tar said, "It seems that someone hit rock bottom with his sounding lanyard." Everyone in the group laughed heartily.

On the other side of the bar, Amos and Amanda exchanged startled glances, knowing that a scream that shrill was a signal for alarm. Amanda commanded, "Angel, you cover the bar; Amos, you come with me." As she sprinted to the back stairway,

Amos paused long enough to grab a cudgel from beneath the bar, as he followed closely behind.

Amos burst through the door at room F, finding Purity cowering in the corner, next to the window, and Sheriff Greenleaf, now fully clothed, with exception of his boots, yelling at the young girl. Her perfumes and hair brushes were strewn on the floor, the looking glass shattered. Greenleaf turned, glaring in defiance at Amos's intrusion. "Get out, you black bastard! I have unfinished business with this little strumpet. Now get up, you little – "

Amos raised the cudgel, rushing toward the bootless sheriff. Suddenly, Amanda appeared from behind Amos, stopping his advance with a yell. In the deepest voice she could muster, she said, "What in hell is going on here?" Looking at the helpless girl, now sitting on her heels in the corner, she asked, "Purity, are you all right?"

Purity murmured, "I'm fine. But he refused to pay my fee. And I did him good, I did. It was a right righteous tumble, it was."

Greenleaf, regaining his composure and straightening his brocade coat, commanded, "Someone run outside and fetch my boots. Meanwhile, I am arresting this little strumpet. Now be quick about it." He glared at Amos. "And what do you propose to do with that club? Perhaps I should arrest you also."

Amos, his fist clenched in frustration, turned to leave. "Stay where you are, Amos," said Amanda loudly. "And close that door."

Greenleaf growled, "And just who do you think you are, other than the mother superior of this nunnery?" To Amos, he commanded, "Open that door, boy. I'll take care of you later."

He had taken one step toward the doorway, when Amanda said mockingly, "You leave this room now, and you do so at the peril of your reputation, my lord sheriff."

Sheriff Greenleaf halted and turned with a glare, "And what is that supposed to mean?"

"Just this; I'm certain you value your high station in Boston, which you have had years to cultivate. It would be a shame if certain newspapers were informed of your twisted delights here at the Snug Harbor," cooed Amanda.

"You wouldn't dare. Why, I would have you shut down within moments of any word of this outside this room. Don't try to threaten me, you lousy strumpet."

At the doorway, Amos raised the cudgel, but Amanda raised her hand to stay his advance. To Greenleaf her voice hardened, "This is no threat; it is a promise. On my way to the *Boston Gazette*, I will personally stop to speak with your wife. I'm certain she and Purity here will have much to discuss, as they compare your perverted proclivities."

Greenleaf turning a bit pale, muttered, "Now you know that is against every ethical part of your business, Amanda. You can't do that sort of thing."

"It isn't ethical for you to scare poor little working girls either," said Amanda defiantly.

"Well, she expected me to pay for what's always been a right of passage; you know, our understanding about the free shaggin' and all. We must be reasonable, Amanda," said Greenleaf soothingly.

"Your days of free shaggin' are over; and also the free pints and quarts," said Amanda boastfully. "Now pay Purity before you go, and we can almost forget this happened."

Greenleaf reluctantly fished in his purse, tossing a half crown on the dressing table. "This is robbery; a half crown is far too much for what is normally a shaggin' for a shillin'."

"That's the price. And remember that you now will also pay for all your drinking spirits, and that goes for all those who work for the Crown," said Amanda triumphantly.

Amos stepped aside as Greenleaf slouched through the doorway. "This is the last time I'll be in this dirty little grog shop. There are many other places to whet my appetite," he said, regaining his composure.

Amanda glared back at him, her face filled with enmity, "Don't be surprised if you and yours get the same treatment elsewhere in Boston. Until you bring to justice the murderer of Charity, you will find no place to take off your boots . . . other than your humble cottage. And I seriously doubt you get the same services from your spouse as you get from the likes of Purity here. Now be off with you."

Greenleaf's eyes burned at the insult, but the sight of the massive Amos standing at the door, cudgel in hand, made him think wiser of his thoughts. He turned on his stocking feet, cloak in hand, to exit down the back stairway to retrieve his boots in the mud below the window.

Amanda immediately turned her attention to Purity. "A half crown! Why, you little devil you!"

Purity, her face ashen, responded defensively, "Well, you said to charge him for services, and I just thought he could afford more than a shillin', and so I – "

Amanda laughed heartily. "What I mean to say is that, why didn't I think of charging a half crown. You are a wonderful girl, Purity; hereafter, all those in the employ of the Crown shall pay a half crown." To Amos, she added, "Don't forget to charge for all their spirits. And thank you, Amos, for being here; I know it wasn't easy."

Amos returned to the taproom, as Amanda helped Purity clean the mess in room F. Upon her arrival to the taproom, she found Imp mixing a flip with Angel behind the bar. "Imp," she said, "I want you to rush over to the Bunch of Grapes and find Big Bessie Clump."

Imp cringed and wrinkled his nose. "She always slobbers on my face. Can't you send someone else?"

"No, you are my man for the job. Now you must tell her the good news. The new price is a half crown for a tumble for all men in the employ of the Crown. Tell her to get the word out, and I will do the same," said Amanda proudly. "And they also pay full price for drinking spirits."

Imp donned his small foul weather cloak made of sail cloth, and shuffled out into the rainy night and up Fish Street toward the Bunch of Grapes. *What's the big deal about a tumble that a man would pay a half crown?* he wondered.

Little did he realize that his life was about to change. One of the high Sons of Liberty left the Snug Harbor, following him at a discreet distance. His orders were to ensure the safety of this little man; Revere and Adams had insisted that no harm ever come to him.

ΩΩΩ

Two days later, the streets of Boston were still quite muddy, but the rain had finally ceased. The windows of the Old State House were open to the brisk salt air of October, as Governor Bernard rummaged through routine customs documents and affairs of the colony at his large desk, cluttered with papers. *Where was Slank when he needed him?* he wondered, when suddenly the door burst open.

Alarmed at first, he smiled broadly as his wife appeared at the door. "Darling," she said boastfully, "I just had to come by and thank you for the lovely gold necklace. But you shouldn't have; our anniversary isn't until next month. You are such a dear."

She couldn't see his look of puzzlement as she kissed his cheek. Recovering from his surprise, he said almost casually, "Nothing gives me greater pleasure than to give you pleasure, my dear." Clearing his throat, he asked, "I am a bit surprised that your gift arrived so early; exactly who delivered it?"

"Oh, there was simply a rap on the door. When I opened it, I found this small package just outside," she responded, seating herself in an oversized chair for her oversized bulk, as she fingered her new necklace which was partially concealed in the many folds of her jowls and neck.

"There wouldn't have been a bill for the – ," he began asking when his thoughts were interrupted by incessant rapping at the door. "Come in," he ordered, smiling wanly at his wife, and at the seeming chaos of his interrupted routine.

Hubert Slank entered, saying formally, "Governor, allow me to announce – "

"Oh, forget the formalities," grumbled Sheriff Greenleaf, followed by Hutchinson. At the sight of Mrs. Bernard, they both halted abruptly and bowed courteously. "Please forgive the intrusion, Mrs. Bernard. We thought the governor was alone. Please let us come back at a more convenient time," said Hutchinson in a mellow tone of self-control.

"That will not be necessary," said Mrs. Bernard, rising from the chair. "I merely stopped to thank my husband for his kindness," she said, proudly showing her new gold necklace. "I am most fortunate to have a man so generous. Now I must be off. I shall see you at dinner, my dear."

When the door shut at her departure, Greenleaf leaned over the desk, and glowering at Bernard said, "Governor, we must do something about this strumpet thing."

As he spoke, Hutchinson seemed to glide over to a sideboard to pour a tumbler of Madeira wine, smiling to himself. "Governor," he said chuckling and holding up the decanter, "perhaps I should pour you one of these. You will need it, after you hear this tale of woe."

"This is no laughing matter, Mr. Hutchinson. It has become a giant case of domestic tranquility gone awry," said Greenleaf earnestly.

"What are you talking about?" asked Bernard, rising from his desk. "Strumpets? Domestic tranquility?"

Hutchinson handed him a tumbler of wine. "Let us sit in an easy chair, Francis. This you must hear from the sheriff himself. After he shared this with me, I felt you should be included because God only knows how to deal with it."

On cue, Greenleaf rambled, "It seems that a number of my deputies have been ill treated by the taverns of Boston, sir. I am sorry to admit that some have taken advantage of the lustful services provided at some establishments. Now these doxies vow to tell the wives of these noble public servants, unless – " He stopped, as if looking for the right words.

"Unless what?" pursued Bernard.

Looking for help from Hutchinson and seeing none available, Greenleaf continued, "Unless we solve the case of the murdered doxy."

Bernard looked furtively at Hutchinson, then sympathetically back at Greenleaf. "Just how important are these deputies in the giant scheme of public safety, Sheriff?" asked Bernard. "Actually, I thought this doxy business was a dead issue!" he added, laughing at his gallows humor.

Hutchinson added, almost too casually, "I am sorry to report that I received similar news from a few customs officials and even the town crier. Perhaps we took the visit of those two strumpets sometime ago a bit too lightly."

Bernard looked piercingly at Greenleaf. "Besides deputies and the other lower civil servants, is there anyone of consequence at risk here?"

Clearing his throat, the sheriff murmured phlegmatically, "We must assume that there are . . . but they haven't come forward . . . to my knowledge . . . sir."

Hutchinson raised his eyebrows at that and placing his tumbler on a small table said, "Sheriff, as a judge of the superior court, let me suggest that I discuss this with Governor Bernard privately. Together, I am sure we can come up with a legal remedy to put this case to bed, so to speak. Please excuse us."

Greenleaf lifted his bulk from the chair and lumbered to the door. "My men would be most obliged if you could remove this onus from their lives. Most are petrified that their wives would learn of a simple indiscretion of a little tumble in a tavern, if you get my meaning."

The sheriff was gone only a moment, before both Bernard and Hutchinson were doubled over with laughter. Hutchinson chortled, "It seems that the good sheriff is afraid to admit that it was his wicket that was caught shaggin' with the wrong doxy."

Bernard, still smiling, said, "It is a concern, however, when you think of how many men this could actually affect. The doxies are normally mute about their shaggers, in order to keep them loyal. Maybe someone should answer for the death of that Charity girl, after all."

Hutchinson, his smile now fading to his judicial look of consternation added, "No doubt you are right, Francis. But who could that 'someone' be?"

After a gentle rap on the door, Hubert Slank entered with a sheaf of papers. "These need your signature, sire. Please forgive the interruption," he said in a monotone.

As he turned to the door, Bernard said haltingly, "Slank, don't go just yet. I think we have a task for you."

"Sire?" queried Slank, his eyes shifting from Bernard to Hutchinson.

Bernard cleared his throat, "Slank, it would be in the best interest of the Crown if someone, preferably someone of little consequence, would pay the price for murdering that unfortunate doxy down on Hancock's Wharf. Do you know of anyone who could find this . . . person who did it? Our good sheriff seems to be unable to solve this dastardly crime on his own."

Slank, again shifting his eyes as if looking for an answer in the air, said, "I suppose my old sailor friend could dig deep into the waterfront. How soon do you need results, sire?"

Hutchinson quickly retorted, "The sooner the better. It is a case that must be solved – without involving the justice system."

Slank, a sly leer overtaking his face, said, "Then the penalty for this crime has already been determined by the courts; is that correct?"

"You could say that," said Hutchinson. "It would be unfortunate, if the criminal were to pay for his crime prior to trial. Of course, if that did happen, I am sure the court findings for the miscreant would be justifiable homicide."

"My old sailor would prefer to remain anonymous, sire," said Slank.

"And he shall. Tell him that whatever happens, the official findings shall be placed in the hands of Sheriff Greenleaf. He will gladly take the credit for solving a crime and the courts can attribute the execution . . . er, death, to resisting arrest."

Slank said, "A few golden guineas for his work would be most appreciated, sire."

"Of course," said Bernard. Draw up the necessary documents for the expense under the usual stores of the Crown, and I'll sign it."

Slank, providing a rare smile said, "Consider the job already completed, sire. If you will now excuse me, it seems there is much to do!"

ΩΩΩ

Three days later, Governor Bernard sat at his desk reading the following headline below the masthead of the *Boston Gazette*:

MURDERER BROUGHT TO JUSTICE: ON THE WATERFRONT

Sheriff Greenleaf reports that a Northside ruffian and sometime sailor named Jesse Adair was nearly arrested on Hancock's Wharf for the murder of a fair damsel named Charity. Unfortunately, while resisting arrest, Adair was mortally wounded as the sheriff's deputies defended themselves.

Greenleaf told our reporter that Adair said that he didn't really mean to kill the doxy, but she assaulted him and tried to rob him. Sadly, his day in court will not occur. But justice has once again prevailed in Boston. Adair's body was hung, nonetheless, and it can be observed in the gallows at Boston Neck.

The sheriff again notes that the men and women of Boston can be guaranteed that the streets shall be safe for *all* citizens. Thomas Hutchinson, of the Superior Court, added that he only wished that this sort could have come to trial in order to learn all the facts.

He placed the newspaper aside and smiled broadly at Hutchinson. "Well done, if I do say so myself."

Hutchinson nodded in agreement. "I would like to meet Slank's old sailor friend. This man gets results. He could be a great asset to Omega; don't you think?"

Bernard grinned. "Who's to say he isn't already an Omega, Thomas?"

"Do tell!" said Hutchinson, with a conspiratorial grin. "Who is he?"

"Only Slank knows," replied Bernard. "The old tar feels it best to remain in the shadows. I use him sparingly, but Slank guarantees his prowess on the waterfront."

Hutchinson, again grinning, said, "Join me for dinner at the British Coffee House, Francis. It is time to celebrate. The strumpets should be happy about justice having been served, and I understand that the dead criminal, this Adair fellow, was one of the Sons of Liberty. Come, we can watch the Bunch of Grapes from the window of the British Coffee House; with luck, we might see Greenleaf himself enter there for a bit of amusement."

Bernard shook his head. "I shall pass on dinner, Thomas. I have something more urgent to care for at the moment. Perhaps I will meet you there later."

"Very well, perhaps later," said Hutchinson. He danced his way out the door without a care in the world. Conversely, Bernard sat down heavily behind his desk to again read the document delivered by some unknown urchin that afternoon. It was a demand for seven pounds in payment for a gold necklace. "But I didn't order this necklace!" Bernard said to himself.

The note instructed,

> *Place an envelope with seven pounds payment in the alms box of the Old North Church; the poor of Boston thank you. If payment is not made promptly, the gold*

necklace in question shall be redeemed in a most tasteless and public fashion, certain to embarrass you and your wife.

Bernard exited out the back door of the Old State House and casually made his way to the Old North Church. After a brief prayer, he deposited an envelope with a most generous donation in the alms box.

Shortly thereafter, while having coffee with Hutchinson at the British Coffee House, he asked, "If you were to purchase fine jewelry, Thomas, who would you go to in this colony; that is, if you couldn't get it from London?"

"I hate to admit it, but the best goldsmith and silversmith I know is Paul Revere. I still go to him for repairs and small baubles. Why do you ask?"

Bernard frowned, "Never mind. I was just wondering."

ΩΩΩ

That evening at the Green Dragon Tavern, Paul Revere sat at a corner table with Sam Adams and Hancock. "It worked just as you said it would, Sam," laughed Revere. He placed an envelope in the center of the table. "The vicar watched the governor place the envelope in the alms box as expected."

Adams opened the envelope with seven one pound notes saying, "John, here's the three pounds you put up for the actual cost of the necklace. Paul, here's two pounds profit for you and your work. I'll take one pound back to the church, and the remaining pound will pay for our dinner."

Hancock chortled, "Imagine that! The governor presents his wife a gold necklace, and in the process helps a poor Boston goldsmith, the church, and the Sons of Liberty. He's really quite a generous man."

Sam added, "It's merely an annoyance for Governor Bernard, but anything to make him feel less secure suits me fine." They all laughed as they ordered another round.

ΩΩΩ

January 1767,

The howling wind of a winter nor'easter rattled the windows, and the driving sleet added a rhythmic tattoo. A slight draft whistled through cracks in the window frame. Amanda sipped her warm flip, listening intently to the tirade of her friend Bessie Clump. "I don't believe them for one moment," grumbled Big Bessie, her brassy voice echoing off the walls of her small bedroom in the upstairs of the Bunch of Grapes. "I tell you, Amanda, that Adair fella was no more guilty of killing sweet Charity than I am."

Amanda couldn't help but smile at the animated gyrations Big Bessie demonstrated. Her huge breasts seemed to dance in her bodice, as her arms flailed with each agitated sentence. The contents of Bessie's tankard of ale, clenched tightly in her pudgy fist, spilled from one side of the bed to the other.

Bessie suddenly lowered her voice, "What exactly are you grinning about, Amanda? This is serious."

"You must forgive me, Bessie; but this I must know. How do you possibly entertain any gentlemen with your room in this condition?" asked Amanda, mustering as much tact as she could.

Bessie followed her gaze. "What's wrong with it? And what 'gentlemen' are you talking about?"

"Why, this place is a mess, Bessie. Half your clothes are on the floor, with dirty food platters and half-drunk pints and quarts strewn about. And look at your perfume bottles, half spilled on your little dresser there," she said, pointing from one mess to the other.

"What's that got to do with business? The men I see don't come up here to do my laundry; it's only one thing they want, and that don't take too long, if you get my meanin'," replied Bessie sternly, wagging her finger in front of her face.

"But the smell," said Amanda, holding her nose. "Ale, morsels of old fish on these dirty platters and your perfume all put together make something awful."

"It ain't no better than the way these old sailors smell; you know that," grumbled Bessie. "I'll clean up, when they clean up."

Sitting back in a moment of deep thought, Amanda said, "You have something there, Bessie!"

"Got something where? What do I have?" asked Bessie, an incredulous look on her face. "Does it show much?"

"No, it's not on you; it's in your head, silly. Listen to me. What if we tell our girls to stay clean and wash every day? Then we can insist our customers stay clean and wash," Amanda said triumphantly.

"You mean that you expect to tell a man to take a bath before he takes a tumble?" asked Bessie. "You must be dreaming. These blokes sometimes might bathe once a month, for god's sake. In fact, some of those rustics in the farm country might take a bath in May and another in October. If it wasn't for the occasional swim in the river, they could be a walking garden plot."

Amanda stood, gazing around the room. "That's exactly what I mean; but even more so. How about we provide the baths for the men?"

Bessie, warming to the idea said, "We could charge extra for the baths."

"And even more," added Amanda, "what if the girls take a bath with them?"

"We would be the most squeaky-clean strumpets in Boston, Amanda," said Big Bessie, as she assessed herself in the looking glass. "I think I'll need an extra large tub, if I'm gonna climb in it with one of my regulars," she chortled, smiling at visions she chose not to share.

"You have regulars?" asked Amanda, innocently.

"Don't we all?" retorted Bessie. "Of course, my regulars are those who like extra special treatment that the other girls don't exactly care to provide, if you get my meanin'," continued Bessie with a knowing wink.

Amanda, electing not to continue this line of thinking, said, "It's agreed then. I'll get tubs, if you get tubs, and we charge for baths."

Nodding in agreement, Bessie added, "But what about the Charity situation? Adair didn't do it and – "

"We both know that," interjected Amanda soothingly. "But the town seems satisfied that justice has been served, with his body hanging down by Boston Neck. We best let the Sons of Liberty deal with it; he was one of their own. We can help if needed."

"Perhaps you are right. At least, we now charge the sheriff and the other Crown officials, and no more free pints and quarts," said Bessie proudly.

They left the bedroom arm in arm, headed for the taproom. "It's the same at the Snug Harbor, Bessie. But we now charge the same as everyone. Purity's 'half-crown tumble' helps with the profits, but some are still back to shaggin' for a shillin'," said Amanda in a resigned tone of voice. "I guess I should get back to the Snug Harbor," she added. "We can use Imp to pass messages, if we have to communicate. And, by the way, he hates you mauling him, Bessie, and he's growing, in case you haven't noticed."

Big Bessie grinned sheepishly, standing at the bar. "He's such a precious little boy; I just want to mother him. But you're right; lately, he's been tweaking my chest a bit when I hug him. It won't be long before he can see over the bar to get a pint of ale."

Amanda laughed. "It won't be long, and he'll be ready for everything we have on the menu."

They were both laughing heartily as they wandered to the door. They made little note of the red-capped old sailor, who seemed to be innocently reading the paper at the end of the bar. After Amanda departed, the old sailor left, heading toward the Old State House. *Who is Imp?* he wondered.

ΩΩΩ

CHAPTER 7

1767
Boston, Massachusetts

AS GOVERNOR BERNARD predicted, a period of comparative peace prevailed in the colony of Massachusetts. Much to his disgust, Sam Adams could do little to provoke his fellow radicals to any action in the name of liberty. John Hancock and his Merchants Club happily returned to the business of trade, with the tacit popular approval of their continued smuggling to avoid British taxation. Everyone benefited with lower prices passed on to every household in the colony. This tranquility continued through the end of 1766 and into the spring of 1767.

On February 3, 1767, Maude Aikins, a tenant of John Hancock and the proprietor of a small bake house on the waterfront found herself in the middle of a disaster. As the *Boston Gazette* reported, it seems that Maude was tending to one of her small children, when an errant spark from her bake oven created a small fire on her table cloth. The small fire jumped to the drapery, creating a larger fire. When she discovered the problem, the walls were aflame, and she was forced to evacuate with her children in tow.

The final assessment was the loss of twenty buildings, many belonging to Hancock. Fifty families were homeless. In traditional charitable fashion, the General Court appropriated four hundred pounds for relief of the homeless; this was supplemented with a hundred guineas from Hancock's private holdings. Stacks of firewood, food, clothing, and shelter were also provided to the needy. The New England winter was particularly harsh that year, and the firewood was greatly needed.

Once again, Adams found no reason to criticize and every reason to praise the Crown for its support, much to his chagrin.

ΩΩΩ

February 1767
London, England

King George III stood gazing out the windows of Buckingham palace at what he could see of the Thames through the pouring rain. He was lost in thought, when Charles Townshend, the new chancellor of the exchequer, entered the room, as expected. Townshend had replaced William Pitt who was an acknowledged friend to the American colonies.

The king, dressed in a fine gold brocade coat and blue silk waistcoat, turned slowly to the new arrival, knowing full well that the longer you left underlings waiting, the more regal you appeared. But, on the other hand, he thought, *Why spend any more time with this nasty business than necessary?* "What do you have for the Crown today, Mr. Townshend?" he asked, sipping from a crystal glass of claret.

Charles Townshend did all he could to conceal his disdain for the king, whom he secretly referred to as His Corpulence. "If Your Majesty pleases, it seems that the royal coffers are still suffering, and the recent lowered real estate taxes for the landed peers of the realm have not helped us one farthing. But I think I have a solution, sire," he said.

King George's bulging, languid grey eyes seemed to pierce Townshend's head. "If you recall," said the king, "it was Parliament who insisted the land tax be lowered so that more money could trickle down to the London streets. It seems that the London mob has stopped its rioting, which seemed to start at the slightest provocation. Hence, we have reaped the desired effect!"

Townshend smiled. "Your Majesty is entirely correct. The mob is quiet, and the landed gentry are happy, paying less to the Crown. However, the deficiency must be made up, and I have a plan," he said proudly.

King George smiled, taking another hearty sip of the claret. "Please do go on, Mr. Townshend. Just whose pocket do you plan to pick in order to replenish the royal coffers?"

Townshend, realizing he now had the king's undivided attention, said, "We must revisit the support we get from the American colonies, sire. Despite the repeal of the Stamp Act, which was opposed by merchants in both America and London, we must exercise the Declaratory Act, which gives you and Parliament the right to make any laws it sees fit for the colonies."

The king leaned forward, a sudden burning in his otherwise languid eyes. "And just what new laws do you see fit for my colonies, my dear chancellor?"

Townshend reached into his valise and retrieved the documents he had prepared. *Now was his moment to shine in the eyes of the Crown,* he thought to himself. "If I may say, Your Lordship, the American protest of the Stamp Act was an affront to the Crown. However, if we tax commodities they need and cannot manufacture, by law, we shall have the funds we need in no time at all."

"What commodities do you have in mind exactly?" asked the king.

"We shall place impost duties on glass, white lead, red lead, paint, all paper and tea," responded Townshend eagerly. "These are goods that must be purchased through London by a law that is already established. We already have a monopoly, and we can capitalize on it."

The king wrinkled his nose, as if offended by a foul odor. "Let me remind you that most of these goods are readily smuggled into America, according to the regular reports from our customs officials. The American colonists seem to be little more than a thieving gaggle, my lord minister."

Again Townshend smirked, as his beady blue eyes scanned his prepared documents. "Your Majesty is again correct. In fact, the New York colonial legislature has refused to provide for the king's troops who are stationed there, in violation of the Quartering Act. The solution is simple; we will have the royal governor of New York suspend its legislature, hence, removing them from power."

"And what of the smuggling?" asked King George.

"The greatest violator is the port of Boston, where we have only two customs commissioners and no royal troops. We should send at least six additional commissioners with a complete staff of supporting clerks. We will empower them to inspect any vessel, warehouse, or even their homes, if they feel the need to do so," said Townshend, his voice rising triumphantly.

King George smiled, rubbing his hands together in joy. "This will certainly rile those rascals in Boston. We will no doubt hear of the heat in Boston created by the likes of Sam Adams and that dastardly Hancock. By the way, I met this Hancock fellow at my coronation; did you know that?" Waving his hand, as though erasing the comment, he continued, "It's of no consequence. Be certain to alert Governor Bernard of our plans with these new taxes but to keep it secret until the official announcement. Get this passed in Parliament, and I shall sign it. You've done well, Mr. Townshend. Now I've had enough of this; you are excused."

On May 13, 1767, the Townshend Act passed. As with most legislation, it took more than a month for the news to arrive in the colonies and months more before bureaucracy could turn the wheels of enforcement. Little did Townshend realize that he was providing the very disturbance Sam Adams needed to rekindle the flames of discontent that had become a mere ember of hope for liberty.

ΩΩΩ

July, 1767
Boston, Massachusetts

The news of the Townshend Act arrived in the official packet for Governor Bernard and via copies of the *London Times* for all in the colony to read. Upon arrival of the news, Sam Adams immediately rushed a copy from the wharf to Edes & Gill for reprinting and editorial comment in the *Boston Gazette*.

Despite his Puritan ethics, Adams said, "Curse the dirty bastards to hell. Just who in hell does the king think he is dealing with here in Boston?"

Benjamin Edes looked up slowly from his copy of the *London Times,* saying, "Are you speaking to me, Sam?"

"There is no one else in this damned place," said Sam, his voice bouncing off the walls as he stepped to the window. "How can you be so calm, when our freedoms are being trampled upon? This is an outrage. If we don't take action, the next thing you know, we'll have redcoat bayonets up our sweet English asses! I tell you it's time we armed ourselves."

Ben placed the newspaper aside and said with an impatient sigh, "Sam, you forget that I am on your side. You'd best call our friends together and set a meeting of the general assembly. You're the secretary. Meanwhile, I'll reset the presses. You can start writing an editorial, using whatever fictitious name you are using lately. And don't worry! All of Boston will know quite well who wrote it, including the governor. Meanwhile, I suggest you forget about arms and cannon and such. How could we ever hope to stand up against the greatest army in the world? In fact, it's the same army we fought beside in the French and Indian War. It's, in fact, our army! They should be considered our friends, shouldn't they?"

"You best remember this little conversation, Ben. And when a redcoat sticks his bayonet in your ass, will you be content to know that it's a bayonet, thrust by your friend wearing a red coat? I sincerely doubt it. Now I need someone to notify the others of a meeting," retorted Sam with a tone of disgust.

Ben thought for a moment. "Why don't you send little Imp? He's just down below, getting the next issue organized to deliver. He's perfect for the job and knows everyone, and I mean everyone."

"Grand idea! I thought we had already put him to work. Fetch the lad," said Adams, seemingly lost in thought.

At that moment, John Hancock rushed up the stairs two at a time, laughing heartily. "How can you find joy at a time like this?" grumbled Adams, "Haven't you heard about this Townshend mess?"

Not deterred, Hancock continued, "I'm as distressed as you, if not more so, Sam. But in the midst of all this bad news, there is some news that will bring a smile to your face."

Ben interjected, "We could use some good news to print, John. What is it?"

"Glad you asked, Ben, because the Snug Harbor Tavern and the Bunch of Grapes will soon have news to share with the town."

Adams muttered, "Parliament is taking over, and you have news about taverns. What can you be thinking, John? This is not the time for trifling tidbits."

"This is not trifling, Sam. One of my ships just unloaded two cast iron bathtubs to be delivered to those very same taverns. Can you believe it?" laughed Hancock.

Edes grinned. "By god, that is news."

"So now we have bathing doxies," murmured Adams. "What's the big news about that?"

Hancock smiled knowingly. "Not only will the strumpets be clean, but I understand that the customers will be equally scrubbed down." All three men suddenly burst out in laughter.

Adams, turning serious said, "Let's be sure to share this with the others later. I'm sending this Imp lad to summon everyone to discuss this Townshend Act."

"Using Imp, eh?" queried Hancock. "Not a bad idea, at that!"

ΩΩΩ

At that same moment, Governor Bernard was reading the exact same *London Times* article, spelling out the specifics of the Townshend Act. Thomas Hutchinson sat in an easy chair across from his desk perusing the official dispatches from Parliament.

Bernard threw the *Times* to the floor, stepping briskly to the sideboard, pouring a large tumbler of claret. Hutchinson smirked, "That's something I normally do, my dear friend. But it's a bit early in the day for you, isn't it?"

Francis Bernard scowled, "Hell with the time of day, Thomas. Do you realize what Sam Adams and his rabble will do with this Townshend nonsense? What could Parliament be thinking?"

Hutchinson, helping himself to a small tumbler of claret and gulping it quickly, said in a calm voice, "I don't think we should alarm ourselves just now. It will be a few months before the new customs commissioners arrive. Meanwhile, we can do whatever possible to mollify Adams and his small gaggle, if that's what you want to do. Actually, I would prefer to have the king's troops come with the new commissioners and force the Townshend Act down Adam's throat with a bayonet."

Bernard grimaced, as he downed his own tumbler of wine. "Our real problem, Thomas, is that we will now lose the support of Hancock and the other merchants. I fear that Townshend has put a match to a bit of kindling."

Hutchinson refilled his glass, saying, "These past few months have been very calm, and I fear we have been remiss in keeping our network alive. Perhaps it is time to revive Omega."

"You are correct. Summon Slank for me," commanded Bernard. Hutchinson stepped into the hallway, returning with Bernard's secretary.

Slank, maintaining his subservient demeanor, said, "I understand you are in need of our special services, Governor."

"Yes," said Bernard, now looking out the window down the length of King Street toward the harbor. "I feel it is time to awaken Omega, Slank."

"Does this include the entire network, or the inner circle, sire?" asked Slank.

Hutchinson interrupted saying, "This time we will need all of Omega. That includes all strumpets and barmaids."

Bernard added, "And get that candlemaker mingling with the rabble on Hancock's Wharf. It is time we put him to work."

Slank replied, "I'll get the old sailor to make the rounds. I will need a few golden guineas to whet a few appetites."

"Take what you need from our tax collections and charge it to Crown supplies. Tell Omega to keep their eyes on Adams, Hancock, and Revere; where they go; the trouble will begin. I've heard rumors that Adams has suggested a call to arms. Find out if they have any weapons to speak of; not that it matters, if the king's army was to come ashore."

Slank bowed courteously, gliding out the door.

Hutchinson, gazing at the closed door, said, "You must forgive me, Francis, but there is something peculiar about that man, Slank. There is something about his eyes that I find unsettling."

"Relax," said Bernard. "His loyalties lie with us. And I've learned that he works best, when no questions are asked. Let's put it this way; if anything remiss or illegal were exposed, we can truthfully say we knew absolutely nothing. Somehow, Slank will take the brunt of any blame." They both laughed heartily at the folly of underlings.

Little did they realize that at that particular moment, the old sailor in the red cap was passing by the governor's doorway. His evil glance at the door spoke volumes of the possible retribution to come should he be betrayed by those in power.

ΩΩΩ

August, 1767

Sam Adams again was pacing the floor in the upstairs room of the Green Dragon Tavern. The sun was just setting over the western mountains and noise from the streets coming through the open window seemed to ebb by the moment. John Hancock, James Otis, and Paul Revere sat there silently in thought, hardly aware of their friend's meandering about the room.

Breaking the silence, Otis said, "Face it, Sam. We've done our best, from a legal standpoint. We've nominated our best men to the governor to fill the general court."

"And that bastard Bernard vetoed every one of those nominations," snapped Adams, raising his shaking hand.

"And we, in turn, have refused to fill the vacancies; thereby, bringing activity of the court and all legal activity to a screeching halt," said Hancock. "Hell, we should have done that long ago, now that I think about it," he added with a broad smile.

James Otis, a barrister of great repute sneered, "Thanks for kind words, John. You have effectively denied my livelihood as a lawyer."

Revere laughed aloud and then became quite serious. "Just listen to you, gentlemen. I am with you about our legal issues in the assembly and courts, but please don't lose sight of the real problem. This Townshend Act has crippled the average colonist with these taxes. You know that quite well, don't you, Mr. Hancock?"

Rising from his seat, Hancock downed his glass of wine and stepped slowly to the window to gaze at the harbor. "Paul, I have two ships docked at my wharf with cargo from the Indies. I will have a hard time selling it, due to the financial burden of this Townshend Act. I am befuddled as to what to do about it."

Sam Adams grinned. "We know how you cope, John; you simply smuggle around the customs agents or pay them off. Then you can charge less than the competition; I suppose you call that buying power, eh?"

Otis mused, almost to himself, bringing the group back to the problem at hand, "The next move rests with Governor Bernard, gentlemen. Now that we have tied his hands politically and legally, he must take action."

"And I fear that action will include the king's troops somehow," growled Adams, hammering his fist on the table. "I tell you that we should call the countryside to arms."

At that moment, the door opened. Dr. Ben Church waddled in, a mug of ale in his meaty fist. "What is all the pounding about, gentlemen? I could hear you howling in the hallway, Sam. Am I missing something?"

Sam Adams looked at Church, shaking his head in disgust. "For god's sake, Doctor. Is that all you do is eat and drink?"

"As a man of medicine, I have learned that one must look first to his nutrition and personal health," responded Dr. Church with a smile. "But that's not why you were howling a moment ago, Sam. What's wrong?"

"You know damned well what's wrong, Ben. Our economy is a mess with this Townshend Act, and the governor does nothing," said Otis. "He's actually part of the problem."

"Part of it?" yelled Adams. "He's probably the ring leader. I sincerely think he takes delight in abusing our rights as Englishmen. And the next thing you know, he'll have the king's troops in our lap."

Revere's eyes narrowed, and he slowly and distinctly asked, "Do you really feel that is possible, Sam?"

Hancock laughed as he interrupted, "Hardly possible at all, Paul. We're Englishmen, and the king knows it. He would never assault his own subjects, let alone loose the wrath of his army on us."

Adams rumbled, "I still feel we should be ready with a call to arms. Paul, perhaps you and the other Sons of Liberty should look to expanding and organizing the High Sons in the small towns outside of Boston. We need contacts in Charlestown and possibly extending all the way to Lexington and Concord." Looking to the others, he saw a look of incredulity. "What? Gentlemen, there is nothing wrong with our preparing for the worst. I only wish we had access to cannon and powder."

Ben Church chortled, "Now he wants to blow up the Old State House, with the governor in it, no doubt. How ridiculous!"

Hancock didn't miss the silent nod of agreement between Revere and Adams. "Ridiculous or not, Ben, preparation has never been a bad idea. As for cannon and powder, the king's troops would certainly have an answer – more cannon and more powder. I think we should stick with the Nonimportation Agreement. Stifle London's commerce, as we did with the Stamp Act, and the merchant's demand for action in Parliament. Governor Bernard will become a mere puppet to the demands of commerce and the rule of the almighty English pound in London. Trust me!"

ΩΩΩ

September 1767

Governor Bernard began to pace the floor of the Old State House, occasionally pausing at the window to stare at the harbor. Thomas Hutchinson, seated in an easy chair, frowned, "What are you so agitated about this time, Francis?"

"I just received this letter from Lord Shelburne in England. Now this brings our constant bickering to a head, and I guarantee the Liberty Party will not like it one iota," said Bernard, shaking the sheaf of documents in his hand.

"Who cares what Sam Adams and his rabble like or dislike? And since when is it your job to make them happy?" responded Hutchinson, acerbically.

Bernard went to the sideboard near his mahogany desk and poured himself a crystal tumbler of Madeira. "What's aggravating is that I'm drinking a wine provided by that smuggler Hancock while my wife and children are being cared for by that backstabbing Dr. Joseph Warren. The whole damned town knows that Warren writes those Paskalos letters, and Hancock is the chief financier of the Liberty Party."

Hutchinson grimaced, "We are all in the same quandary, aren't we, Francis? What exactly did Lord Shelburne have to say that seems so very troublesome to our not-so-loyal opposition?"

Bernard glanced at the documents in his hand and continued as if he hadn't heard a word from his lieutenant governor, "If you recall, I vetoed the House's nominations to the General Court, and in response, they refused to fill the vacancies, despite my request to do so. I referred the problem to the home office in London and the colonial secretary, suggesting a change in the Massachusetts Charter."

"I know all that," said Hutchinson, pouring himself a tumbler of claret. "But what did Shelburne say?"

Bernard, glancing at the letter again, said, "He sends royal approval of my veto of councilors who harbor private resentments and who might be induced to embarrass the administration and endanger the quiet of the province. What do you make of that, Thomas?"

"Endanger the quiet of the province?" echoed Hutchinson, raising his voice. "Hell, these letters in the *Boston Gazette* are screaming for your head and seem to be a mere syllable away from unabashed treason and rebellion!"

Governor Bernard looked up from the letter, grinning. "You have no reason to be upset, Thomas. To date, the Liberty Party has aimed its venomous pen at me and me alone. It seems that they somehow trust you." Pausing to scratch his head, he pondered a moment, adding, "Perhaps we can play on the trust they have in you personally. Let's get the fat man to dig a bit deeper on this. I could care less if they like me personally. But if we can quiet them with your homegrown colonial appeal, we might get the better of Adams and his mob, yet. It seems that your being born here carries a bit of sentimental value, and we should exploit it as much as possible."

Hutchinson nodded, deep in thought. "I still don't trust them. They demolished my home and my belongings and my records. More importantly, they scared the hell out of my family. Their apologies can be damned!" Rising suddenly and sauntering to the door, he continued, "Francis, I think I have found a new weapon to use against our radical friends." He opened the door adding, "Slank, please send in our friend."

In short order, Slank wandered into the office trailing a broad-shouldered, slightly rotund, yet quite dignified gentleman. He was dressed in a dark green brocade suit, trimmed in white piping. The lace at his throat and cuffs were of the finest work, and his walking stick was corded from Scottish heather and capped with a small ball of gold. His shoes were adorned with gold buckles. He stopped to stand before Bernard's desk, his piercing blue eyes locked with the governor's.

Hutchinson enjoyed the momentary silence, as the two men appraised each other. Finally, he said, "Governor Bernard, I have the pleasure of introducing Mr. John Mein, recently emigrated from Scotland."

Extending his hand across the desk, Bernard said, "It is a pleasure, sir."

John Mein shook his hand and bowed courteously. "The pleasure is all mine, Governor Bernard."

Hutchinson smiled broadly. "I thought it wise for the two of you to meet. You see, Governor, Mr. Mein here is proud owner of the London Book Shop, and he also provides a small lending library."

"How very nice!" said Bernard, drumming his fingers impatiently.

"More than 'nice,' Governor," continued Hutchinson, pouring a glass of wine for Mein. "You see, Mr. Mein has just begun publishing a small biweekly newspaper here in Boston."

"Just what we need," said Bernard sarcastically. "Isn't the *Gazette* enough of a pain? Er . . . forgive my forwardness, Mr. Mein. No offense intended!"

"None taken." John Mein smiled, sipping his wine as he eased himself into a chair. "Let me clarify something for you, Governor. You see, in my short time here in Boston, I noticed the heavy hand of your radical element here, especially in the *Boston Gazette* you just mentioned."

"Let me help you with this, Mr. Mein," interjected Hutchinson. "In essence, Francis, our good Mr. Mein here has agreed to publish a new weekly newspaper, the *Boston Chronicle*, which will present the Tory point of view and by coincidence, our viewpoint. At last, we will have a publication that doesn't pander to the fleet rabble out there."

Bernard smiled broadly. "Mr. Mein, I thank you for being here. It is high time the Crown have a vehicle to share the truth of government to the people. You just cannot fathom the lies that *Gazette* prints in the name of Publicus, Junious, and all those other mendacious penmen."

Mein downed his wine saying, "Gentlemen, this will be easy. As a loyal subject of the Crown, I agree with you. Furthermore, I find the activities of Sam Adams and his friends to be an abomination. I promise the *Boston Chronicle* will provide the king's truth. I've even employed a candlemaker's apprentice to deliver the *Chronicle*. He's a fat little kid named Emmet Glunt. If you have any news or opinion worthy of print, be assured that I will be happy to share it with the good citizens of Boston."

Raising his finger, Bernard interrupted, "Let me assure you of our cooperation, and thanks, Mr. Mein. Let me also assure you of threats, fire, and brimstone from Sam Adams and his cabal of criminals."

"I don't fear the threats of any radical, Governor; I can take care of myself. But if they are criminals, why don't you have them arrested?" queried Mein.

Hutchinson smiled. "Perhaps the term 'criminal' is a bit strong. Let us just say that we are in agreement that this radical element needs to be challenged, and we will do everything we can to support your efforts, Mr. Mein. In fact, speaking for Governor Bernard and many others, I can assure you that we will provide you exclusive access to any news from London, the Parliament, or elsewhere in the colonies."

Mein arose and headed to the door. "The first issue comes out next week. I'll be certain to have Glunt deliver a copy to this office. You will enjoy what you read; I assure you, gentlemen."

Staring at the closed door, Bernard smiled. "This should prove interesting, Thomas. Let's be certain to have Omega keep an eye on Mr. Mein. I would hate to see anything interfere with the *Boston Chronicle*. Get the old sailor to ensure his safety."

ΩΩΩ

Saturday, October 29, 1767

A thick evening fog obscured the view from the second-story windows of the Green Dragon Tavern, as Paul Revere squinted trying to identify the stocky short figure in the shadows of the street below; a man who seemed to follow his every move throughout the late afternoon. "Damn, the fat little bastard," grumbled Revere, turning to the leaders of the Liberty Party. "Every time I turned to see who it was, he seemed to vanish into the shadows."

Ben Church laughed heartily, as he licked his meaty fingers of excess chicken grease. "May I humbly suggest that you might be imagining things, Paul? Why, for god's sake, would anyone follow you?" Turning to Dr. Warren, he added, "Paranoia, Joseph; that's what it is – paranoia. We are beginning to see spies all around us since news of the Townshend Act has been spread about."

Dr. Warren, rising from his chair with a tankard of ale in his fist, smiled. "You may be right, Ben. But on the other hand" – turning to Revere – "our friend Paul here is no man to bear false alarms. He knows the streets."

"The streets be damned!" sneered Revere. "I swear that somehow I was followed as I rode the countryside. From Charlestown to Concord, I had this uneasy feeling of being watched; as though there was an evil eye of sorts. Now I have the same feeling here in Boston."

Warren grimaced, as he opened the newspaper. "Paul, there is certainly something blowing in the wind these days, and I don't like the smell of it. Have you read this new *Boston Chronicle?*"

Ben Church, sipping his tankard, responded, "Not much, Joseph. I personally prefer the *Gazette* where I can relish the gossip of your writers with the Roman names."

Frowning and sticking to the point, Dr. Warren added, "This John Mein seems to see the news from a different angle than any sane man in Boston. For god's sake, if I were to believe him, the Crown and the governor can do no wrong."

Revere, sipping from a tankard and peering through the window, said, "I met this Mein fellow once. Seems a decent sort; I made a few gold buttons for both him and his wife. I can say this; he pays his bills on time."

Warren just glared, "I still don't like his politics, and I feel he bears watching. Perhaps I should get Jim Otis and Sam Adams to write a small note about this man and his gibberish rag of a newspaper." He wadded the paper and threw it across the room.

ΩΩΩ

March 1768

"Just look at this despicable rag," grumbled Governor Bernard, as he paced the floor of his office. He threw the latest copy of the *Boston Gazette* on his desk in disgust.

Looking at the *Boston Chronicle*, Thomas Hutchinson grinned. "It's amazing how the same story can be reported in two very different ways, Francis. I suggest you relax. From what I read here, John Mein has done a marvelous job of vilifying our radical friends in the *Chronicle*."

Gesturing toward the *Gazette*, Bernard continued to growl, "You know as well as I what the rabble out there on the street are reading, Thomas; and it isn't the *Chronicle*. Sure, our loyalists will refuse to read this rag, but the common folk are slaves to the propaganda of Edes & Gill."

"For the record, Francis, let's be clear about how this mess began. If I recall correctly, at the beginning of the year, the Crown decided to create a new position, secretary of state for the colonies, which was filled by the Earl of Hillsborough," said Hutchinson.

Still pacing, Bernard interjected, "Quite right! Then our dear Sam Adams decides to stir things up with his circular letter to the other colonies. Hell, this man did all he could to create public insurrection against the Townshend Act. This blatant affront to legal taxes is a slap in the Crown's face. The bastard waited till the loyalists went back to their country homes, then reconvened the House to pass his circular letter movement by a vote of ninety-two to seventeen. It was a legal disgrace and a breach of legal form. Now we have all the colonies joining this illegal nonimportation movement."

"Calm down, Francis. Your head will burst. Here, let me pour you a glass of Madeira. Now, you know as well as I that this circular letter is a problem for Hillsborough, and not one for you personally," responded Hutchinson.

"On the contrary, it is my problem. It was Hillsborough who ordered me to dissolve the General Court and forbid the meeting of the House," muttered Bernard defensively.

Hutchinson frowned, "So that's why Edes & Gill have attacked you in the *Gazette*."

"Yes. Those damned propagandists have caused the shut down of representative government and have nefariously placed the blame squarely on my shoulders, when I merely follow the orders of the Crown," said Bernard, pounding his copy of the *Gazette*.

Hutchinson retrieved the copy and glanced at it. "Seems that Edes & Gill don't particularly care for you personally, Francis. Let me see here. You are accused of cruelty, on a path of malice, enmity, a thirst for mischief, and obviously, a man hater." He paused to sip his wine. "It seems to me that you are not a nice person, if you read this," he added sarcastically.

"Easy for you to make fun, Thomas! It's not your life in the balance; you know the capabilities of the Boston mob. Remember your own house during the Stamp Act," stated Bernard, still pacing as he fiddled with the lace at his cuffs.

"You have a point. I have numerous complaints on the court docket. One addresses about one hundred of the town dregs marching with fife and drum passing the Council Chambers. Another complains of about sixty ruffians pounding on Commissioner Burch's home with clubs. The poor fellow had to get his wife and children out the back door for their own safety. And the last was a blatant unloading of a cargo of Madeira, duty not paid. The report said that forty of the rabble paraded the wine through the Boston streets at high noon. As they were carrying bludgeons of some sort, no commissioner would dare approach the parade," said Hutchinson. "The list seems endless."

"A lot of good Sheriff Greenleaf is against a mob like that," said Bernard disgustedly. "The city of Boston has become a government of the mob, by the mob, and for the mob, so help me God."

Pouring another glass of wine, Hutchinson smiled. "I have an idea, Francis. First, we can have John Mein elaborate on the fact that Hillsborough is the cause of the closure of the House meetings. Second, and you will love this one; I, as head of the Superior Court, can indict Edes & Gill."

"Indict them for what? I don't think they have been part of the mob," queried Bernard.

Laughing half to himself, Hutchinson continued, "I wish I had thought of it before. You see, ever since Henry VIII, it has been illegal to libel a public official. The *Boston Gazette* is literally filled with libel against you."

"That might do the trick, Thomas. Meanwhile, let's get Omega working on another task," said Bernard, eagerly shuffling through a few documents on his desk.

"What do you have in mind?" asked Hutchinson, downing his wine.

"The Earl of Hillsborough has decided to take action against anyone involved with this circular letter. He wants the instigators taken on charges and possibly sent to England for trial. I guess the charge could be treason. What do you think of that?" stated Bernard triumphantly.

"How is it that Hillsborough is taking action so quickly?" asked Hutchinson.

"I have had many correspondences with him and many others in London. I refuse to be duped and abused by a gaggle of colonial rustics, Thomas. Now let's get Omega to collect more information on the real instigators. Sadly, they use many pseudonyms in their correspondence."

"Consider it done, Governor. I'll get the old sailor and the fat man on it immediately," said Hutchinson, as he left the room.

ΩΩΩ

April 8, 1768

John Hancock sat at his desk in his third floor warehouse office, looking at his ledgers in disgust, and scratching his wigged head. Sam Adams sat in an easy chair, trying to conceal his smile. Not that he enjoyed Hancock's pained look, but he knew that this financial strife imposed by Parliament was rapidly driving his rich friend deeper into the radical camp of the Sons of Liberty.

"Those bastards in London have done nothing to eliminate this Townshend Act, and it is getting worse. I've had to raise prices to accommodate the taxes, and now my warehouse is full of glass, paint, and all the red and white lead you can imagine," muttered Hancock, half to himself. "I've written letters to every factor I have in London, and no one seems to care. Damn that Charles Townshend! These new taxes in the Townshend Act are choking our trade and demoralizing the people."

Adams slowly arose from his chair, looking out the window to gaze out at the wharf and Boston Harbor. "Try to relax, John. There are many ways to handle this, and you have simply learned that Parliament could care less about your bombastic letters." Turning from the window, he added, "Actually, I'm more concerned about the propaganda machine created by John Mein and his dastardly *Boston Chronicle*. The man is a graven image of the Crown itself, and he has the audacity to support this Townshend mess. Now he publicly vilifies our circular letter."

Hancock smirked, "It's only words, Sam. He has his freedom of the press."

"Damned his freedom," grumbled Adams. "Just remember what happened last January, that bastard Mein assaulted our own Benjamin Edes; a much smaller man, I might add."

"Hell, Sam. The *Boston Gazette* called Mein a contemptible Scot, a traitor, and, if I recall, even hinted at his being a Roman Catholic, God forbid. What would you do?" asked Hancock in a matter-of-fact tone.

Sam grinned. "Our friend Edes refused to even acknowledge Mein, and he never would divulge that it was Jim Otis who wrote that article under the name of 'Americus.'" He added as he paced the floor and wagged his palsied hand, "It still gives him no right to assault little Ben Edes. Perhaps we should get Mackintosh and the Sons of Liberty to impress our concerns on Mr. Mein. Mackintosh is a little more his size, if you get my meaning." He wandered back to the window with a view of the harbor.

Hancock, scratching his quill across a document and without looking up from his work noted in a firm tone, "I could really care less about John Mein. It's Townshend and his damned act that stick in my throat."

"We are doing what we can with our Nonimportation Agreements with the other colonies, John. We've gone so far as to tell the citizens to eat less mutton so that local artisans will have more wool for local production. All we have to do is become more self-sufficient and patronize our local producers of goods. And as for Townshend himself, please keep in mind and be satisfied that the fellow died last September," said Adams. "God rest his sinful soul!"

"At least he can't do any more damage to my accounts where he now lies," said Hancock, picking up his quill pen to make a note.

"By the way, did you hear that Hutchinson and his Superior Court indicted Ben Edes and John Gill for libel against the governor?" queried Sam.

"Libel against the governor, eh? The bastard's lucky to be alive. I suppose we should get Jim Otis and John Adams to provide a legal response," said Hancock.

"I already spoke to them. And they both suggested that we ignore the whole thing. Some legal rot about Henry VIII and a lousy law. We should just leave the legalities to them. They are the best we have," said Adams.

"Fine for them! As for me, I have ships to refit and men to pay. These new London taxes and your nonimportation rules are choking me. I have to do something," muttered Hancock.

Adams grinned. "You've made your feelings well known publicly in the general assembly when you said that you would not suffer any of the royal customs officials to even board one of your London ships. By the way, isn't that one of your ships tied to the wharf, as I speak?"

"Yes," said Hancock, "that's the *Lydia*. She just arrived last night with a cargo from London."

Abruptly, the office door crashed open, and a young sailor, panting from rushing up the flights of stairs, said, "Mr. Hancock, sir. Captain Scott sends his regards, and he says there are agents from the customs commissioners now boarding the *Lydia*, and he thought you should know about it, sir."

Hancock dropped the quill and arose from his ledgers. "I told you, Sam! Those six new customs officers and their bloated staffs would come to no good for this port. I have work to do, and dirty work it is," he said, donning his purple coat and grabbing his gold-knobbed walking stick. "I'll talk to you later, Sam," he added, as he rushed out the door and down the stairs. Adams smiled broadly, again looking out the window. *This was working out better than he could have dreamed,* he mused to himself.

As Hancock approached the ramparts of the *Lydia*, he heard Captain Scott saying to someone he didn't recognize, "You will have to wait for Mr. Hancock, my good man. I have no authority to permit you to inspect anything."

"I am not your 'good man,' and I have the authority of the king's commissioners. Besides, you are the captain of this ship, are you not?" asked a man dressed in upscale homespun, obviously trying to be more than his station warranted.

At that point, Hancock boarded his brig to the surprise of all concerned. With Hancock's arrival, a sudden quiet pervaded the deck of the *Lydia*. "Tell me, Captain Scott, exactly what is this all about?" queried Hancock, his eyes burning.

"Mr. Hancock, I'm so happy to see you. A short time ago, these two men boarded our *Lydia* with the intent of checking our cargo. I told them this was against your orders," said the captain.

"Speaking of orders, we have our orders from the Crown customs commissioners, Mr. Hancock," said one of the strangers, trying to use an unfamiliar bombastic tone. "And those orders are to check the cargo of this ship."

"And just who are you exactly?" asked Hancock sternly.

"I am Owen Richards, and this is Richard Jackson. We demand, by the authority of the customs commissioners and the Crown, to go below and inspect your cargo," responded Richards, raising his voice with a bit of false bravado.

"I see. I'm sure you have your duties; however, they will not be completed here and now," Hancock responded in a firm soft tone. "Captain Scott," he continued in measured tone, "get these men off the *Lydia* and use whatever force you deem necessary."

At a nod of the captain's head, the crew immediately rushed menacingly toward Richards. "No need for that," said Richards, warily raising his hands in surrender, "we'll leave with no trouble." The crew laughed as they retreated away from the wharf. Hancock joined in the merriment, saying, "Captain Scott, post a watch for the evening and treat the men to an extra ration of rum." He gazed at the waterfront and added, "Take them to the Snug Harbor. Inform the proprietor to send me the bill."

ΩΩΩ

It was just past high noon of the following day when Imp Smythe swaggered into the Bunch of Grapes to deliver the latest issue of the *Boston Gazette*. He took little note of the two men sitting by the window overlooking King Street, as he was beckoned by Big Bessie Clump at the far end of the bar. As he handed her the *Gazette*, he said boldly to Abigail Stuff, who was behind the bar, "I'll have a tankard of ale."

Bessie glowered at him countermanding, "Give Imp his usual mug of cider." She half read the *Gazette*, as her attention was actually riveted on the two men at the other side of the taproom.

It was Owen Richards and Richard Jackson seated near the window, mired in conversation. "The damned commissioner said we don't get paid unless we get into the hold of the *Lydia* and inspect her cargo. All of Boston knows that Hancock is a damned smuggler, and he thinks his high and mighty ass is above paying the import taxes. At least, that's what I learned at customs," said Richards, sipping his ale.

Big Bessie watched them from her perch at the far end of the bar. Imp was sitting alongside her sipping his cider, when she called to Abigail and whispered, "Abby, go check that pair at the window. I know it's early, but offer them a discounted early-afternoon tumble. And listen to what they are saying while you bargain. I swear I heard them say something about commissioners!"

Abigail Stuff puffed her bosoms near to spillage, exposed her shoulders, and glided over to Richards and Jackson. She gently pressed Jackson's knees apart, sat on his lap, and fondling his black greasy hair, said, "Hello, darlin'. My name's Abby Stuff, and I was wondering what a fine specimen of a man like you is doing without me? Buy a girl a bit of grog, would you?"

Richards looked annoyed at the interruption, but Jackson, with Abby's breast in his face, ignored him. "I'm afraid it's a bit early in the day," he stammered. "Did you say 'Abby Stuff'?"

Abigail wiggled into the depths of his lap, saying, "That's right. And I call the business Struttin' My Stuff." She giggled loudly. "If you get my drift." She began to finger his hairy chest, as she continued, "Darlin', normally it's half a crown for a tumble, but it bein' early in the day, we can shag for a shillin'. Now how about that grog, before we go upstairs to my little crib, where we can find a bit of heaven? I just know you want to check out my 'stuff.'"

Owen frowned, shifting uncomfortably in his chair at the spectacle of passion. He said impatiently, "We don't have time for this, Richard. The *Lydia*! Think about the *Lydia* and the commissioners."

Jackson, smiling at Abigail and feeling a bit flushed, nuzzled her chest and said, without looking up, "I'll tell you what, Owen. You go ahead and check the *Lydia* tonight. Meanwhile, I'll tell the commissioner what we are about. That is, after I take care of sweet Abby here." Abigail gave a surreptitious wave, and Big Bessie delivered the grog.

"Are we having a restful afternoon, gentlemen?" asked Bessie. "Have all your needs been met?"

"We soon will be restful," answered Abigail, "Isn't that right, darlin'?" she added to Jackson, nibbling on his earlobe.

Big Bessie, looking at Owen and faking a look of concern, asked, "And what of you, my good man? How can it be that your friend is enjoying life, and you are not? And just who is this Lydia, may I ask?"

"I have important customs business," said Owen with a bit of bravado, ignoring the question. With that, he arose from his chair, adding, "Jackson, I'll take care of the *Lydia* late tonight. One man alone might be best and certainly would not be noticed on the wharf. Enjoy yourself." With that said, he downed his rum and departed.

Abigail, running her fingers through Jackson's greasy hair, said, "Now, darlin', about that shaggin' for a shillin'; let's go enjoy the spice of life." She then gently guided Jackson up the stairs, holding his hand.

Bessie smiled as the couple ascended the stairs. "Imp, get over to the Snug Harbor and tell Amanda that some commissioner's rat plans to visit the *Lydia* tonight. Tell no one but Amanda; she will know what to do. Now, be quick about it." Imp nodded and ran out the door, turning right down King Street toward the wharf.

All the other sailors, tradesmen, and ropemakers, idling the day away with their pints and quarts, seemed to ignore Abby's hustling, as a normal part of the day. And the skinny old salt, wearing a red stocking cap, garnered little attention as he half staggered and shuffled out the door. He paused for a moment in the street, watching Imp scamper toward the wharf.

ΩΩΩ

At eleven o'clock that evening, Owen Richards kept to the dark shadows of the towering masts, silhouetted in the moonlight, as he crept among the barrels and crates of Hancock's Wharf toward the *Lydia*, berthed at the far end. The noise of his footsteps was obscured by the lapping of the waves against the hulls of the ships berthed along the wharf.

Little Imp stood beside John Hancock at the third floor window of his office on the wharf, watching for any activity down below. At this hour, the only normal waterfront activity was in the numerous inns and taverns.

The sudden scurrying of little furry wharf rats, disturbed by Owen's creeping in the shadows, denied him the secrecy he so desired. In the darkness of the office above, Imp pointed out the sudden movement. "That's him down there, about midway up the wharf on the far side," said Imp, pointing into the darkness.

Hancock smiled. "Good eye, lad. You get back to the Snug Harbor now, with my thanks to Ms. Griffith."

Imp objected, "But I want to go along and catch this rascal."

"I don't want this man to know you are involved. Your eyes are too valuable to us, Imp. Now, do as I say and get over to the tavern. Tell Amanda I will need you here tomorrow morning," said Hancock.

On the main floor of the warehouse, Hancock appraised the gathering of his ten best men; all strong dockworkers. To his slave of many years, he said, "Cato, you hold the lantern. Now men, we need not harm the man. But he will not inspect the cargo of the *Lydia*, is that clear?"

Meanwhile, Owen Richards had boarded the *Lydia*, thanking his luck that no night watch was posted. The stomping of approaching boots made his stomach begin to churn in fear, as he rushed into the *Lydia*'s steerage to conceal himself. He mopped the sweat of his brow with his forearm. *How could he be sweating*, he thought, *in the chill of the night sea air?*

With Cato leading the way with his lantern, Hancock's men poured aboard and soon found Owen, quivering in fear in the steerage. Hancock demanded, "Mr. Richards, how strange to find you aboard my *Lydia* at this time of night. Tell me, what you are doing trespassing on my private property. Are you perhaps a thief?"

"You know very well what I am about, Mr. Hancock. I am with the customs officials, and I demand to inspect your cargo down below," said Owen, somehow mustering bravery and overcoming his churning belly.

"I am surprised that you dare anything! Let me see your Crown credentials, Mr. Richards," ordered Hancock. Owen handed over his papers, which Hancock held up to the lantern light. "It seems that there is no date on this document, Mr. Richards. These papers are not official in the true sense, and I must order you to limit your inspection to the upper deck."

Owen timidly declined and looking at the angry men arrayed about him, said, "It seems that would not be a healthy thing to do. I bid you good night, sir." With that, he backed across the gangway and skulked meekly back into town. The remaining watch on the *Lydia* laughed and scoffed loudly at the retreating figure. By then, a large crowd had gathered in the vicinity of the Snug Harbor Tavern at the land side of the wharf. A female voice from the crowd yelled, "Shall we permit these damned commissioners to abuse Mr. Hancock in this fashion? We should march to the Customs House and let them know how we treat trespassers."

Hancock rushed to the crowd and raising his hands, said, "My good friends, this business is finished, and the *Lydia* is secure. Let us all return to our merriment and forget this man. He is nothing." The crowd, which was prepared to march through the Boston streets in protest, grudgingly adjourned to the smoky, cozy confines of the Snug Harbor Tavern, while Hancock made his way home to Beacon Hill.

ΩΩΩ

The next morning, the customs commissioners immediately contacted Attorney General Jonathan Sewell, regarding the illegal manhandling of an agent of the Crown and Hancock's liability for prosecution. Sewell was brother-in-law to Dorothy Quincy, and all of Boston knew quite well that there was an informal "understanding" between Ms. Quincy and Mr. Hancock. In fact, she had been his houseguest for a time. But no one thought to voice any concern about a potential conflict of interest.

Sewell scanned the commissioner's petition carefully. "You are correct that the law specifies that customs men can go on board a ship to inspect cargo and observe unloading. But it seems there is a question as to the meaning of 'on board'," said Sewell. "It could mean on deck or in the hold. But the law is not clear on this; hence, we really have no case." The issue was closed, with commissioners retreating in anger.

In the Old State House, the customs commissioners continued to voice their concerns to Hutchinson and Bernard. "What kind of justice do you have here in this colony, Governor?" they asked collectively. "Your Attorney General Sewell is absolutely useless. This would never happen in London," they continued angrily, with a tone of disdain.

"It seems that your good friend, Hancock, is spitting in the eye of the Crown, Governor Bernard, and getting away with it," asserted Hutchinson, with a barely concealed smirk.

Bernard bristled, both at the attitude of the commissioners and at the news, as he paced the floor of his spacious office. He suddenly stopped pacing and smiled, saying, "Let us look at it this way," he said, with his index finger raised to make the point, "to avert a legal skirmish, which we might lose. We could say that Hancock was merely protecting his interest and his private property. And I might add that he quieted that mob, according to the reports. This shows that he fears the real power of the Crown, and he doesn't want things to get out of hand. Let us forget the incident for what it is – merely an assertion of property rights. If it happens again, the full force of the law will rain down on him." To the commissioners, he added, "Keep a close eye on all Hancock ships, especially those arriving from England." Thus assured, the commissioners departed to the customs house, not too far distant.

After they left, Hutchinson said, "Governor, I think it is time for the fat man to get back to work. I've learned that the candlemaker had the fear of God put into him over that dead doxy, so we have permitted him to sit tight these many months. Now is the time to resurrect that nest of nosy creatures. A few golden guineas in the right hands will assure that we know more about the activities of our brazen Mr. Hancock."

Bernard looked at his lieutenant governor with his eyes narrowed. "Yes, get the fat man on it. It's a blessing that Sam Adams isn't involved with this. Thank God he doesn't own a ship; we would be dealing with the Sons of Liberty, for sure."

"I wonder about that," said Hutchinson, thoughtfully. "It has been very quiet these many months, but I still don't trust that sneaky buzzard. I'm certain that it is his agitated writings that appear in that rag, the *Boston Gazette*. Nonetheless, I'll get the fat man to put a fire under the candlemaker; it seems that he knows a few rascals down at the Snug Harbor."

"Let us be careful. We don't want anyone of significance seen in the vicinity of that iniquitous place," added Bernard.

ΩΩΩ

That evening, Big Bessie sat with Amanda in her upstairs sitting room at the Snug Harbor Tavern. "Things didn't go too well for the customs commissioners and their henchmen, did it!" exclaimed Bessie, half laughing.

Amanda smiled, rubbing her hands together in joy. "It's about time that they pay in some way for the loss of sweet Charity. By god, it's been more than a year since she was murdered, and nothing was done. That sham execution of Adair still makes me sick. In fact, that fat sheriff hasn't been here since."

Bessie, scratching her midriff, added, "This is just the beginning. Those customs swine will never let up, and that is their weakness. We must keep a keen eye between us, Amanda. That little Imp is a wonder!"

Amanda paced toward the window, overlooking the wharf. "I don't like the idea of using Imp, unless we must. He is so little and could get hurt if he is found spying for us against the Crown."

Bessie frowned, "That's what makes him perfect. No one would suspect Imp of doing anything important. And, thank God, Abby Stuff was able to drag the particulars of the *Lydia* inspection from that Jackson fella, so we could get the news to Mr. Hancock. I swear she can get anything from a man, especially just before she trims his mainmast, and that includes all the secrets he might have."

"I'm still concerned about Imp, and I have a better idea," said Amanda. "My bargirl Angel would be a better conduit for our work. She can mingle with the other girls, gathering information easier. And the Crown officers would never think anything strange of another woman walking the streets."

Big Bessie retorted, "I thought you said that Angel wasn't shaggin'."

"She ain't shaggin'," said Amanda, laughing. "That's the beauty of the whole idea. She would be perfect because her contact with people is limited to the taproom. These men never see anything but her cleavage while they haggle with the girls. Angel simply listens, and she doesn't drink anything but cider, so she's clearheaded. From now on, I'll have Angel spend part of her time at the Bunch of Grapes; she will be our messenger."

Bessie asked, "Exactly where did she come from? What's her story?"

Amanda glared into Bessie's eyes. "I have a policy of asking no questions, and I suggest you do the same. Her story is interesting, but I'm sure that most of it is forgotten by everyone concerned. Angel is our girl!"

"I'm wondering!" said Big Bessie, scratching her head, "What if your Angel sort of arrived in town all spruced up as a lady of high station? She could get into places none of us could even dream about."

"Let's save that plan for the future," replied Amanda. "Right now, we need daily communication between our nunneries. Between Imp delivering papers, and Angel quietly working both taprooms, we can watch the Tories and the Crown. Someday the sheriff himself will answer to his neglect of duty. Someday he will be caught with his breeches at half-mast!"

ΩΩΩ

While Amanda made plans for Angel's future duties at the Snug Harbor Tavern, Sam Adams was sitting at his favorite corner desk in the second-floor offices of Edes & Gill, editing his latest addition to the next issue of the *Boston Gazette*. Ben Edes gazed at the copy, and his eyes paused at the signature. "So this one was written by Publicus; you do have a liking for those Roman names, don't you, Sam?"

"It makes me feel like a Roman senator or something like that," Adams responded, with a toothy grin. "This business with Hancock's ship is a real puzzlement for the officials. The Crown's officers can't let him get away with this; it's a matter of principle. They will make trouble, and we must be alert. I predict you will soon have much to print, my good friend," he added. "Meanwhile, we must keep our enemies to be perceived as in the wrong – and keep them there."

ΩΩΩ

The next morning, the sun was burning the morning fog and sea mist from the air, creating that freshness that all denizens of coastal towns have learned to love. Sadly, Zeke Teezle was toiling with tallow in the heat of his candle shop, mired in the mixed odors of hot wax and body sweat. "Glunt, I expect you to take more than one bath a year, hereafter. Cleanliness goes with godliness, young man. And it seems you have forgotten both. We bathe in the months of May and October, and you will do the same. It's our custom, and I have my eye on you," he said, wiping the sweat from his brow with his sleeve and holding his nostrils as Glunt passed by.

Almost casually, Gerty Teezle waddled into the back workroom with a note in her hand. "What's that you have there, Gerty?" asked Teezle, as he continued his work.

"How should I know, Zeke? This one has a red wax seal. It was dropped off by an old sailor with a red stocking cap," she said tartly, as she casually scratched her huge buttocks.

Teezle stopped his work, gazing at the sealed note. "Did the sailor say anything?"

"Something about a fat man, then he just slinked out the door, like he was late for a ship or had the runs or something. Not sociable at all. And you know I try to be friendly with most everyone," she said belching.

Teezle stepped out the rear doorway into the sunlight, breaking the wax seal. A golden guinea fell into his hand from the folded note. His palms began to sweat, and his lips quivered, as he read,

Teezle!

As you know, we have removed the problem of the dead doxy. We have protected you from prosecution. But now, it is time for you to repay us. You will now make new friends at the Snug Harbor Tavern and the Bunch of Grapes. You will sell your candles at those taverns and also at the warehouse of John Hancock.

We have arranged for you to have a tumble with Hope at the Snug Harbor every Thursday evening. This service has been prepaid for you. You will leave a note of all you see and hear of the Hancock business. The candles are your innocent excuse to be there. Hope will give you privacy . . . and a smile. We expect our first report next Thursday. It would be a shame to have the case of the murdered doxy come back to haunt you. There could be more! Destroy this note.

Ω

Why don't they leave me alone? thought Teezle. *I didn't ever see that damned doxy. Now I have to deal with this Snug Harbor place again.*

"Is there something I can do for you, Mr. Teezle?" interrupted Glunt, standing in the rear doorway, digging wax from his fingernails.

"No," muttered Teezle, "I have to go down to the waterfront for a while. You keep busy with the tallow, and I'll be back shortly." He took off his leather apron, then he turned saying, "If Mrs. Teezle asks anything, you don't know where I went. You understand?" He tossed the note into the fire.

Glunt just nodded and returned to his duties. "God save me from any marriage such as this mess! How could anyone be married to the likes of Dirty Gerty," he muttered to himself.

ΩΩΩ

After making arrangements with the agent at Hancock's warehouse to sell his candles on consignment, Teezle paused to take in the multitude of waterfront sights, noises, and activity. The smell of salt air combined with the carts of fish and lobster assaulted his nostrils. *He was far more accustomed to the stench of sheep tallow and suet in the stuffy confines of his shop,* he thought to himself. He found it hard to sort his thoughts about the threatening note, with all the shouting from the sailors in the ship rigging and the dockworkers loading and unloading cargo.

Gathering his wits, he shuffled across Fish Street to the Snug Harbor Tavern. He hesitated at the doorway, thinking that this tavern has created nothing but trouble for him. *How could he make this work?* he wondered. Sighing, he walked slowly into the coolness of the taproom. Unlike the evenings, it was quiet, with few patrons sitting at their tankards of ale. Teezle took little note of the lone old sailor wearing a dirty red stocking cap, sitting in the darkness of a far corner table, seemingly busy with a newspaper and a mug.

Amos was busy mopping the floor while Angel beckoned Teezle to the bar. "And what can I get for you, my good man?" she asked in her sultry voice.

"I came to see Ms. Griffith – on business," he muttered.

"I'm sure you did, but Amanda – er, Ms. Griffith usually takes care of 'business' in the evening. Just now, she happens to be out. Maybe one of the other girls could take care of your 'business,'" she said with a sweet grin. "Now, what will you have to drink? Taking care of 'business' can make a man mighty dry in the throat, you know."

Hearing this, the red-capped sailor peered over the edge of his newspaper, nodded to one particular buxom girl, his eyes again retreating behind the paper.

Teezle, involuntarily ogling Angel's ample cleavage, said, "Nothing to drink. I guess I'll come back when Ms. Griffith is available to talk about . . ."

"Talk about what, you sweet thing?" came the husky voice from behind him. Teezle turned to find what some men would consider a wonder of the world and others might consider a nightmare from hell. Hope was dressed in her day clothes; hence, not ready for the bedroom trade. But Teezle could only notice that she towered over him, as Hope was well over six feet tall. In comparison, the average man in Boston stood a mere five and a half feet. Adding to his confusion, Hope had taken a moment to "punch up her bodice," making her bosoms come to full bloom. Teezle found his chin resting in her cleavage.

"Easy, big fella! These puppies ain't for munchin'; at least, not yet. Why don't we sit down here with a tankard of ale and talk about our future together?" whispered Hope, as she reached out, holding his chin where she had his undivided attention.

Teezle turned helplessly to Angel, who was grinning behind the bar. "I suggest you sit down with Hope and have a tankard of ale. What do they call you, my good man? Ms. Griffith would probably like to know, and sometimes Hope forgets those little details," said Angel.

Teezle mumbled back to Angel, almost pleading for help, "The name's Zeke Teezle, and I really must go to – "

Hope gently grabbed his arm, guiding him to a table in the dimness of the back wall, near the stairway to heaven. "Make that two tankards, Angel! Me and Mr. Teezle here have business to discuss. Ain't that right, you big hunk of man."

Amos delivered the tankards with a friendly shrug toward Teezle, saying, "Hope don't understand the word no."

Hope now had Teezle seated against the wall and began to whisper into his ear, which, to the casual Snug Harbor observer, would be considered a normal amorous adventure. Teezle learned there was nothing amorous about it when Hope bit his earlobe gently and whispered sternly, "Listen, you little twit. You almost ruined things for me with that mess you made with the notes. Lucky for me, Amanda couldn't make any sense of them, and I guess threw them out. Now, we have a date every Thursday, and don't you forget it. Those are the orders. What you see and hear, you tell me and only me! Do you understand?"

Teezle could do little but nod in agreement while he meekly cowered into his chair.

"It will be best if you write a note. I sometimes forget things. Can you write?" asked Hope. Again, Teezle nodded, gazing around the room, his eyes wide.

Hope smiled. "I like a quiet man, especially one who agrees with me like this. We will make a fine team, Mr. Teezle, or should I call you Zeke? Who knows, I might even enjoy you in my little crib up on the second deck. Keep in mind that our Thursday date will be in the evening, say, nine o'clock, and we will be shaggin' in room C. Be certain to bring a half crown for the shaggin'."

Teezle, somewhat recovering from the physical and verbal onslaught, said, "But I thought the tumble was paid for. And what if I have nothing to report and I have no note?"

"You come anyway. And everyone pays for their own shaggin' around here; this ain't no charity. Besides, don't you think a working girl deserves a half crown? As for our meeting regular-like, there might be a message for you. Ain't you the lucky one; you get to shag with me while you work for the fat man. Business and pleasure all wrapped in a nice little package," whispered Hope. She glanced at the red-capped sailor, then added, "And remember, you talk only to me here at the Snug Harbor and no one else." Pointing her finger and touching the tip of his nose, she added, "If any of the other girls try to get into your knickers, you tell them that you want your package wrapped by Hope. Now, finish that ale and get out of here. I'll see you Thursday night."

Teezle immediately did as he was told, leaving a shilling on the table for the ale, before he stumbled over his feet in his rush for the door.

Hope glided over to the bar, saying, "Angel, you are so smart to stay on that side of the bar. That little weasel or beezle or whatever his name was didn't have the shillin' for the shaggin'. Its getting mighty thorny for a girl to make an honest living these days."

With a smile on his face, the old sailor shuffled out the door, turning toward the business end of Boston. Hope said, "I'll clear the tables for you, Angel." No one noticed when she picked up the newspaper, which had been folded neatly by the sailor. She gripped it tightly, noting the feel of cold coins. The paper disappeared into her bodice.

However, Angel did observe part of the paper sticking above Hope's cleavage, and said with a laugh, "Do you expect these men to read the paper as they nuzzle your goodies, Hope?"

"Oh my!" Hope shared the laughter, nervously. "I expect to take time to read this later in my room. Most of my regulars can't read, so I read to 'em – among other things. I'll be in my room, if anyone needs me." With that said, she retreated quickly up the stairs.

Amos followed her with his eyes, shaking his head, "That girl is a wonder. I never saw her with a newspaper before. Amanda made sure the girls can read, but the onlyest time they do it is at Sunday meetins." Angel looked at the empty stairs, lodging her observations in her fertile mind. Her meeting with Amanda and Big Bessie had made her more aware of the waterfront world. They had introduced her to Abby Stuff, learning the best way to gather information with the aid of rum. *She had become a solo audience to a sneaky stage play,* she thought to herself.

Amos grinned knowingly. He too had been told about the new assignment for Angel. And he naturally realized that he would ensure Angel's safety as well as Imp's.

ΩΩΩ

Later that evening, Sam Adams tried to settle his shaking hand, as he sat at the long table in the second-floor meeting room of the Green Dragon Tavern with James Otis, John Hancock, Dr. Ben Church, Dr. Joseph Warren, and Paul Revere. Once again, a window was open to vent the pipe smoke that obscured everyone's vision and ability to breathe.

"Thanks for the Madeira, John," said Dr. Church, "This must be the only place to get this private stock outside of your estate on Beacon Hill or perhaps the governor's office."

"There may be another place or two," said Hancock, smugly.

"I would rather have ale myself," added Adams sarcastically. "But that's not why I called this meeting." Pointing across the long table, he said, "Revere, tell them what you told me earlier."

Paul Revere, flexing his broad shoulders, barrel chest and massive arms, inherent to those who worked with metal, arose slowly from his chair, saying, "Gentlemen, I may have stumbled upon a situation sometime ago that might prove quite useful to us."

It was seldom that the silversmith had much to say, and everyone at the table paid close attention. He continued, "More than a year ago, I had finished meeting with a customer at the Bunch of Grapes when, upon stepping out the doorway, I noticed two ladies leaving the Old State House."

"Get on with it, man," Adams interrupted, spilling ale with his shaking hand.

Frowning, Revere said, "I didn't think much about it at the time, but the ladies stopped at the door of the tavern, not more than five feet away; so I could not help but hear them speaking."

"On with it, Paul!" exclaimed Sam, impatiently. "Forget the politeness and proprieties."

Ignoring him, Revere continued, "It seems the ladies were most angry with Governor Bernard, the sheriff, and the Crown, in general."

Dr. Church asked, "Why would two nice ladies find fault with the Crown?"

Otis, adopting a pompous stance, added, "Yes, and what in hell were two ladies doing in the Old State House? That's a man's work, dealing with the Crown!"

Adams chuckled loudly and with a knowing smile said, "Paul, tell them who the *ladies* in question are."

Paul, clearing his throat, said, "Not that I make it my business to know these people, but the ladies were not *ladies* in the true sense. Actually, it was Ms. Clump from the Bunch of Grapes and Ms. Griffith of the Snug Harbor Tavern. That's why, I never mentioned it till now; I know you men would never deal with this normally and certainly not personally."

The room erupted in laughter. When the noise ebbed, Joseph Warren pondered aloud, "Tell us. What business would two doxies have at the Old State House?"

Otis responded, "What other business do they know? They must be servicing old Governor Bernard himself!"

Adams, raising his shaking hands to quiet the musings, said, "I really doubt it. Paul forgot to mention that both were wearing their mourning black, and they were talking about that dead doxy."

Revere added, "I would guess they wanted to know about that murdered strumpet."

Otis, in a tone of annoyance, asked, "What murdered strumpet?"

Hancock, speaking for the first time, said, "Last year, they found a doxy dead in the harbor, floating face down near my wharf. It seems she didn't simply drown, and the crime was never really solved. Sure, the sheriff claims that the murderer was somehow killed after confessing; Adair, I think his name was!"

Revere sarcastically interjected, "Wasn't it convenient that Adair just happened to be one of the Sons of Liberty?"

Otis flippantly remarked to everyone at the table, "Well, who cares about a dead doxy anyway?"

Adams retorted very loudly and emphatically, "The other strumpets care!"

Dr. Warren added, "By god, Sam, you're right. I see some of these girls for medical reasons, and some still talk about the tragedy of the dead girl." Ben Church nodded in agreement.

Revere continued, "I might add that a few of the Sons of Liberty know them better than most at this table. The Boston doxies are still downright angry with the sheriff."

Adams lowered his voice conspiratorially, "Gentlemen, we can use these women. They can be a source of much information, especially if the Tories and Crown officers use their services."

Otis asked, "Who would dare approach these riffraff with such an idea?"

Everyone's gaze shifted from one to the other in silence. Finally, Dr. Church said, "As Dr. Warren said, these women come to us for medicine. I will have them contacted somehow and report at our next meeting. Perhaps it's best that only I know who is checking with these women of low breeding. It wouldn't do for any of you to get involved, for propriety's sake."

James Otis raised his tankard, saying, "We thank you, Dr. Church, for the kind personal sacrifice. The last thing any one of us needs is the scandal of visiting one of these nunneries. Just be certain that you personally don't indulge in their services." All in the room laughed heartily. Church merely sipped his drink with a smile.

As the meeting adjourned and everyone trooped down the stairway, Adams pulled Hancock aside, asking, "What do you know about this Griffith woman? The Snug Harbor Tavern is on your wharf, isn't it?"

Hancock looked at him in surprise, "Why Sam! How would I know anything about that nunnery and a common doxy? I don't patronize those waterfront taverns. However, the Snug Harbor Tavern is near my warehouses, and I have enjoyed a tankard of ale there occasionally. I promise you that I will ask around down there to learn what I can." That said, he patted Adams on the back and rushed out the door.

Adams, standing in the smoke-filled taproom of the Green Dragon, saw that Revere hadn't departed with the others and had, in fact, joined a few Sons of Liberty at the bar. Sam joined him, saying, "Paul, I think it wise to keep an extra eye on both the Bunch of Grapes and the Snug Harbor Tavern. Get a few of the dockworkers we can trust to spend more time at both places and make close friends there, if you get my meaning. Meanwhile, please continue to keep a man shadowing this Imp."

Revere pondered. "I thought Dr. Church was taking care of this business."

Adams grinned. "He is. And I know he can be relied on. But we must face the fact that a man in his position could never be seen in that low company. On the other hand, we have those who could mingle easily. Your men will simply add manpower and protect the image of Dr. Church, if he should be implicated in anything amiss. He is too valuable to our business, Paul."

Revere gave a thoughtful nod, "I know just the people to handle this. Don't ask who."

ΩΩΩ

CHAPTER 8

THE MONTH OF April 1768 was a blur of activity for Sam Adams. The Townshend Act had moved much of Boston to boycott the imports from London. The merchants grumbled that they couldn't sell their merchandise and sadly, had no other access to this material except British ports. Hancock did his best to keep his Merchant's Club in line, reminding them of his problem with the *Lydia*. The normal blatant smuggling had fallen to a mere trickle. Adams, meanwhile, was not content with the boycott in Boston. He had opened correspondence with Patrick Henry in Virginia and John Dickinson in Philadelphia in order to create a more expanded boycott of British goods throughout the colonies. It was clear that the circular letter had served its purpose.

Meanwhile, Governor Bernard and Thomas Hutchinson were content with the uneasy calm that prevailed in the streets. The Tories had acquiesced to the added duties of the Townshend Act, and the radicals seemed powerless, leaving them to grumble, at best. The *Boston Gazette* continued to publish the invectives and complaints written by Publicus and "Vindex," whom everyone knew were the poison quills of Sam Adams and Joseph Warren.

The fireplace was ablaze in the library of Thomas Hutchinson's home, as he scanned the pages of John Mein's *Boston Chronicle*. He laughed aloud. "I just love this man."

"Who's that?" asked the fat man, sipping a glass of claret.

"John Mein, of course! His interpretation of the law and this *Lydia* affair is in line with those of the commissioner and, coincidentally, my personal interpretation," muttered Hutchinson. "How London could deny the commissioners' appeal and let Hancock get away with his blatant smuggling is beyond me."

"Face it, Thomas. The customs agent went below decks without authorization. It was a fine point of the law, but it still supports Hancock's rights," said the fat man. "I'm no lawyer, but it makes sense to me."

Rising to recharge his glass, Hutchinson grumbled, "You may be right. But you can be certain that sooner or later Hancock will defy the law again. And I will be there to snare his pompous ass."

"Such a vengeful sort you have become, Thomas," chortled the fat man sarcastically. "Why don't you leave this to me and Omega?"

"That's why I asked you here, my friend. What exactly is happening on the streets of Boston? The governor and I are cornered at the Old State House," said Hutchinson, as he took the liberty to refill the man's glass.

The fat man arose from his chair to stand before the glow of the fireplace. "The old sailor tells me that this candlemaker has been taken by the charms of a doxy at the Snug Harbor Tavern. This has enabled him to get close to Mackintosh and the Sons of Liberty; and that puts us closer to Revere, Hancock, and the rest."

"Wonderful!" exclaimed Hutchinson, rubbing his hands together in glee.

"That's not all, Thomas. You see, the doxy and this Teezle have learned that the real objective seems to be the removal of Governor Bernard."

"You mean to tell me that if Bernard was replaced, we might have peace in Boston?" asked Hutchinson.

"The alternative, and I've heard this personally, is that Sam Adams expects to arm thirty thousand rustics from the entire colony and have him forcibly removed. Can you believe it? The man is insane," said the fat man, with a half laugh.

"With that kind of thinking, I'm convinced that we need the protection of the Crown troops in this colony. If we can only get the governor to see it our way," he grumbled.

The fat man shook his head. "It seems that the governor is more concerned about being liked by the citizens. I doubt he will press for the use of troops."

"It may be out of his hands, ultimately, my friend. We have correspondence with London, General Gage in New York, a Lieutenant Colonel Dalrymple in Halifax, Commodore Hood, and others to the effect that troops and the navy are available. In fact, the commissioners have demanded troop support because of the poor treatment they have received from the mob. I have reports of intermittent broken windows, open threats, and even the occasional tar and feathering of the poor bastards. Now I ask you, how can any government operate like this?" muttered Hutchinson.

"Those decisions are yours, Thomas. I suggest you think of the future. Governor Bernard may not be long for his position, leaving the door open for a replacement. Meanwhile, Omega stands at your disposal. I'll keep the old sailor and the others informed," said the fat man, candidly. "Thanks for the wine. And now, I must depart. There is a meeting with the loyal opposition." He laughed loudly, as he closed the door.

Hutchinson poured himself another glass of wine and simply stared into the fireplace, deep in thought.

ΩΩΩ

May 9, 1768

The crew of the sloop *Liberty* was working in the hot afternoon sun, easing her into a berth alongside Hancock's Wharf. She had just returned from the Madeira Islands with a consignment of wine.

John Hancock, dressed in a new purple silk brocade coat, boarded the *Liberty* once she was tied off, to greet Captain James Marshall, the *Liberty*'s master. Marshall was a large burly fellow, with heavy-lidded blue eyes, common to men of the sea, who spend a lifetime squinting into the weather and the sun. After a short meeting, Hancock departed, saying, "I'll meet you at the Bunch of Grapes, Captain Marshall, at six o'clock."

Shortly after his departure, a man representing the customs commissioners came aboard. "Good afternoon, Captain. I am Thomas Kirk, and I wish to welcome you and your good crew back to Boston Harbor. What cargo from Madeira do you have to declare to customs?" he asked courteously.

Marshall smiled, boldly saying, "We have twenty-five casks of wine in the hold to declare, my good man." Sailors, handling the ship's lines, began to chortle among themselves.

Kirk looked keenly into Captain Marshall's eyes. "Are you certain that is all you have to declare? It seems to be a very small cargo for such a long voyage on such a large sloop."

"Mr. Hancock insists that we load only the very finest wines. Sadly, I am told that the fruit of the vine in Madeira was of poor quality this year, due to bad weather. Only a few acres yielded a crop worthy of fine wine," responded Marshall. "Hence, I was forced to leave port with a hold less than full."

Kirk shrugged his shoulders. "Very well," he said. "We shall forward the customs bill to Mr. Hancock, after you unload your cargo. Thank you, Captain. I shall submit my report to the commissioners." He departed with a formal bow. Watching him walk down the wharf, back to the customs house, Marshall joined his crew in a hearty laugh.

ΩΩΩ

At six o'clock, Hancock was sharing an early dinner with Captain Marshall at the Bunch of Grapes, when a dark-haired buxom lass delivered a note to his table. "Mr. Hancock, you should find this worthy of your attention," she said and quickly departed. There was something vaguely familiar about the girl, he thought to himself. His bewilderment of her dissolved upon reading the note.

"Captain," said Hancock, after scanning the note, "it seems that our *Liberty* will have a visitor this evening. It seems that the customs agent you met this afternoon was not convinced of your cargo declaration. I suggest you arrange for a reception committee."

"I'm surprised," said Marshall. "The agent, his name was Kirk, seemed reasonable. Perhaps a bottle of Madeira will keep him quiet, and we can go about our business as usual, Mr. Hancock."

"Offer the wine." Hancock smiled. "But be prepared to take action and unload the sloop without his being wiser than he is. Do whatever it takes, Captain. Is that clear?"

"Aye," said Marshall. "Whatever it takes!"

When Captain Marshall departed, the raven-haired serving wench delivered another tankard, taking the opportunity to join him at the table. Hancock looked a bit surprised at the intrusion. "Forgive my interrupting you, Mr. Hancock, but I want to thank you again for the second chance I now have in Boston," she said.

Moving the candle closer to her face, Hancock could clearly see the green eyes, perfectly framed by the black tresses. He smiled. "Why, Angel! I didn't recognize you. What are you doing here at the Bunch of Grapes? I thought you made arrangements at the Snug Harbor with Amanda."

"I split my time between the two places. It's a plan worked out between Amanda and Big Bessie. But enough of me; what have you been doing? And why don't you stop to visit me?" she asked, reaching for his hand and clutching it to her bosom. "I owe you my life and would like to repay you somehow," she continued in her most sultry voice.

Hancock gazed briefly about the taproom, but everyone seemed to be too preoccupied to notice Angel's not-so-subtle advance. Pulling her hand back to the table, he responded, "Well, I didn't realize that – "

"Realize what, Mr. Hancock? Does it surprise you that I would find you a most attractive man? Actually, I need your help – in a professional sense. My benefactor in London recently sent me a sizeable amount of money, which was discovered among my late father's holdings. It seems these funds were missed in the accounting at his death. Now, I need good advice to handle it wisely; I feel that I can trust only you, Mr. Hancock." Again, she drew his hand to her cleavage.

Regaining his composure, Hancock said, "You are very wise to be careful with any inheritance, Angel. And I would be delighted to help you in every way possible. However, let me find a way to be certain Dr. Church has forgotten you. I shall call on you soon." With that, Hancock stood and briskly marched to the door.

Two people watched the exchange at the table, as Angel arose, returning to the bar. One was Big Bessie, sitting on her usual perch at the end of the bar. Saying nothing, she made a mental note to tell Amanda of the rather intimate exchange. She had never seen anyone approach Hancock like that; let alone, their trusted Angel.

The other observer stepped out the back door of the Bunch of Grapes shortly after Hancock left. Abby Stuff, while clearing his table, returned to the bar for a towel saying, "Some lousy slob left a pile of wax in the middle of the table. Now why would a bloke play around with candle wax? And I'm the one to clean it up – when I could be shaggin'."

"What was that all about?" asked Bessie, her curiosity getting the best of her, when Angel returned behind the bar.

"Just telling Mr. Hancock how we learned about the customs folks and the *Liberty*," said Angel innocently.

ΩΩΩ

At nine o'clock that night, Thomas Kirk walked slowly alongside the *Liberty*, noting that there was no night watch. He had just boarded the sloop, when, within minutes, he was joined by a gang of waterfront ruffians. In short order, Captain Marshall joined the gathering on deck. "What have we here?" asked Marshall.

Kirk, mustering an authoritative stance, ordered, "I demand, by order of the Crown, to inspect your cargo hold, Captain."

Marshall laughed, kindly saying, "Mr. Kirk, you have our declaration. What more could you need? We are all men of honor, are we not?"

"Perhaps so! But, nonetheless, I must inspect your hold because it is not reasonable to have so small a bill of lading for such a large vessel."

"Reasonable or not, that is the declaration. Now why don't you accept a bottle of Madeira as a gift and go about your business ashore while we unload our small cargo."

"Not a chance," said Kirk, raising his voice.

With a nod of Marshall's head, the gang of toughs grabbed Kirk by the arms and legs. "Where to, Captain?" asked one of the sailors.

"Haul him to the cabin and nail the companionway shut. Then let's get the cargo unloaded," said Marshall.

With Kirk stowed, the gang worked until midnight unloading the precious wine. Afterward, Kirk was invited back on deck. "Now, Mr. Kirk, let us not mince words here," said Marshall, firmly. "You saw no wine unloaded, and the reported amount is correct. That will be your story. If it is otherwise, it is quite possible that you could lose all your property." A grizzled ruffian in the gang added, "He could even lose his life, if'n he ain't careful, Captain."

Kirk, his ashen complexion apparent, even in the moonlight, nodded nervously in agreement. Upon his release, he ran down the wharf toward land amid the gang's laughter. "Well done, lads," said the captain, smiling.

ΩΩΩ

In the following weeks, the *Liberty* was reloaded with cargo, destined for the West Indies, and no mention was made of the customs incident. On the morning of May 26, Hancock arrived at his warehouse to find most everyone in a solemn mood. "What's wrong with everyone today?" he asked, as he seated himself behind his desk.

His chief clerk, a dour look in his eyes, said, "I'm sorry to report that Captain Marshall was found dead in his berth this morning, Mr. Hancock."

Hancock involuntarily cradled his head in his hands. "This is a great loss," he said somberly, his voice cracking. "Make arrangements to have the captain's bonus money sent to his widow. Have the offices clad in black, and black ribbons will be worn by us all, until he is buried. Make all necessary arrangements, with the bill sent to this office."

ΩΩΩ

June 6, 1768

It was nearing sunset, and Thomas Hutchinson stood with a spyglass in his hand, scanning the harbor from the upstairs window of the Old State House. "There she is, Governor. The *Romney* has just dropped anchor in the harbor."

"Well, we shall finally see what the radicals are really made of," said Bernard, grinning broadly. "Now the customs commissioners have the backing they have so desperately needed." The HMS *Romney* was a fifty-gun frigate of the Royal Navy, sent for just that purpose.

"I'll prepare a welcoming gala for the *Romney*'s captain and officers," said Hutchinson, with a note of glee in his voice. Bernard nodded, "You do that, Thomas. On your way out, tell Slank I need to see him."

In a moment, Slank entered, closing the door behind him. "You wish to see me, sire?"

"Yes, Slank, prepare a message of welcome to Captain John Corner of HMS *Romney*. We will be happy to officially welcome him with all pomp and ceremony tomorrow morning at Long Wharf, just south of Hancock's Wharf," ordered Bernard.

"Will that be all, sire?" asked Slank, a sly tone in his voice.

Bernard looked keenly at his aide. "Slank, sometimes I think you are reading my mind. Actually, the arrival of the *Romney* should rile our radical friends a bit. It would be wise to activate Omega. If the radical pot gets stirred, I want to know who is doing the stirring."

"I'll get the old sailor on this immediately," said Slank, stepping toward the door.

"And don't forget the fat man," added Bernard. "It's time he earned every golden guinea the Crown has provided."

"Yes, sire," said Slank. "The doxy can handle that for us."

"Spare me the details," retorted the governor. "I need only the results. These tawdry people annoy me. Suffice it to say that their loyalty can be purchased for a few coins."

"As you wish, sire," said Slank, with the hint of a sneer in his eye. He closed the door quietly and rushed down the stairway. *The sun was setting,* he thought, *and there was little time to waste. Time for the old salt to get to the waterfront!*

ΩΩΩ

No one in the Snug Harbor Tavern noticed the presence of the lanky old sailor wearing the red stocking cap, as he sat nursing his mug of ale, while he scanned the latest issue of the *Boston Gazette*. No one, that is, except Hope. She was perched on the lap of an old tar, nuzzling his ear, saying, "Goodness, luv. You know that you are the only man for me. I've been true to only you since you set sail four months ago."

The salt gave her a wide grin, exposing his solo gold tooth, which glistened in the candlelight. "You mean you waited just for me?" he slurred.

"I tell you I'm almost virgin again, waitin' for you, luver!" she exclaimed, nibbling his earlobe. Suddenly, she noticed the red stocking cap at the table against the far wall. She arose abruptly, saying, "I'll tell you what. I have a few things to look into; then I'll be right back. We can then go bite the clouds together, luv." Not waiting for a reply, she casually sashayed over toward the red-capped old sailor.

As she approached his table, he arose and walked toward her. Amid the raucous noise and dense crowd, their body's crushing together was considered normal. Unobtrusively, he placed the folded *Gazette* into her hand, and she reflexively filed the paper into her cleavage. The sailor continued to the bar to get another mug of ale while Hope hustled up the back stairs to room C.

In her room, Hope opened the *Gazette* to find a golden guinea and a sealed note, which read,

> *It is time to alert the fat man and the candlemaker. With the Romney in the harbor, the radicals will act. We must know who will act and their intentions. Destroy this note.*

Ω

Meanwhile, Amanda had settled herself behind the bar to help Amos, as she kept a keen eye on the taproom activities. She was always alert to anyone mistreating her little sisters of tenderness. At the first sign of trouble, she could send Amos to the rescue. A portion of the *Romney*'s crew was given a night's liberty, and every tavern on the waterfront was alive with new blood – Royal Navy blood. "Keep a keen eye, Amos. There could be trouble with the king's sailors mixing with our own unemployed tars."

Amos simply gave her a wink. "Anyone I can't handle, I just pass on to Hope; she can whip their asses!"

Amanda scanned the entire taproom. "Now that you mention it, where is Hope?"

Amos shot back, "She's right over – she was over there with the toothless one."

"Oh, there she is, coming down the stairs," she said to Amos. Hope had just alit from the stairway.

Amanda summoned her to the bar with a subtle wave. "Hope, you know better than to take anyone to your room without letting one of us know about it. It's for your own safety; you know that," said Amanda sternly.

"I didn't take anyone up there. It was a break to color my cheeks; I must look good for old toothless over there," she said, laughing. "Send another round to his table; they have a few more shillings, before they are broke." She winked, heading toward the action of the crowd. No one noticed her tossing the note into the fireplace. She smiled smugly to herself, as she thought of alerting the fat man tomorrow.

ΩΩΩ

At that same moment, Sam Adams paced the floor of the Long Room in the upstairs of Edes & Gill. Joseph Warren sat with his silver-buckled shoes propped up on the table, observing Adams's agitated behavior in his clinical manner. "Sam, you will die an early death, if you don't learn to settle yourself."

"This is an invasion, dammit! The Crown has cluttered the harbor with a warship, and you tell me to 'settle myself.' By god, this is war."

John Hancock's laughter jarred him from his tirade. "Sorry to interrupt your declaration of war, Sam. But how do you expect to sink the *Romney*, may I ask?"

"Laughter? Do I hear laughter?" screamed Adams. "The bastardly Royal Navy is marching about the waterfront, and you laugh. Am I the only one who sees what is happening? By god, I told you when the Stamp Act was repealed that we should have hidden a cache of cannon, shot, and powder. But no, I was overruled."

"I was just down at the wharf, Sam. And they're not marching; in fact, they are staggering. The king's sailors are drunk, and that is not the way they fight a war, if I recall my readings at Harvard," said Hancock, chuckling.

Warren, in deep thought said, "He's right, Sam. It's too early to say what this is about. We need to wait and see what they do. On the other hand, I agree that we should take steps to arm ourselves well. We need to get cannon, shot, powder, and muskets distributed into the countryside."

Sam smiled. "All right. I'll wait and give them a few days. But I tell you those fifty guns are not here to celebrate the king's birthday. Mark my words, this means trouble. Meanwhile, we should have a meeting to plan how best to sink that damned warship, if necessary."

Hancock smiled. "Let's get over to the Green Dragon and have a mug of rum. This war talk has made my throat dry."

As they left, Sam Adams began to mumble about arming the Sons of Liberty and every household in Boston.

ΩΩΩ

Their mugs of tea were getting cold, as Amanda and Big Bessie Clump sat at a table near a window. The *Romney*'s sailors, in their blue and white dress uniforms, were marching in a show of force down King Street for all the citizenry to see. Both ladies sat there with their chins in their hands, a look of disgust on their faces. For the moment, nothing was said, but their silent communications spoke volumes.

Amanda mused, speaking to the window pane, "Look at it, Bessie. Now, the Royal Marine contingent, in their regimental red and gold, is passing by. And that pompous ass Bernard, dressed in his finest gold silk brocade, had the audacity to greet Captain Corner of the *Romney* at Long Wharf, saying that all of Boston was happy to have him here."

Big Bessie responded, speaking to the same window pane, "I personally don't know anyone who is happy about this. Well, maybe the Crown officers and the Tories; but I don't know them personally. Face it; we were both surprised to see even Mr. Hancock there to greet the *Romney* captain."

Amanda looked at her comrade in business. "Yes, I wonder what goes through Mr. Hancock's mind at times; he stood right next to the governor. But, hell, we must admit that last night we both gathered a bundle of golden guineas from those sailors off the *Romney*. But it still makes me sick; them being here," she muttered. "As for Mr. Hancock, I know where his heart is, as well as other parts of his body," she added, with a knowing wink.

"The governor announced a formal ball for the *Romney*'s captain and officers, Crown officials, and all those in the provincial assembly at Faneuil Hall this evening. What I wouldn't give to see what goes on there!" added Bessie.

"That goes for me too," said Amanda. A moment passed before she added, "Wait a minute. We *can* be there; or at least we can send an agent."

Bessie responded, "What have you put in your tea, Amanda?"

Amanda smiled. "Think about this possibility. Angel can be our agent."

Bessie shook her head. "It's not possible. Angel's just another hard-luck harpy, who doesn't have the sense to shag her ass. I've been in this business ten years longer than you, Amanda, and I can read people. There is something peculiar about this Angel."

Amanda gave a knowing grin. "Not really. Keep this to yourself, Bessie. But our Angel was really groomed in London to be a lady. It's a long story, but she has all the training and education to fit right in with those uppity bastards. We must get her into that party tonight at Faneuil Hall."

Bessie began to laugh. "I think she would need an invitation, my dear friend. And she would need the right clothes. How do you plan to arrange that?"

Amanda responded, "If I can get the invitation and the dress, will you help?"

Bessie peered at her friend. "You're serious, aren't you? Well, yes. I'll help, if you really think it can be done. Hell, I'll teach the bitch to do the minuet, if you like." Turning serious, she added, "I've learned that we can trust Angel. After all, she passed that customs information to Hancock when the *Liberty* was in trouble."

Their privacy was suddenly interrupted when Abigail Stuff entered from the crowd watching the parade of marines on King Street. "Did you get a load of all that new talent that has just landed in our laps?" she queried to no one in particular. "Oh! Good day to you, Amanda."

Big Bessie asked, "Where have you been this early in the morning, Abby? It's too early to be shaggin' a marine."

"I have been to see Dr. Church about a cough. I always seem to get whatever crud these sailors bring in the door," responded Abby. "Seems that you have the same problem at the Snug Harbor, don't you, Amanda?"

"What do you mean?" asked Amanda, quizzically.

"Well, I saw your gal Hope at the doctor's office this morning. I just figured she got the same trouble," said Abby. "Of course, bein' a lady, I don't ask personal questions."

Amanda, rubbing her chin, said, "I didn't know that Hope was feelin' poorly; I'll have a talk with her later. She then arose, saying, "I have work to do. I'll contact you this afternoon, Bessie. Have you seen Imp? That little fellow is never around when I need him and always around when the girls are running about naked." She sprinted out the door, laughing as she headed toward the Snug Harbor.

ΩΩΩ

The morning sun was beaming a bright yellow hue through the third-floor windows of Hancock's warehouse offices, overlooking Hancock's Wharf. Sam Adams cursed, as he stood at the window. "This spyglass is useless. I can't see a thing down there, John, with the sun's glare off the harbor waters."

Hancock chuckled at his friend's frustration, as he sat in a captain's chair, his feet propped on his desk. Twirling a quill pen in his hand, he said, "Now Sam, you must learn to relax. Looking at the *Romney* will not change its being there in the harbor. Besides, what can you learn by looking at it?"

Sam glared at him, "It somehow makes me feel better knowing someone is watching, especially if that someone is me." He belligerently put the spyglass to his myopic eyes once again. "And that reminds me. Exactly what were you doing, standing next to Governor Bernard, when the officers of the *Romney* officially arrived at Long Wharf this morning?"

Hancock, still twirling the white quill, said, "I was doing what you should be doing, as secretary of the Massachusetts Assembly. The only way to learn what evil lurks in their cunning minds is to be among them. The governor invited me to attend – and I did. Actually, Captain Corner seems to be a refined gentleman, and I will see more of him at the gala this evening at Faneuil Hall."

"Now you are going to a ball with these plotting bastards. Sometimes, Hancock, I think you are becoming one of them," said Adams, tartly.

Suddenly, the office door banged open, followed by little Imp Smythe, who was immediately nabbed by a panting clerk from the lower floors. "I'm sorry, Mr. Hancock. But this little urchin would not listen when we told him you were too busy to see his sort. He simply scampered up the stairs." To Imp, he added, "Come with me, you little gutter rat."

Laughing, Hancock arose from his chair, saying, "That's quite all right. I'll take care of this; you may go back to your duties." After the door closed, Hancock looked sternly at Imp. "You must learn to mind your manners, young man. Now, what is the meaning of this intrusion?"

Adams interrupted. "Hancock, we don't have time for this!"

Imp, ignoring them both, blurted, "Ms. Griffith needs your help – now!"

"What could be so very important at the Snug Harbor Tavern that would require my attention?" asked Hancock.

Imp looked at Adams, with a sideward glance. "She said the news was for you."

Hancock smiled and was about to respond when Adams said, "Did you say the Snug Harbor, John?"

Turning to Imp, Hancock said, "What does Ms. Griffith need? You can speak in front of Mr. Adams."

"She said something about a dress for Angel and a party. I don't know any more than that," said Imp. "She said to hurry, and I hurried!"

"You certainly did, Imp," said Hancock. He turned to Adams, saying, "Sam, I think it's about time you met a friend of ours. Grab your walking stick and come with me and Imp."

ΩΩΩ

Amanda arrived at the base of the creaky stairway at the rear of the Snug Harbor, patting her hair into place. She had donned a purple satin dress, knowing that it would match Hancock's purple silk brocade coat and breeches. She wasn't disappointed, as Hancock's blue eyes seemed to feast on the way her buxom figure accented his favorite color.

Abruptly, her smile faded, as she noticed an older man in a well-worn, almost threadbare brown coat and faded tricorn hat, standing at Hancock's elbow. Hancock noticed the change, as he smiled, saying, "Ms. Griffith, I would like you to meet Sam Adams."

Adams stepped forward, extending his hand and bowing, "Charmed, I'm sure."

"A pleasure, Mr. Adams; I've heard much about you," responded Amanda in an exaggerated curtsy. Both parties were obviously assessing the other.

Imp interrupted the mutual gaze, saying, "I got 'em as fast as I could."

"You did fine, Imp. Now go help Amos." To Hancock, she added, "This way, Mr. Hancock. And I suppose you also, Mr. Adams." She led them to her room on the second floor.

When they entered, they found raven-haired Angel standing on a pedestal, wearing white pantaloons, while squirming into a billowy white satin dress, which covered most of her head at the moment. "I'm sorry, gentlemen," said Amanda. "I was sure that we would be presentable by now." Adams had turned abruptly, facing the door, his face suddenly a brilliant shade of crimson. Conversely, Hancock savored every moment with a steady gaze, which Amanda noticed with a disapproving frown on her face.

"You can open your eyes, Mr. Adams. We are fully dressed now," said Amanda.

Adams turned, looking at Hancock, as if to say, "What have you gotten me into?"

In a steady businesslike tone, Hancock said, "What is this all about . . . er, Ms. Griffith? And, by the by, Mr. Adams here is quite interested in what happens here. But first, do tell us your story."

Amanda eyed Sam Adams suspiciously as she said to Hancock, "We decided that someone has got to get into the governor's party tonight. And Angel here is the only one who knows how to fit in that high brow . . . er, sorry, but you know what I mean. Why is the *Romney* here, and what does this mean to our business on the wharf?"

Hancock was about to answer when the door burst open, and Big Bessie Clump collided with Sam Adams. Her ample bear hug kept him from landing on the floor. "My, my!" she exclaimed. "This place is getting crowded – with men." To Amanda, she said, a lilt in her voice, "This is no time to hustle your tail, my friend. We have to get this girl ready." She paused with her hands on her hips, assessing the two men.

Amanda did little to conceal her laughter. "Bessie, this is Mr. Adams and Mr. Hancock." Nodding to Bessie, she added, "Gentlemen, this is Ms. Clump. Perhaps you have seen her at the Bunch of Grapes."

Both men nodded politely while Bessie said, "I've seen you gentlemen at my place, but sadly, I haven't had the pleasure of doing 'business,' if you know what I mean." She gave Adams a gentle nudge in the ribs as she chuckled knowingly.

With a polite smile, Hancock said, "You needn't concern yourself, ladies. I will be at the governor's party personally, and I will get the information we need."

Heretofore adopting a quiet stance, Adams interrupted confidently, "Mr. Hancock, I think the ladies have a good idea here." He massaged his chin with his shaking hand, pondering the possibilities.

Bessie said confidently, "You're damned right it's a good idea. Don't think for one moment that Mr. Hancock can learn what our little Angel here can learn. By god, we women know how to make men spill the beans about anything."

Hancock looked at Adams, a frown on his face. "Are you thinking what I'm thinking, Sam?"

Adams nodded. "Ladies, we are aware of your past visit to the governor and the death of your friend."

Bessie interrupted angrily, "And the damned sheriff didn't do a damned thing about it, except place the blame on some convenient patsy and then conveniently kill the poor bastard. Ah, but that was a long time ago."

With a calming gesture of his hand, Adams continued, "This might be the best way to learn more about the inner workings of the Old State House. But it cannot end tonight. Your . . . er, our Angel there should become part of their society." Looking keenly at Angel, he said, "Are you up to the role of a new lady in town? You might have to do this for weeks or even months."

Before Angel could respond, Amanda said, "You bet your ass, she can; she's a lady of high breedin' from London. Just ask Mr. Hancock there!"

Adams looked questioningly at Hancock, at which Hancock said, "I'll tell you about it later, Sam. Meanwhile, let's look at our newfound lady of high society."

"How are you going to get her into the party? That's the question," said Big Bessie, impatiently.

Adams spoke up in his schemer's voice, noting, "We must make her a woman of mystery from another colony. How many people really know her in Boston?"

"Damned few," answered Bessie. "And no one in the biblical sense; for god's sake, by my standards, she's a virgin."

Angel interrupted, "If I'm going to do this, I will tell you how it should be done."

Everyone's attention was riveted to the new voice.

"First, I need an escort for the night; second, a new high-sounding name; third, to be sure I don't get recognized, I need my hair to be blond and reset high off my shoulders or maybe a wig; fourth, a new place to stay, if we are to make this work for a few months."

Amanda smiled. "The hair color is easy; I have a blond wig that I use on Purity for special guests." Bessie added, "Let's give her a fashionable mole on her left cheek. Men are suckers for that look in a woman!"

Sam, looking at Hancock, said, "How would it be if a visitor, let us say, Angel Wexford from London was here for a long visit?"

Hancock responded, "I don't expect a visitor from London."

Amanda smiled. "You do now!"

Angel asked, "Do you have business agents in London? Perhaps I could be related."

"It would be a sin to leave a visitor alone while you go to a gala. You simply must take the lady," said Adams. "And she can stay with you on Beacon Hill for a while . . . with Aunt Lydia."

Amanda frowned at that statement, giving Hancock a demure look. "I suppose it's for the best," said Hancock. "Angel, my coach will pick you up at my warehouse this evening at six o'clock. Meanwhile, ladies, I suggest you get my new houseguest ready." He and Adams rushed out the door.

ΩΩΩ

CHAPTER 9

A SMALL CROWD, most of who were dressed in dirty brown or tan country homespun, had gathered near the entry to Faneuil Hall to watch the parade of dignitaries invited to attend the governor's gala reception, honoring the captain and officers of the HMS *Romney*. There was an audible murmur from the ladies in the crowd at a most scandalous sight.

John Hancock smiled broadly as his escort took his offered arm. They proceeded abreast, toward the entrance, where two Royal Marine sentries stood at attention, resplendent in their red and gold tunics. The night was warm, with a gentle breeze flowing from the harbor. He paused, savoring the moment, as he adjusted his lace cuffs, which accented his navy blue silk brocade coat and breeches. This was trimmed with gold piping, the entire suit framing his gold silk waistcoat.

Clutching his arm was Angel Wexford, wearing a white satin dress, adorned with blue ribbons. Her bleached blond wig was nearly platinum, piled in ringlets high on her head with banana curls nearly touching her naked shoulders. The dress was cut low into a deep V, the point of which accented her ample cleavage, stretching the satin material to its limit. The addition of a false mole on her left cheek completed the stark change in her appearance.

They advanced through the array of military honor guards, which consisted of red-and-white-uniformed Royal Marines and blue-and-white-clad Royal Navy sailors, spaced along both sides of the foyer. Angel mumbled, "What were those rustic women in the crowd outside cackling about?"

Hancock grinned. "It seems that the good citizens of Boston are a bit upset with my being with the most beautiful lady in town – and me being a bachelor."

Angel chided, "Such a scandalous thing to do!"

In the shadows of the main archway leading to the grand ballroom, they paused to be formally announced by the major domo. "John Hancock, Esquire, with Ms. Angel Wexford of London," the major domo barked to the large gathering. A hushed silence pervaded the large assembly, followed by a barely audible grumble of female voices in the crowd of dignitaries.

Angel asked, in whisper from the side of her mouth, "Now, what is that entire hubbub about?" She silently gasped at the sea of dress color in the ballroom; it seemed to be an ocean of plum, apricot, lime, blue, and gold silks, satins, and velvets. No cost was spared to impress the Royal Navy.

Hancock grinned. "It's obvious that we are the last to arrive! That's what the 'hubbub' is about. I told you that we would be late, but you were busy preening before the mirror. Now they are mumbling about our scandalous behavior."

"What scandalous behavior?" asked Angel.

"We are here, two single people in polite Puritan society, with no chaperone to protect your virtue," said Hancock, taking pride in the impropriety of it all.

Angel said tartly, "These folks need to visit the Snug Harbor for an education."

Hancock frowned and scolded, "Let me remind you, Angel, that this is the mystic land of Puritan values and proprieties. Keep in mind that you are visiting from London, as we discussed with Amanda, and you don't even know that the Snug Harbor exists." Angel nodded in understanding.

As they proceeded further into the candlelight of the ballroom and descended the red-carpeted staircase, a few baritone voices seemed to join the gossip of the soprano variety in the crowd of onlookers. "*Now* what did we do?" asked Angel, tightening her grip on Hancock's elbow.

Again, Hancock grinned. "It seems, my dear, that the Royal Navy has just discovered you. Keep in mind, this is a formal reception, and there are few single ladies here. These men have not seen a woman in a few months, having been at sea. Now they feast their eyes on you." *This should work out better than I thought,* he mused to himself.

A steward guided Hancock to the official receiving line of dignitaries. "Governor Bernard and Lieutenant Governor Hutchinson, I am delighted to present Ms. Angel Wexford, a niece of my factor in London," said Hancock, politely observing all the expected proprieties, with an exaggerated bow.

Bernard bowed politely. Hutchinson also bowed and, taking Angel's hand, added, "Did you say 'Ms.' Wexford?"

Hancock again grinned proudly. "I did, Mr. Hutchinson. Adam Wexford, my factor in London, felt it was time for his niece to enjoy a visit to the American colonies."

Bernard, giving a perfunctory cough, said, "Mr. Hancock, let me present Captain Corner, commander of His Majesty's ship *Romney*."

Captain Corner, attired in his royal blue and buff dress uniform with gold striping up to his elbow, gold-hilted sword, and medals straining the integrity of the cloth, bowed, saying, "I recall our brief meeting this morning on Long Wharf. I was told that you were wealthy, Mr. Hancock, but I didn't realize you also had wealth in beautiful ladies." He had spoken to Hancock, but his eyes were riveted to Angel.

Again, Hancock smiled. "Captain, let me present Ms. Angel Wexford."

Corner, with a bit of a leer in his eyes, said in his deepest commanding voice, "Perhaps Ms. Wexford would be kind enough to save a dance for me later, after these formalities are completed."

"Indeed I shall, Captain; a pleasure meeting you," said Angel, smiling coquettishly.

As they continued into the crowd, Bernard, Hutchinson and Captain Corner shared a knowing look. "So that's your smuggler," said Corner, half to Bernard and half to himself.

Hancock and Angel advanced arm in arm to the gathered assembly, where he retrieved two glasses of punch from a tray proffered by a liveried servant. They were soon joined by members of the Merchant's Club, who seemed to be mired in small talk. Learning that Angel was newly arrived from London, they were eager to discuss the latest London fashions while the merchants expressed concern about the *Romney*'s presence in the harbor.

As if awaiting their turn, Dr. Joseph Warren and Dr. Ben Church pulled Hancock aside to add their concern about the *Romney*. Warren said, "You were at Long Wharf this morning. What did they say? Why are they here?"

Hancock, carefully noting the official receiving line as guests continued to arrive, said, "I'm not really sure. The captain was a bit secretive, hinting that it was merely a port visit to rest his crew."

Warren noted, "Do they really expect us to believe that?"

Dr. Church, a glass of punch in one hand and a turkey leg in the other, said, "Perhaps I can learn more in the next few days. As you both know, I am the family physician to the governor's family. I shall invent a reason to visit the State House tomorrow and let you know what I might learn. The *Romney* is here for a reason, and it is not simply for crew rest and relaxation." He continued to devour the turkey leg, wiping his greasy mouth on his sleeve. Ogling the bevy of women, Church added, "John, you must introduce me to the young lady in white; I understand she is from London."

Hancock did his best to conceal his disdain for the suggestion, as he responded, "Why, of course. Ms. Wexford is staying with us for a short time." He waved, beckoning Angel to join them.

Church licked the chicken grease from his blubbery lips and his fingers, as the ladies approached. After the introductions, he took Angel's hand in greeting, as he bowed profusely. "It is indeed a pleasure to meet you, Ms. Wexford. Seldom do we get to meet a lady from London, and I'm sure that London's loss is our gain."

"You are all too kind to a visiting stranger," she said to everyone in general, doing her best to avoid close contact with Ben Church. She was keenly aware that his roving eyes were closely appraising her from head to toe. Addressing Dr. Warren, she added,

"My friends in London would be quite surprised at the size of Boston. Though not as large as London, I am quite surprised at the vast trade you have in this port."

Warren responded, "Let me remind you that London has existed for more than one thousand years, Ms. Wexford."

"Actually, I expected to see little more than farms and countryside," said Angel, doing her best to keep a distance between Church and herself.

Church interrupted, "If you would like to see the countryside, I would be happy to – "

Hearing that, Hancock spoke up. "I shall be taking Ms. Wexford to visit the rustics shortly. I have planned a short visit to relatives in Lexington this coming week."

With a furled brow, Church said, "Perhaps some other time then, Ms. Wexford, before you return to England." Turning to Warren and Hancock, he added calculatingly, "I should go speak with the governor to arrange my meeting with him and his family tomorrow. It will be easy to invent a medical reason, and then I'll learn more about the *Romney*."

The receiving line had broken up, just as he approached them. Hancock watched the verbal exchange between Church and Bernard. A moment later, Ben Church nodded surreptitiously to Hancock and Warren, after which he departed.

Warren, pulling Hancock aside, said, "Ben Church is one sly fellow. As attending physician to the governor, he is our best source of inside information."

Hancock nodded in agreement, "I don't know what Sam Adams would do without his connections." As he spoke quietly with Dr. Warren, his eyes maintained a constant vigil about who Angel encountered. His attention was drawn to the not-so-subtle maneuver of one naval officer. Hancock added, "Joseph, let's join the ladies. It seems that they will soon become the victims of a naval blockade."

Attired in his dress navy blue and buff, the young officer bowed courteously to all and specifically to Angel, saying, "Permit me to introduce myself; I am Lieutenant Robert Spitz of His Majesty's frigate *Romney*." Spitz was tall, almost reedy with a large nose, resulting in his having a nasal twang in his high pitched voice. "I notice that my fellow officers have been remiss in providing you a proper naval escort this evening."

Before anyone could respond, a small military band began to play a minuet, with the audience enjoying the combination of harpsichord, flutes, violins, English horns. and drums. As if by magic, Captain Corner appeared at Angel's side saying, "I see one of my junior officers has discovered you, Ms. Wexford, and I trust you recall that you promised me a dance."

Again, using her best coquettish smile, Angel handed her glass of punch to Lieutenant Spitz without looking at him, saying, "But, of course, Captain; how could I forget such an honor. Please excuse us." She took his arm, as they proceeded to the dance floor.

As they maneuvered through the intricate paces of the dance, Angel was well aware that every woman was assessing her every move. Looking into Corner's eyes, she said, "Tell me, Captain. What exactly brings a Royal Navy warship to Boston? I'm told this is a first for the port of Boston."

Corner smiled condescendingly. "Why would a lovely young lady such as you be concerned with naval activities?"

"For myself, Captain, no reason whatsoever; however, my father's business life is totally reliant on maritime trade. The Royal Navy enjoys great respect in my house, as supreme protector of the sea. What could we do without you? Hence, I am simply a curious young lady, Captain," said Angel, fluttering her eyes, as she glided to the paces of the music.

Again, Corner grinned. "If you must know, Ms. Wexford, we have put into port for provisions, minor repairs, and a bit of shore leave for the crew. The bonus is meeting you."

The minuet came to an end, and the audience applauded the musicians. With that encouragement, they struck up a lively Scottish reel, at which Captain Corner said, "Thank you, Ms. Wexford. This is a bit more than my legs can handle, and this sword hampers the enjoyment; shall we join your party?"

"As you wish, Captain," said Angel. Placing her hand on his chest of medals, she added, "I was wondering, I've never been aboard a warship before. It must be exciting to have all those cannons and muskets and powder about. Would it be possible to ever go aboard such a fine ship of the line as the *Romney*?"

Corner was grinning broadly as he returned Angel to Hancock's side, saying, "Ms. Wexford, thank you for the dance." Turning to his junior officer, he added, "This young lady seems to be interested in His Majesty's frigate." To Angel, he continued, "Lieutenant Spitz will be happy to provide a short tour of the *Romney* tomorrow. A ship's launch will retrieve you at high noon at Long Wharf; if that meets Mr. Hancock's approval!" John nodded, exchanging glances with Angel.

To the small party, he said, "Now I must return to the governor. I'm sure you understand the duties of office." Looking piercingly at Hancock, he added, "Mr. Hancock, I'm sure we will see each other again."

Hancock, his eyes level, replied firmly, "I look forward to it, Captain."

Lieutenant Spitz, not missing the verbal swordsmanship and bowing courteously, said, "I had hoped to enjoy a bit of dancing, but we have a ship's tour to prepare. Good evening, ladies and gentlemen."

ΩΩΩ

June 10, 1768

Early the next morning, Captain Corner stood staring out the second-floor window of the governor's office. He sipped his sweetened tea, as he glared at the assembled customs commissioners and then at Bernard and Hutchinson. "It seems, gentlemen, that there is really nothing for the *Romney* to do here. I was advised that there is a problem with smuggling, but now you tell me that we have nothing to report at this moment. I could be more useful if I remained in New York harbor; those bastards had refused quartering of the king's troops. The mere sight of the *Romney*'s cannon kept the radicals in line."

Hutchinson stood as he replied, "Captain, that is precisely why we need you here! The commissioners need you. Smuggling is rampant here in Boston, and it has been impossible to enforce. But now that you are here, that will change. No one would dare defy the *Romney*."

Corner peered again out the window at the harbor in the distance. "Besides the *Romney*, there are four vessels in port; one sloop and three brigantines. To my knowledge they have all been unloaded and cleared by customs, with no difficulty. So where is the smuggling, gentlemen?"

Governor Bernard arose from his chair, "You fail to understand the – "

Rapping at the office door drew everyone's attention. Bernard growled indignantly, "What is it, Slank?"

Slank entered, followed by an unshaven, disheveled tidesman, who clutched his tattered tricorn hat timidly at the doorway. With a half bow, Slank said, "I beg your pardon for the interruption, Governor. But this man came to the door just now, with a story I think you should find noteworthy, sir."

Hutchinson stepped forward, "Slank, you know better than to interrupt a meeting such as – "

"Please, your lordship," said the tattered stranger. Turning to the commissioners, he added meekly with a perfunctory bow, "Mr. Hallowell! Perhaps you have forgotten me, but I worked for you last month."

Joseph Hallowell, the short, portly chief collector of customs arose and, peering, asked, "Is that you Kirk?"

"Yes, sir, and please forgive my appearance, but I was required to leave Boston in haste for my safety. The *Liberty* captain said I would die if I told the truth," said the stranger, his voice becoming more assured.

Hallowell, turning his attention to the others said, "Gentlemen, this is Thomas Kirk." This news was received with a blank, uncomprehending stare. "Thomas here is our agent who disappeared suddenly last month – after the *Liberty* unloaded her cargo."

Captain Corner impatiently injected, "I'm sure this reunion is touching, but I have important business to – "

Hallowell, suddenly comprehending, said, "Captain, this is precisely why you are here." Looking at the tidesman, he added, "Mr. Kirk, please tell Captain Corner about the *Liberty*."

Kirk, still fidgeting with his tricorn hat, told them how he had been confined to the cabin of the *Liberty*, while Hancock's crew unloaded the cargo, and of the subsequent threat to his life and property. "Captain Marshall declared only twenty-five casks of Madeira, but we knew there was more. Sadly, everyone on the waterfront protects Mr. Hancock."

Corner asked impatiently, "What does Hancock have to do with this?"

Hutchinson smiled. "This is what we have been waiting for, Captain. We now have a witness to Hancock's smuggling and violation of the king's law. Hancock owns the *Liberty*."

Bernard added, "The Townshend Act requires that the ship be confiscated by the customs commissioners. And this is where you and the *Romney* come into play. You are the muscle, the enforcement arm of the king. I suggest that you take action this evening when the dockworkers have retired to the taverns."

Hutchinson, with a sardonic grin, said, "Slank, take Mr. Kirk downstairs. Feed him and get him into clean clothing. We will need him as a witness in the superior court, when we convict John Hancock of smuggling."

ΩΩΩ

As ordered the previous evening, Lieutenant Spitz ordered the small launch from the *Romney* to be tied at the end of Long Wharf. He gave a conspiratorial wink at the launches crew, as he observed the approaching carriage. Even at a distance, he could see her blond hair shimmering in the bright noonday sun. His broad smile faded, however, when the carriage neared, and he realized that Angel was not alone.

The carriage came to a halt, and Spitz noticed the gold H emblazoned on the door. Angel said, "Good day to you, Lieutenant Spitz. Mr. Hancock sends his regrets that he could not join us, but he was kind enough to send Master Smythe here as my chaperone."

"Hello, Lieutenant Spitz. My friends call me Imp." As he said that, Imp jumped from the carriage, following Angel.

Spitz concealed his annoyance with a half smile, "This way, Ms. Wexford and you also . . . er, Imp!" Angel sat next to Imp aboard the launch, further aggravating Spitz, who obviously had plans for a private moment with her.

Once aboard the *Romney*, Imp said to all within earshot, "Look at the size of this ship! I bet it holds tons of cargo."

Lieutenant Spitz, waving a crewman closer, whispered, "Simmons, do what you can to occupy that wharf rat; I have better things to do." Glancing at Imp and then at Angel, Simmons grinned. "Aye, sir. I'll take him forward; you might want to show the lady the gun deck." Turning to Imp, he said, "Come with me, lad."

Spitz wordlessly led Angel below to the gun deck, where she found sweaty crewmen swabbing the deck on their hands and knees while others polished the brass cannon. Meanwhile, near the foremast, Imp was introduced to sailors mending sail and sanding the deck.

Imp looked at Simmons, "Is it always like this; all this work? I was going to go to sea, but I'm not so sure now."

Simmons, the tallest man on deck, laughed. "No fear, lad. You are much too small to be an able seaman in His Majesty's navy."

Within earshot, a seaman sanding the deck mumbled, "He can take my place; for god's sake, most of us were impressed."

Hearing this, Imp looked curiously, "What is 'impressed'?"

Simmons yelled to the crew, "Get your backs into it, you swabs." Smiling at Imp, he said soothingly, "He was sayin' that he is impressed and proud to serve on the *Romney*."

"Oh!" replied Imp. "Can I see the cannon, Mr. Simmons?"

"Come with me, lad. I'll show you how to climb the main mast and into the rigging," said Simmons.

Meanwhile, below on the gun deck, Angel asked, "How far can these cannon fire, Lieutenant?" Smiling and peering through the gun port at Boston, Spitz said proudly, "We could easily demolish any building in this town, especially that tall-spired church on the north end."

"My, my! I pray that is not why you are here, Lieutenant," she said, fluttering her eyes and fanning her face with her lace kerchief. "The mere thought of violence strikes my soul with fear. And please, not a church."

"Call me Robert, Ms. Wexford. And have no fear of violence." Gently tugging her arm to whisper in her ear, he added, "Captain Corner has told us that the Boston radicals actually have no heart for a fight. We are here to stop the smugglers."

Angel, carefully counting the cannon and crew, smiled again. "How could anyone resist this massive show of power?"

"That's exactly what the captain said," boasted Spitz. "If any smuggler tries to make a run, we will easily blow him to the bottom of the sea. We have fifty cannons to do it. Confidentially, I hope these rustics try something; there is nothing like the odor of gunpowder and the roar of cannon. After a few broadsides, we could sail back to England, leaving all of Boston ablaze in a pile of smoke and rubble."

"My, aren't we the bloodthirsty one, Lieutenant . . . er, Robert?" interjected Angel.

"Nothing personal, Angel – Ms. Wexford. I can tell by your breeding that you are superior to this colonial rabble," said Spitz, gently massaging her arm.

"Why thank you for the kind words, Robert. I sometimes wonder how these rustics can be so unlike the London crowd and still call themselves Englishmen," Angel said, searching his eyes. "It would be exciting to sail back to England on the *Romney*; I would feel so safe with you around personally to protect me."

"Have no fear, Angel. The Royal Navy and the *Romney* will make this port bow to the king's will. As for you sailing with us, that is the captain's decision. But I'll put in a word; he usually takes my advice," he said, exaggerating his influence.

Suddenly, a commotion was heard on the main deck. "Perhaps we should get to the upper deck," said Spitz, a tone of urgency in his voice. Surprisingly, he sprinted ahead toward the ladder way.

Angel took the opportunity to glance back at the seamen toiling on the deck and whispered, "If you get ashore, try the Snug Harbor Tavern. The ladies would treat you right!"

Arriving on deck in the sunlight, Angel found Captain Corner issuing orders. "Get that wharf rat out of my rigging. What is he doing aloft? And get that woman off my – " He suddenly noticed her standing near the ladder way. "Aye, there you are, Ms. Wexford. I trust that Mr. Spitz has treated you properly, and you enjoyed your visit aboard the *Romney*."

"Oh yes, Captain. I do thank you and Lieutenant Spitz," said Angel in a formal curtsy.

"Unfortunately, my crew has much work to do at this moment. I will have Mr. Spitz take you back ashore in the launch. Have a good day." To Spitz, "When you return, see me in my cabin."

After Angel and Imp were put ashore at Long Wharf, Lieutenant Spitz found himself standing at attention in the teak paneled captain's cabin. Captain Corner sat at his highly polished desk, with a glass of claret resting in gimbals within easy reach. The cabin was small, but neatness was the rule with Corner. All charts, logs, and ledgers were stowed; the captain lived by the rules he mandated for the entire crew of the *Romney*. "At ease," said Corner, smiling. "Did the visit go well with that Ms. Wexford?"

"Yes, sir," said Spitz. "As with most ladies, she was most impressed with the cannon."

"Did she ask anything out of the ordinary?" asked the captain.

"Not really. She was a bit curious about our mission here, sir," said Spitz.

Sitting forward and suddenly glaring, Corner said firmly, "I'm sure you told her nothing. Please tell me I am correct, Lieutenant!"

Clearing his throat and shifting his feet, Spitz said firmly, "I told her absolutely nothing, sir . . . either about our intent or the *Romney*'s capabilities."

"Good," said Corner. "Because I was reminded today by Governor Bernard that she is currently the ward of John Hancock."

"He's that wealthy merchant. May I ask why that is important, Captain?" said Spitz.

With a broad grin, Corner beckoned Spitz closer; and in a conspiratorial tone, he said, "This evening, we will confiscate the sloop *Liberty*, which is berthed at Hancock's Wharf. It seems that our Mr. Hancock is a smuggler, in violation of the king's law; he owns the *Liberty*. Organize a crew to go into action two hours before sunset; I want a bit of daylight to get this done well. And I want the locals to know exactly who they are dealing with. Get Simmons and others you can trust; leave the impressed sailors aboard. Now be quick about it. Dismissed!"

ΩΩΩ

Hancock's carriage had been waiting at the end of Long Wharf, when Angel and Imp were put ashore. The driver delivered them both to Hancock's warehouse on Hancock's Wharf. When they entered his third-floor office, they found Hancock looking through a spyglass at the harbor.

Standing near the door, Imp spoke up. "Did you wish to see us, sir?"

Hancock turned, smiling. "I am simply curious. Did you learn anything interesting aboard the *Romney*? It seems to be a busy crew out there in the harbor."

"I was high in the riggin', and you can see all of Boston, including your mansion on Beacon Hill," said Imp excitedly.

"And you . . . er, Ms. Wexford?" Hancock asked, reminding himself to maintain the ruse.

Angel looked at Hancock and furtively shifted her eyes to Imp. Hancock smiled. "Imp, I need you to report to Ms. Griffith and tell her everything they told you on the *Romney*. Remember, you are my eyes here on the waterfront. Now go lad; be quick about it." Imp scampered out the door saying, "Aye, sir!"

Hancock turned to Angel, "I suppose you needed to speak more privately. That Lieutenant Spitz didn't do anything improper, did he?"

"Goodness no, Mr. Hancock," said Angel. "But there are some things a young boy might not understand." Hancock motioned for her to sit, "Would you care for some tea, Angel? And please do go on with your story."

"Thank you, kindly," said Angel. "I visited what they call the gun deck, and Lieutenant Spitz tells me they can destroy the city, if need be."

"Why would the *Romney* want to do that?" asked Hancock, again using the spyglass to survey the harbor.

"He said that their reason for being here is to help the customs commissioners and sink the smugglers," added Angel, watching Hancock's reaction to the news carefully.

"I suppose that's to be expected. Did you learn of anything more?"

"Only that the crew was working hard on the cannon and the decks. They didn't seem happy about it," Angel noted.

Hancock chortled, "It seems that sailors live to complain, and some more than others. The carriage will take you back to Beacon Hill, and I'll tell you of our plans for 'Ms. Wexford' later. While you wear that wig, I remind you to maintain your London airs; when there is occasion to return to the Snug Harbor, you become the Angel we have grown to know and love again. We are sorry to put you through this, but it seems an effective way to learn about the Tories and the Royal Navy."

"What should I do now?" asked Angel.

"For the time being, you shall be my guest on Beacon Hill; my carriage shall take you there now. We can discuss your personal accommodations at dinner. Now, I have work to do, including a way to secure your newfound fortune."

Angel smiled broadly as she left the warehouse and boarded the Hancock carriage, knowing full well that her activities were being observed by Purity in the upstairs window of the Snug Harbor Tavern.

ΩΩΩ

Meanwhile, Imp was sitting on the bar at the Snug Harbor Tavern, sipping a mug of cider. It was cool inside and too early for the dinner crowd to arrive. "I tell you

Amos, them sailors work mighty hard on the *Romney*; they was sandin' the decks and swabbin'. I was in the riggin', and you can see the whole town."

Amanda, wearing her scrubbing clothes and mobcap, grinned at his enthusiasm. "Did you get below decks, Imp?"

"No. But that Ms. Wexford lady got down there with the lieutenant. And I wanted to see them cannon, but I only saw them from outside the ship."

Amos asked, "Are you still bent on goin' to sea, Imp?"

"Not no more. They work too hard. They might be impressed to be there, but swabbin' and scrubbin' ain't my idea of fun," said Imp.

Amanda leaned forward, her elbows resting on the bar. "Did you say 'impressed'?"

"Yes. That Mr. Simmons, one huge fella like Amos, said they was impressed to be in the Royal Navy," responded Imp proudly. "I still can't be impressed with swabbin'." Looking curiously at Amanda, who seemed to be lost in thought, he asked, "Now can I have a tankard of ale?"

"When you can see over the bar," said Amanda tersely. "And, just so you know, 'impress' means that those men were kidnapped and forced to serve as seamen in the Royal Navy. Now I need you to get back over to Mr. Hancock and tell him I need to see him at his earliest convenience." Turning to Amos, she added, "Give him a tankard of cider to wet his whistle, Amos. I have work to do upstairs."

ΩΩΩ

Amos poured the cider as he watched Amanda disappear up the stairs. "You best mind your manners when Ms. Amanda is around," said Amos, giggling. Amos stood six foot four inches when standing on his right foot and six foot three inches when he stood on his left foot. This was the reason for his uneven and sometimes shuffling gait. As he looked at Imp sipping his cider, his mind wandered back to his own youth.

He had been a slave to a captain Miles Reed, having been acquired on the island of Jamaica in 1732, when he was merely a youth of nine years old. And "acquired" was the proper word; he certainly had not been purchased.

It was a hot, sultry summer day on the docks of Kingston harbor, where Captain Miles Reed was preparing to leave port with a cargo of slaves and molasses. As he was concluding business, a tall lanky man wearing a broad-brimmed straw hat and carrying a riding crop, scrambled by in a rush to the end of the pier. Reed's conversation with the slave agent was suddenly interrupted by a child's loud scream.

"I'll teach you, you little black heathen! Amos, this will be the last time you ever waste daylight sitting on your little black ass, fishing on the pier," shouted the tall man in a rage. It seemed that with each word, the riding crop slapped into some part of little Amos's scrawny, malnourished body. Dragging the little waif by the arm, the lanky fellow, clad in white, added, "Your job is to gut and clean fish, and you'll do what you're told. Do you understand me?"

A crowd had gathered to witness the beating and the guttural screams coming from the poor boy. "What is wrong with you people?" muttered Captain Reed, as he muscled his way through the crowd. Reed was rather short in stature, but he had a barrel chest and arms as solid as the main mast of his ship. As the riding crop came down once again, Reed grabbed the lanky man's wrist and twisting in a vise grip with his left hand, he launched his right fist into the man's testicles. He then grabbed him by the belt and heaved him howling into the harbor. Utter silence pervaded the dock, as the crowd stood in awe.

Captain Reed looked down at the scrawny little black boy and said, "Come with me, lad." Leading the boy by the hand, Reed stopped by the gang plank and commanded, "Get aboard!" He then turned to his slave agent and added, "It is obvious that the little boy is the property of that lanky bastard. And it is also obvious that he knows little about their value. Otherwise, he wouldn't be beating the life out of them. Tell him for me that I will be happy to pay the going price for the boy when we next meet." He took a moment to gaze at the water in the harbor. "I guess this concludes our business, and it is now time for me to get underway; the tide is just about right." He turned sharply, crossed the gang plank, and shouted, "Hoist anchor and set sail. Helmsman, get us out of this harbor. Our next stop is the American colonies."

Once out to sea and under full sail, Captain Reed called the little boy to his cabin. Sitting back in his captain's chair behind a table strewn with maps and charts, he assessed the scrawny little black boy who stood there before him. "What would your name be, laddie?" asked Reed in a soft mellow tone, well marked with his Scottish brogue.

"I be called Amos," muttered the little boy. As the ship rolled with the sea swells, the little boy started to lose his balance, and he grabbed the table to stay on his feet.

Captain Reed laughed loudly. "You will get used to the roll of the ship, laddie, as she dances through the waves. As for your name, Amos is as good a name as any. You will now serve as my cabin boy, until you grow into a man who can carry his load as a sailor on this ship. Meantime, I don't want you mingling with the slaves in the hold or sticking your fingers in the molasses. Is that clear?"

Amos simply nodded in agreement, as he stared at the charts and the swords, pistols, and muskets mounted on the bulkhead. Watching his eyes, Captain Reed added, "Don't get any ideas about weapons at this time. The day will come when I will teach you how to use them. I have a funny feeling you will be with me for quite some time."

That was the beginning of a long and fruitful relationship. Captain Reed was true to his word, and over the years, he taught Amos all there was to know on a sailing ship. He became one of the most able and loyal seamen to sail the seas between the American colonies, the African coast, and the West Indies. At the age of twenty-one, Amos was given his freedom. He refused, however, to leave the service of Captain Reed. Many sailors laughed when they saw the captain and Amos standing beside one another. Amos had grown into a giant of a man, in great contrast to the small stature of Reed. Many sailors regretted their laughter.

In 1760, Captain Reed had put into Boston Harbor for a load of rum. While he was concluding business with the House of Hancock, his crew was loading cargo. Amos was working deep in the hold, when a line snapped and a barrel came crashing down on his left leg. His fellow crewmen carried him to the Snug Harbor Tavern, where Dr. Benjamin Church was called to set the leg. After concluding his work, Dr. Church said, "I'm sorry to tell you Captain, but this man's sailing days are ended for now. He will probably heal, but I doubt that he will ever be able to scamper around the rigging of a ship again."

Captain Reed, shaking his head in disdain, looked at Amos sorrowfully. Amos, lying on a cot in the back storeroom, grimaced in pain. "It seems I won't be able take you with me this time, Amos," muttered Reed. "I'll leave you in the good care of the doctor here. Now don't you worry about a thing; I'll see you as soon as I return with the next cargo." With that, he turned and rushed to the taproom.

Amanda, in her mobcap, was standing behind the bar wiping out pewter mugs. Lying in a basket at the end of the bar was a small baby boy happily making gurgling noises. "Sorry to see that happen to a good sailor, Captain," said Amanda casually. "Let me draw you a tankard of ale.

Reed looked at the basket, asking, "What do you call this little sailor?"

Amanda smiled, smoothing the child's hair. "We call him Imp. His father was a sailor who never returned, and I have no desire to send him out on those ships to suffer the same fate. I plan for Imp to make something of himself . . . no offense intended, Captain." Shifting her gaze to the back storeroom, she asked, "What do you propose to do with the injured man?"

"I really don't know," answered Captain Reed in a sorrowful tone. "All I really know is that he can't sail with me." He took a heavy swallow of ale and gazed around the taproom. Turning slowly, he gazed into Amanda's deep blue eyes. "This is a mighty fine place you have here, Mrs. Griffith. What would you say to taking on a bit of extra help?"

Amanda gazed back at him, not answering right away. She glanced at the stairway, and she glanced at the doorway to the storeroom. "I have a sneaky suspicion, Captain, that you are suggesting I take that sailor in. The last thing I need here is a big burly slave like that to cause trouble. He's fine for now, being injured, but when he's healthy, how could I possibly handle a man that size?"

Captain Reed smiled. "Actually, Mrs. Griffith, he is not a slave but rather a free man. And I promise you that he would be the finest worker you could ever have. With your permission, I'll have a talk with him. I promise you that when he is on his feet and working behind this bar, no one would dare lay a hand on either you or your girls – ever! God only knows he saved me a few times."

Amanda pondered for a moment and said, "All right, Captain Reed. You have a deal. You take care of the doctor's expenses and provide the crutches. I will be certain that he is fed and has a roof over his head. When he is back on his feet, he will repay me with the sweat of his brow. I only pray that he is as good as you say he is."

Two years later, Captain Reed finally made a return trip to Boston. His first stop was the Snug Harbor Tavern, where he found Amos working behind the bar. Amos smiled broadly at his old mentor, as he rushed around the bar to embrace him in a bear hug. At the end of the bar, they shared a tankard of ale, as the captain told him about his latest adventures. After the second round of ale, Captain Reed stared curiously at Amos. Gazing around the taproom, Reed asked casually, "Are you ready to come back to sea with me, Amos?"

Placing the tankard of ale down carefully on the table, Amos gave an audible sigh. He too gazed around the taproom, inhaling the aroma of fish, bread, and stale ale. With a pained expression on his face, he answered, "I hate to tell you this, Captain, but the Snug Harbor Tavern has become home to me. With my bad leg, I get around pretty well in this taproom. And the girls around here need me. Besides, I wouldn't be much use to you in the rigging of a ship, shuffling around as I do."

Captain Reed gazed out the window at the harbor and then turned his eyes to Amos. He smiled, saying, "I guess it's for the best, Amos. And actually, I should be thinking about settling down myself. I'm getting a bit old for the pitching deck of a ship, and the warmth of the West Indies has become much more appealing in my old age. It's my guess that this will be the last time you will ever see of me here in New England. I wish you well, my old friend." With that, he downed his tankard of ale and, patting Amos on his broad shoulders, he sauntered out the door toward his ship docked along Hancock's wharf.

As Amos gazed out the door at the fading image of Captain Reed, Imp, little more than two years old, scampered from the back storeroom and clasping Amos's meaty hand, asked, "Who was that, Amos?"

Wiping a tear from his eye, Amos said, "That is an old friend of mine, Imp!" Looking down at the little boy, he added, "Now I gotta focus on my new friends. And my newest best friend is you, Imp."

His reflections of the past were interrupted by Imp's pounding on his arm, making him aware of the present. "Are you listening to me, Amos?" asked Imp.

"What was that you said, my boy?" replied Amos.

"I was just wondering how you managed to survive at sea all those years when you were a kid like me. Those men out on the *Romney* didn't seem to be a happy crew," said Imp.

"I reckon happiness depends on who you serve with aboard ship," muttered Amos, as his mind wandered to the image Captain Reed, standing at the helm. Looking again at Imp he added, "Now you get your little butt over to Mr. Hancock, like Ms. Amanda said."

ΩΩΩ

It was that special time of the day when the sun was still peeking over the western hills of farm country, creating an orange glow that sparkled on the placid harbor waters and highlighted the sails and rigging of the ships. As the sun was setting, so the workday seemed to ebb and the mood of Boston to calm.

The taverns were lighting their window candles, inviting the dockworkers, sailors, lobstermen, and fishermen in for a tankard of ale or a warm flip; dinner would come later. At the Snug Harbor Tavern, Amanda stood leaning in the doorway with a mug of cider in her hand, gazing at the orchestrated, yet unrehearsed, march of men from Hancock's Wharf. She smiled broadly at each group of men who entered, as Purity's banter from above drew them into the taproom.

Purity, wearing an off-the-shoulder yellow silk dress that displayed her perky little cleavage, had assumed her perch in the second-floor window, hailing the regulars as they marched from the day's toil. "Come on up, my boys; stop friggin' in the riggin' and start shaggin' for a shillin'. So grab yourself a tankard, and I'll grab ya for a tumble," she spouted for all to hear.

Ever vigilant about the unusual, Amanda noticed a small group of men wandering in the opposite direction toward the *Liberty*. "Amos," she yelled, "where's Imp?"

"He's upstairs helping Ms. Purity," replied Amos from the bar.

"Tell him to get up to Beacon Hill and fetch Mr. Hancock; there might be trouble aboard the *Liberty*. I'll watch the bar," she commanded.

Meanwhile, Joseph Hallowell and his brother Benjamin, comptroller of customs, with a small entourage of customs clerks were busy painting the white broad arrow on the side of the *Liberty*, which was berthed alongside the wharf. Ben turned to the gathering crowd, boldly declaring, "The broad arrow, as you all know, makes the *Liberty* official government property as of this moment."

The crowd only half heard his declaration as they watched a detachment of the king's marines from the *Romney*, the sun glistening off their bayonets and bright red jackets, march down Hancock's Wharf. Lieutenant Spitz, with a condescending leer at the crowd, commanded, "Men, board that sloop and clear the decks of anyone aboard. Cast mooring lines to the barges." Three barges had been aligned on the starboard side in order to tow the *Liberty* to a mooring under the guns of the royal frigate. As the crew cut the *Liberty* loose from her berth, the irate mob began pelting them with stones. Spitz, in a sudden rage, yelled, "Fire your muskets, marines. Fire! Damn you, fire!" The marines slowly lowered their muskets with their bayonets fixed and took aim, but no one fired. Instead, they looked again at Lieutenant Spitz in astonishment. They had never fired on unarmed civilians, and though they had been ordered to fire, it did not fit their training. As moments passed, the barges made way toward the mooring under the guns of the *Romney*. Spitz, regaining his composure, said, "Well done, men. That noisy mob cowered at the mere sight of our arms."

Realizing that any assault on the king's navy would be fruitless, the irate gaggle turned its attention on the Hallowells. "Now the commissioners think they can steal our ships, do they? We'll show them! Tar and feathers! Get them," the voices screamed in unison. The Hallowells sprinted past the Snug Harbor Tavern, heading for the safety of their homes. The mob pursued them through the town, hurling bricks and stones. Arriving at the gates of Joseph Hallowell's home, the yelling and threats intensified.

Hallowell, cowering with his family behind the door yelled, "Disband you rascals, or I'll call the sheriff." The response was raucous laughter, "Did you hear that? He's going to call the sheriff." A voice, familiar to most in the mob, said calmly, "It would be easier for the sheriff to hear Mr. Hallowell, if the windows didn't muffle his voice." At that a heavy volley of stones shattered every window in the house.

Satisfied that they had made their point, the crowd marched back to the waterfront and the Snug Harbor Tavern. With rivulets of sweat flowing into her exposed cleavage, Amanda used a bar rag to daub herself dry as she listened intently to the small groups of rioters bantering. The more ale they drank, the louder they spoke. "I tell you, Amanda, you shoulda' seen them damned commissioners run," howled one old sailor. "The bastards got the *Liberty*, but we showed 'em!" At that point, Hope appeared at his side and, winking at Amanda, said, "Evenin', handsome. Why don't you order me a tankard of ale, and you can tell me all about those dirty commishes. Were you there to clobber them personally?"

Short in stature, the old sailor smiled as his nose was nestled in Hope's chest. "Why not, you gorgeous creature? Give the lady an ale," he slurred, unable to peel his eyes away. He replied boastfully, "You bet your life I was there; me and all me mates. Just look at them there."

Hope smiled, massaging his balding pate. "You big brave man. I would have been scared to death to defy the Crown. What is your name, luv?"

The old man laughed. "Darlin', I can't say, as my wife would kill me if she knew I was even here." He pointed to a table surrounded by a group of sailors and ropemakers, as they ogled Purity dancing on the tabletop. They sang in unison:

> *Whether a saint or whether a villain.*
> *You simply got to be willin'.*
> *From soft to rigid.*
> *From hot to frigid.*
> *You get your shaggin' for a shillin'.*

"What ship do you serve on, and when do you sail next? I want to see more and more of you," asserted Hope, ignoring his protests and fondling the hair on his chest.

"I was set to sail on the *Liberty*, but I'm not so sure now. We aim to get her back for Mr. Hancock in short order, that's for certain," slurred the sailor. "But we showed the commish, we did! We dragged his big old boat over to the Common and set it ablaze, we did."

Hope smiled. "Why don't you come up to my crib and tell me all about it." As she spoke, she took him by the hand and led him up the back stairway. Amanda chuckled to herself, shaking her head in disbelief. Hope sure knew how to bring those shillings into the Snug Harbor.

Just as Hope disappeared up the stairs, Imp came dashing down. Glancing about, he rushed behind the bar. "I got him," he said, panting to catch his breath.

"Got who?" asked Amanda, as she delivered a tankard of ale across the bar.

"Its Mr. Hancock, just like you asked," yelled Imp impatiently, over the noise of the taproom.

Amanda placed her hand gently over his mouth, glancing about to see if anyone heard. Fortunately, everyone was rapt in their own conversation or wrapped in the arms of one of the girls. "What do you mean 'you got him'?" she asked, as quiet as she could.

"We came in the back stairs; he's in your room. How did he know it was yours, now that I think about it?" said Imp, a curious look in his eyes.

Amanda began to pat her hair and take off her apron. "Just look at me!" she said to herself. "Amos, I have something to do; give Imp a mug of cider," she yelled over the din of the crowd. Amos simply nodded.

As Amanda passed the door to Hope's room on the way to her own, she heard the sailor slurring, ". . . and there was Caleb and Homer and . . ." She entered to find Hancock dressed in a dark plum-colored silk brocade, pouring a glass of Madeira. "May I pour one for you, Ms. Griffith?" he asked in a most casual fashion. She slowly crossed the room, took the glass from his hand, and placed it on the table and pressed her lips to his.

After a long moment, he held her at arm's length saying, "I wish I had time for this, but it seems that I have a ship missing. Please tell me what you know; Imp seemed to know very little."

"When I sent for you, I wasn't really sure what was happening, but the crowd in the taproom is speaking volumes," she said. Amanda then related all she knew of the confiscation of the *Liberty*. "Furthermore, Imp tells me that while he was aboard the *Romney*, the seamen told him that they could destroy all of Boston, if needed. And, although he doesn't understand its meaning, Imp learned that many in the crew are impressed seamen. Captain Corner must be using press gangs to man the *Romney* as he sees fit."

"Angel has told me much of the same – and more," said Hancock, a frown on his face. "Tomorrow, I will call on the commissioners to get the *Liberty* back."

Amanda blanched at the mention of Angel's involvement and pondering for a moment, said, "They have painted the broad arrow on the vessel, and they have the power to keep it under the cannon of the *Romney*."

Hancock frowned and angrily said, "I'll take care of that. Those commissioners will regret the day they challenged me."

Amanda, gazing out the window in thought, asked, "And just where is Angel at this moment, John?"

Hancock said nonchalantly, "If my guess is correct, she is probably the victim of Aunt Lydia's personal interrogation at this moment. I sent Angel to my home on

Beacon Hill for the time being; it seems the only safe place, with the officers of the *Romney* watching her so closely. Actually, who can really blame them?"

Biting her lower lip, Amanda tried to control her anger. "If you think for one moment that you expect to put your shoes under my bed while you share another with her, you are badly mistaken, Mr. Hancock!" she exclaimed, stomping her foot.

"Mr. Hancock? A moment ago it was 'John,'" said Hancock defensively, yet smiling. "Put your mind at rest, Amanda. If I know Aunt Lydia, she will personally guard Angel's room, armed with a musket on her shoulder and the bayonet fixed. Besides, it is only a temporary accommodation; trust me!"

"Trust you! Somehow, I recall hearing those words from men before," replied Amanda, maintaining a cold distance between them.

"But you must. Keep this in mind; we need her to complete our plans. You should have seen her at the *Romney* reception, my dear. The entire Tory contingent was captivated by her charms. It will be easy for her to mingle in their society in the near future. I tell you, Amanda, if she can get aboard the *Romney*, she can easily wheedle her way into their hearts and minds. We need information of what they are thinking and planning; you know that. It is crucial now that they have my *Liberty*."

"All right," said Amanda, surrendering to his pleading eyes. "I'll accept this 'arrangement' – for a short time only. Now I have an idea to learn what the commissioners are really about. What we might do is . . ."

ΩΩΩ

The rain was pouring that evening, and Dr. Benjamin Church was busy shaking the water from his rain-soaked cloak and tricorn hat as he entered the second-floor meeting room of the Green Dragon Tavern. The meeting of the Caucus Club was already in session and the stern eyes of the pacing Sam Adams spoke silent volumes at his being late. Quietly, Church slid into a seat at the long oak table as Adams continued his tirade. "I tell you, this is the last straw. If that damned Captain Corner thinks he can casually confiscate private property, especially a sloop that belongs to a leading citizen, he's asking for war. The time is near for the shedding of blood. I'm certain we could raise thirty thousand men armed with muskets and seize all the king's officers. Who could resist such a force?"

Dr. Church, observing the empty plates on the highly polished table, interrupted, "Is it too late to order a bit of mutton?"

"Mutton hell!" growled Adams. "Ben, forget your appetite for a moment and focus on this dastardly breach of the peace."

Dr. Joseph Warren whispered with a grin, "I'm sure a serving wench will arrive soon to recharge our mugs, Ben. Meanwhile, our friend Sam here is about to declare war on the entire British empire."

Adams stomped his foot and, turning his back on them to gaze out the window at the teeming downpour, said coldly, "Mark me, gentlemen. If we let this pass, we will most certainly suffer even greater loss and insults in the future."

At that point, John Hancock entered shaking the rain from his cloak, followed closely by a short squat serving maid. The men at the table became temporarily mute as she cleared the plates and recharged the ale and rum tankards. On her way out, Dr. Church ordered a platter and Hancock whispered, "A glass of brandy would be much appreciated." He waved his hand to clear the smoke as he made his way to a chair. "Sam, while you're standing there, please crack open a window; it would be nice to breathe a little fresh air."

When the door closed, James Otis asked, "How did your meeting with Governor Bernard go this afternoon, John? Will he release the *Liberty*?"

"I must admit that the meeting did not go well, I'm afraid," said Hancock somberly. "It seems that the arrival of the *Romney* has stiffened the spine of the customs agent who inspected the *Liberty* last month."

"And who exactly is this agent?" asked Paul Revere, rising from his seat with a knowing glance at Sam Adams.

"The man's name is Kirk," said Hancock. "And he alleges that more than one hundred pipes of Madeira wine came ashore without paying a customs duty."

James Otis, with a tired expression on his face and using his barrister's tone of voice, said, "I'm sure you made your customs declaration at the time the *Liberty* put into port, did you not?"

Hancock grinned. "According to my records, the *Liberty* paid a duty on twenty-five pipes of Madeira, as declared by Captain Marshall." At that moment, the serving maid returned, placing a platter before Dr. Church and handing a glass of brandy to Hancock, who merely nodded his thanks.

Church coughed phlegmatically and, wiping his mutton splotched lips with his sleeve, said, "Pretty scant cargo for an Atlantic passage, if you ask me, John."

Adams scowled, "Scant or not, a duty was paid and accepted. The ship is confiscated and, by the eternal, we should hang the commissioners for common thievery."

Hancock added, "The twenty-five pipes of Madeira simply show that it must have been a bad year for the grape harvest in the Madeira Islands."

Dr. Warren asked, "What does the captain of the *Liberty* have to say about the customs declaration?"

"Actually, he doesn't say much these days . . . because he is dead," he responded, gazing blankly at his glass of brandy. "But it seems that this Kirk fellow claims he was poorly treated, imprisoned in the ship's cabin, and threatened by Captain Marshall on the day of the customs inspection. Can you imagine such a fabrication?"

Adams grimaced, "Is there no limit to their mendacity? Now they condemn and malign the dearly deceased!"

Otis, becoming more agitated, asked, "What else did Bernard and his band of thieves have to say, John?"

"They want a full confession and payment of a hefty fine, plus customs fees. Only then will they consider the return of the *Liberty* to my keeping on the wharf," said Hancock, shaking his head. "Otherwise, Hutchinson is prepared to go to court, and God only knows how long that will take."

Otis stood, pounding his fist on the table, "Perhaps I should represent you on this, John. Hearsay of a dead man's activities is pure hogwash! By god, I'll bury the bastard in writs of English law until he chokes on them."

Hancock quickly responded, "I might just pay the fine, James. Time is of the essence, and I need the *Liberty* back in service, customs be damned! I'm losing money with that ship moored with the *Romney*."

Adams began pacing faster. "Pay the fine! Pay the fine? Don't even think it, John!" He had become even more animated, shaking his hand in the air to everyone and no one in particular.

Otis added, "Sam's right! It's the principle of the thing. Let me go with you to the superior court. We can put the commissioners in their place. We can fight this."

All at the table began speaking at once, sharing their varied opinions. Abruptly, a short stout balding man seated next to Sam arose, "Gentlemen, perhaps I can be of some help. My cousin has been updating me of your activities here in Boston."

Sam Adams smiled; and to the others seated at the table, he interjected, "Gentlemen, most of you know my cousin John Adams from Braintree. I have consulted him about the continued abuses of power by the Crown." Nodding to Otis, he continued, "Our friend Jim Otis here, as we all know, has been a thorn in the Crown courts for some time. Perhaps it is time for a new face to tweak the governor's nose. I suggest that my cousin John here represent us in this *Liberty* confiscation."

Otis coughed audibly, "I have no problem with that. In fact, John and I can work together; that's entirely up to Hancock there. But we shouldn't lose sight of the bigger picture. The *Liberty* situation is but a dastardly omen of what is to come from London. I still go on record that Parliament is comprised of a gaggle of buttonmakers, pinmakers, horse jockeys, gamesters, pensioners, pimps, and whoremasters. And I don't care who hears these words. Who could ever trust those rascals?"

Again, a strange quiet pervaded the table, as every eye seemed to rest on John Hancock. He took his time to note the expression on every expectant face before he said, "It is actually contrary to my better business judgment, but you just might be right. Perhaps we should go to court and fight this."

Dr. Church, licking mutton juice from his fingers, asked patronizingly, "What will Mr. Adams do that is different from the talents of Jim Otis here? What would be the point of adding another lawyer?" Looking specifically at John Adams, he added, "No offense intended, sir."

Sam Adams stood again, "It is time for a new face. The Tories hate James Otis, and we all know it! Sorry, James. But you must admit the truth." He continued shaking his finger in the air to emphasize the point. "Furthermore, I've finished our letter to Parliament telling them they have no right to impose taxes, if the sole purpose is to raise money. This taxation to pay the salaries of governors and judges is a blatant violation of natural law. That should be the function of local assemblies."

Dr. Warren laughed. "If Governor Bernard sees that letter, he will have a seizure. Isn't that right, Benjamin?" Dr. Church chortled as he nodded, licking his fingers of mutton grease.

John Adams added, "Mr. Hancock, I suggest we meet with the chief justice of the superior court, who, as we all know, just happens to be Lieutenant Governor Hutchinson, in order to inform him of our decision to rescind your settlement agreement and schedule a court date."

Paul Revere added, "While you play with legalities, I think that we should find this Kirk fellow and explain the facts of life to him."

Sam Adams, with a conspiratorial grin on his face, added, "This is a job for the Sons of Liberty, Paul. But don't you get personally involved." Revere, grabbing his cloak, tricorn hat, and walking stick, crossed to the door, saying, "I know just where to find our high Sons of Liberty at this time of the evening, and I'll let you know of our dealings with Mr. Kirk."

As he departed, Sam noted, "Revere continues to amaze me. He somehow manages to bridge that gap for us between the educated, the tradesmen, and the unwashed masses. I don't know what we would do without him."

Dr. Church added, "You mix pretty well yourself, Sam. Maybe it's because you didn't collect all those taxes. It's a good thing you still have interest in that brewery of yours." Everyone laughed, as John Adams and Hancock privately met at one end of the table.

ΩΩΩ

Revere made his way to the Snug Harbor Tavern within fifteen minutes. He paused at the doorway, his eyes peering through the smoky taproom, searching for the right men among the crowd of revelers. He found his mark at a raucous party near the fireplace, which always maintained a small blaze to heat the loggerheads.

Behind the bar, Amanda, wearing her white mobcap, took note of Revere's arrival, saying, "Amos, draw me a mug of ale. I'll deliver this one personally." Amos shrugged in surprise.

"Mackintosh, my good man, how goes it with you this fine evening?" asked Revere casually as he joined the table.

"Good evening, Mr. Revere. Please join us," said Mackintosh, a key leader of the Sons of Liberty. "You know most of these fine fellows. Let me introduce you to our newest 'High Son'; this is Zeke Teezle. He's a candlemaker from the south end."

Revere, after a prolonged pause to assess who could be trusted, said, "Good evening to you all." Pulling his chair aside, he muttered to Mackintosh, "Mac, what is wrong with you? Teezle is a known Tory."

Mackintosh laughed for all to hear, "Teezle, tell Mr. Revere what happened to you last week."

Teezle, clearing his throat, looked at Revere warily, "I don't want to say this too loudly, sir, but the Crown has raised my taxes, and I am tired of it."

Mackintosh added, "Don't you see? Old Teezle here used to be a king's man, but he has seen the error of his ways." He added loudly, looking around the taproom, "Let's have another round! Where's that serving wench when I need her?"

Revere, leaning on the table, said quietly to the small group, "We have a task for you men. It seems that . . ."

Suddenly, Amanda appeared at his elbow. "Good evening, Mr. Revere. We seldom get to see you down here at the wharf."

Revere smiled. "A silversmith must go where his customers are, ma'am. Thank you for the ale." He abruptly turned to the table dismissively, and Amanda retreated back to the bar, eyeing Teezle warily. Revere continued, "Let me remind you, gentlemen. Nothing you hear leaves this table." He gazed piercingly at Teezle. "Absolutely no one must know of our activities." He then proceeded to tell them about Kirk, the customs agent. "We must find this Mr. Kirk and learn what he knows about the *Liberty*. And I don't care if he is bruised in the process. Is that clear?" he added firmly. The briefing concluded, Revere seemed to relax and join the merriment.

In short order, as if on cue, a tall buxom lass dressed in a red velvet off-the-shoulder gown joined the table and sat on Teezle's lap. Puffed with the extra female attention that seemed to be exclusively his, Teezle said, "My friends, this is Hope. Isn't she delightful?" As he nuzzled Hope's bosom, everyone laughed uproariously. She whispered in his ear, and they both stood, holding hands. As she led Teezle to the stairway, she glanced over her shoulder, winking, "I won't keep him long, gentlemen. This will take only a moment." More laughter echoed across the Snug Harbor Tavern.

The only one not laughing was a lanky sailor seated at a corner table, wearing a red stocking cap, who seemed totally absorbed in the latest issue of the *Boston Gazette*.

ΩΩΩ

Five hours later, at nearly three o'clock in the morning, Amos was alone, cleaning behind the bar. He had just stoked the fire again and cleared the tables. As he wiped down the bar, he thought to himself how strangely quiet the taproom became after such a noisy evening.

Suddenly, he heard a light tapping at the door. He immediately picked up his wooden cudgel from behind the bar, expecting to find a drunken unruly sailor seeking an extra drink. He unlocked the door, holding the cudgel at the ready in his other hand. To his surprise, he found a tall black man, gasping for air, and drenched from the rain. As Amos lowered the club in stupefaction, the tall stranger rushed past him into the taproom, muttering, "Close the door and get away from the window!"

Standing by the door, his cudgel raised, Amos said, "And just who in hell do you think you are, bustin' into my taproom? If you a runaway slave, you best get your black ass outside my taproom now. You may be my color, but I won't have no trouble here at the Snug Harbor. Do you understand me?"

Crossing the taproom and warming himself at the fireplace, his wet clothes dripping on the hearth, the stranger whispered, "I need help! And only a black man can help me; at least, that's all I can trust for now. And I ain't no damn slave!"

Amos turned, and after craning his neck outside to see if anyone had followed the man on Fish Street, he locked the door. Pausing for a moment to gather his thoughts, he hurried to the far end of the bar and gestured with his hand saying, "Come with me back here and sit at this table out of sight from the windows." He filled a mug, adding, "Here's bit of rum to warm your insides. Now you just sit here for a minute; I'll be right back." He returned from the back storeroom with an old shirt and an old pair of trousers. "Get out of those wet clothes and put these on. They should fit because we look to be the same size."

After the stranger seemed settled, Amos sat down next to him and said, "Now what is your story? And you best be tellin' me the truth."

The black stranger tossed down the remainder of his rum and said in a quiet tone, "The name is Crispus Attucks. These past fifteen years, I was a harpoon man on a whaling ship sailing out of Nantucket. The ship put in this afternoon for food and stuff down at Long Wharf, and I decided that I'm just too old for that way of life anymore. Besides that, I can't stand the smell of whale blubber burning on them decks."

Shaking his head in bewilderment, Amos sat back in his chair and responded, "Now what's that got to do with me and you at this hour in my taproom? Besides, every path has a few puddles. And I've heard too damn many sob stories in this taproom to need yours added to the list."

Looking a bit agitated, Crispus said, "Could I please have another mug of rum? It's been a long time, and it tastes mighty good."

Amos said proudly, "I can do better than that. Let me fix you a flip. I promise this is the best you can get in Boston and then you best leave."

Sipping his flip, Crispus continued, "This is what happened. I was a slave back in 1750; I think it was. I belonged to a man named William Brown in Framingham. In those days, I was an expert trader of horses and cattle. My daddy was African, and my mamma was a Natick Indian. They taught me real good, and I knew my stuff. We did a lot of business with white folks. But I didn't like this Brown fella, and I wanted my freedom from Framingham real bad, so I runned away when I visited Boston and saw all them ships in the harbor."

Amos asked eagerly, "What did that Brown fella do after you ran away?"

"I can't read, but I learned that Mr. Brown went to the *Boston Gazette*, describing me as a mulatto fellow, about six feet and two inches high, with short curly hair. I am told that he described my knees as being nearer together than common. He put a ten-pound reward for my capture, and I had no choice but to stow aboard the first ship out from Boston. That ship took me to Nantucket, where I learned to handle a harpoon pretty good. But now I am back . . . and thinkin' about Mr. Brown."

Amos rocked in his creaking seat, thinking. Finally, he leaned forward, saying quietly, "I think it best if you just forget about this Mr. Brown. It don't take a very big man to carry a grudge, and you seem to be mighty burdened." Sitting back in his chair, sipping his flip, Amos gazed into the stranger's eyes and took good measure of the man. He added calmly, "It seems to me that our stories ain't too far different. We both have messed up legs, and we both did slave time," said Amos. "But there ain't much I can do for you here."

"All I needs is a place to stay for the night. I promises to be gone before daybreak because I think I still have friends living in the north end of Boston," replied Crispus with his eyes pleading.

With his eyes glancing up the stairway, Amos nodded, "All right! But this is just between the two of us. You can spend the night on the floor of the storeroom where I sleep. After you settle yourself in the north side, you can drop in for a pint."

"I didn't catch your name, and it seems I owe you so much," said Crispus.

Again, glancing upstairs Amos, replied, "Amos is the name. It's only right to take in strangers who need help from time to time." As he shuffled to the rear of the taproom with his uneven gait, he added, "Now you be extra quiet in the storeroom because I shares it with a small white boy, who just happens to be my best friend. And, speakin' of names, you best change yours. That 'Crispus Attucks' sort of dances in the mind. You need something more common so as not to draw attention to yourself."

Pondering for a moment, Crispus grinned. "How about 'Johnson'? I once sailed with a fella by that name. He was Scotch-Irish or somethin' like that." Scratching his head, he added, "Yea! That's it! Michael Johnson. The 'Michael' part comes from that angel I heard about in the white folks' Bible."

"You don't look like no Scotch-Irishman to me, but that name is fine as any I heard around here!" exclaimed Amos.

ΩΩΩ

The rain had ceased, and the sun was burning off an early morning fog, as Governor Bernard peered through his spyglass at the ships in Boston Harbor. "I tell you, Hutchinson, the creation of Omega was our best idea ever in dealing with these radicals," he said smiling. Turning to the fat man seated in a corner chair, he continued, "So they plan to threaten our Mr. Kirk, do they?"

"Exactly right, Governor! I'm not exactly sure who it will be or when. But I understand the Sons of Liberty are involved," said the corpulent man, clearly concerned.

Hutchinson, pacing the floor, said disgustedly, "That could be almost anyone who works on the docks. What else do we know of their plans?" he asked the fat man.

Proudly, the fat man arose from his seat and poured himself a glass of claret from the lead crystal decanter. "You can expect another meeting with Mr. Hancock; only this time, he will be accompanied by John Adams."

Bernard, lowering the spyglass, glanced over his shoulder. "We know Sam Adams, but who is 'John' Adams?" he asked with a curious tone in his voice.

"He is Sam Adams's cousin, a lawyer from Braintree. Sam seems to think that a new face, replacing James Otis, will make the case more 'congenial,'" added the fat man, sipping his claret.

Bernard raised his eyebrows, glancing at Hutchinson. "With you as superior court judge, I am sure that this John Adams will bring no new challenges to the court. Besides, we already have an agreement with Hancock, and he is expected to pay a hefty fine."

The fat man downed his claret, saying, "Forget about it. Adams will cancel that agreement, and Hancock will ask for a court date."

Hutchinson glanced at Bernard. Then opening the office door, Hutchinson said with a tone of dismissal, "Thank you for coming, my friend. But please continue to use the usual Omega channels of communication, if possible. We should keep these personal emergency meetings to a minimum. Here's a small token of the Crown's appreciation." He handed a small pouch of heavy coins to the fat man as he departed.

Closing the door, he turned to Bernard, asking, "How does this information match that from the other Omega agents?"

"The old sailor tells us much the same. It seems that our candlemaker has been adopted by the Sons of Liberty, and he is filled with Hope, if you know what I mean." They both laughed heartily as Hutchinson poured them both another glass of claret.

Bernard said, "Let's get Kirk out to Castle William in the harbor or aboard the *Romney* for his own protection. He can join the commissioners and their families as they hide from the wrath of the town mob. Kirk's testimony is crucial to the *Liberty* case."

Hutchinson chuckled, "If Hancock thinks he will ever get the *Liberty* back, he is dreaming. I'll find every legal hurdle you can imagine to block him; this John Adams notwithstanding!"

Bernard sipped his glass of wine. "At last, we have found their weakness. Hancock will do nothing if it affects his wealth and pompous image. When he finally realizes that we could ultimately confiscate all his ships, he will yield to our way of thinking, and this radical cabal will simply dissolve for lack of the pound sterling," said Bernard. He glanced again through his spyglass at the harbor, laughing. "As long as the *Liberty* is moored alongside the *Romney*, we own John Hancock."

Hutchinson frowned, "We should keep in mind that more than a thousand Boston families depend on Hancock for their daily bread and provisions. And he also contributed more than a thousand pounds sterling to the Brattle Street Meeting House. With all that, he is quite popular with the town rabble."

Bernard nodded, "You have a point. All the same, we will squeeze him gently . . . in the courts, Mr. Chief Justice."

ΩΩΩ

It was near high noon when Amanda, wearing her white mobcap, scrubbing clothes, and leather bodice to support her breasts, barged into the taproom of the Bunch of Grapes, carrying the latest issue of the *Boston Gazette*. Big Bessie, sipping a cup of noon tea, smiled. "Why, Amanda, what a pleasant surprise!" Looking her up and down, her arms akimbo, she added, "You must be in a hurry. I seldom see you dressed so informally, my dear."

"I didn't come here to find someone for a bit of shaggin'," said Amanda sarcastically. "But I need to talk with you – privately." Big Bessie guided her to a private corner table, far away from the bar and the front door.

"What is this about?" Bessie asked in a whisper.

Amanda frowned, "It's a bit personal, but I have an uneasy feeling about our mutual friend Angel."

Big Bessie said, "Wait a minute; I think we need something stronger than tea." She waddled to the bar, returning with two tankards of rum. "This should help us think more clearly. Now what is this about Angel?"

"As of now," said Amanda, "I don't think we will see much of her. Would you believe that rascal Hancock has moved her into his mansion? He claims it will be for a short time, but I don't trust her one bit."

Big Bessie burst out laughing. "I'm sorry if my amusement offends you, Amanda. But just look at yourself; you are in a huff about a simple trollop. Besides, if I recall correctly, you helped organize that arrangement with Angel and Hancock for the *Romney* reception party."

"But I didn't expect that hussy to move in with him," retorted Amanda, pouting.

Placing her hands under her chubby layers of chin, Big Bessie asked, measuring her words carefully, "Do you mean to tell me, Amanda, that you and Hancock got a 'thing' going on at the Snug Harbor? Are you shaggin' that rich rascal?" She paused with a mock glare and her brow furrowed, "Now you be honest with your friend, Big Bessie."

Sitting back in her chair heavily and taking a hefty gulp of her rum, Amanda said, "It's just between us here at this table, but the short answer is . . . yes; we've been tumblin' for quite some time, actually."

Big Bessie, with a conspiratorial grin, asked in a whisper, "What's he like? Is he different than them kinky sailors we are so familiar with? Tell me! Tell me!"

"Never you mind what he's like under the covers! Besides, it's more than that, if you really must know," replied Amanda, a coy look on her face.

"What do you mean, 'it's more than that'?" asked Big Bessie. "With men, that's the only thing. And, trust me, I know something about men." She leaned back in her chair, gulping down her rum.

Leaning forward, Amanda said, "Actually, Hancock is my landlord and my major supplier of goods and provisions. So we have a business relationship."

"You got more than that, it seems," replied Big Bessie. "And our regular business and romantic business don't usually mix too well. You know that all to well, Amanda."

"The real problem is that I really like the man, Bessie," added Amanda, somberly. "Now this 'Angel' has entered the picture, and I don't exactly like the way she looks at him. And, dammit, as we speak, she is living under his roof up there on Beacon Hill."

It was now Big Bessie's turn to sit back heavily in her chair. Looking at the rafters, she reflected on the encounter Angel had with Hancock in her very own taproom. Now, she pondered, her suspicions were noteworthy. "Has that rascal promised you anything beyond what we usually expect, Amanda? This is important because we could ruin that man, if we cared to."

Amanda stood in anger, "I don't want to ruin him, you dolt!" A group of tradesmen, sitting at a distant table, looked up from their chowder at the commotion. "And just what are you looking at, you bastards?" growled Amanda.

"Sit down," commanded Big Bessie. In a calming voice, she added, "It seems to me, Amanda, that you have a rare disease."

"A disease? What in hell are you talking about?" asked Amanda, petulantly.

"It's something that women in our business can ill afford. I think you're in love, Amanda. The big ugly, jealous, possessing, craving-lusties kind of love," said Big Bessie. "Now the symptoms are worse because of a festering wound called Angel." She ordered another round of rum before she continued, "If you really want this rich bastard, let me tell you what you have to do. You must . . ."

ΩΩΩ

CHAPTER 10

July 1768

GOVERNOR BERNARD SAT in his office, glaring at Thomas Hutchinson and the other members of the Council. "Gentlemen, I think you will agree that this continued mob rule and sporadic rioting must cease. It is for that reason that you must recommend that I request troops from the Crown."

"Nice of you to ask, Francis," said Hutchinson, "but you can do this of your own volition as governor. Why do you need us?"

"The answer is simple. You all know the mentality of this town mob. I will not be singled out for their abuse. I will request the troops, only if you agree to share the blame for their arrival. It is simply good politics for us all. We must stand united," he said firmly.

Looking about the room, most members of the council gazed at their hands, the floor, and any other inanimate object they could find in the room. No one was willing to look him in the eyes. Finally, Hutchinson, speaking for them all, said, "It seems that we prefer not to have our heads bashed in, sir."

"And neither do I," responded Bernard tersely. "Perhaps it's best if I simply write a letter to London hinting at the need for soldiers. I'll include our latest report from Omega that the Sons of Liberty have guaranteed death to the man who requests British troops to patrol the streets of Boston."

$$\Omega\Omega\Omega$$

July 1768
New York

Major General Thomas Gage, Britain's commander of Crown forces in the American colonies, straightened the lapels of his spotless crimson uniform coat, as his valet brushed his back clear of any errant traces of lint. He continued to preen himself in the looking glass, when Lieutenant Colonel William Dalrymple entered with a handful of documents saying, "General, pardon the interruption, but I think these dispatches warrant your immediate attention."

Gage, dismissing his valet with a wave of his hand, said, "What is it, William, that could be so urgent? You know it's time for my morning ride."

With rigid military bearing, Dalrymple said, "Your adjutant brought these to my attention. These are not the usual messages. and all are sealed for your eyes only, sir."

Breaking the wax seals and scanning them quickly, Gage said in an aggravated tone, "Would you listen to this, William! Three letters with the same basic message! The first is from the customs commissioners in Boston; they insist that the entire British army come at once to harness an unruly mob. The second is from Governor Bernard of Massachusetts; he merely hints that a contingent of the king's forces might be helpful in restoring order, but he would prefer that I act on my own initiative. And last is a letter from Lord Hillsborough in London. It seems that the king and Lord North have appointed him to a new office, that of secretary of state for colonial affairs."

"Exactly what does Lord Hillsborough think of the situation?" asked Dalrymple.

Gage arose from his desk and gestured to the sideboard. "Pour us both a tankard of rum, William. It seems that our Lord Hillsborough is a dynamo," he said with a broad grin. "He has heard from the Boston commissioners and has ordered me to deploy a regiment from Halifax to Boston. As we both know, that is your particular command. In addition, he has ordered two regiments based in Ireland to set sail for Boston."

Handing a tankard to Gage, Dalrymple asked, "Do you plan to personally meet these detachments in Boston, General?"

"I don't feel that is necessary. I'll remain in New York while you take command of those three regiments in Boston. You will have your own forces from Halifax to combine with those from Ireland. I expect it should be easy for you to crush this mob of Boston rascals once and for all," said Gage, smugly.

"Thank you for the opportunity, General. But it seems like overkill to send that many troops to handle a few ruffians," added Dalrymple.

"You should be able to establish peace rather quickly. The mere sight of a British bayonet should terrify them. There is a group known as the Sons of Liberty providing most of the trouble; actually, a mob of hooligans. When you arrive, you will coordinate your activities with Governor Bernard. I anticipate that you should arrest the leaders of this group in the name of the Crown," said Gage, speaking with brutal detachment.

"It shouldn't take more than a month or two to clean up the entire affair. I hear that there are many Tories on our side to provide whatever intelligence we should need," added Dalrymple, smiling.

"Just keep your eyes on our Irish regiments. They can be quite unruly, especially if they've been drinking. I want our men to function as peacemakers, not troublemakers. Do you understand?" said Gage in a commanding tone. "You should make plans to meet and take command of these regiments around the middle of September. That should give you adequate time to arrange your personal affairs, and it will take that long for the Atlantic crossing anyway. Meanwhile, I will communicate with Governor Bernard about our plans. Any questions, William?" Without pausing, he added, "Send a courier in on your way out."

"I'll put a plan together for your approval before departure, General," said Dalrymple, downing his tankard. "Boston will finally feel the wrath of the British Crown. And I might add that it is about time."

General Gage shook his head uneasily. "I hope you're right, William. You realize that I am sending you into a hornet's nest. I trust your keen judgment in dealing with this. These New Yorkers are tame when compared to those Boston radicals. So take the time to learn all you can from Governor Bernard; I hear he has a good spy network up there. If you need additional help, simply send a dispatch rider or use Commodore Hood's packet ships."

Dalrymple nodded, "I'll send Captain Preston to arrange for quarters in advance."

"Smart idea," said Gage. "A captain will be less likely to alarm our radical friends."

Dalrymple smiled, saluted, and strutted out the door, a man on a mission.

ΩΩΩ

September 1768
Boston

It was high noon when Imp scampered into the Snug Harbor taproom, stopping at the near end of the bar to catch his breath. Amanda, seated at a corner table, looked up from her ledgers, a glare of agitation in her eyes. Gazing around the taproom, she took note of a few patrons she did not know. As Imp took a hesitant step toward her table, she shook her head and pointed to the stairway. Catching on instantly, Imp casually sauntered to the back stairs and up to Amanda's room. She appeared within moments.

"You know better than to rush about like that, Imp. I've told you before that you must remain inconspicuous and act casual at all times. Do you understand me?" said Amanda, shaking her finger at him.

"What does inconspic – whatever that word is – mean?" asked Imp defensively.

"It means I don't want anyone to ever notice you – whatever you are doing. Never rush; never hurry; never yell. If you are to be useful, you must look like the Imp we all know. Don't draw attention to yourself," said Amanda, firmly. Calming down, she added in a low voice, "Mr. Hancock has told me that you have been serving as an informal messenger for him and Mr. Adams and their friends. So it is most important that you don't pass messages for all to hear, as you almost did down in the taproom."

"They told me I was the best to be a messenger because I deliver the *Gazette* and know most folks," said Imp proudly, with obvious innocence in his voice.

"That's why you have to be casual about your movements. We can never be sure who could be watching you. It's for your own safety, Imp; very few people know about you being a messenger, and I want to keep it that way. Now, what are you in such a rush about?" asked Amanda, reverting to her tone of concern.

Imp stood, recovering from his chastisement, "You'd be in a rush too, if you just heard what I just heard, Ms. Amanda."

"Well! Out with it already!" she exclaimed.

"It finally happened. The regulars are on the way to Boston," stammered Imp.

"When? Where did you learn this?" asked Amanda.

"I was on the docks. A Crown sloop just berthed at Long Wharf, and the sailors were boastin' that they just put a captain ashore," said Imp.

"What's the big deal about one captain coming ashore?" asked Amanda, impatiently.

"He ain't no ordinary soldier. He told the sailors that he was here to make quartering arrangements for the arrival of the king's troops. Seems he was right proud of the fact that they were comin'," replied Imp.

"How many are coming? When? Did he say?" probed Amanda, suddenly in a rush.

"I don't know. Everyone on the dock was askin' the same questions," Imp replied.

Scratching her head through her mobcap, Amanda seemed lost in thought. "I want you to deliver this same news to Mr. Hancock right away; you should find him over at his warehouse office. Be quick about it but don't run. After you deliver that message, you come right back here. There is more for you to do," added Amanda. The concern on her otherwise passive demeanor was apparent. Imp rushed out.

ΩΩΩ

September 12, 1768

Once again, the Caucus Club convened in the upper room of the Green Dragon Tavern. "I told you! I told you! I told you! There is no end to the arrogance of the Crown," trumpeted Sam Adams, again in state of severe agitation, his quaking hand seemingly working overtime.

Dr. Ben Church stood at the far end of the table. "For god's sake, keep your voice down, Sam. The walls have ears!"

"I don't care who hears me. In fact, someone better listen to me. No one else seems to care," yelled Adams, defiantly.

"But we do care," interrupted Hancock. "The point is there's no sense in giving anyone more evidence to arrest you – or us, for that matter. Secrecy is still our most potent weapon, Sam. Keep a cool head about yourself!"

Paul Revere added, "It's agreed then! I'll have the Sons of Liberty hoist a barrel of turpentine onto a pole on Beacon Hill. At first sight of the king's troops coming into the harbor, it will be ignited as an alarm for the entire countryside."

Adams glared at his trusted friends. "That's not enough. We should demand that Governor Bernard convene an emergency session of the House and Council."

Nodding his head in agreement, James Otis added, "Sam's right! It is a simple point of law. The king cannot impose his army on a colony without consent of the colony's representatives."

"But Bernard has refused to convene the House without the consent of the king," said Dr. Joseph Warren in a matter-of-fact tone.

Sam Adams paced the floor again, "This is nonsense. We are elected as the colony's representatives, and we are now meeting, are we not? That's a legal meeting of Englishmen, the way I see it."

Church said, licking his fingers of lamb chop residue, "But we are meeting illegally. We can't tell the governor of our discussions without admitting our violation of his banning our meeting in the first place."

Otis, scratching his head, asked, "Are we certain the king's troops are really coming, Sam?"

Hancock, clearing his throat with a polite cough, interjected, "It is most definite, James. My contacts on the dock and a few brash Tories inform me that this Captain Preston met with the governor to arrange quarters for a few regiments. It seems he was the messenger of a Colonel Dalrymple. The regulars are coming; you can be sure of it."

Adams, becoming ashen in his anger, said, "Quarters? It will be a rainy day in hell before we provide quarters for one damned redcoat. I tell you, now is the time for action. Let us arm every citizen of Boston with muskets from the town armory. As an excuse, we could tell them that a new war with France is imminent."

John Adams, now pacing at the same rate as his cousin, said, "We've already taken our muskets from the storehouse on the pretext of cleaning them. Do you really want to lie to your neighbors about a French invasion? Be sensible, Sam!"

Revere added, "We all saw it at the town meeting at Faneuil Hall. They voted not to take up arms at this time. I'm not so sure that our friends are in the mood for insurrection, Sam."

Sam paced again. "There were too dammed many Tory farmers at the meeting! That's the problem. I tell you that now is the time to act. Soon it will be too late."

Dr. Church said, "The representatives have voted, Sam; let's forget it and hope for the best. Don't forget, we are Englishmen. What redcoat would dare harm a fellow Englishman?"

ΩΩΩ

September 16, 1768

Lieutenant Governor Hutchinson stared out the window overlooking King Street, toward Long Wharf, while Governor Bernard sat in the largest easy chair in his office, sipping a tumbler of claret. "Well, Francis," said Hutchinson, "it seems that all of Boston is now aware that the king's troops are on the way. I've heard rumors that Adams and his cronies plan to raise thirty thousand armed men to oppose them."

Bernard frowned and gulped his wine, setting the glass aside. "Thomas, just between the two of us, I'm both happy and sad that it has come to this. But you are correct; our friend Teezle heard Sam Adams spout that he plans to destroy every soldier who places his foot ashore."

Hutchinson nodded, "He might say that, but mark me well; at the first sight of our troops, this mob will disappear. Adams claims that the arrival of the British army is akin to a foreign invasion. Can you believe such nonsense?"

"Has he forgotten that he is an Englishman, for god's sake?" asked Bernard. Rising to recharge his tumbler, he added, "Nonetheless, I purposely let the word leak out with our Tory friends, hoping to soften the reaction of the troop's arrival. In a few days, I'll make the formal announcement. By then, all the bluster from Adams will fall on deaf ears, I hope."

"And the sight of those redcoats and the Royal Navy frigates will send him scurrying for cover. All his words in the *Boston Gazette* are no match for British bayonets and cannon. I guarantee it!" added Hutchinson, smiling.

Bernard joined Hutchinson at the window. "Let's get the latest news from the street as soon as we can. When the commanding officer arrives, I want to provide him the best information we have on all radical patriot activities. Get Omega to do a little more probing. I'll talk to the fat man. Meanwhile, you get the old sailor on the street again. I don't want these soldiers to suffer some sort of ambush when they arrive."

Hutchinson downed his claret. "I'll get right on it. And don't worry about an ambush; Adams and his friends will probably run for the hills. I can almost guarantee it!"

ΩΩΩ

October 1, 1768

A heavy dawn fog shrouded all of Boston Harbor as the small skiff put ashore at the edge of Long Wharf. Lieutenant Colonel William Dalrymple, commander of the king's troops assigned to Boston, jumped ashore with a lone junior officer at his side. He paused briefly at the entrance to Long Wharf, assessing the situation. He had been briefed that all of Boston had been the scene of rioting and unrest. He gazed up King Street, noting that it was devoid of humanity as far as he could see through the mist. Not a soul was stirring. He told the crew to stay with the longboat, as he glanced at the harbor behind him. He could barely discern the shapes of the small armada, but he knew it was there.

The evening before, the citizens of Boston had quietly witnessed the orderly arrival of the British ships. Now, the harbor had become a forest of masts and spars. A fleet of twelve British men-of-war had moored around Boston, and they were prepared for action. Dalrymple knew that their cannon were loaded, and the ships had springs put on their cables in order to maintain a broadside profile to the town. On board, his command was comprised of two full regiments – the Fourteenth and the Twenty-ninth, along with a portion of the Fifty-ninth and a train of artillery. Each man was supplied with sixteen rounds of powder and ball.

Dalrymple marched with his aide up the middle of King Street as the sun began to make its presence known in the east. The fog was beginning to burn off, and he could observe only a few furtive curious glances from windows. He realized that the eyes of Boston were upon him as he arrived at the Old State House door, where a reed-thin doorman greeted him. Dalrymple barged past the man, saying, "Where's the governor?"

The liveried man bowed courteously. "My name is Slank, sir, secretary to Governor Bernard, who unfortunately is not in at the moment."

"This is ridiculous! Where is he? I have a – "

"Perhaps Lieutenant Governor Hutchinson could be of assistance, sir," interrupted Slank, again bowing.

"And just where is this Hutchinson chap? Let's be quick," grumbled Dalrymple.

"This way, sir!" Slank led the way to the second-floor offices, ever so slowly and deliberately. Impatiently, Dalrymple opened the designated door without knocking, his aide in tow.

"I told you, Slank, that I did not want to be – " Hutchinson didn't finish his sentence. He instantly arose from his chair with a broad smile.

Dalrymple paused, as the door was silently closed behind him; Slank had disappeared. "I am Lieutenant Colonel William Dalrymple, and I am here to speak with Governor Bernard," said Dalrymple. "Where is he?"

Hutchinson cleared his throat. "First, let us be clear about something, Colonel. I am the lieutenant governor of this colony, and I suggest you slow down a bit and adopt a more genial tone."

Suddenly smiling, Dalrymple seemed to glide over to the windows overlooking King Street and the harbor. Slowly, he said, "Forgive me Mr. Hutchinson, but I have been at sea with my regiments for some time, and I am quite anxious to get them ashore. My frigate arrived in the harbor near nightfall, but I felt it wise to meet with you at first light rather than come ashore in the darkness. I assume Governor Bernard has arranged quarters for my troops."

Clearing his throat uncomfortably, Hutchinson muttered, "Unfortunately, quartering seems to be a bit of a problem at the moment, Colonel. Governor Bernard will return from Jamaica Plain tomorrow. Hopefully, we can resolve the issue then."

Looking around impatiently, Dalrymple responded tersely, "This is one rotten way to greet the king's forces, Mr. Hutchinson. I was advised of rioting for which His Majesty's navy and I had prepared." He glanced out the window. "Now I find a quiet town, basically deserted and the governor himself absent. And now you tell me that quartering is delayed. How should I feel, Mr. Hutchinson? How would you feel?" grumbled Dalrymple.

Wandering to the sideboard, Hutchinson said casually, "Let me pour you a glass of brandy, Colonel." Handing him a tumbler, he added, smiling, "Have a seat, sir. You should know that your mere presence has tamed this town, Colonel, and I personally am most happy to have you here." Without asking, he also handed a tumbler to Dalrymple's aide, adding, "Congratulations, gentlemen! Without so much as a word or a drawn saber, you have suddenly quieted the radicals of Boston, and I pray it stays that way."

Dalrymple took the proffered glass. "That's all well and good, Mr. Hutchinson. But now that we are here, what are your plans for us?"

"Governor Bernard will clear that up tomorrow in this office, let us say, at one o'clock in the afternoon. Meanwhile, I would like you to disembark your forces from those beautiful men-of-war as soon as possible and march your regiments slowly and smartly down the center of King Street. Continue past this building to Tremont Street. You then turn left and in short order, you can encamp on Boston Common – for only a short time, I assure you."

"Well, as long as it is for a short time. General Gage in New York will not like this, I assure you. I certainly do not!" said Dalrymple.

Hutchinson seemed to ignore the issue, eagerly adding, "Please, Colonel, make a big display of your forces when marching up the street. I want flags unfurled, fifes, and drums and fixed bayonets; let's not forget the bayonets."

Dalrymple smiled, setting his glass aside. "Mr. Hutchinson, there is no one on the street to see anything."

Hutchinson laughed heartily. "Colonel, you are the biggest news in years. Behind every door and window, there is a radical Son of Liberty. I want them all to shudder at the sight of you and your men."

"I'll do as you wish, Mr. Hutchinson. We shall meet again tomorrow." Dalrymple placed his gold-trimmed tricorn on his head and opened the door.

Hutchinson's melodious voice caused him to pause, "Don't forget the bayonets, Colonel Dalrymple."

The colonel merely shook his head on the way down the spiral stairs. After his exit, Hutchinson called for Slank, who slowly shuffled into the office. "Is there something I can do for you, sir? That soldier seemed quite agitated."

"Never mind that, Slank! We need to have the key members of Omega here tomorrow at one o'clock for a meeting with our new friends in the red coats," said Hutchinson proudly. He stepped to the window, watching Dalrymple and his aide march back to Long Wharf.

"As you wish, sir. I'll speak to the old sailor immediately."

ΩΩΩ

Big Bessie Clump glared over the rim of her tankard of ale, as she watched the parade of soldiers marching down King Street. Sitting across from her at the window table at the Bunch of Grapes, Amanda Griffith held her chin in her bunched-up fists. Both were clad in mobcaps and scullery clothes, in stark contrast to the bright red coats, chalk white breeches and black hats of those marching by with military precision.

Leading the vanguard of the Fourteenth and Twenty-ninth regiments were the fife and drum corps. Comprised of black musicians clad in bright yellow uniforms, they created a mysticism and precision to the procession that instilled both fear and awe in the few inhabitants watching the parade on the fringe of King Street. The music, combined with the glistening bayonets, and the intermittent barked orders of the sergeant majors to the seemingly endless ranks of redcoats, was intended to inform the populace that the king meant business and that no violation of civil law would be tolerated. The two leading regiments were followed by a portion of the Fifty-ninth and a train of artillery.

"If I was a man, I'd put a stop to this, Bessie. This is an affront to the entire colony, for god's sake. Just look at them struttin' down the middle of town like they own it," grumbled Amanda. "It seems the only ones brave enough to face them on the sides of the street are citizens the size of Imp there, sitting at the doorstep." It seemed that every apprentice in Boston had found a perch along the length of King Street to watch the long line of soldiers as they marched to the Common. Not a word was uttered.

"Let's face it," responded Big Bessie. "Right now, the redcoats do own the town. But time will tell. You must admit it, though; they sure are pretty." She took a heavy swallow from her tankard and pointed through the window with her chubby arm. "Just look at those big burly grenadiers; with those bearskin hats, they look to be ten feet tall. I wonder if everything they have is big!"

Amanda turned her eyes from the street and looked intently into Bessie's eyes. "Forget about what's 'big,' Bessie. Just what do you mean 'time will tell'?"

Bessie patted Amanda's hand and spoke firmly. "Now you settle down and face the facts! Right now, no man in the colony could possibly stand up to them, Amanda. They're too ready for trouble, and it's what they want. A soldier wants to get the fightin' over with as soon as possible. A long wait is their worst enemy."

Amanda shared a knowing grin. "You know, Bessie, sometimes you really surprise me. By god, you're right! Within a week, every redcoat marching out there will be sufferin' the craving lusties for what we have and forget all about fightin'."

"You bet your sweet arse," blubbered Big Bessie, laughing. "I'll bet we could make most of them claim a new religion and trade their Brown Bess muskets for one good shaggin."

Amanda added, "Maybe our Sons of Liberty can't do much right now, but we can get the job done on our end."

"Be kind to our Boston men, Amanda. Remember, they don't have the same ammunition we have. Our weapons are far more potent!" said Bessie, with a brassy laugh as she juggled her pendulous breasts.

Staring with an analytical eye at the passing parade, Amanda added in a cunning tone, "We should advise our girls to keep their ears open with this new opportunity. Business will be great, and there is much to learn; shaggin' seems to make a man talk. I best get over to the Snug Harbor. We'll both be needin' more rum, ale, and beer with this gaggle." She rushed down King Street to the sound of drums and fifes.

Meanwhile, across the street at the British Coffee House, Paul Revere sat with Dr. Benjamin Church. The contrast in style was obvious; while Church was resplendent in pale blue satin brocade and flashing his gold signet ring, Revere was quite relaxed in the attire of a tradesman, with only gold buttons accenting his waistcoat as a small sign of status. Church, taking note of the gold, said, "Paul, what would you charge to provide me gold buttons like yours? I've come into a bit of money and – "

"Not now, Dr. Church!" said Revere tersely. "Let's focus on this dastardly parade. It has been nearly four hours that they have been marching by, and only now do I finally see the end. What is our final tally?"

Biting into a pork chop and downing his pint of ale, Church responded philosophically, "It really doesn't matter, Paul. The number of the king's troops in Boston is an obvious overkill. Look at them! Bayonets glistening in the sun, the wary eyes; these men are ready for trouble. It is best that we remain out of sight."

"By my count," said Revere, ignoring his comments, "I find more than one thousand men, including a company of artillery. That's more than two complete regiments. Where will they stay? That's a lot of men to quarter."

Church, licking his fingers in a nonchalant manner, said, "It seems they've marched over to the Common. I guess they will probably pitch their tents and build their fires there for now."

With that said, Revere arose from the table. "I'll see you later, Doctor. I'm off to the Common to finish my count."

"Go with God, my good man," said Church, waving with his mouth full, "and be careful of those bayonets. I shall remain for a small serving of plum pudding."

In a matter of minutes, Revere found Sam Adams and his cousin's small son John Quincy standing on a knoll above the Common, not far from the Hancock mansion. "What do you think, Sam?" asked Revere, with a tired gaze.

"A lot of good that barrel of turpentine on that pole did!" exclaimed Adams, disgustedly.

"Lighten up, Sam. You know very well that Sheriff Greenleaf finally mustered up enough courage to take the barrel down. And, besides, all the turpentine had leaked out anyway," said Revere defensively.

Ignoring his comment, Sam Adams grumbled, "Where's the insurrection? What happened to the Sons of Liberty?"

John Hancock joined them, staring at the assemblage of white tents and red uniforms, arrayed in neat rows on the community grazing land. Without preamble, he said, "Face it. We did what we could, Sam. We argued with the governor to keep these redcoats billeted on Castle William in the harbor, but it seems that this Lieutenant Colonel Dalrymple has countermanded that order. Bernard wouldn't put them right under my nose here on Beacon Hill, would he? It had to be the colonel."

Adams, with a vacant stare, said, "We have much to learn about our new adversary, John. In my opinion, Governor Bernard has the innate ability to say one thing and do another. As for the redcoats, I suspect that Lieutenant Colonel Dalrymple is merely a puppet. It seems to me that this General Gage, commander of all the king's troops in the colonies, is pulling the strings and will probably dictate to Governor Bernard before long, even if he is in New York."

Little John Quincy Adams said, "Those redcoats certainly look sharp down there, don't they? What's that song they keep singing?"

Sam patted his head. "Remember this moment, John Quincy! That song is 'Yankee Doodle Dandy,' and it is intended as an insult to us all. They don't belong here, and I promise they will not be here very long, if I have anything to do with it." Turning to Hancock, he said, "I have another letter for the *Boston Gazette* to write, or I should rather say 'Vindex' has a letter to write. I'll see you tomorrow, John."

Hancock smiled, patting Adams on the back. "Relax, Sam. A small setback – for now! Sadly, most of the populace has gone to ground. But I trust they won't stand this insult for long. Besides, we must prepare for another governor's reception in appreciation of the army's arrival. First, the Royal Navy; now, the king's army! How honored we should feel!" he added sarcastically.

Turning back, Sam said after a moment's thought, "A formal party? You should bring your friend Angel out from hiding. She helped with the navy on the *Romney*; perhaps her charms can now be unleashed on the army." At that, he kicked up his heels. "When is this party?"

Laughing, Hancock added, "I am merely speculating, Sam; no formal announcement has been made about the governor's gala. But you know Bernard. He won't waste this opportunity to cram his new force down our throats, with all the cordiality he can muster."

Adams pondered a moment in silence, "You are probably right, John. Let me know if you hear of a formal date for this sham of a celebration. But don't forget that girl . . . that Angel. We could use her."

"I was thinking the exact same thing, Sam. Right now, Angel is in Lexington, visiting my cousins in the countryside for a while. I had to get her out; Aunt Lydia was having fits with that beauty under our roof. I can get her back to Boston whenever she is needed. By the way, if you are ever going to a reception, you should get a new suit of clothes. As secretary to the House, you should make a fashion statement. It is your duty to impress the governor and his friends," Hancock added, laughing aloud.

"Hell with new clothes! And hell with the governor! I'll leave high fashion to you and your merchant friends," yelled Adams, as he headed off for Queen Street and the presses of Edes & Gill. "Yankee Doodle" echoed from the Common as he marched off.

ΩΩΩ

2 October 1768

Lieutenant Colonel William Dalrymple stood beside the governor's desk, a tankard of rum in his left hand; his right hand fondling the silver and gold hilt of his saber. "Now that we are here, Governor Bernard, I must tell you that I am quite concerned about the quartering of my troops. Already there is the hint of winter in the night air, and I cannot, in good conscience, leave my regiments camped in tents on your pasture land."

Thomas Hutchinson smiled. "Colonel, we can easily billet one regiment in Faneuil Hall."

Immediately, Sheriff Greenleaf arose, objecting loudly, "If you want to create a revolt, that is certainly one way to start it, Mr. Hutchinson. We all know that the Sons of Liberty have claimed informal ownership of the place. I doubt we could gain approval for this in the Council."

Governor Bernard raised his hand in a calming manner. "Now, Sheriff, we must look at the big picture here. The colonel is right. The troops cannot be expected to remain in tents. And you are right. Using Faneuil Hall will certainly tweak Sam Adams's nose a bit." Recharging his tumbler with claret at the sideboard, he added, "So that's what we shall do – tweak his nose." Turning to Dalrymple, he said, "Colonel, I think I can convince the Council to allow the use of Faneuil Hall eventually. Just give me time. Unfortunately, the balance of your force will still remain encamped on the Common along with the housing on Castle William. I need time to get the Council behind me on this quartering issue. I must keep Sam Adams quiet on this problem if possible."

Dalrymple said, "I'm not pleased about my men in tents, but I expect you will work on it. Now, please tell me more about this Adams character, Governor Bernard. You men talk like he is the devil incarnate."

A portly gentleman in the back of the room raised his ample girth from his chair and wandered to the sideboard. As he poured himself a tumbler of claret, he said, "Colonel, I feel it is safe to say that I know Sam Adams better than most men here." Glancing around, all nodded their assent. "I feel it is fair to say that you can rely on him to do all in his power to make your stay in Boston a most unpleasant one."

Dalrymple smiled. "And just how many men in arms are with this Mr. Adams that I should fear him so?"

The fat man continued, "I doubt that you will find a frontal assault from him. His best weapon is his pen."

Hutchinson interjected, "And his pen is full of lies. You can trust that it won't be long, and you shall read things about you and your army that you never thought possible. Adams will do his best to turn the town against you."

Again, Dalrymple smiled. "From the preliminary reports I'm getting, a good part of Boston has welcomed us quite well. The local taverns seem more than happy to have us around."

"We have a network of people watching these places, Colonel Dalrymple. I would advise your men to stay clear of two places in particular; one is the Bunch of Grapes on King Street, and the worst of all is the Snug Harbor Tavern down on Hancock's Wharf," said the fat man.

Dalrymple, bristling at being ordered about, said sternly, "Just who are you, my dear fellow, that you feel qualified to dictate the comings and goings of the king's army?"

Governor Bernard interrupted. "Colonel, perhaps it would be best for you not to know everything and, especially, everyone. You see, our mutual friend standing here is part of a network we refer to as Omega. They are comprised of many well-placed men and women to keep us advised of this radical patriot activity. We will provide you all the information we have, as it becomes available."

After a polite knock on the door, Hubert Slank entered quietly. "Pardon the interruption, gentlemen, but I was informed that you needed me for something."

"Yes, Slank, I do. While Colonel Dalrymple is here, do you have any news from the old sailor?" asked Bernard.

"Yes we do, sir. It seems that our candlemaker has been ordered to patrol the streets on occasion with the Sons of Liberty, just to keep an eye on the 'redcoats'. Beg your pardon, sir. No offense meant by that. As for our strumpets, it seems that the prices are going up at the Snug Harbor. The girls have been told to keep their eyes and ears open for any information."

Hutchinson grinned. "Just as we suspected! If your men do visit the Snug Harbor, I suggest they keep their mouths shut while their breeches are off, Colonel." All in the room laughed. It seemed that they had the situation well in hand.

ΩΩΩ

Lieutenant Colonel Dalrymple stared out the windows of the British Coffee House on King Street as he shared a table with Captain Preston. "Captain, I'm sure that the men will soon be properly quartered, at least before the snow falls around here. Meanwhile, we must ensure their best behavior, especially in their off-duty time in the taverns."

Preston smiled. "I'm sure this rabble will create no problems for us, Colonel. Now that we have found four hundred muskets hidden right here under our noses in Faneuil Hall, these farmers and clerks have no arms to resist the might of our force. I predict these colonials will cower at the first sight of our men up close."

"After speaking with the governor, I'm not so certain about that. I'm told they have arms caches everywhere, especially in the outlying towns. Tell our men to be alert for trouble, in particular, if they go to a place called the Snug Harbor Tavern. Apparently, it has been a hotbed of trouble in the past," corrected Dalrymple.

Captain Preston sipped his tankard of ale saying, "I'll be sure to have our sergeants peppered throughout the town to defuse any incidents between our men and the locals. When I consider the pugilistic capabilities and drinking habits of my Irishmen, I shudder!"

Dalrymple grinned. "Add random visits by our junior officers, Captain, including yourself, of course." He paused to order another round from a serving wench. "We need someone to keep our sergeants out of trouble also," added Dalrymple with burst of laughter. "And by the way, Captain, I am preparing a reception at Lieutenant Governor Hutchinson's mansion; all officers shall be present in their best uniforms on the evening of Friday, October 21. The Royal Navy shall be there also, and I expect us to look our very best. The intention of the reception is to honor the arrival of General Gage from New York and to settle the nerves of the local Tories. The general will arrive on October 15, so have the men ready for inspection."

"Lovely! General Gage, the Royal Navy and a bunch of Tories! Please tell me that we might find a few ladies to make us feel welcome as well, sir," said Preston with a smile.

"I'll see what I can do in that regard, Captain. I am sure that a few colonial lasses would be most obliging to meet the king's officers," said Dalrymple.

ΩΩΩ

That evening, the Snug Harbor Tavern found itself wall-to-wall in redcoats. Amanda Griffith, her dark hair cascading over her breasts, which stretched the limits of her form-fitting red satin dress, stood at the end of the bar of the taproom, sipping a tankard of cider. Her usual taciturn face was twisted with mixed emotions. Amos, sweating behind the bar, had stocked extra beer and ale in expectation of the new business. Gazing about the room, Amanda said with a broad smile, "Amos, we could easily use at least ten more girls in this little nunnery of ours." Two girls were occupied in their cribs while the others had their choice of the next patron.

On the other hand, she listened keenly to the guttural conversations among the troops, and the hostile content could not be more pronounced. Near the doorway, Sergeant Major Sean Delaney, his halberd propped against the wall, boasted at his table to anyone within earshot, "We should have these radicals shackled to the pillory in short order, I tell you. And, failing that, they could find themselves on the business end of a bayonet."

Sitting on his lap, Hope, with her green dress hiked to midthigh, ran her fingers through his hair. "My, my, sergeant, aren't we the mean one tonight? But I declare, I see you don't even have a bayonet."

Delaney, overtly fondling her breast, said with an ale-induced slur, "Dearie, my bayonet is in my breeches. As for a weapon, we sergeants prefer to use that long halberd there." He pointed his wavering finger at the six-foot-long rod, with a jagged battle axe at the end. His men pounded the table and, laughing uproariously, howled, "More ale! More beer! More rum!"

Hope, with a knowing smile and nibbling on Delaney's earlobe, whispered, "Why don't you take me up to my crib and show me that 'bayonet' of yours."

Delaney, with a lustful grin displaying a row of rotten teeth, arose to his full six-four stature, hefting Hope in his arms in the process. "Show me the way to the 'bayonet practice field,' you gorgeous piece of womanhood." Hope pointed the way to the back stairs, winking at Amanda as she passed.

Amanda grinned. "Amos, let me tell you this, no one enjoys her work more than Hope." Amos laughed and, pointing to the stairs, added, "With the possible exception of Purity."

At that moment, Purity came down the stairs looking quite bedraggled, with her dress slightly askew, as she tucked her perky little breasts into her bodice. Wandering quietly over to Amanda, she spoke just loud enough to be heard above the din of the taproom, "That's the fifth one this evening." She wiped her brow on her sleeve.

Amanda smiled. "The evening is young yet, Purity. It seems these soldiers have quite a hunger tonight."

Pursing her lips, Purity said quietly, "I can handle the traffic, Amanda. The problem is that almost every private in the rear rank is talking about desertion."

Amanda furrowed her brow and tried to smile. "We had a little of this during the French and Indian War years ago, Purity. They should settle down soon; remember, this is their first week here, and I suppose we should expect it."

"I don't think so, Amanda. Two of them left my room and scampered down the rear stairs, complaining about someone named Delaney. They asked for directions to Boston Neck and the countryside," added Purity. "One of them even tried to sell me his Brown Bess musket! Would you believe that, Amanda? Of course, I told him that I was sellin' and not buyin'."

After a long pause of deep thought, Amanda's smile disappeared, and she responded in a calculating tone, "If that happens again, Purity, I want you to ask them how much they want for the musket. You understand?"

Purity looked at her, a puzzled look on her young face, "Why would we be interested in a musket, Amanda?"

"Protection! Simply protection, Purity!" said Amanda, her smile returning. Purity arose from her seat and, smiling broadly, said, "Well, back to my little sea of red bodies." She howled over the din, "Shaggin' for a shillin'!" In a matter of moments, she found herself perched on another soldier's lap as she donned his black tricorn hat.

Amos edged his way toward Amanda, scratching his head, "Have you noticed that not one of our regular customers has been here this entire evening? What's that all about, Ms. Amanda?"

Again, seemingly lost in thought as she surveyed the taproom, Amanda pursed her lips. "Amos, you're right! Early tomorrow we must take steps to change that. We should have a breakfast meeting, and be sure Imp is there also. I have work for him." The redcoat revelry and singing continued until almost daybreak.

> *The king had simply unshirted,*
> *And the queen was already unskirted,*
> *The bed slat was broke,*
> *But he doubled his stroke*
> *He cried, "Wait, I ain't been inserted.*

ΩΩΩ

While the Snug Harbor Tavern was bulging with redcoats, the Green Dragon Tavern was replete with a contingent of the Sons of Liberty. In the upper room, Sam Adams was sitting next to Dr. Ben Church and quietly sulking. Paul Revere, standing at the window with a tankard of ale in his heavy fist, said, "Our men in the taproom down below are ready for war, Sam. Mackintosh and the Northside gang have already loaded their muskets. You need only say the word, and they will seize the streets."

Adams looked sideways at Church, his brow furrowed in annoyance, when Hancock burst into the room with Dr. Joseph Warren, who literally spat his words, "Three men, John! There were three, I tell you! And I bandaged them as well as I could."

"This is just the beginning, I tell you," responded Hancock in agitation. "The men on my wharf are ready to explode."

Rising from his seat, Adams asked, "What are you two talking about?"

Hancock looked at the others sternly, "Haven't you heard? It seems that the king's troops got the better of a few good men this evening."

Adams, with a half grin, responded, "A fight? With the redcoats? You mean a few of our 'innocent citizens' might have been harmed?"

Revere growled, "Where did it happen? How?"

Dr. Warren said calmingly, "It seems these men had been drinking all afternoon at the Snug Harbor Tavern when a few sergeants from the Twenty-ninth Regiment arrived. Our men said something about their Irish ancestry and shabby red coats."

Revere chortled with a mischievous grin, "What's wrong with that?"

Dr. Church, shaking his head in annoyance, asked, "Were they hurt badly, Joseph?"

Warren, in a reassuring tone, said, "Not really! Cuts and bruises; but nothing broken! More wounded pride than anything, Benjamin!"

Adams arose from his seat again. "I believe it would sound better if they were injured defending the honor of our sweet innocent women of Boston," he said with conviction peppered with a tone of conspiracy.

Hancock responded, "I assume that is the version of the story we shall read in the *Boston Gazette*. Is that a fair assumption, Sam?"

Adams smiled. "I can almost guarantee it! Of course, the names will be omitted to protect the innocent. I think 'Vindex' will write the editorial for Edes & Gill."

Dr. Church said, "Is anyone hungry? I'm going to the taproom for an order of lamb chops. Where is that serving wench, when you need her?" He continued, mumbling to himself, as he waddled out the door to the taproom.

Hancock, raising his finger in thought, said, "Sam, let's be careful with our words just yet. The governor has invited the Merchant's Club to his reception to honor General Gage and the arrival of the king's troops. It is scheduled for the evening of October 21 at Hutchinson's residence."

"And the Royal Navy! Don't forget that wonderful squadron of twelve frigates in the harbor," added Adams in a tone of revulsion as he ignored the suggestion of a party. "The ships of the line of battle have anchored with springs on their cables so that their gun ports could face the town." The threat was obvious, and all of Boston was well aware of it.

Dr. Warren, a sly grin on his face, said, "Wouldn't it be delightful if we could somehow arrange to get invited to this little soiree at Hutchinson's home?"

Ben Church suddenly appeared in the doorway. "No lamb tonight, gentlemen. But I do have a platter of pork chops, with more ale and wine on the way," he said in a singsong voice. "And what was that I heard about the governor's soiree?" He added, "I've heard about it, and you must be dreaming about our getting invited. What could possibly cause the governor to invite us, of all people?"

"What if I suggested to Governor Bernard that the elected officers of the House and Council should be present to show a united front of peace and cooperation?" queried Hancock.

Dr. Warren added, "Be certain to assure them that a bevy of young colonial ladies would be invited; that is our daughters, nieces, etc. Keep in mind that the king's officers have not seen a respectable lady in some time. That alone should get us into the enemy camp."

"And what of that lovely child we met sometime ago, that Wexford girl, Mr. Hancock? I believe that is her name. The last we saw of that beauty was at the *Romney* reception," stated Church, licking his bulbous lips.

John grinned. "She spent a few months in Lexington, staying with the Reverend Jonas Clark. He married my cousin sometime ago and took over the parish house. Actually, Aunt Lydia sort of insisted that it would 'look better' if Ms. Wexford didn't share my roof for too long a time."

Revere laughed. "And if Aunt Lydia isn't happy, no one is happy on Beacon Hill!" All joined in the laughter.

Hancock added, "Now that you mention her, I'm reminded that she really enjoyed the *Romney* party, and I thought she would certainly enjoy this one. I sent for her a few days ago, figuring she was probably terribly bored with Lexington and all those rustics by now."

Church smiled. "She is quite easy on the eyes, John. When will she be here?"

Hancock returned his crooked grin, "Just remember that you are a happily married man, Dr. Church." At that comment, Church averted his eyes to the floor.

Hancock continued, "As for the Wexford girl, I am sorry to report that she departed Lexington a month ago. I'm told she went to the Buckman Tavern on Lexington Green, where she paid a farmer to bring her back to Boston. No one has seen her since. I've asked around, but it seems that she just vanished."

Dr. Church belched, "Perhaps she took passage back to London. Women are a bit fickle you know?"

Adams downed his tankard of ale. "Hell with the wench!" he interrupted. "Our main concern is that we all agree for the time being. We'll put a stop to any hostilities. Paul and I will speak with Mackintosh to make sure there are no more injuries to our men. At least until we can learn what the army intends to do in Boston. John will try to get us into that little reception for General Gage."

Church added, sipping his claret, "Who knows what can happen, gentlemen? If we show them a face of peace and cooperation, they could very well set sail for London, just like Hancock's little lady."

ΩΩΩ

CHAPTER 11

October 1768

GERTY TEEZLE GRIMACED as she dabbed at Zeke's open wound. "Of all places to be struck, Zeke! How did you manage to get cut on your skinny arse?" she grumbled impatiently while busy soaking the rag in a bowl of hot water laced with liniment.

"Frankly, Gerty, I didn't realize a saber was quite so long, and I can't run as fast I once could. Ouch! Be careful with that liniment, Gerty. Can't you be a little tender about this? I'm not a damned horse, you know!"

At that moment, Emmet Glunt appeared at the top of the stairs, panting at the exertion of getting there. The sight of Teezle bent over a chair, his pale pink buttocks arched into the air, and Gerty dabbing at the ragged gash, stopped his advancing into the room any farther. Aghast, he muttered, "Oh my god! What happened?"

Gerty glared, "Get the hell out of here and get some work done, you fat little bastard!"

"I knew you shouldn't be running with Mackintosh and his gang, Mr. Teezle," he prattled, turning on his heels in retreat.

Alone again, Gerty slapped Teezle near his open wound. "What was he talking about, Zeke? Mackintosh and his gang?"

With a sheepish grin, Teezle said, "I weren't with them, Gert; I just happened to be too near them when trouble arrived at the same time."

Gerty, finished with her bandaging, commanded, "Pull your breeches up, Zeke." Her arms folded across her ample, flaccid bosom, she continued, "Now where were you exactly, when this butt butcherin' happened?"

"I already told you; I was down on the waterfront," said Teezle defensively.

"How could such a thing happen on Long Wharf?" asked Gerty, thinking aloud.

"It wasn't exactly Long Wharf; it was a little farther north . . . a bit," said Teezle, gesturing with his fingers.

Her arms on her hips in agitation, Gerty screamed, "You mean it was Hancock's Wharf, don't you? Were you at the Snug Harbor Tavern? Down there minglin' with those dockside drunks and doxies? What in hell were you doing there? Up to no good, I expect!" With that said, she threw her pan of bloody water and rags at him. "What will my friends say when they hear of this, Zeke?" she added loudly, her eyes blazing.

Teezle, regaining his dignity with his breeches up and his shirt tucked, said in a calming voice, as he wiped his face with his sleeve, "Easy, Gerty! Take it easy! I was selling candles; that's all! As luck would have it, Ebenezer Mackintosh and his gang were just leaving the Snug Harbor Tavern when I was entering. They were actually running out, with a gaggle of redcoats on their tails. I was an innocent bystander; I promise you, Gerty!"

Cooling a bit, Gerty gave him a toothless grin. "It is a bit funny; you gettin' jabbed in the arse like that, Zeke." Grabbing his hand, she added with a wink, "You know, pattin' your arse like that sorta got me in the mood, and it's been quite some time since we did something ticklish in the crib, if you get my meanin'."

Teezle wiped his brow with his sleeve again. "You know you are the only woman for me, Gerty."

"Are you sure you didn't see any doxies down there on the wharf, Zeke?" she asked in a mellow undertone.

"How could I ever even look at another woman, Gerty? Now let's get down to our tumblin'!" he said, with a lecherous gleam in his eye.

Giggling, she grabbed his hand. "Come with me, you stallion you!"

Meanwhile, down below in the candle shop, Glunt, upon hearing a noise in the front of the shop, rushed from the back. To his surprise, no one was there. Scratching his head in bewilderment, he looked about only to find a note with "Ω" imprinted in the wax seal. It was addressed simply "Teezle."

ΩΩΩ

Thursday, October 9, 1768

A fire blazed in the hearth of the taproom to fight the early-morning chill, as Amanda, seated at a table near the door and clad in mobcap and a blue woolen dressing gown, sipped a cup of hot tea. Hope and Purity had joined her after a late night of record business. Purity said with a shiver, "I don't really mind the redcoats so much, Amanda. And I thought you would be happy with all the business we have now. After all these years of embargos against English goods, we now have the king's own army spending all their shillin's right in our laps, literally."

"I agree," said Hope. "I've never made so much hard money and enjoyed it so much. These soldiers, along with the Royal Navy, are here for fun."

Amanda frowned, "Let me remind you that they are not here for fun. They came here as a show of force. It just doesn't sit right with me. Just look at the harbor! A squadron of twelve frigates ready to give Boston a broadside with God only knows how many cannon. And doesn't it annoy you that the very same redcoats you entertain are bragging of their readiness to do harm to all your past paramours?"

Hope grunted, "Our local men don't have the shillin's these redcoats have, Amanda."

"I realize that, but I think it's time to take advantage of an opportunity here," said Amanda.

Purity responded, "I am taking advantage. In fact, I'm takin' as many advantages as I can muster into my crib every evenin'."

Glaring, Amanda continued, "I'm happy we are making money. But I also want us to focus on disarming these redcoats."

Hope muttered, "Disarm them? How do we do that?"

"Listen to me carefully. Purity put the idea in my head," said Amanda. "Many of these privates want to desert. So I have decided that we will help them. Part of the cost will be that they part with their Brown Bess muskets. Then we can give them to our own men of Boston, specifically the Sons of Liberty."

ΩΩΩ

Friday, October 10, 1768

Lieutenant Colonel Dalrymple marched into Governor Bernard's office unannounced, with Captain Thomas Preston in trail. Neither man said a word.

Governor Bernard, seated at his desk, watched in awe, as the soldiers took off their rain-soaked capes and tricorn hats. Slank, standing at the side of Bernard's desk with a sheaf of papers in his hand, shook his head in disgust at the trail of mud from their boots.

Overcoming his surprise and regaining his composure, Bernard arose from his seat and, quietly dismissing Slank with a wave of his hand, asked in an almost casual tone of voice, "So, to what do I owe the honor of this unexpected visit, my dear colonel?"

Dalrymple just opened his mouth to reply, when the office door opened again. This time Slank entered, followed by Lieutenant Governor Hutchinson and a very corpulent gentleman. "Sorry for the interruption, Governor Bernard," said Hutchinson, "But – Oh! I see you already have company." Smiling at Dalrymple, he continued, "It is just as well that you are here, Colonel. Actually, you are the real reason we are here." The fat man and Slank had quietly retreated to the far end of the room, somewhat preoccupied in their own private hushed conversation.

Bernard, coughing for attention, said, "Gentlemen! It seems that this rainy day is bringing more than its share of surprises. Would someone be so kind as to tell me why I must suffer this interruption? You are all aware that appointments are to be arranged through Mr. Slank, my secretary. But now that I have been so rudely interrupted, what can I do for you on such a miserably rainy day?"

Dalrymple, having helped himself to a tumbler of claret at the sideboard, groused, "It is indeed a miserable day, Governor. And it became more miserable when I received my most recent personnel roster today. It seems that my officers," he continued, glaring at Captain Preston, "have been remiss in reporting an alarming rate of desertions among my troops."

Bernard, straightening his lace cuffs, smiled condescendingly. "Colonel, I suppose you should normally expect to lose a few men when you deploy for any lengthy period of time to foreign shores."

"I have lost more than fifty men in less than two weeks of our being in Boston," growled Dalrymple in a rage. "This is appalling, unacceptable, and certainly unprecedented. A few men, yes. But more than fifty is an abomination. Never in my military career have I – "

Bernard interrupted, "Where could fifty men have gone, Colonel? Boston is basically an island, connected to the rest of the colony by a narrow neck of land. And, if I recall correctly, you placed sentries at Boston Neck upon arrival."

Captain Preston, maintaining his military bearing proudly interjected, "Fortunately, not all these scoundrels have disappeared. We have captured more than seven deserters; they will all rue the day they decided to run from their sworn duty to the Crown."

Hutchinson, shaking his head in disgust, said, "We all saw your so-called military justice, Captain. Having a man tied to a wagon wheel and flayed with one hundred lashes is a bit excessive, isn't it?"

Dalrymple, downing his claret and handing the tumbler to Preston for a refill, barked, "What would you have us do? Perhaps we should promote them for returning to duty; or maybe a gala party and killing of a fatted calf for our poor wayward prodigal sons?"

The fat man at the rear of the room raised his voice, "What good are these men after suffering under the lash to that degree, Colonel Dalrymple? How could they possibly serve the Crown after such poor treatment?"

Glaring, Dalrymple strode toward the fat stranger, his fists clenched. "And just exactly who are you to judge, my good man?" he growled.

Hutchinson arose from his easy chair and stepped between the two men. "Please forgive our zealousness, Colonel. My friend here provides a valuable service here in Boston and understands the pain of his fellow man. Please indulge us a bit, sir!"

Turning and raising his hands, Dalrymple commanded, "Very well! Captain, hand me that tumbler of claret." Taking a hearty gulp, he added to no one in particular, "My friends, apparently you do not understand the mentality of the king's troops. These ruffians respect only one thing: fear. They have learned to impose fear upon their enemies, and I have learned to impose the same upon them. Every lash a deserter endures will guarantee that another will think twice before deserting his post."

The fat man commented innocently, "It wouldn't surprise me if a man died with that degree of punishment."

Captain Preston piped up, "If he dies, he dies!" Dalrymple gave him a half grin, adding, "It should not come as a surprise to you, gentlemen, that the lash is considered minor punishment to our troops. The firing squad is always a consideration, and our men know it well."

Hutchinson, in a calming tone, said, "That's all well and good for the king's army. But the crowd of citizens witnessing such a spectacle has created its own minor disaster for us in Boston, Colonel."

"Disaster my arse!" yelled Dalrymple. "The point is this: how are my men evading the sentries and getting out of this town?"

Bernard and Hutchinson glanced furtively at each other. After a mutual nod, they both stared at the far end of the room. Slank and the fat man nodded in acknowledgment. Bernard responded with measured words, "Colonel, perhaps we can help find the answer to that question for you."

Dalrymple peered around the room. "It seems to me that I am in the midst of a conspiracy. The looks on your faces tell me there is much to learn about this town."

Hutchinson smiled. "Please forgive us, Colonel! But we have a small network of men and women in Boston. They should be able to get to the bottom of your desertion problem. It will take a bit of time, but I assure you they are quite resourceful."

"And just who, may I ask, are these 'heroes' of the Crown?" queried Dalrymple.

Slank, speaking for the first time and gazing at Governor Bernard, muttered, "Please permit me, sir, but I think it would be best if the identity of our agents remained a secret."

"I agree, Mr. Slank!" stated Bernard, authority in his voice. "Colonel, please indulge us. It has taken years to organize the Omega, and the fewer who know of its details, the better for us all."

"In fact," added Hutchinson, "most of us don't know everyone involved. Our pockets of agents work independently and report through different channels. If the Sons of Liberty knew of these people, they would find themselves floating in Boston Harbor." He paused to look around the room for agreement. "On a lighter note, Colonel, I am looking forward to meeting General Gage later this month. We have planned a fine gala for his arrival, and we expect your contingent of officers to join us the evening of October 21."

"General Gage will be here, sir, in order to inspect us and affirm our quartering arrangements for the winter," stated Dalrymple bluntly.

"At the suggestion of Mr. Hancock, I have taken the liberty of inviting Sam Adams and a few of his radical supporters. It would be interesting for you to meet your adversaries, who normally find it convenient to hide behind their quill pens," added Hutchinson with a sardonic grin.

Arising in dismissal, Colonel Dalrymple strode to the door. "That should certainly make the general's reception interesting. Come along, Captain Preston. And, Governor, I thank you for the fine claret on this rainy morning. For now, I'll trust you to help with this desertion problem. Meanwhile, the floggings shall continue despite your criticisms and concerns. As I said earlier, it makes most men think twice about leaving the service of the Crown." He and Preston departed, slamming the door behind them.

Staring at the closed door, Bernard looked to the far end of the office, "Gentlemen, it is quite clear what we must do. Slank, get everyone in Omega on the streets. We must find out where and how these troops are leaving Boston."

Hutchinson, sipping a tumbler of Madeira, queried, "Governor, do you think it was wise to mention 'Omega' by name to the colonel?"

"Perhaps not, but I had to tell him something. We can't afford his next step, which would probably result in random and wanton shooting of our citizenry. If that happened, God only knows what our patriot scoundrels would do."

Hutchinson frowned, "Right you are! We must keep our people reasonably quiet. Who knows what Adams and his radical friends could do if really provoked by the king's troops. That's why I agreed to invite a few of those rascals to the party."

The fat man, polishing his gold signet ring, added, "I told you it would be a wise thing to do, Thomas. If they actually meet these officers, I am certain they will crawl back into their holes and hide. They might grumble, but they will not dare raise a hand against a greater force. Now, I have a meeting to attend with you-know-who this evening. I'll relay messages via the usual channels."

Slank added as he sauntered to the door, "I'll get the old sailor to check our sources on the waterfront."

"And don't forget our friend, Teezle; it seems he's in the right spot with the right connections," said Hutchinson. "Now is the time for him to deliver."

ΩΩΩ

October 10, 1768

An Atlantic squall pounded the New England coast and continued into the early afternoon, driving everyone indoors after all hatches had been battened down and the ships secured. With most dockside activities cancelled, the denizens of the waterfront had headed inland, away from the angry wind and surf.

The door to the Snug Harbor taproom crashed open, accompanied by a heavy gust of wind-driven rain. Private Hugh White stood in the doorway, straightening his shoulders, as he struggled with his heavy Brown Bess musket. He did his best to maintain his military bearing, despite his soggy red tunic and his dripping black tricorn hat. There were no other patrons and Amos, in his leather apron, was busy cleaning behind the bar.

Faith, Chastity, and Purity, sipping hot tea at a rear table near the back stairs, began to laugh at the vision before them. Faith chortled, "Just look at him, Purity. His musket is bigger than he is, for god's sake."

Purity, a frown on her face, said, "Have mercy, Faith. Perhaps the man's other weapon is equally large; you never know about these things." She strutted over to the doorway and, stopping with her hands resting on her hips, added sarcastically, "Well, if it ain't the lord protector of the Crown. And what can I do for you, my good man? And where are all your redcoat friends?"

Shuffling his feet awkwardly, Hugh began mumbling a response when his attention was drawn to a commotion at the rear of the taproom. "Amos, we must get everyone busy cleaning the rooms on the second floor; it's a pigsty up there!" grumbled Amanda, loudly, as she stumbled down the stairs hurriedly, clad in her woolen dressing gown and mobcap. "And close that damned door; it's pouring rain out there, you know!" Suddenly noticing the presence of a redcoat at the door, she adjusted her mobcap and smoothed her dressing gown. Looking askance at Amos, she mumbled, "Why didn't you tell me there was a patron in the place, Amos?"

At that moment, Purity, having gotten to know him briefly and holding his hand, guided him to the bar. "Amanda," she said with mock formality, "may I present Private Hugh White of his majesty's Twenty-ninth Regiment. And isn't he just the cutest thing you ever saw?"

Amanda smiled and, sharing a quick glance with Amos, said soothingly, as she appraised the soldier with her blue eyes, "Amos, why don't you make one of your famous flips for Private White here. This weather must have chilled him to the bone." Turning to White, she added, "Now, Mr. White, tell me how it is that you find time to join us this miserable afternoon while all your comrades in arms are otherwise occupied in the streets of Boston."

The red-hot loggerhead made that tantalizing sizzling sound as Amos, with a toothy grin of pride, delivered the steaming flip. Taking a hearty draught, Hugh White licked his lips and graced the room with his first smile. Looking up into Amanda's eyes, while Purity pressed her perky breasts against his arm, White said, "Well, you see, my Twenty-ninth Regiment is pulling regular duty today. But I stood a double sentry duty at the Custom's House all night."

Amos, usually a man of few words, asked, "Mr. White, I'm just a might curious and forgive me for askin', but ain't you a bit short for army life? I mean, most of your friends are quite tall like me, especially them grenadiers."

White, rising to his full five feet in stature, slammed his drink on the bar, growling, "I'm as good as any man in the Twenty-ninth Regiment and a better marksman with my Brown Bess than most."

Purity, running her delicate fingers through his wavy black hair, said in a cooing tone, "Now, Hughie baby, you just relax. Amos didn't mean nuthin', and you must admit that you are no taller than me; actually, I sorta like it. It's not often that I can look directly into a man's eyes, when we are both on our feet, if you get my drift."

With that, she gently and surreptitiously massaged his inner thigh, causing White to loosen his grip on his Brown Bess.

Amanda, nodding to Amos to refill the soldier's tankard, said almost too casually, "Tell me, Mr. White, do you really like army life?"

With Purity's female ministrations, a broad grin returned to White's face. "Actually," he responded, "I rather enjoy the army. Of course, we all hate chalking our breeches and shining our brass. And for the life of me, I don't understand the need to keep shifting our left and right boots all the time; it seems they don't want them to wear uneven like." He took a moment to gulp his flip. "The scariest thing is the floggin's; you don't ever want to be caught leavin' your post or desertin'. Floggin' is as close to death as you can be. Even so, this army life sure beats starvin' on the family farm in Cork, Ireland. I get paid a shillin' a day." Musing for a moment, he added wistfully, "I do miss the old sod, though. I hope me mother and father are all right. With feeding six children, it was the best thing I could do when I enlisted in the army; one less mouth to feed, you know! At least now, I get a shillin' a day from the Crown, and that's better than starvin'."

Purity, nuzzling his ear, asked, "Why don't you take off that wet red coat and warm yourself by the hearth, Hughie? Or . . . even better, we could go up to my crib, if you have a mind and a shillin', of course."

Shaking his head dejectedly, the little soldier frowned, "Sorry, but all I have is five shillins to last me till next pay; I lost most of my money playing cribbage with the sergeants."

Realizing that no money would change hands, Purity instinctively took a step back. Taking note of this action, Amanda suggested, "Why don't you take off that wet coat, Mr. White, and sit by the fire; you must be quite tired." With a nudge of her elbow, she added, "Purity, help Mr. White with his coat. And, Amos, place his musket behind the bar in a safe place."

Purity placed his dripping red coat on a peg near the hearth as he sat down with his second steaming tankard of flip, warming himself by the fire. "Now this is the life," he said, propping his feet on a bench. "I've been pondering this moment all night as I stood sentry duty in the pouring rain."

Looking at him from the side of the hearth, Purity sighed deeply. She had grown accustomed to the brazen attitudes and coarse ways of the soldiers, sailors, and ropemakers. Now, her eyes came to rest on this lonely young soldier. Her mind flashed to her days as a young girl on a farm in Concord, realizing that it was not much different than his life in Ireland. Poverty had driven her to Boston, leaving one less mouth to feed on the farm. *He was no older than she was*, she mused, *and so sweetly innocent, sitting there with his eyes closed.*

Hugh White had nearly nodded off, mesmerized by the crackling of the fire, the smell of burning pine, both combined with the mixed aroma of baking bread and clam chowder simmering in the kitchen. Purity sidled over to him and gently whispered in his ear. White opened his eyes, a look of disbelief on his face. Gently, Purity held his hand as he arose from his seat. Hand in hand, they made their way to the back stairway. Pausing at the foot of the stairs, they both turned to look at the bar. Amanda and Amos were both smiling at the way the coupling had progressed.

Amanda quipped, "It seems that Purity is adopting a payment plan for our young soldier, Amos."

They had no sooner disappeared up the stairs, when the door again burst open. Ebenezer Mackintosh and six of his friends from the South End mob stumbled in and rushed to the bar. Looking about the warm cozy taproom, Mackintosh said, "Where in hell is everyone?" Where are the lord protectors of the realm? Where are the damned lobsterbacks? They must be afraid of a little Boston drizzle, if you ask me. Where are all the weak-kneed tars of the docks? I told you, lads, that we was probably the only ones brave enough to come down here for a wee dram to quench our thirst."

Squinting at Amos through bloodshot bleary eyes, he waved his arms and roared, "Tankards of ale for all my friends!"

As he guzzled his ale, Mackintosh staggered over to the hearth saying, "Let's gather over here by the fire, lads; that damned rain has me soaked and chilled to the bone, by god."

Rubbing his hands briskly in front of the blazing fireplace, he suddenly noticed the red coat hanging on the wooden peg. Hefting the small coat in his meaty hands, he yelled, "Teezle! Get your skinny arse over here and look at this. I'll bet a shilling it would fit you; and if it does, it's yours for the askin'. Such a fine red coat! I wonder who could have left it behind; it's my guess, he sure was a tiny fella."

As Zeke Teezle wiggled his skinny frame into Hugh White's red coat, Amanda casually walked from behind the bar and, with her arms folded across her chest, stated defiantly, "There will be no taking of anything that doesn't belong to you. Is that clear?"

Teezle halted his wiggling abruptly with one arm in and one out. He said, "Fine with me, Mrs. Griffith. I really don't want the damned thing. I already got my arse cut once by a bayonet, and I'm not warm about a second chance, if one of those redcoats was to catch me wearin' it."

Mackintosh glared at Amanda and, while maintaining hard eye contact with her, growled, "I said put the damned thing on, Teezle!" A deadly quiet pervaded the taproom.

Amos stealthily reached for his heavy wooden club behind the bar. "The silence sure does get loud in here at times, don't it, gentlemen?" said Amos, to no one in particular.

The six Sons of Liberty exchanged nervous glances, wondering where this unexpected confrontation was headed. Mackintosh, not one to be intimidated by anyone, let alone a woman, stepped toward Amanda, "If you think for one minute that – "

His motion was halted when the door again crashed open, reminding everyone of the blustery weather. Standing in the doorway was Paul Revere, his tricorn hat dripping and his riding boots quite muddy. "I thought I'd find you here, Mackintosh," he said casually. To the others, he nodded. "Teezle, men, how are you all this fine evening?" he added with a note of sarcasm. Shedding his oiled slicker and dripping tricorn, Revere strode to the bar, his eyes taking careful note that he had obviously interrupted something.

Mackintosh, assuming an easy gait, wandered to Revere's side at the bar, his eyes still wary of Amanda's hostile glare. Looking between the two of them at Teezle, Revere said, "Obviously, I have stepped into the midst of a manure pile. What is going on here? And, Teezle! What are you doing in that red coat, which obviously was not tailored for you? Hell, the arms barely reach beyond your elbows."

Looking at Teezle, Amanda couldn't contain her smile. With a dismissing wave of her hand, she said, "Mr. Teezle, you look ridiculous. Put the coat back on the peg."

Mackintosh commanded with a growl, "You keep the coat on your back, Teezle!"

Amanda looked hard at Revere, shaking her head slowly. Amos again exchanged a hard look at Mackintosh, his hand on the cudgel. The tension in the room had returned. The seconds seemed to tick slowly.

"Mackintosh," said Revere, breaking the silence in a calming tone barely audible to anyone else, and easing himself toward the far end of the bar. "Come over here for a moment." In a whisper, he added, "What are you trying to do here?"

Ignoring Revere's whispered tone, Mackintosh grumbled for all to hear, "I will not be dictated to by a common harbor strumpet, by god!"

Revere, in a rare display of emotion, quickly elbowed the large mob leader in the ribs, which silenced his bravado. "Now listen to me," said Revere, angrily through his gritted teeth. "First, Mrs. Griffith is not a common strumpet. Second, this place is the best place to learn about our redcoat friends; they come here to play. Mrs. Griffith and her girls help our cause with more information than you could ever gather in a year. Do you understand me, Mac?"

Looking incredulously from Revere to Amanda, Mackintosh whispered, albeit with a slur, "Do you mean to tell me that . . . oh my god!"

Nodding, Revere said, "That's exactly what I mean. Mr. Hancock and Mr. Adams would be very displeased if you made a mess of things here. If she wants that red coat to remain, it remains."

Mackintosh replied in a pleading tone, "Well, what about – ?"

Revere interrupted, shaking his head, "That is all you need to know, Mac. Let the redcoats think that the Snug Harbor is a safe harbor. I need you to pay attention to the redcoat patrols and where they store their cannon and powder. And one other thing, we want you and the others to keep a friendly protective eye on that young Imp, who lives here. He runs messages for us now and again, so no harm must come to him, especially if you see him with a red feather in his hat."

The muted discussion continued for a few moments. Then, rising to his full height and straightening his shoulders, Mackintosh stepped toward Amanda and doffing, his tricorn hat, said, "Beg your pardon, ma'am. I just didn't know which way the wind was blowin'. Please accept my humble apology." Turning to Teezle, still standing at the hearth with one arm in the sleeve of the red coat, he added, "Zeke, take off that ridiculous red coat and put it back where you found it on that peg. We won't be needin' it tonight." Looking again at Revere for approval, he added, "We'll be leavin' now. Let's call it a day, lads." The group departed as abruptly as they entered.

As the door slammed, Revere turned to Amanda, smiling. "They won't bother you again, Mrs. Griffith; I'm sure of it."

"Call me Amanda," she responded, smiling, "and have a tankard of ale on me. I don't know what you said to Mackintosh, but I thank you just the same. A missing red uniform coat could cause trouble for me and many others."

Revere took his tankard to a small table near the back stairway, where Amanda joined him, casually saying, "I've seen you in the streets and have visited your shop on occasion, Mr. Revere, but this is the first time you have graced the Snug Harbor Tavern with your presence. To what do I owe the pleasure of your patronage today in the midst of this miserable weather?"

Leaning forward and glancing about the taproom to ensure their privacy, Revere said, "Actually, Mrs. Griffith, I'm here on business, and I felt this squall might give me the chance to do so without anyone around to notice. If anyone asks about my being here, you will please tell them I have merely delivered a few silver buttons that needed repair. In reality, I'm here about Master Imp; I understand he lives here."

Sitting heavily back in her chair and biting her lip in thought, Amanda responded protectively, "And just what might you have to do with Imp?"

Paul Revere grinned. "Relax, Mrs. Griffith! We know that you have been his guardian and protector. And I give you my personal assurance that he is better protected than anyone in Boston."

"What does that mean?" asked Amanda, petulantly. "And you still have not answered what Imp has to do with you."

"At Mr. Hancock's suggestion, your Imp has been selected to serve as an official messenger for us," whispered Revere.

"I've heard a little about this already. Now just who is 'us'?" asked Amanda tersely. "I know Mr. Hancock, but this 'messenger' business is not clear. Imp could be put in danger, if I'm not mistaken!"

"Let me put it this way," Revere continued, "First, a group of patriots finds it most important to know about the comings and goings of our redcoat visitors. Second, it seems they have adopted the Snug Harbor Tavern as a place to relax. Third, we have people watching them and, at times, it is necessary to share important and timely information around town."

"What has this to do with Imp?" asked Amanda, impatiently. "Can't someone else do this messenger business?"

"Imp is the perfect lad to pass information. He delivers the *Boston Gazette* and is accepted well in most establishments, both high and low. He will not draw attention to himself," replied Revere, downing his ale.

"This sounds dangerous. Imp gets around," said Amanda. "and many times he is busy running errands for me. How would anyone know when he is passing official information? He would need a friendly eye on him for protection. If the redcoats ever found out, he would suffer terribly." Shaking her head negatively, she added, "I still think this is really a man's job."

Revere frowned. "No! A man would be noticed by prying Tory eyes. And everyone knows where Mr. Hancock, Adams, and I stand. We can't move without someone taking note. As for protecting Master Imp, I just spoke with Mackintosh. He and his mob will assure Imp's safety." At that point, he reached into his pocket, retrieving a goose feather. "When he is running messages for us, Imp is to place this feather in his tricorn. That will be the signal for all concerned to keep an eye on him."

Amanda took the feather from Revere's hand, noting the delicate fingers attached to a strong fist. "My god!" she exclaimed, "this feather is red."

Revere smiled. "We needed something distinctive for the lad. Again, no one will know what the red feather means, except those who need to know. Keep this hidden and tell him not to wear it unless he is on official business. Is that clear?"

Amanda gave him a trusting smile and, nodding her ascent, said loudly, "Amos, bring another tankard of ale for Mr. Revere." She patted the silversmith's hand. "Is there anything else you would care to enjoy here at the Snug Harbor Tavern, Mr. Revere?" she asked coyly.

Revere, trying to conceal a sheepish grin, said, "Mrs. Griffith, the charms of the Snug Harbor Tavern are very well known among my circle of friends. And I am personally very flattered at the kind offer. But, you see, my lovely wife, Sarah, would suddenly find herself in the castrating business if she learned of such a dalliance. Hence, I must kindly decline the fine offer."

Amanda smiled. "I certainly respect your fidelity to your wife, Mr. Revere. My only family seems to be Imp, but I don't think he realizes it."

Revere leaned forward, again sipping from his tankard. "Our children are the reason for this struggle, Mrs. Griffith. I personally have five little lambs; four girls and a boy. Little Mary was born just this past March, and Deborah, the oldest, is ten years old."

"That's quite a large family," said Amanda, "it must keep your wife very busy."

"We lost our first Mary to the fever back in '65. It seems that if a child can survive the first few years, they have a chance," added Revere with a note of melancholy. "I suffer great fear whenever Sarah gives birth; it's like I suffer every pain with her. That's why we serve the New Buck Church, you know, the Cockerel every Sabbath. God must have His hand in our lives."

Suddenly, Revere jumped to his feet at the crashing of the door. Amanda could see the tension in his arms. She placed a staying hand on his elbow, as she smiled at the new arrivals. Standing in the doorway stood Sergeant Major Sean Delaney, halberd in hand. He marched to the bar with three privates in tow. Behind them, entering at a slower yet more commanding pace, a British officer appeared; his tunic more crimson than the faded redcoats of his small contingent.

Amanda glided across the floor, hiding her apprehension of the intrusion. "Good afternoon, gentlemen. Why Sergeant Major Delaney, we haven't seen you here in quite a few days. Where have you been?" she queried nonchalantly.

"Good evening, ma'am," greeted Delaney with surprising politeness, standing almost at attention. "May I introduce Captain Thomas Preston of the Twenty-ninth Regiment." At that, Delaney took a step backward with a perfunctory bow.

"Thank you, Sergeant Major," said Preston. "Mrs. Griffith, it is indeed a pleasure to meet you. Your reputation as a gracious hostess precedes our meeting, and I wish to personally thank you for the kindness you have shown to my troops. Being so far from home and living a Spartan army life can certainly wear on a man's morale."

Amanda smiled as Preston kissed her proffered hand. "It is indeed a pleasure to provide whatever meager hospitality we can to the king's troops, Captain," retorted Amanda.

The scraping of a chair behind Amanda drew everyone's attention. Revere, donning his black coat and tricorn, smiled as he eased his way toward the door. Blocking his path stepped Sergeant Major Delaney. At six feet four inches, he was easily the tallest man in the room, and he was not one to move for anyone, least of all, a short colonial with muddy boots. Revere, a man of middling height, paused, saying to Amanda, "I thank you again, ma'am, for the business. If you need more buttons, please don't hesitate to call on me. Forgive me, gentlemen, for the intrusion; I'll be on my way." He then glared up at Delaney for a long moment. At the same time, Delaney appraised this man, noting the broad shoulders, thick neck, and muscular arms. Experience had taught him not to underestimate an adversary, regardless of stature, and the eyes of this man told him to be wary.

Noting the awkward challenge, Captain Preston ordered with a smile, "Sergeant Major, let the man pass. Can't you see you're blocking the way, for god's sake?"

Striding to the door, Revere said, "Thank you, Captain."

"Sir, before you depart, let me formally introduce myself. I'm Captain Thomas Preston in His Majesty's service, and you are?"

Revere made a half turn toward Preston and, smiling broadly, said, "Revere. Paul Revere, silversmith to the masses. If I can be of service to you, my shop is just around the corner, Captain Thomas." Touching his tricorn and pausing at the door, he added, "Good evening to you all." The opening and closing of the door reminded everyone of the heavy storm on the waterfront.

"Did you see who that was, Captain?" spouted Delaney. "Paul Revere himself! We were told that – "

"That will be all, Sergeant Major," stated Preston icily, shaking his head. "Why don't you and the men grab a table over by the fireplace while I speak with Mrs. Griffith privately." Turning to Amanda and nodding at Amos, he said quietly, "Tankards of ale for my men please, and a private moment with you, Mrs. Griffith, if I may."

Trying to hide her anxiety, Amanda said, "Please join me at the corner table, Captain." After they were seated, she added, "Now, what can I do for you on this rainy evening?"

"I am here to seek your help with a problem regarding the king's troops, Mrs. Griffith," said Preston, sitting back in his chair while extending his crossed legs in a relaxed fashion. He took a long draught of his ale as his eyes remained locked on hers, looking for any reaction as he added, "You see, it seems that many soldiers in the king's army have been brazen enough to leave the service without permission; desertion, you might call it."

Amanda, maintaining the obvious visual and verbal sparring, responded almost casually, "I'm sorry to hear that, Captain. And I'm shocked that anyone could even think of leaving the king's service. But what could that possibly have to do with me, the poor owner of this little grog shop?"

Preston's eyes narrowed. "Possibly nothing; possibly everything!" he retorted. "You see, we have reason to believe that this is the place many of our men were last seen, prior to their abrupt disappearance. I'm sure you can understand our concern. Actually, we are not sure whether these men have left us voluntarily or if they were kidnapped or even killed, God forbid."

Amanda did her best to smile, saying, "Why Captain! Are you accusing me of kidnapping and murder?" She continued, laughing out loud, "You can't be serious. How could a house full of ladies ever do such a thing? Besides, I personally appreciate your being here. Business has never been better here at the Snug Harbor Tavern, and my girls have never been so busy. In essence, we have everything to lose by your loss of men. Actually, I'm sorry to hear of it. Now what exactly can we do to help you?"

Preston smiled and leaning toward her said, "I'm glad you put it that way, Mrs. Griffith. I told Lieutenant Colonel Dalrymple that you were probably a reasonable lady." In a whisper, he added, "What I really need you to do is keep your eyes and ears open. If any of the king's own even so much as mentions leaving us, you must bring it to my attention personally."

Her smile becoming broader, Amanda leaned forward, touching the back of Preston's hand ever so delicately. As she glanced over her shoulder, nodding toward the redcoats laughing over their ale by the fireplace, she whispered in reply, "I promise you that I will personally see to it, Captain. Not one of them will leave your service."

Preston, placing his free hand over hers in a patting gesture, said, "Those men are officially with me, looking for deserters. They know nothing of our new arrangement, and I would prefer that we keep it that way."

Amanda gave his hand a suggestive squeeze, as she eyed him coquettishly. "I promise to keep everything strictly between us. And I mean everything!"

"Good," said Preston, rising from his chair and smiling broadly. "I can be contacted at the Customs House near the Old State House on King Street. I'm in charge of the guard there."

Sergeant Major Delaney arose with the small contingent, when he suddenly noticed the red coat hanging on the wooden peg. "Now what have we here?" he asked of the entire taproom.

Captain Preston immediately turned his attention to Amanda, his eyes asking the same question. Amanda fluttered her eyes and smiled. "Gentlemen, that red coat obviously belongs to a man in the king's service. He is currently enjoying the company of one of the ladies upstairs. The coat was simply hung to dry, as you can see."

Delaney, taking deliberate strides toward the stairway, said, "I don't believe that for one moment; I'll check for myself. And he best not be shaggin' my Hope; I've taken a liking to that big girl."

Amanda sidestepped into his path, "You'll go no farther, by god," she said defiantly, her eyes blazing.

Delaney halted, as Captain Preston interrupted loudly, "That won't be necessary, Sergeant Major. We have no reason not to believe Mrs. Griffith. And besides, how would you like to be interrupted while you enjoy the charms of a provincial beauty." He added firmly, "Now, sit down by the hearth for a moment and finish your ale, Sergeant Major." Taking Amanda gently by the arm, Preston guided her back to her chair at the table, where he continued in a soothing tone, "This may seem a bit forward, Mrs. Griffith, but I have one more favor to ask, if I may."

"And what could that be, Captain?" asked Amanda, calming down as she stared past Preston at Delaney.

Following her eyes, Preston said, "Forget about him; I'll handle it. As for my request – "

The scraping of chairs across the room told him that his men had finished their ale. He whispered quickly into Amanda's ear.

She stood back a moment and after a brief pause, said, "I would be delighted, Captain Preston." She took his hands in hers and nodded.

Smiling broadly, he bowed to Amanda saying in a more commanding tone, "Let us take our leave, men. We have yet to check the Bunch of Grapes before we return to our quarters."

Delaney, returning the red coat to its peg, said, "Whoever wears this is a little squint; I'll tell you that. Hope that strumpet upstairs enjoys small arms inspection." At that, all the men joined in laughter. Delaney, turning to Amanda and touching his silver-trimmed tricorn, added, "We'll be back shortly, madam, as patrons, as soon as this patrol is completed. I'm certain Hope will be waiting for me." The men formed up and marched out with military precision.

The sudden silence in the taproom was stifling, as Amanda and Amos exchanged glances. "Where's Imp?" she asked instantly.

"He's cleaning in the kitchen, just like you told him," responded Amos, replacing his cudgel.

"Get him out here, and be quick about it," commanded Amanda, as her gaze rested on the door. She picked up a small sheet of paper from behind the bar, scribbling a note.

In a few seconds, Imp appeared, a towel in his hands, saying, "I'm doin' like you said, Ms. Amanda. What's wrong?"

"Forget the kitchen chores for now. I need you to run – and I mean run – over to the Bunch of Grapes. Give this note to Big Bessie. Use the back alleys; it will be quicker. And after you give her the note, leave her place by the back way. I don't want you to be seen by that redcoat patrol; do you understand?"

"Yes'm!" said Imp, turning on his heels toward the storage room and the back door.

Amanda yelled as he disappeared, "Don't forget to wear your slicker in all this rain." To Amos, she added, "Make us both a flip, Amos. I have a feeling this business is about to become more trying on us all." As Amos mixed the flip, Amanda, lost in thought, glanced at the red coat on the peg.

Amos, with a broad smile and sliding a tankard of flip across the bar, said, "I don't know why you didn't just tell them redcoats to git the hell out, Ms. Amanda."

She grinned. "Sometimes life is simpler when you plow around the stump, Amos. And they have hard cash to spend. Besides, not all those redcoats are bad, not bad at all." She sipped her drink with a contented sigh.

"What are you up to, Ms. Amanda? That officer told you somethin', and I see that sneaky look you sometimes git," mumbled Amos.

"Don't you worry yourself about my sneaky looks, Amos. Don't you worry," she muttered, lost in thought.

ΩΩΩ

CHAPTER 12

Tuesday, October 11, 1768

T HE COBBLESTONE STREETS of Boston were slippery, and those not paved were a quagmire of mud following the all-night storm. The sun beamed down, creating a steaming muck for the street vendors and their pushcarts, while young boys splashed playfully in puddles of water. The upstairs room of Edes & Gill and the *Boston Gazette* was abuzz with activity, as it was most Saturdays. At a corner table, lit by sun streaming through the windows, Sam Adams gripped his quill pen tightly, as his palsied scrawl ripped across the parchment. He was lost in thought and oblivious to the presence of others in the room.

Benjamin Edes wiped his sweaty brow as he toiled with the layout of the coming issue. Looking up from his work and wiping ink from his hands, he smiled at Joseph Warren who was sharing his table while at work on his next editorial. "Just look at him, Doctor. He seems to be lost in a world that I can't comprehend." He gestured toward the corner table.

Glancing over at Sam Adams, Warren replied, "You're right, Ben. And actually he is. Sadly, as you well know, the presence of the king's troops has set us back on our heels so to speak. Our only recourse is to propagandize and disturb this menace to our society."

Without looking up from his labors across the room, Adams grumbled, "That is exactly what I'm about today, gentlemen. Now that we control both the assembly and the council, Governor Bernard will play hell getting permanent quarters in this town for those damned troops. They can rot during the day and freeze at night on the Common, for all I care."

Answering Benjamin Edes unspoken question, Warren added, "It's easy to understand the situation, Ben, if you study it closely. Sam and I have noted that if we can keep the redcoats out of Faneuil Hall and from billeting in any other buildings or homes, we can place His Majesty's troops in a quandary. This leaves them with the option of moving the garrison to Castle William in the harbor or to force the Quartering Act, whereby the troops will be forcibly moved into the private homes of the citizens. The Castle William option effectively removes them as a threat. And the quartering option will most certainly cause such anger that we will finally move the entire populace out of their submissive stupor and into the realization that their rights have been violated and usurped by this unjust government."

Adams stood up from his labor and, holding his quill pen above his head in triumph, stated, "That's all quite true, my dear friend. However, what I've just written is the best I've come up with in some time, if I do say so myself." He crossed the room to get closer. "You see, I've learned that our own dear Lieutenant Governor and Superior Court Justice Thomas Hutchinson received a trunkful of ordinary cloth bandanas in shipment for resale by his sons."

Ben Edes, inking the printer, asked innocently, "So pray tell, why is that inconsequential bit of news worthy of note?"

With a sly conspiratorial grin, Adams announced, "Don't you see this is a blatant violation and disregard of the Nonimportation Agreement? And, furthermore, they are not really cloth bandanas but fine silk scarves from – oh, let us say, Lord Clive in London, as personal payment for keeping his foot on the throats of the poor wretches of Boston. How does that sound for the next issue of the *Boston Gazette*?"

Edes stood there, his mouth agape. "But none of that is actually true, is it?"

Doctor Warren responded with a hearty laugh, "Of course, it's not true, Ben. But what does the truth have to do with it? Sam has just created a giant dose of envy and blatant violation of the fairness doctrine. When the common man on the Boston streets reads about this, he will be ready to march on Hutchinson's home and raze the damned building like they did years ago." He made a full bow from the waist in the direction of Adams. "My good man, I salute you for your genius. I assume this will be penned by Vindex, as usual."

"But of course," responded Adams. "Who else could write such a crass thing? Certainly not Sam Adams or the trusting, loyal Dr. Warren. Let us keep in mind that we must put our adversaries in the wrong and keep them there. The public perception of reality will always trump all logic and legality."

Ben Edes just shook his head in surrender. "You write it, and I'll print it, gentlemen. God only knows what Governor Bernard and Mr. Hutchinson will do in reprisal. I've always been a member of the Loyal Nine, but I still have my business to think of."

Warren patted him on the shoulder. "Courage, my good man, courage! I guarantee that the *Boston Gazette* is the first paper the governor reads. How can he resist? If Hutchinson protests, it will be perceived that he has been lying about his business anyway. Remember that perceived reality is what really counts. The people will believe you, Ben; trust me on this."

"How can you be so sure that you know what the governor and Mr. Hutchinson are thinking?" asked Ben.

"Actually, we can learn firsthand because we have been invited to General Gage's formal reception. We have ten days to tweak his nose, until we dine with him in his own residence. What do you think of that, Ben?" boasted Dr. Warren.

Ben shook his head, "Do you mean to tell me that they had the courage to invite old Vindex over there?"

Adams glared across the room. "You think I will not fit in?" He laughed. "After I thought about it for a while, I realized Hancock was right. We need to meet these people eye to eye; and it is probably best to do it in a festive atmosphere, where they are expected to be polite and kind. It might lower their guard, and who knows what we could learn about their intentions."

Edes looked incredulously at both men. "Just don't mistake kindness for weakness, Sam. Actually, I would love to write about that meeting personally."

"You won't, but 'Vindex' will. You can trust me on this," said Adams with a sly grin.

ΩΩΩ

October 11, 1768

The heat of the midmorning sun had created a steaming mire of mud puddles amid the cobblestones on King Street. The hucksters and the peddlers yelling, "fresh lob" and "fresh fish," with bells on their carts, created a heavy din of music, as Big Bessie Clump stared vacantly at Amanda. She was still dressed in her night shift and mobcap, as she poured tea at the window table at the Bunch of Grapes. "I tell you, Amanda, there's gonna be hell to pay with these redcoats throwin' their weight around like they are. If you hadn't sent Imp like you did last night, there would have been a bloodbath right here in this taproom."

"We almost had a riot at the Snug Harbor last night too. But what is it that happened here, Bessie?" asked Amanda, also clad in her mobcap and brown homespun cleaning dress.

"Well, Sam Adams was sitting here with Mackintosh and his gang when Imp showed up in that downpour. Everyone except Adams was pretty well into their ale by that time, and I had a hell of time getting them to leave by the backdoor before that party of redcoats showed up from your place," said Bessie, scratching her midriff. "That big old Sergeant Major Delaney barged in like he owned the damned place, looking for deserters."

"What did you tell him?" asked Amanda, leaning forward eagerly.

"Absolutely nothing! What do you expect? I told him we was loyal to the Crown and wouldn't tolerate no desertin' of the king's troops at the Bunch of Grapes," said Bessie triumphantly with a sly grin.

"I'm glad that Imp got here to warn you," said Amanda, smiling.

Bessie grimaced, "I'm concerned about only one thing." She leaned forward pressing her huge breasts against the table. "I'm hoping that my Abby Stuff didn't open her mouth about anything. She's one of them girls who talks too much when she's in the crib. And she took one of those redcoats upstairs, when that officer left for the evening."

"What does Abby know?" queried Amanda, her brow furrowed.

"She knows as much as me about getting those soldiers out of town, and she's good at it. But don't you worry. I told her to stop braggin' while she's shaggin'," chortled Bessie, her flab bouncing in her shift. She waddled to the bar, "Why don't we have a tankard of ale, Amanda? This tea is getting stale."

Amanda followed her to the bar. Getting close to Bessie, she whispered, "You had best tell your girls to keep their mouths closed. If the army learns about us getting deserters out of Boston, we will find ourselves getting flogged on Boston Common. That Delaney chap would take great delight in watching us get our naked asses whipped."

Bessie, downing her ale, chuckled, "Especially if they found out we are keeping every Brown Bess musket those fellows have, in exchange for their freedom from the army."

ΩΩΩ

CHAPTER 13

Saturday, October 15, 1768

I N THE EARLY dawn and without fanfare, one of His Majesty's frigates quietly sailed into Boston Harbor. The crew was under strict orders to keep as quiet as possible as they worked the rigging and eased the vessel into a mooring alongside the HMS *Romney,* which was still shadowing Hancock's *Liberty.*

Imp had arisen before dawn, as he did every Saturday, knowing he first had to help Amos clean the taproom before he rushed over to Edes & Gill for delivery of the afternoon edition of the *Boston Gazette.* He lit a candle in the taproom and sat alone sipping cider at his favorite table at the front window overlooking Hancock's Wharf. He enjoyed the quiet at this magic time of day when the hush of night had not quite released its grip to the bustle of another day. With the front door open to the gray dawn, he savored the smell of the salt sea breeze and the sounds of waves lapping at the dock. The creaking of ships' rigging as they gently rocked against the wharf added to the music of the moment. The only evidence of people stirring on the waterfront was the distant changing of the watch aboard the king's warships in the harbor. Imp smiled at the faint sounds of marine sergeants and navy bosuns barking their regimented orders.

Suddenly, the solitude of the coming dawn was shattered by the clatter of horses' hooves and the rumble of carriage wheels on the cobble stones of Fish Street. As the coach passed, he noted the governor's seal on the side door. It continued down the length of Hancock's Wharf.

Picking up his mug of cider, Imp casually sauntered out the front door trailing the carriage. Not a soul was yet stirring, with the exception of a few fishermen at the adjoining docks. The sight of a long boat from one of the frigates alerted him that something was not quite right. *It was strange,* he thought, *that the Royal Navy would use this wharf rather than Long Wharf, as they usually did and where His Majesty's troops had put ashore just a few weeks earlier. And just what was the governor doing here at this hour?* He crept behind the fish barrels lining the Hancock warehouses.

In the darkness, he could barely make out who was disembarking from the long boat, when from his right he heard the clatter of more horses; and they seemed to be in a hurry. As they drew closer, he could make out one mounted officer accompanied by two mounted dragoons, the scarlet of their uniforms just barely visible in the darkness. The officer's gorget, however, glistened in the moonlight. As they halted abreast the governor's carriage, the officer saluted smartly saying, "Captain Preston at your service, General Gage. Lieutenant Colonel Dalrymple sends his compliments."

In a gruff tone, a tall officer, the gold medals and cord of his tunic glistening, said, "Very well, Captain. Take me to Lieutenant Colonel Dalrymple immediately. At least he followed orders. What is the governor's carriage doing here? I gave specific orders that no one was to know about this visit prior to my arrival."

Straightening his gorget, Captain Preston answered in a quiet tone, "It seems, sir, that Boston is well populated with spies and informers. It is nigh impossible to conceal our movements without a hostile pair of eyes taking note. In this case, sir, it is obvious that someone is keeping the civilian government apprised of the situation."

Preston could feel the general's eyes glaring. "Spies? Informants? Never mind, Captain. Lead this carriage to wherever Dalrymple happens to be at this hour."

The entourage had no sooner cleared the wharf than Imp ran as fast as his legs could carry him back to the Snug Harbor Tavern. He rushed to the back storeroom where he shook Amos awake, as he donned his jacket and grabbed his tricorn hat. "Amos, you gotta tell Amanda that I gotta run to the *Gazette.*"

Amos, sitting up in his cot and rubbing the sleep from his eyes, said, "Miz Manda will whip your hide if you don't do your chores round here, Imp."

With urgency in his voice, Imp responded, "You gotta cover for me, Amos; it's important. Trust me!" With that, he rushed to the door. Suddenly, he stopped in the doorway, snapping his fingers in recall. He knelt down to retrieve a small box hidden under his cot. Opening the box, he found what he was looking for in the dim candlelight. Between his small fingers, he held up a red feather about four inches long, which he secured to the band of his hat.

Amos, getting dressed, observed the young boy on his knees with the red feather. He unconsciously rubbed the ears of his new puppy. The small English bulldog, apparently abandoned, had been roaming the waterfront the last few months, and Amos began to feed it scraps of food and named him Angus. Now the small cur had moved into the Snug Harbor like all the other orphans of society. Nodding, he said, "I understand, Imp. Why don't you take Angus with you? I'll take care of Miz Manda."

"I'll be at the *Gazette,* Amos." With that, he scampered through the taproom with the English bulldog in trail.

ΩΩΩ

As General Gage's carriage slowly made its way down Fish Street, then passing Faneuil Hall and the Old State House, the only other traffic seemed to be a few milk wagons from farms as far away as Lexington, making their way to the Boston market. By the time Gage and his entourage had arrived at Boston Common, the sunrise in the east had exposed the beauty of the hills around the Charles and Mystic Rivers. The leaves on the oaks and maple trees had turned a bright orange, yellow and red, creating a striking panorama to the west of Boston. As Gage alit from the carriage, he paused, saying, "It's hard to believe that anyone could find any rationale for discontent when surrounded by such natural beauty."

By that time, the entire Twenty-ninth Regiment had assembled in time-honored military precision, the morning sun sparkling off the fixed bayonets. Sergeants up and down the lines were barking orders, as troops stood at rigid attention before their neat rows of white tents. The morning serenity was shattered as the artillery detachment honored General Gage with the requisite seventeen-gun salute. The blistering fusillade echoed across the sleepy town.

ΩΩΩ

In the early darkness, Benjamin Edes stumbled across the kitchen of his living quarters at the rear of Edes & Gill, Printers. Standing in his nightshirt at the open door, he bellowed, "Whoever's rapping at my door at this hour had best have a good reason, by god!" It took a second glance downward before he realized it was Imp. Angus gave a little growl at Edes's harsh tone.

"Beg pardon, Mr. Edes," muttered Imp, "but I got news, and I think it's important. I didn't know who else to come to at this hour."

"Important news, eh?" said Edes, frowning. "I'll be the judge of that," he muttered under his breath. With a sudden smile, he added, "Why come on in, lad. I can brew some tea, and you can tell me all about this important news. After all, that's precisely the business we are about, isn't it." As he poured water into a kettle, Edes added with mock seriousness, "Now you sit yourself down there at the table and tell me what could possibly be so important at this hour down at the Snug Harbor Tavern?"

"Well, you see, Mr. Edes, I was sippin' some cider in the taproom when the governor's carriage comes rattlin' down to the wharf and gets General Gage out of a long boat."

Stopping midpour, kettle in hand, Edes froze in place. "Did you say General Gage? Do you mean the same General Gage who commands His Majesty's army in all the colonies?"

"Yessir! At least I think so. That's what they called him, and he had more gold and medals than anyone I ever saw. Anyway, he didn't want anyone to know about – "

At that moment, a loud volley of cannon fire pierced their ears and rattled the windows. Imp jumped to his feet, and Edes dropped the kettle of water, sending Angus scurrying. His eyes wide as saucers, Imp mumbled, "What the hell was that?"

Edes, having served in the militia during the French and Indian War, smiled. "That, my boy, is the distinct sound of His Majesty's cannon. And since no war has been declared that I know of, I would say that your news is correct. Let me get some clothes on, and we can rush to the sound of the guns."

ΩΩΩ

Monday, October 17, 1768

General Gage made his way up the narrow winding staircase to Governor Bernard's second-floor office, following Hubert Slank at his slow deliberate pace. Slank had rid himself of the hunched-over subservient lackey mannerisms and had adopted the shoulders-back military bearing he felt more fitting to the general's presence. Upon their entering the office, Governor Bernard arose from his desk and strode to the door, bowing formally. "General Gage, it is indeed a pleasure to finally put a face with the name. Your fine reputation precedes you, sir."

Returning the bow with equal obsequiousness, Gage smiled. "It is indeed an honor, sir."

"Please do come in and be seated, General." Directing Gage to the most comfortable chair in the room, he said, "Slank, I am expecting Sheriff Greenleaf and Mr. Mein momentarily. Otherwise, we are not to be disturbed." Bernard then turned his full attention upon Gage, introducing the others in the room, including Hutchinson, Andrew Oliver, and a rotund gentleman, introduced only as a coordinator for information gathering.

Gage, accepting a crystal glass of Madeira, said, "A pleasure to meet you, gentlemen. I'm sure you have met Lieutenant Colonel William Dalrymple, commander of the Fourteenth Regiment, and Lieutenant Colonel Maurice Carr of the Twenty-ninth; and this is Captain Preston of the Twenty-ninth. Of course, none of us would be here without Commodore Samuel Hood and His Majesty's ships of the line." He introduced two Royal Navy captains, adding, "I expect to have Commodore Hood here personally with more troops in due time." He casually arose from his chair, taking command of the room, still clutching his glass of wine. He was taller than anyone in the room at a few inches more than six feet, and his standing enabled him to take full advantage of that fact. This seemed to punctuate his authority.

Bernard made a mental note that every aspect of this man spoke of his keen attention to detail. From his powdered wig to his polished boots, his uniform was impeccable. *This man has come prepared,* he thought to himself, *but prepared for what?* He sat back in his chair, listening intently.

Gage continued, "Now the way I see it here in Boston, we are – "

A rap on the door and Slank's abrupt entrance halted Gage in midsentence. His pursed lips indicated his disapproval.

Slank announced formally, "Governor, Sheriff Greenleaf and Mr. Mein have arrived." Both men bustled past Slank, as if he was a piece of furniture. Slank glared, but no one noticed as the new arrivals offered their apologies for being late. Greenleaf went directly to the sidebar and poured himself a tankard of claret while John Mein seated himself next to the fat man at the back of the room.

Bernard, after introducing the two men, said, "General, there is no doubt that Lieutenant Dalrymple has briefed you on our situation here in Boston. And we are all aware of certain issues you wish to discuss. But permit me to share a more detailed account from a civilian perspective."

Gage smiled as he returned to his seat. "Governor Bernard, His Majesty's army and" – gesturing to the naval captains in attendance – "the Royal Navy are at your service. Please, proceed."

Francis Bernard took his seat at his desk and glanced at a few documents. "Perhaps it would be best if we start with Sheriff Greenleaf's assessment. It has been his task to deal with the rabble on more intimate terms than most of us here."

Greenleaf set his drink on the sideboard and shifted his ample girth closer to the governor's desk. "Thank you, Governor. General Gage, I would like to make just a few points. One is that I personally appreciate your arrival. As sheriff, my handful of deputies, and I primarily serve writs for the court and attend ceremonies. I can hardly be expected to cope with the rioting and hostilities of the mob we have so sadly experienced."

Clearing his throat to get attention, Hutchinson interjected, "You can say that again, Stephen. Peacekeeping doesn't exist because that would imply that there was peace in the first place. Between Andrew Oliver here and myself, General Gage, we have suffered the most personally, losing almost everything we ever owned due to mob rule. And you couldn't even find witnesses in this town."

Greenleaf turned crimson. "If you are implying that I'm not doing my job, you are more than welcome to try it on for size. For god's sake, it seems that you and your family have taken almost every other official office in town." He paused to sip his wine, adding in a loud voice, "Besides, when Sam Adams alerts his thirty-thousand man army of radicals from the countryside, you'll have more to worry about than your precious private possessions. That mob out there will have your scalp."

Bernard arose, raising his voice, "Gentlemen, please! Let us keep a civil tone here. General Gage, please forgive this outburst."

Gage looked at Greenleaf, who had retrieved his tankard. "Let me understand this, Sheriff. There is a mob of thirty thousand men out there ready to take up arms against His Majesty's forces? And just who is this Sam Adams?"

Hutchinson didn't give Greenleaf a chance to answer. "Perhaps that could be best answered by our friend from Omega." He glanced at Bernard, who nodded his approval.

Gage, observing the large man at the rear of the room, muttered uncertainly, "Omega? What is that? And what is your name, sir?"

The fat man spoke slowly with a tone of secrecy. "General, my name is not important. And to be brief, I function as a focal point in the gathering of information; spying, if you will, on the radicals of this town. Omega is merely a name for our network." He paused to sip his wine slowly and deliberately. "To answer your questions: Sam Adams is a major agitator, who at times has raged that he can raise a thirty-thousand man army to oppose the royal armed forces. Of course, this is a mere figment of his imagination."

Gage sat back in his chair, gulping his wine. "Thank God for that. I was thinking that I had an inadequate force for a moment there. Imagine my forces confronting thirty thousand farmers with pitchforks." Almost everyone in the room broke out in laughter.

The fat man did not share in the laughter of the others, as he continued, "Let me assure you, General, at this time such a force is inconceivable for Adams and his henchmen. However, he does have the mob, and that is quite real."

Looking at Dalrymple, implying that he should take special note of this information, Gage interrupted, "Tell me about this mob. How large is it? Who controls it?"

The fat man nodded, "You see, General, prior to the Stamp Act fiasco, our fair town of Boston was blessed with not one, but rather, two gangs; the North and Southside gangs. Comprised mostly of rabble, apprentices, and common tradesmen, they were fairly tame with the exception of Guy Fawkes Day. Every November 5, the gangs celebrated the Gunpowder Plot by marching through town with a large statue of the Pope. The problem was that each gang could raise at least five hundred men at a moment's notice, and they each marched from their respective areas. When they met at the center of town, all hell would break loose with many broken bones and broken heads. They actually declared war on Catholics, Irishmen, and Scots. It was insanity until Sam Adams somehow got the two leaders Mackintosh and Swift to sign a truce and merge the gangs. Now when they march, they rarely fight among themselves. They look for a common enemy."

At this point, John Mein interjected, "Sadly for us, they have found a common target, and that has been the tax collectors, customs commissioners, and anyone seemingly loyal to the Crown. Anyone who violates the Nonimportation Agreement will find their businesses splattered with night soil and their windows shattered. God only knows where they find all those chamber pots."

Andrew Oliver added angrily, "Or, as in my case, my image was hung in effigy from the Liberty Tree, and my home vandalized and robbed. I resigned as a commissioner to save the lives of my wife and children. These vagabonds are out of control. Some men have suffered the humiliation of tarring and feathering."

Governor Bernard watched keenly as Gage absorbed the news. "The real problem, as you can see, General, is that any form of civil government has been paralyzed by mob rule. The assembly is ruled by the radicals, with Sam Adams firmly entrenched as its secretary. Even the council is impregnated with them. If I deny them meeting privileges, they merely reconvene as a 'town meeting,' conducting nonbinding legislation. Such meetings are obviously illegal, but what can we do? Ultimately, His Majesty's customs commissioners have escaped for their lives to Castle William in the harbor. If it were not for the presence of the HMS *Romney*, they and their families would have been treated quite harshly."

John Mein added, "Actually, it is the small Tory merchants who have been most hard pressed by the Nonimportation Agreements. Any merchant who sells English imports is subject to the worst possible treatment, including tarring and feathering. The parading through the streets of these poor wretches is most intimidating."

A momentary silence pervaded the room, as Gage looked each man sternly in the eyes, one at a time. Satisfied that they had vented their concerns, he arose slowly from his chair and wandered to the window overlooking King Street. In the distance, he saw the Royal Navy frigates aligned with their cannon trained broadside upon the town. As for the citizenry, they seemed well occupied with their work and trade. Turning to the office, he said slowly, "Gentlemen, I thank you for your candor. I only wish a formal request for His Majesty's troops had come sooner."

Bernard rose to speak, but Gage stilled him with a raised hand. "I know, Governor Bernard! Your formal request of troops in previously unoccupied Boston could have conceivably created a greater problem – even insurrection, if I am to believe what I have heard here today." Pausing in his oratory, he said, "Captain Preston, refill my glass, if you would – Madeira, I believe it was."

Looking at Bernard, he continued, "I am informed by Lord Barrington that your need for troops is not to quell a riot but rather to rescue the government from the hands of a trained mob and restore the activity of civil power, which seems to be severely constricted. Are those not your words, Governor?"

Glancing around the room, Bernard began to rub the back of his neck. He sipped his claret and responded in carefully measured words, "General, it is no great secret that there is great turmoil in Boston. These good men and I have done our best to reason with the rascals and malcontents to no avail. The Stamp Act and Townsend Act have aggravated these people to no end. The added taxes have unfortunately enabled them to ally themselves with Hancock and a few other wealthy merchants. Their propaganda in such trash as the *Boston Gazette* has poisoned the people and their affection for the Crown. If I were to publicly say that I requested your troops, I would quickly find my home burned, with me and my family living aboard one of those frigates in the harbor."

Hutchinson echoed his sentiment in a somber tone of voice. "That would probably be the end for every Tory in Boston."

Gage grimaced. "That leaves us in a bit of a predicament, gentlemen. Captain Preston, hand me that document from Lord Barrington." Scanning through the pages, he continued, "Here it is. The War Office has ordered me to take no step whatever but with the express requisition of the civil magistrate. That includes, Governor, marching and quartering of troops and opposing rioters." Scanning further, he added, "Oh, here it is, this includes your approval to repel force by force, if absolutely necessary." He took a draught of his wine. "As you can see, Governor, although I have every inclination to order my troops to march upon these miscreants, I can do nothing without your specific orders."

Looking down at his desk, Bernard said, "That does present a problem, General, because right now, the mere presence of your troops has sent half the rascals to the hills and the other half to hiding in their garrets. How can I possibly request troops to repel activity that no longer exists?"

Gage merely shook his head. "Well, hopefully we can solve two problems that I present to you, Governor. The quartering of my troops must be addressed. I realize that you have already discussed this with Lieutenant Colonel Dalrymple, but I tell you that the status quo is not acceptable. Winter will soon be upon us, and I still have troops living in tents on the Common. In addition, the desertion numbers are abominable. I am informed that no less than seventy of the king's troops and sailors have left their posts. This could not be accomplished without the help of the townsmen. In fact, on the night of October 9, some villains had the unmitigated gall to ruin the frame of the guardhouse not far from this building; now, it is useless to anyone. How do you propose to resolve these issues, Governor?"

Bernard cringed under the blunt address. "I have been through this with the Council for days on end, General. The votes continue to be against any quartering. The common attitude is to place all your men on Castle William in the harbor. Actually, it is a legal part of the town."

"Unacceptable?" growled the general. "I'll tell you what, gentlemen. I have an appointment with a Mr. John Copley for a portrait sitting. Your tailors are not worth a farthing, but it seems that this man enjoys a fine reputation as an artist. I suggest you find warm shelter for all my troops, or I shall find them myself – at the point of a bayonet. Do I make myself clear?"

"Let me remind you, General, that you and your army serve at the pleasure of the civilian leadership," said Governor Bernard bluntly.

"Then I suggest you start exercising a bit of leadership and unleash the dogs of war, Governor. We will be happy to comply," blurted Gage. Not another word was uttered. Gage retrieved his gold-trimmed tricorn and walking stick as he marched toward the door. "Men, come with me. It seems that our civilian friends have a bit of work to do, and we should leave them to it."

ΩΩΩ

CHAPTER 14

Monday afternoon, October 17, 1768

BIG BESSIE CLUMP grumbled to herself as she trudged up the creaking back stairs of the Bunch of Grapes Tavern. She waddled down the hall, scratching her midriff through her shift, and stopped suddenly. Her fat fists bunched on her ample hips, she muttered, "Lazy bitch!" With visible contempt, she held up the small wooden sign hung by a string on the doorknob, which read, Go Away; Busy Shaggin'. Pounding on the door with all her might, Bessie howled, "Abby, git your ass out of the crib. I know you ain't shaggin' in there. It's well past noon, and we best get ready for the evening." Her tirade was greeted with total silence. After pounding again with no response, Bessie waddled down the hall, yelling down to the taproom, "Did you folks see where Abby has gone to? She ain't in her room."

One of the girls appeared at the bottom of the stairs with a blank stare, "She should be there, Bessie. I know she was entertaining some blokes, but I heard them leave before dawn. You should get those creaky floors fixed."

Bessie waddled back down the hall. "This ain't right," she muttered to herself. "Abby always tells me where she's off to." She hammered on the door again; no answer. Sighing, she violated her own rule that any door with the sign on the knob meant absolutely no intrusion.

She found the room in total darkness, with only the light of the hallway filtering in. As she stepped inside, she slipped on something and crashed into the door jam. Looking down at her feet, she saw candle wax shredded on the floor. "What the hell!" she muttered as she crossed the room and opened the shades. She barked in a jovial tone, "It's time to get your ass moving, Abby. We have – " The next sound she uttered was a shriek.

Abby Stuff lay across her bed, the front of her bodice stained a bright crimson and her eyes wide open in death.

ΩΩΩ

Amanda Griffin, still in her mobcap and day clothes, burst through the door of the Bunch of Grapes with Imp in tow and paused briefly at the bar. "Where's Bessie?" she asked hurriedly. The bartender simply pointed to the back stairs. "You stay here, Imp. I might need you." She then scurried to the stairs, taking them two at a time.

She found Bessie sitting on Abby's bed, the crumpled blood-stained linens wadded on the floor. Bessie was slowly fingering through the few trinkets and baubles that were seemingly Abby's treasured possessions. "Are you all right, Bessie?" mumbled Amanda, as she crossed to sit beside her.

Bessie's bloodshot teary eyes spoke volumes, as she blubbered, "The dirty bastards killed my little angel, Amanda. Abby never did a thing to hurt anyone. Why? Why? Why?" She buried her head into Amanda's neck. "She tried to tell me that someone was getting a bit rough at times, but I just shrugged it off. Why didn't I listen to that sweet girl?"

Looking about the room, Amanda realized that someone had to take control of the situation. "Come with me, Bessie. Let's get down to the taproom and have a small drink – just like Abby would want us to."

Bessie, looking deep into Amanda's eyes, nodded, "Yes. Abby would want that." Amanda held Bessie's arm as she shuffled down the hallway and down the stairway into the taproom. Her sobs had turned to a quiet weeping.

Seated at a table in the taproom, both ladies nursed a tankard of flip. Amanda sent Imp to the Snug Harbor to warn the girls to keep an eye out for each other. She asked, "Did you send for the sheriff, Bessie?"

Bessie didn't smile. "Yes, I did, Amanda. Only God knows why." Raising her finger to emphasize the point, she added, "I recall what that bastard did for your sweet Charity two years ago. In fact, I was told that his fat blubbery ass was just too busy to get right over here. Something about meeting with a general or something! Too busy my ass!"

Amanda frowned, "Maybe we should go visit him like we did before, Bessie. And there is no time like now. You get your mourning clothes on, and I'll run to the Snug Harbor to do the same. I'll be right back." Bessie simply nodded in assent. As Bessie waddled to her room to change clothes, Amanda turned to the bartender. "You get upstairs and put a board across the door to Abby's room. Don't let anyone in there. You can clean it up after the sheriff investigates. Where is Abby's body now?"

One of the girls piped up, "I think she was taken to Dr. Church for examination or some such."

"I'll be right back," said Amanda, rushing out the door. "Don't let Bessie leave without me."

ΩΩΩ

Dr. Joseph Warren leaned back in his chair in the typesetting room of the *Boston Gazette*, lost deep in thought, a look of agitation on his normally taciturn face. "Sam, will you please stop your pacing?"

Adams stopped in his tracks. "It just so happens that I do some of my best thinking when I'm pacing, Joseph."

Running his fingers through a bin of printer's type, John Hancock said, "I don't know why you called for me, gentlemen. Just what do you expect me to do about the arrival of General Gage? It seems to me that he can do pretty much whatever he chooses."

Wagging the index finger, Adams growled, "We have to do something, for god's sake. I tell you we should let the wrath of our colony come down on him, John. With thirty thousand men, we could drive Gage and his army into Boston Harbor."

Warren stood gazing out the window at the harbor in the distance. "Sam, just stop and look out there a moment. I see a forest out there in the harbor. And you know as well as I that the forest I speak of is comprised of the masts of twelve of His Majesty's warships." Pointing for dramatic effect, he added, "Each ship has its cannon trained on Boston, courtesy of Commodore Hood and General Gage. Now how do you think the Royal Navy will respond, if anyone dares to trample into armed rebellion? Think, for god's sake. Think!"

Adams glared. "We can't just sit here like whipped street urchins."

Hancock added, "Hell, Sam, they still have my merchant ship *Liberty*. God only knows how that will be resolved. And, if you haven't noticed, most of our support has evacuated Boston and found refuge in the surrounding towns. What poison do you think the governor, Hutchinson, and the other Tories are pouring into that redcoat skull of Gage? I wouldn't be surprised if they have a warrant for our arrest in short order. Those who left town are certainly of that opinion."

"They can't do anything without real cause. I spoke with Mackintosh and Revere to ensure the rabble and gangs are quiet," said Adams, with a tone of resignation. "For how long, I can't be sure; but, for now, there will be no real altercations. We are Englishmen, for god's sake, and we have our rights. We can't be arrested without due cause or some such legality my cousin is always spouting."

Warren smiled. "Let's keep it that way. Gage won't play his hand unless Bernard says so. And he will probably see the current peace as achieving his goal. We must learn what it will take to get these redcoats out of town."

Hancock laughed. "And my best guess is that we provide no reason for them to be here in the first place. It is only a question of time before they get bored and take their toys back to where they belong."

Sam Adams began pacing again. "You may be correct, John. But I'm not sure how long we can keep a tight rein on Mackintosh and his men."

Hancock pounded the table, scrambling the bins of type again. "I have it. There is no doubt that Bernard will soon announce that reception for Gage and his entourage. As we discussed before, we should be represented at such a soiree and Dr. Church is working on our being formally invited. That is precisely where we can dig for more information, as we appear to meekly accept his presence and politely ask why they are here."

"I'll tell you why they are here!" howled Adams. "It's that bastard Bernard; that's who it is."

Warren raised his hands in a calming motion, as a preacher would calm his congregation. "Sam, cool down, or you'll drift into a fit, and I'll have to medicate you." Looking at Hancock, he added, "You're right, John. Let's leave the impression that we are the most loyal of His Majesty's subjects and attend that – "

The door burst open suddenly, with Benjamin Edes leading Imp into the room. "Sorry for the interruption, gents, but my star reporter here has more news. You should find this interesting." Turning to Imp, he added, "Go on, lad. Tell them your story."

Holding his small tricorn with the red feather displayed, Imp said, "I figured it was important you should know that another strumpet was killed today."

"Who? Where?" came from each man.

"At the Bunch of Grapes it was. And Abby was the nicest lady. She always gave me – "

Hancock interrupted, "Imp, I want you to get back to the Snug Harbor and warn Mrs. Griffith of this. Then I want – "

"It was Miz Griffith sent me here to tell you. She went with Miz Bessie to see the sheriff; they was wearin' their black mournin' weeds and all," said Imp.

Adams said triumphantly, "That should scramble Greenleaf's eggs, if you know what I mean. So much for peace and quiet with the redcoats in town!"

Warren added, "Let's get our people asking questions, Sam. Meanwhile, I'll contact Dr. Church about those invitations to the governor's reception for Gage. He's Bernard's personal physician and is usually invited to those parties. I'm sure he can get us in."

"I'll get to the warehouse on the wharf. It seems that I'll have a rush on black cloth for the funeral," said Hancock. "Imp, you come with me."

As they headed to the door, Ben Edes muttered, "When you get the details, let me know. Meanwhile, I'll reset the headline of the *Gazette*." He turned to his presses.

ΩΩΩ

Despite the loss of one of their sisters in the trade, the ladies of the Snug Harbor Tavern were busier than usual later that evening. The redcoats took little notice of the black drapery about the windows as they were out in force for an evening of revelry. Many tables had been gathered together near the hearth to accommodate a large contingent of the Twenty-ninth Regiment. Amanda made a mental note of the gathering from behind the bar. "Amos, keep a sharp eye on that gaggle by the fireplace. I'll be upstairs."

"Got it covered," said Amos, wiping the bar. "I'll get Angus on them, if they want trouble." Angus, sitting behind the bar, yelped at the sound of his name.

Sergeant Major Sean Delaney was holding court in the midst of the Twenty-ninth contingent. "More grog! More ale! More rum!" he howled, standing with his tankard held aloft. "Can't you see that the king's troops are running dry over here? Where's a serving wench when I need one?"

Faith and Hope laughed heartily, as they worked each end of the tables. Hope cooed, "Seanie, baby. Why don't you bring that big stick of yours up to my crib?"

"Do you mean my halberd?" asked Delaney, slurring his words, "or do you want my big stick?" He grabbed the crotch of his white breeches.

Hope grinned. "The big stick, of course." The entire table laughed, as Amos delivered another round of ale, and they joined in another chorus.

> *My lassie's back home, and I'm braggin'*
> *I finally escaped all the naggin'*
> *I'm safe as a bug,*
> *Right here at the Snug,*
> *And ready and ripe for the shaggin'.*

The door opened, and Zeke Teezle needled his way through the crowd to the bar, as he usually did. Amos smiled a toothy grin. "What's you doin' here tonight, Mr. Zeke? It ain't Thursday, or could I be wrong?"

Zeke scratched his scrawny neck, saying, "Just gimme a tankard of ale, Amos." Looking around the smoky taproom, he asked, "Is Hope in tonight?"

Amos smiled again. "You seem to have a real likin' for that big girl, don't you, Mr. Zeke?" Leaning forward, he added, "Tonight might not be the best time for you seein' Hope. It seems she's minglin' with the redcoats of the Twenty-ninth this evenin'."

Teezle stood on his tiptoes to see through the crowd and the smoke. In doing so, he caught the eye of Sergeant Major Delaney. Immediately, Teezle downed his tankard and turned for the door. Delaney's booming voice halted his exit. "Teezle," he howled, "where you goin', my good man. Git your arse back in here." His neck slunk deep between his collar bones, Teezle threaded his way to the gathering of redcoats."

Delaney pulled an extra chair to the table, saying, "Teezle, my man, you sit yourself right next to me." To the entire table of redcoats, Delaney howled, "Quiet, you rascals, I got an introduction to make. This here's my good friend, Zeke; and I say he's the best colonial in all of Boston." Patting Teezle on his boney back and patting Hope on her ample rump as she perched on his lap, he added, "And this here, Teezle my boy, is the best strumpet on the waterfront. This is my gal Hope."

Before he could mutter a word, Hope extended her hand, "Any friend of Sergeant Major Delaney is a friend of mine." She kissed Delaney heartily as her eyes fixed on Teezle sternly. The message was clearly saying, "You don't know me tonight."

As Amos delivered another round, he heard Delaney slur, "It's not like the other night at the Bunch of Grapes is it Zeke; certainly a little less bloody, ain't it?" His laughter echoed across the taproom. Under his breath, he added, hugging Teezle by the shoulders closely, "If it wasn't for you, Zeke, I would never have guessed that dirty doxy was getting my boys to desert and leave the service of the king. By god, she'll never do that again, will she?" He guzzled his ale, adding, "Now you take my girl Hope here – truly bent on making the king's troops happy. That's what she's here for." He nuzzled Hope's cleavage, with a guttural howl.

Only Angus noticed Amos's short sprint up the stairs and quick return to the bar. Shortly thereafter, Amanda returned to the taproom, stopped at the bar to confer with Amos, and hustled out the door.

ΩΩΩ

Tuesday, October 18, 1768

It was nearly high noon on Battery Alley in the extreme north end of Boston, not far from the Old North Church, as the lanky old sailor made his way to the side door of the Salutation Tavern. After gazing up and down the narrow alley to be certain he wasn't noticed, he straightened his red stocking cap to better conceal his identity and opened the door quietly. It took a moment for his eyes to adjust to the darkness of the tavern taproom. Immediately, he recognized the whispering voice of the fat man. "Over here, to your left."

Sitting at the farthest corner table, lost in the shadows, the sailor whispered, "What are you trying to do? We can't meet like this during the day."

"Hush up and listen," said the fat man. "We have a serious problem." Leaning forward deliberately, he continued, "Yesterday, two harlots stopped by the state house complaining about the death of a strumpet."

"Are those doxies still complaining about that? I thought that mess was finished more than a year ago. If I recall correctly, it was me who provided the man who did it. We both know he wasn't actually guilty. Sadly, he was too dead to be questioned or defend himself," chuckled the old salt.

Shaking his head in irritation, the fat man said, "I agree. We handled that dead doxy as needed; but this is another one."

"Another dead whore!" The old sailor put his hand to his head in thought, sitting back heavily in his chair. "Where did this one happen?"

"You mean to tell me that you don't know about this one?" queried the fat man. Sipping his tankard of ale, he continued, "According to the strumpets at the statehouse, the girl was killed at the Bunch of Grapes. They grumbled about this being the second one and that our sheriff was 'good for nothing.' They were demanding justice from the governor."

"Sorry I wasn't there to hear this firsthand. What did Governor Bernard say?" asked the sailor, scratching his head.

"He promised the usual investigation, of course, and reminded them of the capture of the last criminal who killed one of their ladies." The fat man smiled. He took a hearty draught from his tankard, muttering, "Nonetheless, this was not our doing. One of the girls from the Snug Harbor contacted me this morning, and it seems she is pretty sure who actually did this and why. Now listen to me; this is how we should handle this . . ."

$$\Omega\Omega\Omega$$

Zeke Teezle sat sweating in the back room of his candle shop, the air reeking of tallow. As he pored over his ledgers and figures, he occasionally looked up to be certain that Emmet Glunt was earning his daily bread, when he heard the bell that hung over the front door ring. "See who that is, Emmet," commanded Teezle, without looking up.

Glunt shuffled his chubby bulk to the front, grumbling under his breath, "Glunt do this! Glunt do that! Why can't he move his own shifty skinny arse for a change, I wonder?"

He returned to the back room, saying, "That's strange; there was nobody there. I wonder who rang the bell."

Teezle looked up from his figures. "No one there, you say?"

"Only this on the front counter," said Glunt. He handed Teezle a sealed envelope.

The envelope simply read, "Zeke Teezle." He looked on the back to find a wax seal with the imprint of "Ω." As hot as it was in the room, Zeke felt a sudden chill. He turned ashen and his lips quivered. "When Gerty returns from wherever she has gone to, tell her I had to step out for a while," he mumbled.

"Where you goin', Mr. Teezle?" asked Glunt, feigning concern.

"Never you mind, Glunt; I gotta do something or go somewhere or whatever," muttered Teezle, grabbing his tricorn hat and cape, as he ambled out the door. He yelled over his shoulder, "You be sure to say nothing to Gerty about me gittin' a letter, you hear me, boy?" He paused before his shop on Milk Street, looking up and down the street for a face; not one he would find familiar, but rather someone who might be watching him closely. There was no one. He sauntered across the street on his way to the British Coffee House. "It would be safe there to read this, away from the prying eyes of Gerty and Glunt," he said to himself.

Seated at a rear table near the hearth, Zeke found the British Coffee House nearly empty of patrons this early in the day, as this was the chosen haven for most British army and navy officers and the merchants. Sipping a tankard of ale, he opened the letter and read quietly.

Teezle,

We have it on good word that you have once again murdered a strumpet. You are directed to visit your contact at the Snug Harbor Tavern tonight. She has detailed instructions for you. Destroy this note and keep the appointment. Otherwise, Sheriff Greenleaf could somehow learn of your escapades, you naughty little man. Remember, there is Hope.

Ω

Casually, Teezle guided the note over the burning candle on the table, letting the ashes flutter to the floor. "Damn that sergeant major," he mumbled to himself. He downed his tankard and wandered back to his Milk Street candle shop.

ΩΩΩ

CHAPTER 15

Friday, October 21, 1768

EVERY WINDOW IN Faneuil Hall was lit with candles, and the entire building seemed to exude warmth, despite the cold chill wind coming from the harbor. An honor guard from the Fourteenth Regiment stood at attention, aligned at the main doorway. Their red coats seemed to glow in contrast to the white-chalked facings and their white breeches. It was obvious that hours were spent shining the brass fittings of their belts.

Inside, Sam Adams, standing in the company of Hancock, Dr. Warren, Dr. Church, and his cousin John, said, "I must admit that His Majesty's army and navy certainly know how to dress up a soiree. Did you notice the sharpness of those redcoats standing guard at the door? I'd never really been this close to the bastards." He sipped his punch as he gazed about the hall. He leaned forward, adding in a whisper, "Did you ever see so many Tories in one place? Let's be sure to take note of who is here, and who is complying with the Nonimportation Agreement. And look. There's John Mein. No great surprise to see him here, the Tory bastard. I can just imagine what he will write in the *Boston Chronicle*. No doubt he will describe General Gage as riding into town on a white charger to save the citizens of Boston from some great imaginary evil."

Hancock shook his head, with Dorothy Quincy holding his arm closely. "Sam," he groused, "can't you give it a rest for just one evening? This has turned out to be quite a party, considering they had to move it from Hutchinson's home to Faneuil Hall. Now, just try to enjoy the moment, for god's sake."

"God's sake has nothing to do with it, Hancock. This accolade to an interloping general is really an insult to Boston society. Why doesn't he go back to New York?

Or better yet, back to London? What do you think about this insult, Ms. Quincy?" asked Adams, as his glare shifted from one group to another.

Smoothing her navy blue silk dress, trimmed in shimmering gold ribbon, Dorothy smiled. "Now, Mr. Adams, you know it's not fair to ask me such a question. I'm certain all the other ladies here would echo the sentiment that any occasion to dance and socialize is worthy of the effort. After all, it is merely a social gathering, is it not?" At her side, Aunt Lydia, clad in decorous black, interjected, "I agree with Dorothy." Wagging her finger, she added, "John, you promised that this would be a joyous evening. And, furthermore, I will not tolerate embarrassment to your Uncle Thomas's memory. He was loyal to the Crown all his days, and I expect the same of you and your friends here."

Dr. Church grinned with a feigned bow. "Ms. Quincy and Aunt Lydia are quite right!" Turning to Adams, he frowned, "Now Sam, you promised civility, and I expect you to keep your promise. I got us invited as leaders of the loyal opposition. I emphasize, loyal! Now keep a civil tongue in your mouth, even if you can't keep a civil thought in your head." Looking keenly at Sam in mock appraisal, he turned to his cousin John Adams, "Is that red suit the only set of clothing he has, John? If I didn't know better, I'd say he wants to be a bloody lobsterback himself."

Sam turned, glaring, "I heard that Doctor. And let me remind you that there are some things not to be bantered about. You just never mind my clothing." He added, gesturing to the young merchant, "Do you think I'm some preening peacock like our dear friend Hancock here?"

Dr. Warren said, "I agree with Dr. Church. Let's tone down the verbal banter and save it for the Green Dragon. We are here to keep our ears open and to remind everyone here that we are all loyal to the Crown."

"Speaking of the Crown, just where are the governor and General Gage? It seems strange that they would be late for their own party," said Hancock, as he straightened the lace at his cuffs and throat. His navy blue brocade coat was trimmed in gold piping.

Sam Adams simply rolled his eyes at this preening. "I think I could use another glass of punch. If I didn't know better, I'd assume that both he and Ms. Quincy had joined the Royal Navy," he said to no one in particular. Just then a small entourage of junior officers arrived, resplendent in the red coats of the army and the blue and gold of the Royal Navy. "Would you just look at that," added Sam.

Following his gaze, Hancock suddenly coughed as though he was choking. Dorothy Quincy, still holding his arm, muttered in mock anger, "Easy with that punch, John."

Gazing at the arched entryway, Sam said in a matter-of-fact tone, "I doubt it's the punch, Ms. Quincy." Among the small throng gathered at the foot of the stairs, Hancock and Adams found their eyes riveted on one army captain, the only one with a lady on his arm. The raven-haired woman, dressed in a crimson satin dress with white lace trim, was the center of military attention. Her necklace, fashioned from a gold Spanish coin suspended from a red ribbon, accented the low cut bodice and her ample bosom.

"How very rude to be staring like that, John!" scolded Dorothy. Then leaning toward Hancock to maintain decorum, she whispered, "Who is that dark-haired lady on the arm of that officer? She keeps looking over here." Aunt Lydia frowned conspicuously, saying, "I strongly doubt that my John would know that woman or anyone like her. It is obvious she doesn't come from good family." Squinting with her eyes to get a better look, she added, "With her bosom showing like that, she could possibly be a common doxy, for all we know. Who else would wander arm in arm with a redcoat." Turning to Hancock, she pleaded, "Please tell me, John, that you don't know that woman."

From the other side of the room, clinging to Captain Preston's arm, Amanda Griffith smiled broadly at Hancock and his friends. She then gazed about the room, realizing that more than half the men in attendance, both radical and loyalist, had at one time or another enjoyed the pleasures of the Snug Harbor Tavern.

Adams pulled Hancock aside, asking quietly, "Isn't that the same woman I met at that tavern down on the wharf, John?"

Glancing over his shoulder, Hancock did his best to conceal his amusement and replied, "By god, I do believe you are right, Sam; it could be the same lady."

"Lady my arse," scoffed Adams. "What could that officer be thinking by bringing a woman of that caliber to this dastardly event?"

Benjamin Church rushed to their side to join them, saying, "Gentlemen, do you have any idea who that lady is over there?"

Hancock, squeezing Adams's arm to keep him quiet, said quickly, "What lady are you speaking of, Ben?" Church gestured in the direction of Amanda, to which Hancock added, "No idea whatsoever, Ben. Who could she be?"

"I do believe it's the same woman who runs a grog shop on the waterfront; not that I have ever been there myself, you know." Gazing intently again, he added, "By Jove, I'm certain of it. I've had a few of her girls, er . . . employees, come to me for . . . health issues."

"Imagine that," said Hancock, the mere hint of a smile on his face. He then watched in awe, as Amanda seemed to glide across the floor toward him with Captain Preston. Knowing there was no escape, Hancock returned to Dorothy Quincy's side.

"Good evening, gentlemen, and to you, madam. Captain Thomas Preston, at your service," said Captain Preston with a military bow to Dorothy. "May I introduce Ms. Amanda Griffith? I am with the Twenty-ninth Regiment, and as an officer in His Royal Majesty's service, I would like to thank you for joining us this evening. Forgive the intrusion, but our commanding officer has ordered us junior officers to mingle and introduce ourselves. Hopefully, we can get to know each other better."

Hancock took the lead, introducing everyone, adding, "It is indeed a pleasure to meet you, Captain, and also you, Ms . . . . ? I must apologize. I didn't quite catch your name."

Amanda, a steely grin on her face and her eyes locked icily onto his, said, "Griffith. Amanda Griffith is the name. It is a pleasure to meet you all, especially you, Mr. Hancock. Ms. Quincy here is so very fortunate to have you as an escort this evening." Her eyes were not smiling. To Dorothy, she added, "Mr. Hancock has shown himself to be most generous to those less fortunate on the waterfront, Ms. Quincy. Most ladies in Boston would consider it an honor to merely share a glass of punch with him."

Dorothy blushed, "John certainly is generous to a fault. But look at you, Ms. Griffith; it seems you have the entire British army with you."

Hearing that, Preston smiled. "Not if I have anything to say about it. My comrades in arms can look all they want, but Ms. Griffith here is a very special lady, and she is here with me."

Hancock cleared his throat, "That certainly seems to be the case, doesn't it, Captain?" Guiding Preston away from the others toward the punch table, he added to the others, "If you will excuse us, ladies. Perhaps the captain and I should get more punch for you ladies. And you, Captain, can tell me about – "

Suddenly, the majordomo pounded his staff, announcing the arrival of Governor Bernard and General Gage. The governor's wife was smiling at his side while General Gage had an auburn-haired young lady clinging to his arm.

In the din of the expected applause, John Adams said to his fellow radicals, "Well, gentlemen, there he is in all his red and gold splendor, and here's our opportunity. Who among us shall sally forth to fetch our redcoat-in-chief?"

All the other eyes were riveted on General Gage, who was busily engaged in shaking hands with every Tory in attendance; all except the eyes of Dr. Church, Hancock and Amanda, that is. They stood in amazement at the visage of the auburn-haired beauty at Gage's side. Her hair was upswept with a small replica of the British Union Jack functioning as a hairpin, and her low cut dress was made of white satin trimmed in scarlet ribbon, displaying her more-than-ample décolletage.

Captain Preston and Hancock returned, accompanied by a liveried servant, bearing a tray of glasses. Hancock announced, smiling, "The good captain and I felt it wise for our entire party to recharge our glasses, and this fine man has agreed to assist us." As glasses of punch were passed around, Hancock casually asked, "Just out of curiosity, Captain Preston, I don't suppose you know who that lady in white is at the side of General Gage. Could that possibly be his wife?"

Preston responded for all to hear, "I'm told that is a Ms. Cross from New York. It seems she asked permission to accompany the general; something about business or relations here in Boston." He gazed at Gage and his party adding, "Of course, I'm just a captain and am certainly not told everything, but rumor has it that she has strong contacts in Parliament."

Amanda elbowed Preston's ribs, "Now don't you give me that stuff about you being a mere captain. I bet you're more fun than General Gage on his best day."

"And you are more fun than any London lass with contacts in Parliament, Amanda." Preston smiled, looking into her mesmerizing blue eyes.

Sam Adams nudged Hancock, saying, "It seems we won't have to approach Gage after all. He's making the rounds of the hall with Governor Bernard at his side. Can you imagine that?"

As the honored party approached, Ben Church stepped forward and bowed with a proffered hand, "Governor Bernard, it is indeed a pleasure to see you and your lovely bride once again."

Bernard smiled. "General Gage, this is Dr. Benjamin Church, my family physician. Perhaps he could introduce his colleagues and friends." Looking at Amanda with a half smile, he added, "Unfortunately, I myself do not know everyone here this evening." Church introduced the radicals in their turn, with Sam Adams, and Hancock the last in the queue.

Hancock, gripping Gage's hand firmly, said, "General Gage, may I introduce Ms. Dorothy Quincy. Her father is one of our best legal minds in Boston. And who, may I ask, is this lovely young lady with you this evening?"

Gage beamed, "This, Mr. Hancock, is Ms. Angel Cross. She is on her way back to London and with – "

Interrupting the general's story, Angel stepped forward, her eyes wide in disbelief. Standing between Hancock and the tall redcoat captain, she found Amanda staring with blazing blue eyes. "My goodness, General, these fine people are not interested in me and my travel plans." Looking at the host of patriots, she added, "Would you all please call me Angel? I simply hate this 'Ms. Cross' business that I always hear from these military gentlemen." Feigning a small stumble, she suddenly fell toward Amanda and into the arms of Hancock. She whispered hurriedly, "You don't know me tonight; we can talk later!" Standing again and regaining her composure, she continued, "Oh, how clumsy of me. Please do forgive."

Gage, offering his arm for support, laughed. "Easy, my dear!" To the others, he added, "It seems that Ms. Cross still has her sea legs from her time on His Majesty's frigate."

Offering glasses of punch from the tray, Hancock said casually, "General Gage, we are certainly glad you have taken time to visit our small town. As you know, heretofore, we have never been garrisoned by His Majesty's troops. And – "

"And we are wondering who it is that invited you to invade our small town," interjected Sam Adams.

"Nothing subtle about that," muttered Dr. Warren to John Adams, under his breath.

John responded just as quietly, "Sam was always one for the frontal approach. In the future, let's be sure to keep him writing and not speaking." Just as quickly, he spoke up interjecting himself, "What my cousin Sam here means to say, General Gage, is that many of our townspeople are concerned and even a bit perturbed about this military campaign. Could it be that the French are invading New England again?"

Gage's ready smile was balanced by the shrewd appraisal of his icy grey eyes, "Gentlemen, perhaps your question should be directed at Governor Bernard here. His

Majesty's troops merely serve at the pleasure of the civil authorities. This is certainly no 'invasion,' as you suggest."

With all eyes turned on him, Bernard gave a toothy grin, "It seems, gentlemen, that London has learned of the harsh treatment the tax and customs officials have received by our street rabble here in Boston. I'm really not certain who it is in London that ordered our military friends to Boston, but we must admit that the mob has dispersed, hasn't it?"

Sam Adams, his shaking hand quite evident, responded slowly, "Mob? Did you say mob? Why, Governor! How could we, as members of the Massachusetts Assembly, know anything about the rabble of a mob?"

"Actually, gentlemen, this mob situation seems to be the explanation of why we are here. Unfortunately, I left the original documents ordering our movements in my New York office. But I assure you, as soon as things have quieted for His Majesty's customs officials to do their duty, we shall consider our tasks completed. As for the French, they wouldn't dare consider coming back to these shores," said Gage matter-of-factly. His eyes were cold, measuring each man in the party.

Easing the tension, Benjamin Church smiled. "What is all this talk of mobs and the French? Are we not here to eat, drink, dance, and enjoy the peace that His Majesty's army and navy have provided? There is an excellent menu prepared for the occasion, and I suggest that we all make our way to the tables for a fine repast." Maneuvering between Gage and Angel, Church continued, "Please let me escort you to the dining area, General." To Angel, he whispered aside under his breath, "Ms. Cross, we must speak privately. I will expect to hear from you."

Seeing this, Hancock pulled Church from his position, saying, "Excuse me, General Gage, but I need to speak with Dr. Church for a moment." To Church, he gritted his teeth, "I'm not sure what you have in mind, Ben. But tonight is not the time for it. Do you understand me?"

With a furrowed brow, Church pulled his sleeve away from Hancock's grip. "You forget yourself, sir. Do you recall who that woman is? I was merely – "

"I know exactly what you are thinking, Ben. Let's discuss this later. Meanwhile, keep a smile on your face and imagine that you never saw that girl before this evening. We don't need a scene tonight."

Sam Adams moved to Hancock's side as the crowd made its way to the dining area. "What's going on, John? I recognize that woman and – "

"Later, Sam! Later!" exclaimed Hancock, as he eased his way to Dorothy Quincy's side.

As the group tried to find their seats, Amanda sidled over to Angel Cross and whispered, "You'd best find a way to make it to the Snug Harbor, young lady." She squeezed her hand tightly.

Angel responded with her own terse whisper, "And what exactly are you doing with this captain of the guard, my fine lady?"

Her answer was Amanda's cold icy stare, which was immediately replaced with a broad grin, as she took Captain Preston's arm. Pulling her closer, Preston gushed,

"Let us enjoy this dinner, Amanda. I'm told it will delight the soul. General Gage has brought his own kitchen orderlies to prepare a fine beef dish, and I'm told the plum pudding is to die for."

"Let us pray that no one has to die for anything, Captain," said Amanda, loudly, as she and Preston trailed Angel Cross on the arm of General Gage.

ΩΩΩ

The streets around Faneuil Hall were littered with carriages, as the revelers departed shortly after midnight. The Tories, arm in arm with both army and navy officers, all headed for the British Coffee House on King Street to continue the evening while General Gage and Governor Bernard made their way to the Old State House. John Hancock, helping Dorothy into his carriage, noticed Sam Adams standing there alone observing the mass exodus. "Come along, Sam. You can ride with us. We're all headed to the Green Dragon. I have to drop Dorothy off at the mansion; then we can meet the others."

Adams stood there alone in his red suit, gripping his walking stick like a weapon. "Just look at the hypocrisy of it all, John. After playing niceties with us, Bernard and Gage head back to the Old State House to plan our undoing." He shook his walking stick in that direction.

"Lighten up, Sam. Doctor Warren told you that you could get mired in apoplexy or some such malady. Hell, we just had a fine dinner, and you must admit Gage's chef is a wizard in the kitchen," said Hancock, joyously.

"All right," said Sam resignedly, as he eased into the carriage. "Perhaps you're right. After all . . ."

Just as the carriage was about to move, there was a rap on the door. Frank, the black liveried driver, yelled, "Get back, lad. Do you want to get yourself run over out here in the darkness?"

"What is it, Frank?" asked Hancock, loudly, as he peered out the side window. "Oh! It's you, Imp."

Imp stood at the door, panting heavily with Angus standing at his side. He clutched his small tricorn hat with the red feather in his grimy hands, as if in prayer. "Beg pardon, Mr. Hancock, but I don't know exactly where to go. Have you seen Miz Griffith tonight? I must find her."

Looking at Dorothy with a side glance, Hancock said, "This won't take a moment." He alit from the carriage and guided Imp from the middle of the street. "What are you doing out at this hour, Imp? And what are you doing with the red feather showing? You should know that it is to be displayed only when you are on official business. You'll have the High Sons of Liberty going crazy, trying to protect you." He glanced up and down the street, satisfying himself that all the revelers had departed. "Now, tell me, what do you need to see Mrs. Griffith about?"

Having gained his composure and his breath, Imp leaned forward, speaking rapidly, "Amos sent me with Angus here for protection. It's an emergency at the Snug Harbor."

"Slow down! Slow down! What devastating emergency would make Amos send you out at this hour? Why didn't he come himself?" asked Hancock, calmly.

Sam Adams, showing his head at the carriage window, yelled impatiently, "Come on, Hancock. We don't have time for trifling with young street urchins at this hour."

"Just a moment, Sam; be there in a minute," stated Hancock. Easing himself down on his haunches, he continued, "Now what's the problem at the Snug Harbor that can't wait until morning?"

Imp shook his head impatiently and continued his rapid rambling, "It's the body, Mr. Hancock. We don't exactly know what to do with it. Amos figured we could throw him in the harbor, but Hope and Purity thought we should check with Miz Griffith first."

"Body?" asked Hancock sternly, his eyes widening. "What body?"

"The dead soldier; it seems someone killed him . . . and – "

Hancock stood abruptly, rushing to the carriage door. "Sam, would you mind seeing Dorothy to the mansion? I have a situation that needs tending to immediately."

Dorothy grumbled, "John Hancock, this is turning into a strange evening, if I do say so myself. I can understand your meeting your friends at the Green Dragon. Mr. Adams was kind enough to explain things to me. But now you go traipsing off with this dirty little boy."

Shaking his head, "I'll make it up to you; I promise, Dorothy. Now, Sam, see that she is safe behind doors, and I'll meet you and the others as soon as possible." Adams merely nodded, as Hancock rapped the door, adding, "Frank, get that team moving. You know where to go."

ΩΩΩ

As Hancock and Imp walked quickly through Dock Square toward Hancock's Wharf, Imp shared what he knew of the dead soldier. Stopping for a moment, Hancock said, "Listen carefully, Imp. Do you know where Mr. Revere lives?" Imp nodded. "Walk there quickly, without being noticed. Go to his backdoor, where the kitchen is. Tell Mr. Revere that I need him immediately. Tell absolutely no one but him where you are going. Then bring him to the Snug Harbor Tavern." Imp started to rush off. "Walk, so you won't be noticed, Imp. And now would be a good time to wear that red feather. I'll see you at the tavern."

ΩΩΩ

Candles were burning brightly in the governor's office, as Bernard, Gage, their ladies and the balance of their entourage shared a bottle of Madeira. Half perched on the edge of his dark mahogany desk, the governor said, "Well, General! It seems to me the evening was a profound success, and I'm certain the ladies would agree."

Gage, seated in an easy chair, smiled. "Quite right, Governor Bernard. Now that I see you have significant Tory support, I'm convinced that the reports I've received in the past might have been a bit exaggerated."

"Unfortunately, Thomas Hutchinson was not able to attend this evening due to his judicial duties. I mention it merely because he would take issue with the presence of our radical friends," said Bernard, sipping his wine smugly.

Gage grinned broadly. "If that small rabble of pompous asses is all that stands in the way of His Majesty's troops, we have little to concern ourselves. The picture I was handed gave me visions of ogres behind every corner, armed and ready for insurrection. Now I meet one evil old man, a skinny doctor, a chubby lawyer, and one pompous merchant. It's hardly a formidable force to stand against even the weakest of my men!"

Standing at the sideboard, the fat man adjusted the lace at his sleeve. "I would suggest, General, we exercise a bit of caution; and also let me remind you that small group of men wield considerable influence with the Boston mob and the Massachusetts Assembly." As he refilled his glass, he added, "Not that I wish to put a damper on your enthusiasm, but I know these men well and understand their perception of reality. They understand the mob."

"My good man, I have but one question," replied Gage, "of what Boston mob do you speak? Since our arrival, my troops have yet to encounter one man brave enough to utter one word in opposition to the Crown, let alone raise his hand in anger."

"I pray you are right, General. Perhaps the mere sight of fixed bayonets has tempered the courage of our rabble. But I urge you and your men to remain vigilant," added the fat man, downing his drink and belching audibly.

"Just out of curiosity, did any of you ladies hear of anything regarding any evil plot against us here in Boston?" asked Gage sarcastically.

Angel Cross stood with her small glass of wine, saying, "I met this divine lady this evening. Her name was Quincy. I do believe with Mr. Hancock. She seemed to know absolutely nothing about any discontent whatsoever. Either there is nothing afoot, or these colonials do not speak to their women."

Mrs. Bernard sniffed, "Actually, my dear, there are some things we ladies are better off not knowing. As for this blather of insurrection, the Stamp Act mess is behind us, and this nonimportation of English goods is a bit of an inconvenience for many. Fortunately, we get all we need via British warships these days, thanks to Commodore Hood and General Gage. The Tories of the town seem to be absolutely delighted. Did you hear John Mein at dinner this evening? I swear if it weren't for his wealth, he would gladly enlist in His Majesty's army personally. You have made a great impression, General, and we thank you."

"We can rest easy, General Gage," said Bernard. "No one would dare raise his fist against the finest army in the world. The rabble trembles at the sight of a redcoat, and we had the privilege of stuffing that fact in their faces this evening, along with a bit of beef and plum pudding, I might add." The laughter in the room was contagious, as more Madeira was poured.

ΩΩΩ

CHAPTER 16

"HE'S DEAD ALL right," said Hancock, standing in Hope's bedroom. The blade of the halberd had shattered the collarbone and was firmly embedded in Sergeant Major Delaney's chest, as he lay with his limbs splayed across the floor, a grimace on his face. Hancock, nearly slipping on a pile of candle wax near the doorway, stepped carefully around the thick pool of blood to glance outside at the harbor. "It's just a few hours before daybreak," he said, turning back to the room. Amos stood leaning against the doorjamb with his arms folded, as the girls stood in the hallway behind him.

Amos said, "I got the taproom cleared, and there's no one about that I knows of, Mr. Hancock. But what we gonna do with this body? If the army finds him here, we are . . ." He turned at the rumble of footsteps on the stairs. He too nearly slipped on the pile of candle wax. "What the – ?"

"It's me," yelled Imp. Trailing behind him, Paul Revere stepped into the bedroom and stopped abruptly. "Sweet Jesus!" muttered Revere. Looking at Hancock, he said, "I was going to ask why you summoned me at this hour, Mr. Hancock. But I just figured that one out." He paused to assess the sight before him, then added, "Now I could ask a lot of questions, but looking at this, I figure you might have a few ideas."

Hancock frowned, "I do indeed, Mr. Revere. And thank you for coming. Our immediate issue is to get him out of here without – "

More footsteps rumbled at the stairway. Hancock looked sternly at Amos, "I thought you said – " Suddenly, Amanda rushed into the doorway. Her gasp was quite audible. "What in hell – ?" Looking at each set of eyes, Amanda regained her composure quickly.

Hope suddenly barged in, nudging Amos aside. "Amanda! Thank God you're here. Let me explain. I just stepped out to the privy for a moment and, when I returned, I found the Sergeant Major like you see him, in that pool of blood. I didn't do nothin', I promise!" she said sobbing.

Amanda held Hope by her shoulders, saying, "Don't say another word. We can talk later. Right now, we have to take action." Nodding to Hancock, she said firmly, "Imp, I want you to get yourself down to the main door and make sure no one, and I mean absolutely no one, enters the taproom. Amos, get down to the storeroom and fetch a bucket of water and some rags. Girls, you get to your rooms and clean things up. We can talk later. Now all of you, git!"

Left alone with Hancock and Revere, Amanda said quietly, "Don't ask, gentlemen. I wasn't here all evening. I have no idea what happened here. But most importantly, what do I do with him?" She sat on the edge of the bed, staring at the redcoat body. She shifted her gaze to Delaney's rumpled uniform, which had been tossed across a small chair and then again at the motionless body. Unconsciously, she began to toy with the pleats of her red satin dress, lost in thought, her blue eyes staring at nothing.

Revere stood at the doorjamb, uncomfortably scratching his head, when Hancock stepped to the edge of the bed snapping his fingers, "I've got it! He's simply deserted. As far as anyone knows, it's not his body that's missing; it's him that is missing from duty. Let the redcoats think this one is simply another deserter, lost to the hills of the Massachusetts countryside."

Revere smiled. "Just like all the others, John! It's perfect, as explanations go. I'll arrange for a large fish cart to haul the body out to the countryside for burial. The guards at Boston Neck never check a fish cart, with all the flies and the stink of it all. I'll be back shortly with a few Sons of Liberty."

Before he scurried down the hall, Hancock yelled, "Make sure you get reliable men, Paul. And the fewer, the better! We don't need all of Boston knowing about this. And keep Mackintosh out of it this time. We need sober men for this." Again, he stared at the large pool of sticky blood.

With everyone gone, Amanda looked at Hancock with a pained expression, tears welling in her eyes, "For god's sake, John. If word of this gets out, the redcoats will hang us all."

In a cold steady voice, Hancock said, "Revere will remove the body, and you can forget it ever happened. But first, you must get this mess cleaned up and burn that uniform. Have Amos toss the halberd into the harbor before daylight."

"Thank you, John," mumbled Amanda, still fingering her dress.

Walking to the doorway, Hancock placed his hand on her shoulder and raised her chin to face him. "I recommend you change nothing in your relationships with the Twenty-ninth Regiment and that Captain Preston. To do otherwise would raise suspicion; and that suspicion would guarantee an investigation of this man's missing, no matter what we do. The desertion of privates is fairly common these days, but a sergeant major deserting is quite another issue. I'm certain that his men knew of his whereabouts this evening, as they usually do. The girls had better come up with a common tale to tell, and that goes for Amos and Imp too. As for you, you have the perfect alibi. You were dining with General Gage. Now I have people to see before daybreak, Amanda. We can talk more tomorrow." With that, Hancock rushed down the stairs and through the taproom. He paused at the main door where Imp stood guard. He patted the small boy's head and, resting on his haunches, grabbed him by the small shoulders, saying, "You did well this evening, Imp. Now you follow Mrs. Griffith's lead on this, and no trouble will befall you good people." He stepped out onto Fish Street and headed toward the Green Dragon Tavern. There was still work to do.

ΩΩΩ

Saturday, October 22, 1768

The midmorning sun beamed through the windows of the taproom, washing the whitewashed walls in a warm yellow glow. Sadly, that was the only thing glowing at the Snug Harbor Tavern, as the pall of imminent doom hovered over the sustained silence that permeated the small gathering of people at the rear table. While Amos stood as a sentinel behind the bar, Amanda and the girls sat sipping tea, lost in thought.

Suddenly, the front door crashed open, and Big Bessie Clump rumbled into the taproom. Without losing her stride to the rear table, she ordered, "Punch for everyone, Amos, and be quick about it." She stopped at the table, her chubby arms spread wide. "Well look at this, would you! If I didn't know better, I'd say we were in mourning." Grabbing a tankard from Amos's tray, she took a seat next to Amanda. "Listen, girlie, and this goes for you all; Imp told a bit about what happened here last night and – "

Amanda glared, "That little bastard! I told him not to tell any – "

"Easy, girl! Easy! Don't be a hussy and get your shift in a bundle. I saw him wandering over to the *Gazette* and simply asked how you folks were doing. Seems he needed someone to talk with, and he sure couldn't find it here." Patting Amanda's hand, she added, "Rest easy! I'm the only one he spoke to. No one else at the Bunch of Grapes knows about your dead soldier."

Amanda took a heavy draught of her punch, saying nothing.

"What did you do with the dirty redcoat? Did he leave any hard money behind? Which of you girls killed the bastard? Do you know his name?" asked Bessie in a rapid-fire monotone. Seeing only blank stares, she downed her punch. "What seems to be the problem here?"

Amanda leaned forward, "Bessie, stop and think a moment. I've had a redcoat killed here at the Snug Harbor. Shortly after daybreak, three grenadiers stopped by searching for a certain Sergeant Major Delaney who did not report for duty at his appointed time. They had word that he planned to stop by here last night."

"Holy Mother of God! What tale did you tell them?" blurted Bessie. Adding more loudly, "Amos, another round of punch; I think we need it."

"Amos told them that Delaney stopped by and then left after a tankard of ale," murmured Amanda, sipping her punch. "I don't think they were convinced, but they left to check other places. I have a feeling they will be back."

"So what if they return? Just stick to your story," said Big Bessie, scratching her midriff. "You gotta be bold when you're lyin'."

Amanda shook her head, "Easy for you to say, Bessie. If they look around, we have a lot of explaining to do. We cleaned as best we could, but the blood stain up there is huge. Looks like we were butchering hogs all night."

"He was a mighty big man," added Purity. "I ain't never seen so much blood. I didn't know a body could have that much blood!"

"Enough about the blood already!" shouted Amanda. She added more quietly, "There must be some way to clean that up before the redcoats return. There's no time to replace the boards and, besides, that would be clear evidence of something gone wrong."

Just then two burly dockworkers wandered into the taproom, lugging two small kegs. Amos immediately said sternly, "We are closed right now, gents." Angus growled, as if echoing Amos's words.

Ignoring the comment, one man said, "Where do you want us to put these small barrels?"

Amanda arose with one fist on her hip, "I ordered no barrels of anything. What is this?"

Shrugging his shoulders, the man answered, "Makes no difference to us, lady! Mr. Hancock sent us with these barrels of red paint and these brushes, sayin' you might have need of them. But if you are refusin' them, we can just – "

Suddenly rushing forward, Amanda quickly said in a soothing tone, "Oh, thank you. I simply forgot about this order. Please thank Mr. Hancock for me. We've been meaning to paint this place for some time." Both men doffed their caps, leaving the kegs of paint in the middle of the taproom floor.

Looking at the empty doorway, then the kegs, and then Amanda, Amos asked, "When did you start planning to paint, Ms. Amanda? I don't recollect us orderin' no paint and brushes." He scratched his head in wonder.

Bessie sat with a sardonic grin, sipping her punch as Amanda took charge of the situation. "Girls, get into your dirtiest clothes; we have work to do."

"What kind of work?" they asked in unison.

"For starters, we will paint every bedroom floor. Do you understand me?" stated Amanda.

Hope looked at the kegs on the floor. "But look at this, Amanda, the paint is an ungodly red. Who would ever paint a bedroom floor red?" Suddenly, her eyes brightened. "Oh! I get it. We should do my room first. Come on Faith, Purity, Chastity!" They scampered up the stairs.

Leaning on the bar, his chin buried in his meaty fists, Amos grinned. "What else you plan on paintin', Ms. Amanda?"

Bessie laughed heartily. "Why don't you paint the whole damned place, Amanda. Red would be a great color for our kind of business, don't you think? Hell, if it works for you, I might do the same thing for the Bunch of Grapes."

Amanda joined the laughter, "A red business for redcoats. I wonder what Captain Preston will think about that?"

Bessie suddenly grimaced, "Captain who?"

"Preston," said Amanda. "He's a Captain with the Twenty-ninth."

"That's who I thought you were talking about," said Bessie.

Leaning forward, Amanda added with a note of braggadocio, "You should know that he took me to the governor's reception last night, Bessie. And I met General Gage at the dinner."

"A little out of your league, don't you think?" queried Big Bessie, sipping her tankard.

"What league? I'm as good as any of them snooty bitches in town. Besides, I'm particular who I share my crib with, and it ain't just anyone. You know that!" said Amanda sternly, wagging her finger.

"Don't wag at me," stated Bessie, shaking her jowls. "I'm your friend, Amanda, and don't you forget it. I've been down that road, and I figure that this Captain Preston and his cronies can cause nothing but trouble for you." In a more secret tone, she added, "Besides, I thought you had a sort of understanding with Mr. Hancock; and he's the last man I can imagine sharing his livestock with a redcoat."

"I'm not any man's 'livestock,' Bessie. I deal with whoever I please. And right now Thomas Preston seems to fill my needs quite well, thank you. Besides, that uppity Hancock had the gall to take that prissy Quincy girl to the ball in company with his old Aunt Lydia. What a sight that was!" Looking at the bar, she added, "Amos, bring us another round. All this talking is making me thirsty."

Bessie said, giggling, "Good idea. Now tell me everything, and don't leave a thing out. Who else did you see there at the party?"

Amanda laughed. "Now that I think about it, Bessie, I don't think I have much to worry about. Every damned Tory and ranking redcoat saw me there. Many of those devils were customers of ours. Can you believe that! And I got to see them with their wives. I don't think they will want to make too much trouble for me, as I will promise to testify about a lot of things, if you get my drift." She nudged Bessie with her elbow.

"Now my girl is talkin'," chortled Bessie. She drained her tankard quickly. "I think I'll wander over to Hancock's and see if there is any red paint left. We might start a trend with red paint and red lights, Amanda."

Watching her leave, Amanda turned to Amos, "Let's get these floors painted, Amos. Otherwise, I want you to plan for business as usual this evening. If anyone questions you about a missing redcoat, just ask if this could be simply another deserter.

Now get one of these paint kegs upstairs and the other in the back storeroom." She rushed upstairs with her hands full of brushes.

As Amos easily lifted a keg to his massive shoulders and ambled to the stairway, he mumbled to himself, "Dead body? Deserter? One strange way for white people to desert the army, if you ask me!"

ΩΩΩ

Later that evening, the Snug Harbor Tavern found itself mired in the usual heavy blend of odors and noise. A large fire was ablaze at the hearth and an element of the Twenty-ninth Regiment had arrayed tables and chairs around the warmest part of the taproom. A small contingent of the Royal Navy had joined them in song.

> *While sailin' the sea, we started to grumble,*
> *And once ashore, we all seem to stumble,*
> *After six weeks at sea,*
> *We ain't drinkin' tea,*
> *We're havin' a Snug Harbor tumble.*

Amos laughed heartily as he delivered a round of tankards to the revelers.

"Thanks, my good man," yelled a paunchy private, as he hugged Faith who was perched firmly on his lap.

Handing him a tankard of ale, Amos asked, "What might you men be celebratin' tonight? If you don't mind me askin'."

"Not at all! Not at all!" slurred the soldier. He leaned forward, almost dumping Faith to the floor. "You see, we can't find the sergeant major. The bastard up and disappeared."

"Sorry to hear that," said Amos.

"Sorry? Sorry? Don't be sorry, my good man. Sergeant Major Delaney made our lives pure hell. And besides that, most of my mates here owed him a bundle in gambling losses. Now the poor bastard isn't here to collect. That's why we are celebratin'." He laughed loudly. "Isn't that why we are celebratin', mates?"

Standing at attention, letting Faith fall to the floor, he saluted with his tankard, "Here's to the memory of long lost Sergeant Major Delaney." The entire contingent of the Twenty-ninth Regiment stood at attention, echoing his salute. They then downed their tankards and ordered another round.

The singing continued, as Amos wandered back to the bar. Despite the October evening chill, Amos used a bar towel to mop his sweating brow. He poured a tankard of ale and slid it across the bar saying, "Crispus, you won't believe what them white soldiers is celebratin'."

Crispus Attucks, glancing over his shoulder, gave a toothy grin. "Let me guess; a little time off, maybe?" Leaning forward, he said in a whisper, "It would be best if you called me Michael, my friend. Michael Johnson is what folks know me as, at least for now."

Amos leaned forward, "All right, Michael. Seems they lost a sergeant major, and it's time for the privates to play." They both laughed.

Attucks asked, "How could you lose a sergeant major? You don't just misplace someone. Now aboard ship, it's possible to lose somebody. I seen that happen, but I don't understand this."

Amos winked, "Could be desertion. Lots a desertions goin' on these days. That's a fact."

Attucks turned to observe the redcoats in song. He mumbled to himself, "But sergeant majors don't desert. Leastwise, I ain't never heard of it."

The front door suddenly opened, letting in a draft of cold salt air. Standing in the doorway, Amos observed three tall grenadiers, still wearing their bearskin caps, which made them appear to be eight feet tall. Each was holding his Brown Bess at his side. Amos said, smiling, "What can I give you, gentle . . ." His voice trailed off, as Captain Preston marched in behind the grenadiers and approached the bar. The revelers of the Twenty-ninth had suddenly become quiet. The only sound in the taproom was the crackling in the fireplace and the growling of Angus. Amos picked up the puppy to quiet him.

Just at that moment, Purity came stumbling down the rear stairs, laughing arm in arm with little Private Hugh White. "Oh, Hughie, you little devil, you just say the cleverest things. I bet you must be the smartest soldier in the regiment."

Hugh White laughed boisterously. "You could say that. But for the life of me, no matter how bright I am, I can't figure out why anyone would paint their floors bright red. Whose crazy idea was that, Purity?" Suddenly, they both stopped and froze at the foot of the stairs, as the silence of the taproom assaulted their senses.

After a long silent pause, as everyone seemed to appraise the situation, Captain Preston said in a commanding tone to the grenadiers, "Maintain guard here at the door; no one enters or leaves." Turning to Amos, he asked, "Where is Mrs. Griffith?"

Amos, glaring at Preston, responded coldly, "I'm not exactly – "

"I'm right here," stated Amanda loudly, as she stood midway on the stairway, one hand on her hip. She was wearing a blue satin dress with white trim, her cleavage well exposed. A few soldiers gave an audible gasp, which was immediately muffled by Preston's glare.

Strutting down the length of the bar, passing Attucks as if he didn't exist, Preston pushed Hugh White aside. He paused at the stairway, saying, "We have to talk, madam . . . in private." He turned to stare at the taproom. "You men at the door, don't forget my orders," he pointed.

Amanda turned on the stairs, "This way, Captain!" There was no smile in her voice.

Once in her room, Amanda turned abruptly, "What is the meaning of this, Thomas? I have a business to run. And in the midst of my busiest time, you come marching into my taproom with your dragoons."

"Grenadiers," corrected Preston, taking off his gold-trimmed tricorn.

"What?" grumbled Amanda.

"The men are grenadiers, not dragoons." Preston smiled.

"Goons! Dragoons! Grena . . . I don't give a damn, Thomas. I *do* care about your interfering with my business."

Dispensing with his cordial tone, Preston suddenly pursed his lips, "Listen to me Amanda. I'm doing my best to make this pleasant. My men have been looking for a sergeant major all day, and – "

"I know that," interrupted Amanda, her hands balled into fists. "Hell, this was the first place your goons stopped. It was shortly after daybreak, if I recall. Me and my girls were still in our shifts, for god's sake."

Not smiling, Preston continued, "Our search was fruitless. Most everyone interrogated told us that Delaney was on his way to the Snug Harbor Tavern, and we can find no witnesses of him going anyplace beyond the waterfront."

"Well maybe, just maybe, he fell into the harbor. It wouldn't be the first time around these parts," said Amanda, defiantly. "Most of your men wander around here half drunk. And I have witnesses to prove it." Wandering to her window, she added, "And speaking of witnesses to drunkenness, just go down into the taproom this moment and look at your own men. Your own eyes can condemn them."

Preston donned his tricorn and, providing a hint of a smile, said, "I've learned that Delaney was here and left, according to the official report. However, I have orders to clear the Snug Harbor Tavern of the king's troops, pending an investigation by Sheriff Greenleaf, Amanda." Turning at her bedroom door, he added, "I'll do my best to make a private visit when I can. Meanwhile, I'll do what I can to hasten the investigation and get things back to normal."

Once in the taproom, Preston ordered all military personnel cleared, announcing that the tavern was off-limits until further notice.

When Amanda returned to the taproom, the only customer was Crispus Attucks, still sipping his tankard of ale. Amos continued to wipe down the bar, saying nothing. Around the hearth, the girls sat together grumbling among themselves. Amanda glided behind the bar, saying, "You might as well pour me a flip, Amos." More loudly, she added, "Seems we will be doing without the company of the king's troops for a while. So starting tomorrow, we should get the word out that redcoats will not be found at the Snug Harbor Tavern."

Just then the door opened, with Imp rushing to the bar. "Gimme a flip, Amos. I'm mighty thirsty," he ordered, as he petted Angus.

"Give him a tankard of cider, Amos." Amanda smiled, patting Imp's head. Sternly, she added, "Why didn't you close the door, Imp? That cold salt air is . . ." Her voice trailed away as Paul Revere appeared in the doorway, and marching past him up to the bar, Amanda saw Mackintosh and a dozen Sons of Liberty.

While Mackintosh howled for a round of ale, Revere beckoned Amanda to the end of the bar. Leaning forward, he said, "We heard that a certain tavern in Boston was off-limits to our redcoat friends. It just seems to me that such a place deserves the patronage of Boston's finest, Mrs. Griffith!" Looking at Mackintosh, he added, "If you call that Boston's finest!"

"How did you know about this, Mr. Revere? I myself just learned of it minutes ago," said Amanda.

"Let's just say that we have ears about town, and Mr. Hancock advised me to arrange for some patronage in the absence of the redcoats. I even told my wife I'd be here, and she gave me her blessing. Actually, a better thing couldn't happen for us. It seems no matter where we turned, we were running into redcoats." Revere turned to witness the laughter among Mackintosh and the Sons of Liberty. Imp sat on the bar in their midst while Amos and Attucks continued their private conversation. Amanda smiled as the girls joined the gaggle of shipwrights and dockworkers. Her keen eye noticed Hope giving a big hug to one little fellow at the side of Mackintosh. It was Zeke Teezle, his head buried in Hope's bosom, a weary smile on his face.

ΩΩΩ

Sunday, October 23, 1768

Sitting in the Old South Meeting House on Marlborough Street, Sam Adams and John Hancock listened attentively, along with the other Liberty party members, to the pious ramblings of the parson. Secretly, Hancock wondered how any man could harangue a group of people for so long with threats of fire and brimstone. Out of the corner of his eye, he observed Sam Adams nodding his head repeatedly at every utterance from the pulpit. *Was it agreement or the palsy?* Hancock wondered.

The trials of Jonah and some big fish were interrupted by the stomping of boots, accompanied by the trill of fifes and the beat of drums. The plaintive verses of "Yankee Doodle" filled the air, as the king's troops marched by to the cadence of an experienced sergeant. Adams and Hancock exchanged glances and, excusing themselves, quietly exited out a side door, which faced Boston Common.

Once outside, Adams said, "Let's wander over to the Common to determine who exactly was kind enough to share a tune with the congregation."

Hancock smiled. "Not bad singing, actually. We could use a few of those tenors in the church choir." Looking back at the church, he added, "Actually, Sam, I'm happy to get out of there. If I was to believe our preacher in there, I'm certainly destined for a bed of brimstone as the worst sinner in God's creation."

"Blasphemy!" grumbled Adams. They stopped at the edge of the Old Granary Burial Ground, just overlooking the Common. The white tents were still neatly arranged in geometrically perfect rows. Most of the soldiers were seated around campfires, sharing a Spartan lunch. In the distance, Adams spied a cadre of marchers singing in unison. "Let's wander down there, John. At least, we can get an idea what regiment it is."

As they sauntered along Common Street, more than a few soldiers scowled. "It seems that the king's troops are not too happy camping among us," chuckled Adams.

Hancock, in a more sober tone, responded, "You are correct as usual, Sam. But I wonder just how long General Gage will tolerate his men living in tents, especially with the onset of another New England winter."

"That's his problem," said Adams, without taking his eyes off the bivouacked troops. "All the more reason for him to take these damned redcoats south to a warmer climate." Turning, he added, shaking his walking stick, "That's precisely what we should propose. For the good of the king's forces, they should leave."

"Watch that stick, Sam. You'll put someone's eye out one of these days, and it might be mine, for god's sake," corrected Hancock.

"Huzzah! Huzzah!" came shouts from the other side of the encampment.

"What's that all about?" grumbled Adams. Rushing farther down Common Street, they found the answer. A course had been laid out for a small steeple chase, and the races had commenced. Both sides of the course were lined with redcoats, and the betting was obvious to anyone within eyeshot.

"Damn them! Damn them all!" grumbled Adams. "Imagine the gall. The bastards are having horse races and betting on the Sabbath. May their souls burn in hell," he muttered. Without another word, Adams turned back toward the church.

"Wait for me, Sam," said Hancock, in trail.

Pausing to waggle his finger at the encampment, Adams added, "I tell you, John, I want to see you on Queen Street at Edes & Gill right after breakfast tomorrow. I want you to help me remember what we just saw. A column in the *Gazette* is mandatory. Now, the bastards have brought the example of sinful betting and racing on the Sabbath for our children to watch."

Walking at his side, Hancock said half to himself, "I wonder what kind of odds they were putting out." Sam Adams's glare was scalding. "There goes that brimstone again," said Hancock.

ΩΩΩ

Later that afternoon, at the Old State House, Governor Bernard sat back in an easy chair, smiling broadly. Hutchinson stood at the sideboard, as Slank was pouring Madeira for everyone. The fat man sat in a large chair at the far end of the room, doing his best to seem remote in the shadows. General Gage had perched himself on the edge of Bernard's mahogany desk, with Captain Preston standing nearby.

Gage peered about the room, as though he was appraising a battlefield. "Now what could be so urgent for us to meet on a Sunday, Governor Bernard? From all that I've heard prior to my arrival, one could be pilloried here in Boston for simply discussing business on the Sabbath; something about Puritan ethics or some such rot." He accepted the glass of wine, as Slank played the part of a servant, wandering about the room with a tray. His wanderings halted at the side of the fat man.

Bernard, scanning a document on his desk, said, "General, I am happy to report that we have finally solved our quartering problem for your forces."

Gage sipped his Madeira slowly, "I must say, Governor, it is about time. Already the nights are becoming bitter cold in those tents. My troops are tough, but there is no reason for this poor treatment, especially by one's own countrymen."

"Nonetheless, General, we have reached an agreement with James Murray to move your men into his sugar warehouse on Brattle Street, just a few blocks from here."

Captain Preston asked, "Exactly how many men will this sugar warehouse hold, Governor Bernard?"

Hutchinson answered, "We are told it should accommodate no less than two companies of your troops."

Preston smiled. "I'll move the Twenty-ninth from the Common before the week is out, General Gage."

Bernard smiled even more broadly, rising to pour himself more wine while motioning Slank to remain seated. "The real coup, General Gage, is that we have persuaded William Molineux to lease his warehouse space on Griffin's Wharf." Laughing aloud, he continued, "It should surprise you that Mr. Molineux is a staunch supporter of our radical element here in Boston. In fact, there are those who consider him a major agitator in his own right."

Hutchinson joined Bernard's laughter, "It seems that twenty-five pounds per month is more appealing than the empty gratitude of Sam Adams and his nefarious cronies."

Gage echoed the sentiment, "It seems no matter where we go in the world, the British pound sterling solves most problems."

Preston said, "We can move the artillery and the Fifty-ninth into that wharf area. It seems to me that this will place our forces in a circle, focused on the State House and the Customs House. This is working perfectly, General."

Gage arose with a half smile, "I thank you, Governor. I realize that this wasn't an easy task for you, considering the dissention in your Council. Your administration seems riddled with radicals."

Waxing philosophical, Bernard replied, "The comfort of the king's troops is certainly worthy of the effort and compromise, General Gage."

With a frown on his face, Gage continued as though he had heard nothing, "Hopefully, this will harness the rampant desertion rate we have here." His wilting glare caused Captain Preston to shift uneasily from one foot to the other. "I have learned to expect my lowly privates and corporals to desert on occasion, but today I learned of a sergeant major absent from his post." Again, he glared at Preston.

In the shadows across the room, Slank and the fat man exchanged knowing glances, saying nothing.

Hutchinson volunteered, "We have our very own Sheriff Greenleaf looking into this desertion problem, General."

"Happy to hear it!" stated Gage. "Meanwhile, I have placed this Snug Harbor Tavern off-limits to my troops. It seems that every time some of my men spend the evening there, someone disappears. What in hell could be so appealing about a common colonial tavern?"

The fat man interjected with a slight cough, "Perhaps, General, you should ask that question of your own Captain Preston there at your side. You may not be aware of it, but the proprietress of the Snug Harbor Tavern was clinging to his arm the entire evening of your reception at Faneuil Hall."

Gage again glared at Preston. "Captain, let us depart and leave these good men to their Sabbath. We have quartering arrangements to make. And we have a few things to discuss about your personal social life here in Boston."

After they left, Hutchinson looked across the room. "Slank, would you be kind enough to recharge our glasses. I think – "

Bernard interrupted with a roar, "Be damned with recharging our glasses! What in hell is this about a tavern trollop attending our private party? I thought you men had that Snug Harbor Tavern covered."

The fat man, shaking his heavy jowls, said calmly as he lifted his heavy bulk from his chair, "The problem is greater than you can imagine, Governor. You see, we were ready to take action down there, based on information from our Omega agents."

Slank interjected, as the fat man paused to down his wineglass, "Then this sergeant major starts taking action on his own time, killing a doxy in the process. When he threatened our agent at the Snug Harbor, another agent was forced to kill the sergeant major in her defense."

Bernard growled, "You mean to tell me that we are responsible for the murder of one of the king's own troops?"

"It was the right thing to do at the time, Governor," asserted the fat man firmly, pounding his fist into his hand. "If we can't protect our own secret agents of Omega, what loyalty can we demand or even expect?"

Hutchinson spoke up with a calming motion of his hands, "Gentlemen, arguing among ourselves will solve nothing. Perhaps it is best that this sergeant major did get killed; rumor has it that it was a soldier who killed that doxy at the Bunch of Grapes. Perhaps we can get Sheriff Greenleaf to officially set the blame for her murder on this dead soldier. That will stifle the constant complaining we continue to hear from the common trollops and rabble."

Slank shook his head negatively. "Sadly, Mr. Hutchinson, the army is not aware of the soldier's death. And I'm not so sure it would be wise to let them know about it."

Hutchinson looked at Slank in disbelief, asking, "Do you mean to tell me that we have hidden a dead soldier's body from the army?"

"Not exactly," interjected the fat man. "But we do know who did."

"Well, tell me. Who has the body of this sergeant major?" asked Hutchinson tersely.

Slank stepped to the window, impatiently saying, "Actually, we can't be certain, Mr. Hutchinson." Turning to face his superiors, he continued, "You see, we have learned from our agent that the body has been buried someplace outside Boston."

Hutchinson glared, "Getting a straight answer is like pulling teeth. Who buried the body of the soldier?"

The fat man coughed as he interjected, "We are not trying to be difficult, Mr. Hutchinson. We are merely trying to protect you with a lack of detailed knowledge." He sipped his wine, continuing, "But, if you must know, you will be happy to know that John Hancock and Paul Revere are responsible for the removal of our dear departed sergeant major."

Slank laughed, adding, "It is hard to believe that those two rascals have inadvertently aided Omega in disposing of a dead body."

Bernard muttered, looking blankly at his desk, "The important question, gentlemen, is what do we do next? The last thing we need is General Gage and his staff asking questions about a missing body. Perhaps it's best that we leave them convinced of the sergeant major's desertion from the army." Pausing to stare at each of the others in the eye, he continued, "No, let's keep the army in the dark about the death and tell our Omega agents to keep their mouths shut. If the sheriff or anyone for that matter asks questions . . . well, they know nothing."

Slank responded, "I'll get the old sailor on it immediately."

The fat man merely nodded.

Hutchinson marched to the door, saying, "I'll get Sheriff Greenleaf immediately to inform him that his investigation has officially concluded that the sergeant major has deserted and run off into the Massachusetts countryside with some wench he met on the street. He'll find it easy to share that tale with the army."

ΩΩΩ

Monday, October 24, 1768

It was shortly after high noon, and a brisk autumn breeze was blowing through the open door and windows of the Snug Harbor Tavern in order to air the place out from the smell of fresh paint. The taproom floor and the bar had been painted the same bright red as the bedroom floors. Amos stood behind the bar with Imp perched on it; both were busy wiping paint from their hands and faces. Imp grumbled, "Easy with that rag, Amos. You're getting whale oil in my eyes."

"Sit still, you little wharf rat. This oil is the onliest way I know to get this red paint off. You got more on your face than on the bar. If I didn't know better, I'd swear you was painted like a Mohawk Indian," laughed Amos in his baritone voice.

Sitting at the opposite side of the bar, enjoying a bowl of clam chowder, Crispus Attucks said, "I'd appreciate you bein' careful with that 'Indian' talk. My mother's people, you know!" Both Imp and Amos ignored him.

The taproom was half filled with sailmakers, ropemakers, and shipwrights, enjoying a late noon meal, while the girls congregated at one table doing the same. Little notice was made of the lanky, hunch-shouldered old sailor shuffling to a corner table and sitting alone. His face was hidden by a copy of the *Boston Gazette*, with his red cap low on his brow. Hope, half giggling to the other girls about the call to duty, arose slowly to join the old tar.

After a short chat, the old sailor reversed his tracks out the door, mumbling about the lack of peace and quiet. Again, everyone seemed to ignore the anonymous old salt.

Left alone at the table, Hope grabbed the *Gazette* and hastened up the stairs laughing to the other girls. "Old bastard didn't have a shillin' for a tumble, and all I get for my time with that old tar is a copy of the news. If anyone asks, I'll be nappin' a bit." With that, she scampered up the stairs.

Once in the quiet of her room, Hope sat on the edge of her bed and opened the paper to find a note. The wax seal was embossed with "Ω." She read hurriedly,

> *Nothing is to be said about the dead soldier. Officially, it did not happen.*
> *Say nothing to anyone, especially the sheriff and the army.*
> *We know about you and Teezle, and we will protect you.*
> *As usual, you are expected to destroy this note.*

Ω

Looking about her room, as though someone else was present, she quietly folded the note and tucked it under the goose down mattress. *It was time,* she thought, *to protect herself.* "It seems to me that too many strumpets are getting killed, if they get in the way! By god, it will not happen to me," she muttered to herself.

ΩΩΩ

Thursday, October 27, 1768

It was near midnight, and the noise and singing in the Snug Harbor taproom down below forced Hope to speak louder than she would have liked. With her brow furrowed, she huddled closer to Zeke Teezle seated on the bed beside her. She held a candle between them, murmuring, "Just look, Zeke! The bastards sent you the same note."

"You're right, my lass. Your note and mine are exactly the same. Seems the fat man wants us to be mighty quiet about what happened here," whispered Teezle.

Standing with her fists on her hips, Hope said defiantly, "Zeke, two doxies have been killed in this town. And both killed because of Omega, to my way of thinking." Pacing the floor, she added, wagging her index finger, "Well, it won't happen to me."

With sorrow on his face, Zeke looked up from the bed at the tall strumpet and said solemnly, "I'd be mighty sorry to see anything happen to you, Hope."

"I'd be even more sorry, Zeke. And I'd be dead, if it wasn't for you killin' that bastard Delaney," responded Hope with a half smile.

"I just couldn't let anything happen to you," said Teezle. Standing awkwardly and shifting his weight from foot to foot, he asked, "Did you tell the others what I did?"

Smiling broadly, Hope grabbed Teezle's hands in hers, "Zeke, put your mind at ease. I didn't tell and won't tell anyone anything. My story is that Delaney hit me in the head, and I found him dead when I came to. No one knows about his threats about deserters."

"What about these notes? We should destroy them like it says," whispered Teezle.

"No! Not this time!" exclaimed Hope. "I'll let the fat man know that we have them and that nothing should happen to us. Otherwise, who knows who could get their hands on them?" She laughed aloud. Conspiratorially, she added, "Now this is strictly between us, Zeke. We keep the notes from now on, and we cover for each other. Now let's you and me get down to business. Nothin' wrong with us enjoyin' each other for a shillin', is there?" She tugged Zeke's head into the confines of her ample bosom.

ΩΩΩ

CHAPTER 17

Monday, October 31, 1768

T HE CADRE OF black drummers, resplendent in their yellow and red tunics, maintained a steady beat to quarters while the men of the Twenty-ninth and Fourteenth regiments mustered into their straight lines on Boston Common. A heavy dark overcast with the promise of rain covered the entire harbor and the surrounding countryside, hiding any evidence of the recent sunrise. Sam Adams, standing at John Hancock's side at the parlor window overlooking the Common, said, "It seems we have a storm brewing today, John."

Frowning, Hancock responded, "In more ways than one, Sam. I find this whole thing most distasteful; most distasteful." He gulped his cup of tea. Looking at the clock on the mantel, he noted that it was just after 6:30 AM.

Below on the Common, with the redcoats fully assembled and regimental flags flapping briskly in the autumn breeze, the drumming ceased. Suddenly, a single drum was heard approaching from Tremont Street, as the drummer preceded a guard of six redcoats marching from the town prison. The grenadiers in their bearskin caps, Brown Bess muskets on their shoulders, marched in two files with one man, wearing only his white shirt and breeches in their midst. They marched with precision to a slow, ominous cadence, led by a sergeant major, halberd held high.

As they approached the assembled regiments on the Common, heading for a tall wooden post erected for the occasion, General Gage and his staff emerged from the command tent. Subalterns barked orders, and the entire assembly came to attention. The drummer stopped abruptly, as the prisoner stood before the wooden post. The only sound was the flapping of regimental pennants and the British Union Jack. The tension in the air could be felt all the way up the hill to the Hancock mansion. The slopes around the Common were littered with an equally silent audience of apprentices, tradesmen, and merchants.

General Gage quietly nodded and Lieutenant Colonel Dalrymple stepped forward. Unrolling a document, he spoke loudly for all to hear, "Attention to orders! In accordance with His Majesty's Articles of War and the dictates of British military justice, Private Richard Ames of His Majesty's Fourteenth Regiment has been found guilty of desertion by a military tribunal, meeting in His Majesty's Colony of Massachusetts. It is the decision of this tribunal that Private Richard Ames shall suffer execution in the company of his comrades in arms; such execution by firing squad to occur not later than 7:00 AM, October 31, 1768." Looking up from the document and glancing at the junior officer in charge of the firing squad, Dalrymple concluded, "Signed, General Thomas Gage, Commanding. Detail, carry out the orders forthwith."

With merely a nod from a command lieutenant, two burly grenadiers tied Private Ames to the wooden post. The lieutenant stepped forward to provide a black blindfold. When he had finished, he ordered a small detail of men to clear the far slope of civilians who were in the line of fire. This was done quietly but quickly and with resolve. Not too many noticed this activity, as most eyes were riveted on the squad of redcoats who marched forward in single file, their muskets at port arms. Again, a stillness and heavy quiet pervaded the Common. The commanding lieutenant drew his saber, and with a nod, the drummers began the requisite drumroll. "Ready, aim!" With a cloud of musket smoke and the smell of cordite, it was done. The drums stopped.

As the firing squad cleared the area, Dalrymple again raised his voice. "His Majesties forces gathered here on Boston Common shall now pass in single file to bear close witness to the punishment reserved for those who desert their post. After passing, all troops shall be dismissed."

Without a word, General Gage and his staff did a smart about-face and returned to the command tent. Orders were barked as troops passed slowly by execution site. A short time later, a small detail was observed cutting Private Ames from the post.

Standing in the window, Sam Adams shook his head in sadness, "What a despicable sight that was, John! How do we explain that to our children? Hell, I don't want these soldiers dead; I just want them gone from Boston."

"More tea, Sam?" he asked, as he poured himself another cup.

"Just one more," Sam answered solemnly, still looking out the window. "Then I'll wander over to Queen Street to help Ben Edes write about this debacle for the *Gazette*."

Sitting down at a small table, Hancock said, "I will be interested to read what John Mein will say about this in the *Boston Chronicle*." Straightening the lace at his neck and sleeves, he donned his crimson coat, adding, "Do you have any idea how hard it will be to get a redcoat to desert now, with that sword of Damocles hanging over their heads?"

Adams looked at his young protégé solemnly. "I realize that, John. But we must continue to try. You know as well as I that our best bet is using those doxies to lure them away from this damned encampment." Pausing a moment, he added, "And just what are you doing reading that damned *Chronicle* written by that detestable John Mein?"

"I have learned that it is always wise to know what the opposition is thinking, Sam. It applies to business as well as politics. By the way, I have word that these tents on the Common will be taken down in short order. Our redcoats are striking camp," said Hancock.

"What? How can that be? Have you been holding out on me? Please tell me that General Gage has decided to take his damned lobsterbacks back to New York," chided Adams.

"Not exactly," said Hancock with a sardonic grin. "It seems that some of our leading citizens have decided that a firm grasp of the British pound sterling is better than a grasp of your opposition to the governor. Even Molineux has provided room in his warehouse on Griffin's Wharf for the quartering of troops."

Turning smartly to the door, Adams barked with a grimace on his face and fire in his eyes, "There's not a moment to lose, John. I'll expose these traitors to our patriot cause. By god, the *Gazette* will be my rapier in this duel of ideas. I'll be on Queen Street if you need me." With that, he bustled out the door, his red suit a mere blur. Hancock half laughed, as he paused to take another look at the wooden post down on the Common. The regiment had returned to its normal routine, with the exception of tents being dismantled. He looked up at the overcast, deciding to take his carriage rather than walk down to the wharf. *No sense in getting soaked, if you could help it,* he thought to himself.

ΩΩΩ

Meanwhile, in the command tent, General Gage briefed his staff. "First, gentlemen, I want you to know that I take very little delight in what happened out there this morning with Private Ames. But it is obvious that we had to take strong measures to make the rank and file understand that desertion will not be tolerated. After looking at the eyes of the assembled regiments, I am confident we made a strong impact on their thinking. With the closing off of that Snug Harbor place down on the wharf, I am certain our desertion problem should cease."

Looking at Captain Preston, he added, "Captain, I have taken time to rethink your situation at that den of iniquity. I want you to culture your arrangement at the Snug Harbor with this Amanda woman. See what you can learn about this radical element from her. We have yet to see this mob that Governor Bernard and the commissioners talk about, but I am convinced that there is an undercurrent of activity with the lower classes. See what you can learn – in a covert way, if you understand me, Captain."

"As you order, General. I'll do my best to serve the Crown," replied Preston, to the laughter of all in the tent.

"I'm sure you will enjoy the sacrifice for the benefit of the Crown." Gage smiled. Turning to the others, he continued, "Within the next few weeks and certainly before December, we shall have garrisoned Boston with the addition of the Sixty-fourth and Sixty-fifth regiments. General John Pomeroy and Commodore Hood should be here to take formal command. Then, I, gentlemen, shall be free to return to New York and a more civilized life. By god, these New England puritans are a bit stuffy for my taste." Rising, he stepped out to his waiting carriage, "I shall retire to my quarters and breakfast with Ms. Cross. This evening, I expect to see you all at the British Coffee House on King Street for our evening game of whist; bring your money, gentlemen. Meanwhile, be sure to get these tents taken down and the men quartered properly."

ΩΩΩ

At 11:00 PM, the Snug Harbor Tavern was a crawling mass of ropemakers, shipwrights, and tradesmen. The odious mixture of sweat, spilled ale, fried scrod, fresh baked bread, and pipe smoke was somewhat obscured by the burning embers of pine from the fireplace. In the corner the Sons of Liberty had pulled tables together as they joined in song:

> *The redcoats arrived on parade,*
> > *And they came to the Snug to get laid,*
> *After the squirtin'*
> *They started desertin'*
> > *And ended up diggin' a grave.*

The laughter was contagious, and Zeke Teezle once again found himself sitting beside Ebenezer Mackintosh, with Hope perched firmly on his lap. Mackintosh placed his well-muscled arm across Teezle's bony shoulders. "You know, Zeke, until I met you, I didn't know that candlemakers could be so much fun. How do you get all that ale in that little skinny frame of yours?" slurred Mackintosh.

Hope elbowed Mackintosh, "Now you leave Zeke alone. I can tell you from experience that not every part of his body is skinny; bony, but not skinny." Again, the crowd burst into laughter.

Amos stood next to Amanda at the bar, saying, "Sure is good not to see a bunch of redcoats in our place, Ms. Amanda."

Amanda, keeping her eyes on the crowd, muttered, "That may be so, Amos. But that means that Big Bessie is getting all that redcoat money these days."

"Seems to me we are doin' all right tonight," said Amos.

Shaking her head, Amanda replied, "These local men can afford a pint or a quart, but our real money is upstairs in the cribs. If you take time to notice, every girl we have is in the taproom. I need them on their backs, upstairs; that's where the money is."

No one seemed to notice the door opening and the entry of a short person wearing a black cape and hood, needling their way to the bar. Pulling the hood from her face, Angel Cross peered at Amanda. "Where can we talk?" she muttered without preamble.

Shifting her blue eyes and forcing herself to appear nonchalant, Amanda said, "Follow me upstairs." To Amos, she said, "You didn't see any of this, Amos."

"I'm as blind as a bat," said Amos. "Don't see nothin' or nobody; not me." He closely watched the two women make their way up the stairway.

Amanda entered her own bedroom and turned abruptly, her fists on her hips and her blue eyes blazing. "All right, my fine lady, you have a bit of explaining to do."

With a note of defiance, Angel Cross replied, coldly, "Not that I owe you an explanation for anything, but what exactly would you like to know?"

"First, what is this nonsense with you and General Gage, of all people?" growled Amanda.

Laughing quietly, Angel said, "Oh that! It's nothing, Amanda. Merely a man with a bundle of lusties. A woman like you should know that quite well."

"Don't hand me that," said Amanda sternly. "What exactly have you told General Gage? It's my guess that it's because of you that I have no redcoat trade here at the Snug Harbor. And, furthermore, what have you done to harm the patriots in this town?"

"You'll have to be satisfied with my word that I have told the redcoats nothing about your beloved Hancock and his patriot cause," stated Angel. Observing the wide-eyed response, she added, "Yes, that's what I said – your beloved Hancock. Do you think I didn't see that when I worked here? Actually, I'm surprised all of Boston doesn't know about this little arrangement of yours."

Walking casually to the window, Angel turned abruptly taking the offensive, "Personally, I am bit curious about your clinging to the arm of a certain Captain Preston, Amanda. What's that all about? I am wondering where your loyalties lie these days."

"You have no right to question me, Angel. You know too much about our activities here, and there are many people talking about what to do with you."

Leaning forward, a note of sincerity in her voice, Angel murmured, "That's why I'm here, Amanda. I am afraid that General Gage will learn of my past here in Boston. Don't you realize I'm on your side, for god's sake?" She began to pace, saying, "But Dr. Church saw me at the general's reception and let me know of his recognition. I fear I could be exposed by that fat bastard."

Pondering a moment to clear her thoughts, Amanda half grinned. "If what you say is true, you have nothing to worry about with Dr. Church. The last thing he needs is a scandal about his past activities with you. He couldn't afford a public discussion."

"Perhaps you're right. I'll have to trust in his fear of a tarnished reputation. Now, I don't have much time tonight; General Gage is at the British Coffee House with his staff, and I need to get a message to Mr. Hancock," Angel said urgently.

"I can handle that for you," said Amanda with a note of caution.

"Fine! Tell him that General Gage is leaving at the end of November, returning to New York," said Angel.

"That's good news," said Amanda. "Hopefully, he will take his troops with him."

"Not a chance," added Angel. "In fact, there are more regiments due to arrive before his departure. Please pass this on to Mr. Hancock and his friends."

"It's amazing that the general shares this information with you." Amanda smiled.

"Pillow talk is magic." Angel grinned.

Sitting on her bed in a more relaxed mood, Amanda asked, "Why did you disappear on us so suddenly, Angel? Hancock was worried, although he keeps his feelings close to his waistcoat."

Laughing aloud, Angel said, "It was obvious that I couldn't stay at the Hancock mansion on Beacon Hill for long. Sweet old Aunt Lydia could be a witch when the lord of the manor was absent. He sent me to that little burg called Lexington for a while to keep the peace. I couldn't stand the place; it was nothing but milk farmers and one stopover called the Buckman Tavern. And living with the town minister was no fun at all. Especially after spending time here at the Snug Harbor Tavern." They both laughed heartily. "Now tell me," continued Angel, "what is this with you and that Captain Preston?"

With a conspiratorial grin, Amanda said hurriedly, "I felt it was time to make my Mr. Hancock a bit jealous and collect a bit of military information in the process. You are right; men will tell you almost everything with their head on your pillow."

Seemingly anxious, Angel said, "I suppose I should leave before the general returns to our quarters. You should know that I will not be leaving with him. I will need a place to disappear prior to the end of the month. I was hoping to get my old job back here at the Snug Harbor, if possible."

Answering slowly, Amanda said, "We can discuss that in the next few weeks, but it shouldn't be a problem. Now I suggest you get back to the general. Meanwhile, I'll do what I can to stay in touch, and you do the same. Go out the back way. It wouldn't be wise for the general's lady to be seen in a place like this, would it?"

ΩΩΩ

CHAPTER 18

November 24, 1768

A N ICY WIND accompanied General Gage as he entered the otherwise warm confines of Castle William. It was midmorning and Governor Bernard, seated next to Thomas Hutchinson, laughed as Gage took off his heavy coat, cursing the weather. "It seems to me, General, that you are not too partial to our New England weather. Would you care for a cup of hot tea?" Without awaiting an answer, he placed a steaming cup on the table.

Gage smiled. "I've traveled the world over, gentlemen, and endured many hardships and discomforts in His Majesty's service, but for the life of me, I can't seem to adjust to bitter cold like this, especially when I'm confined to a damned frigate in the middle of an ocean"

Bernard grinned. "At least, it is only a short voyage back to New York. An Atlantic crossing at this time of year would be absolutely miserable."

Gage looked out the window at the warships tossing in the heavy chop of the harbor and visibly shivered. "I can hear that icy wind whistling through the rigging from here. And just look at those heavy dark clouds."

Hutchinson said matter-of-factly, "It's the portent of a nor'easter, General. It's our most miserable winter storm and, seemingly, God's way to make us appreciate our hot summers."

Sipping his tea, Gage said, "Let's get down to business. It seems His Majesty's navy is anxious to set sail, something about tides and such. As you know, I'm needed in New York, and I'm satisfied that my troops are well billeted and quartered here in Boston for the winter; that was my major concern. Brigadier General John Pomeroy is due to arrive shortly with the two additional regiments, and he will relieve Lieutenant Colonel Dalrymple of total command. I expect Major General Alexander MacKay to ultimately take full command, if his transports ever arrive. God only knows where his frigates have taken him. The navy blames tides, winds, and currents. They never acknowledge that they are probably lost at sea half the time. For all I know, MacKay could be floating around the West Indies, looking for a northbound breeze to get him here."

"Speaking of taking people places, General, we were hoping to see Ms. Cross with you today," queried Hutchinson.

Suddenly frowning, Gage said coldly, "I expect this to be strictly between us, gentlemen, but I've simply lost track of the girl. She was most amusing and, incidentally, full of information about your radical element here in Boston. I was surprised what she knew of Adams, Hancock, and the radical fringe. Actually, it was she who recognized that Snug Harbor place to be a den of thieves. I'm glad I placed it off-limits to my men."

Bernard, with a quick glance at Hutchinson, asked, "How would such a pretty lass know anything about a tavern on the waterfront? She seemed such an innocent-cultured creature."

"Let me make it clear, gentlemen; she is quite cultured. But innocent? Hardly! She knows her way around a bedroom, and she's pretty shrewd," chortled Gage. "But enough of Ms. Cross. Apparently, she has already found passage back to London. At least that was her intent when she accompanied me here. In retrospect, she might have proven herself an asset to your Omega thing, if she was around."

A blast of cold air filled the room as an aide entered, saying, "Sorry to interrupt, General, but the navy says we must leave now or lose the advantage of the tides."

Rising and downing his hot tea, Gage said, "Governor Bernard, Mr. Hutchinson, I thank you for your kind hospitality. I trust the king's peace will prevail. Please keep in touch."

"We thank you, General Gage," said Bernard. "Feel free to visit anytime."

Opening the door, Gage laughed. "Perhaps in the spring, when the weather is more agreeable."

Left in the room alone, Bernard smiled. "Well, Thomas, it seems that we finally have control of the situation. Adams and his radicals have retreated to their holes like a gaggle of rats while the king's commissioners are back in business."

"I told you long ago, Francis, that the only thing these so-called patriots would understand is a bayonet," said Hutchinson. "Actually, I'm surprise that we didn't have to use one. The mere sight of the king's power has prevailed."

"Let's get back to town. Lunch at the British Coffee House is on me, as we can sit back and enjoy our Pax Britannica. So much for Sam Adams and his thirty-thousand man army we heard so much about." They both laughed heartily.

ΩΩΩ

January 1769

As promised, Brigadier General John Pomeroy arrived in the company of Commodore Samuel Hood and the additional regiments. With all their men properly garrisoned for the winter, they settled into what was considered a normal routine.

The citizens of Boston were well accustomed to a challenge from the night watchman during their nightly excursions. However, any challenge that came from a redcoat sentry was greeted with disdain, silence, or, in extreme cases, outright hostility. The redcoats, under strict orders, maintained their requisite military discipline, responding to any personal abuse with stoic tolerance.

Josiah Withers, the town watchman, carried his lantern in his mittened hand, as he held the lapel of his heavy coat tightly against his neck. His head was half concealed by his heavy scarf while his woolen tricorn hat was pulled down tightly, bending the tops of his ears, in response to the bitter cold enhanced by a heavy sea breeze. He made his designated rounds in a plodding manner. "Ten o'clock, and all's well," he howled for the citizens to hear.

Meanwhile, in a dank cell of the Queen Street jail, three men convicted of thievery were busy plotting their escape. "What we need is a diversion to get them to open these cell doors in a hurry," said a shivering Private Bryan Donnelly, the only soldier in the group. "In London, I heard about some poor fellows using a fire."

"We can't do that," said another inmate, rubbing his arms to keep warm. "If the jailer don't get here in time, we could end up dead – I mean burnt to a crisp. I only have a few months to go in this place."

"Don't worry about it," said Donnelly, his hot breath visible in the cold air. "We have our water bucket here. We can use wet straw; it creates more smoke than fire. Time is on our side, lads; and, once we are out in the street, be sure to mingle with the crowd before you disappear. I guarantee that you will never see me again."

In a few moments, the jailer reacted in response to hearing screams. "Fire! Fire! Get us out of here." He stumbled through a wall of smoke to unlock the cell, only to be greeted with a smack on the head with a water bucket. The inmates stepped over his body out into the street continuing to yell, "Fire! Fire!"

The watchman barely heard the cries of "fire," but it was loud enough for him to take action when he saw the smoke coming from Queen Street. He rang the fire bell, alerting the whole town. Immediately, every man and boy ran out to confront the emergency, as they had been trained.

Ebenezer Mackintosh found himself working side by side with a redcoat sergeant, as they and their men fought the blaze. It was evident that every redcoat and every Son of Liberty could work in unison when they had to for a common cause. In no time at all, the fire was out, leaving only the walls of the jail still standing. Mackintosh found himself shaking hands with every redcoat he could find, knowing they had saved the entire town from disaster. The flames had been confined to the one building.

The next day, the *Boston Gazette* ran the following headline:

GAOL FIRE EXTINGUISHED: CITIZENS AND TROOPS SAVE THE TOWN

"That says it all," muttered Sam Adams, sitting in the back room of Edes & Gill. "These damned redcoats don't make it too easy to hate them."

Hancock grinned. "You must admit it, Sam. The rank and file shouldn't be blamed. It's the Parliament and the Crown we have an issue with."

"Perhaps you're right, John. But it is our effective use of the *Gazette* and the Sons of Liberty that will force the redcoats to take hostile action." Rising to look out the window at the falling snow, he added, "Actually, I'm convinced that if we can rid ourselves of Governor Bernard, we can improve things around here."

"Do you really feel that we can work with Hutchinson, as Bernard's obvious replacement?" asked Hancock.

Laughing under his breath, Adams looked over his shoulder at his protégé, saying, "Not really. But Hutchinson is born of Massachusetts, and we might find a way to make him one of our own. Don't forget that he and his sons are merchants like you. Pursuit of the almighty British pound will triumph ultimately. Otherwise, I'll figure some way for Ben Edes to print our own currency, if need be."

"Sounds like treason!" exclaimed Hancock.

"Does it now?" said Adams. "Fortunately, you are the only one to hear it. Hence, I can deny I said it. Let's get over to the Green Dragon to meet the others. We have to figure a way to rile the citizens of this town. This so-called peace is making me nervous."

ΩΩΩ

April 1769

Amos smiled broadly as he wiped down the bar. "It sure is good to have you back with us, Ms. Angel. Where exactly did you go off to for these many months? If you don't mind me askin'."

Angel, rinsing out the pewter mugs, smiled. "Let's just say that I had important business in New York, Amos. Then for the last few months, I was visiting friends in Lexington, courtesy of Mr. Hancock."

On the other side of the bar, Amanda summoned her with a wave of her hand. Sitting at a back table, she reached out, touching Angel's hair. "Welcome back. I hope your stay in Lexington wasn't too boring for you."

"Actually, I hate that place. But Mr. Hancock said it was the safest place to disappear until the memory of my face with General Gage had faded," said Angel.

"Now that I'm back, I need all the friends I can find; and I consider you my best friend in Boston, Amanda." She primped at her raven hair unconsciously.

"The black hair looks good, Angel. If it wasn't for Dr. Church being so curious about you at General Gage's party, you could probably keep your natural color," said Amanda, analytically.

"My peace of mind is what's important to me now, Amanda. And I want to thank you for taking me back in. The Snug Harbor Tavern is beginning to feel more and more like a second home," responded Angel. "I'll stick with the Angel Black name, as it seems some folks still remember me."

"You can fix Charity's room anyway you like. I never did find a permanent replacement for her. The one thing that stays, however, is the red floor. And don't ask why; just accept it," said Amanda.

Leaning forward, she added, "Now for the touchy part, Angel. With the redcoats off-limits here at the Snug, there isn't a real need for you to tend bar more than some of the time. Big Bessie Clump would like to borrow your services over at the Bunch of Grapes because she has all these lusty redcoats, and she lost Abby Stuff a while ago. So how about it?"

Leaning back slowly in her chair, Angel frowned. After a long moment, she said in a calculating tone, "As you know, I'm not warm and fuzzy about the crib business. However, if that's what it takes to survive, I'll do it – for a while."

"That's fine," said Amanda flatly. "One rule is that you stay away from Mr. Hancock and Captain Preston. I'm sure you understand that and why."

"Crystal clear to me!" exclaimed Angel. "When do I spend time at the Bunch of Grapes?"

"She will need you on Friday and Saturday nights," said Amanda. "Otherwise, you can consider the Snug Harbor your home."

At that moment, Imp rushed into the taproom with a bundle of newspapers under his arm. Striding directly over to Amanda, he yelled to the bar, "I'll have a tankard of ale, Amos."

Amanda countermanded with a smile, "Make that a cider for the lad, Amos."

"Ms. Amanda, I think you should look at this. I can't read all the words, but those folks that did read it seemed a might upset about something," said Imp. He handed her a copy of the *Boston Gazette*.

Gazing at the front page, Amanda said, "I can see why, Imp." In a louder voice, she barked, "Listen to this, my dear friends. It seems that our own Governor Bernard has been writing private letters to Lord Hillsborough in London for some time now. In fact, there are six letters printed here, and not one says too many nice things about the citizens of Boston." Turning the pages rapidly, she continued, "It's little wonder that Parliament has sent the redcoats. This traitorous bastard Bernard has painted us to be the worst Englishmen in the entire empire. According to him, we aren't worthy of the courtesies provided to common slaves, and we sure as hell can't be trusted."

Looking over her shoulder, Angel added, "It seems that he fears that an army will come down from the hills to remove the king's governor, the commissioners, and all his other officers. What's this about subverting royal authority? No wonder they sent Gage and his troops."

Amanda looked at Amos. "Get an extra barrel of rum for tonight, Amos. I have a feeling that there will be some mighty angry and thirsty men in here tonight."

ΩΩΩ

Laughing heartily with a spilling tankard of ale, Sam Adams said, "This evening, gentlemen, the ale is courtesy of the Adams Brewery and Distillery." He gazed around at the members of the Caucus Club and the Masons in the upstairs of the Green Dragon Tavern, as they reveled in the official reading of what they referred to as the Damning Bernard Letters.

Joseph Warren acknowledged, "We can thank Dr. Ben Franklin, our agent in London, for expediting copies of these letters to us. Now, I realize he asked, in fact, insisted, that they not be shared with the public, but – "

"How can we control the colonial free press?" interjected John Hancock, sharing the gaiety.

Pounding his tankard, Paul Revere asked, "How do you suppose Governor Bernard will react to this salvo against his pristine reputation? Mackintosh and the Sons of Liberty are prepared to burn his house down around his ears."

Dr. Church stood up somberly, "Let's not forget, gentlemen, that the governor has more than one thousand redcoats out there to defend him. I suggest we temper our men on this. Otherwise, we could find ourselves with a very large burial detail."

Adams echoed the sentiment, "He's right, Paul. Let's just sit back and wait to hear from our governor. If we don't hear something soon, we'll approach him officially with his malicious lies."

ΩΩΩ

Governor Bernard paced the floor of his office, ranting at the top of his lungs. "How in hell," he screamed, "did the *Boston Gazette* get copies of my personal letters to London? Is nothing in this world sacred, for god's sake?"

"Take it easy," said Hutchinson in a calming tone. "If you are confronted with these letters, you can simply deny that it was you who wrote them."

"If I'm confronted? If I'm confronted? The real question is 'when' I'll be confronted, Thomas. And it's obviously a simple matter for you to say 'take it easy.' It's not your bacon in the frying pan, is it?" Bernard continued screaming.

John Mein, seated across the room, responded, "Governor, let me assure you that the *Boston Chronicle* will print a broadside stating that this publication of letters in the *Gazette* is false, malicious, and full of venom and mendacity. Furthermore, I can say that the mere printing of such trash is meant to insult the intelligence of the average citizen of Boston and that the populace should stop reading their fictions and fabrications of the truth."

The fat man, sipping a glass of wine, casually added, "I'll get the Omega agents to spread equally effective counterpropaganda in support of your historic loyalty to the best interests of the citizens of not only Boston but all of Massachusetts. How does that sound?"

"In the meantime, I suppose I can look forward to the Boston mob razing my home," said Bernard sarcastically.

"I understand, Francis; that very thing happened to me and my family years ago, as you may recall. It might be wise for you to find official business on the other side of the colony for a week or so, until this news cools down," suggested Hutchinson. "Meanwhile, as head of the court, I'll alert His Majesty's army to maintain extra vigilance around your home and the State House. The assembly will be denied the right to convene in your absence."

John Mein added, "I'll cover and justify your 'official' absence in the *Chronicle,* and before you know it, we'll be back to business as usual."

"Very well, gentlemen," said Bernard with finality, "I suppose that is the best way to handle it. I thank you for your support. My wife and I will leave immediately for business in Worcester."

CHAPTER 19

Wednesday, July 26, 1769

AGAIN, THE STENCH of tallow mingled with the odors of fish mongers and vegetable hucksters from out on Milk Street and pervaded the hot, stuffy back room of Zeke Teezle's candle shop. Wiping the sweat from his brow with his sleeve, Zeke was absorbed in alignment of his strings of wick, when Gerty barged into the doorway barking, "All right, what is this all about?" She was holding a note with a red wax seal on it. The seal was imprinted with "Ω," and it was broken open. "And who in hell is Hope?"

Stepping from the privy in the rear of the shop and hearing Gerty's grumbling, Emmet Glunt stopped in his tracks, near the rear window. The last thing he needed was to step into the midst of another Teezle argument. *Actually,* he thought to himself, *it was a shame that Zeke never seemed to stand up too well against Gerty's tirades. On the other hand, Zeke was a bastard to work for and probably deserved it.* He strained his ears to hear Teezle, as his voice lowered to almost a whisper.

"Sit down, Gerty. It's time I told you what has happened. If I don't tell someone, I'm going to burst," murmured Zeke. Gerty waddled across the room, moving a chair closer to where he was sitting. Zeke reached for the note, but she quickly held it behind her back, out of reach. "Not so fast, Mr. Teezle! Now start talkin'." She leaned forward with an elbow on her knee, her legs apart like a man, and her unencumbered pendulous breast clearly visible through the sweat-soaked cotton homespun dress.

"Well, cutting to the chase, Gerty," said Teezle, "you might recall that last October, a redcoat turned up missin'."

244

Gerty grumbled, "Zeke, don't waste my time. There's redcoats missin' all the time in this town. At least, there was before they executed that one poor fella."

Shaking his head impatiently, Zeke continued, "Listen to me for once, will you? This redcoat was special. He was a sergeant major . . . and . . . I . . . killed him." He buried his face in his waxy hands, his visible balding head glistening with rivulets of sweat.

"You did what?" muttered Gerty, sitting back in her chair. "How in hell could you possibly do such a thing? And, for that matter, why would you do such a thing? You're a candlemaker, for god's sake!"

"I had to kill him, Gerty. He was gonna kill Hope at the Snug Harbor Tavern, just like he killed Abby," sobbed Teezle. "Hell, I'm so damned scared, Gerty!"

She sat there with her mouth agape. "Who in hell is Abby? I'm trying to get to Hope, and now you throw in someone named Abby – and a dead redcoat to boot. And what's that about the Snug Harbor?" grumbled Gerty, scratching her midriff.

"Sounds pretty bad, doesn't it?" said Zeke.

"Bad? Bad? It's more than bad," Gerty growled. "Who are these women?"

"Oh, they're just some strumpets, that's all," explained Teezle.

"Strumpets!" howled Gerty. "What in hell are you doin' with strumpets? As if I didn't know, Zeke Teezle!"

"Stop it, Gerty. There's more! I gotta think. There's this Imp kid with a red feather and messages for the Sons of Liberty. Mackintosh told me to keep an eye on him. I forgot my schedule on that. I should be out there right now."

"Imps? Red feathers? Strumpets? Killing redcoats? Have you lost your mind, Zeke?" howled Gerty.

"Now take it easy, Gerty. You see the fat man made me do it," continued Zeke.

"Fat man? What fat man?" asked Gerty.

"I'm not really sure, but – "

"Not sure?" queried Gerty. "I'll tell you what this is, Mr. Teezle. It's a love letter from this Hope. The rest of your story is a damned lie."

Suddenly, grabbing the note from her hand, Teezle screamed, "Shut your mouth for a moment, Gerty. Let me read this." He smiled as he read,

Hope,

You may keep your note as insurance, if you like. No harm will come to either you or the candlemaker. Continue your Thursday rendezvous and keep us informed of the patriots. Soon they will all be in the Tower of London, awaiting the hangman. Show this to the candlemaker and then destroy it. We are in this together.

Ω

Looking up from the note, Zeke stood and tossed it into the fire. Gerty stood abruptly with her chubby fists clenched. She was surprised when Zeke stepped forward, hugging her closely.

"What in hell are you doing, Zeke? Who is Hope? I – "

"Just be quiet, Gerty. That note tells me that all is well. I can now take steps to get out of this mess."

ΩΩΩ

That evening, sitting at the kitchen table, Emmet Glunt finished his evening meal of fish and bread with Zeke and Gerty. "Is there something wrong, Mr. Teezle? You folks are mighty quiet this evening," asked Glunt, quietly.

"Everything is fine," muttered Zeke, as looked warily at Gerty.

"Well, the shop's cleaned up. So I'm going down to Long Wharf to do some fishin' before the sun sets, if it's all right with you," said Glunt.

"Take off, lad," said Teezle, almost too cordially. "We'll see you later."

Immediately, Glunt darted for the door. Zeke and Gerty failed to notice that Glunt departed without a fishing line of any sort. Once out on Milk Street, Glunt rushed over to Marlborough Street then right to the Old State House. He stopped before the side door on King Street, noting that candles were lit in the windows. He rapped on the door loudly. A few yards away, a redcoat sentry said, "What are you up to, lad, at this hour?"

Glaring, Glunt said, "None of your bloody – "

Suddenly, the door opened, and a tall lanky man stared down at him. "What is it?"

Taking off his tricorn hat, Glunt said, "Beg pardon, sir. I'm lookin' to find the sheriff."

"Now what would a small lad like you be needin' the sheriff for at this hour?" said the tall fellow.

Glancing over his shoulder at the sentry, Glunt stepped up on the stoop to the State House and whispered, "I know who killed a redcoat and – "

Placing his finger to his lips, to silence him, the man said, "Do come in, lad. This sounds to be very important."

Feeling a bit puffed, Glunt stepped into the side door and followed the man up the narrow winding stairway. On the second floor, the man seated himself at a small secretary desk, saying, "Now tell me, lad, what is your name? and what is this about a killing?"

Looking around the strange surroundings, Glunt murmured, "Name's Glunt. Emmet Glunt. I was lookin' for the sheriff."

"Well, Master Glunt, unfortunately the sheriff is out for the moment, but you can talk to me. I am Mr. Slank, secretary to Governor Bernard."

"The governor? Wow!" exclaimed Glunt.

"Now what is this about a killing? I need the whole story to share with the sheriff," said Slank in a voice of authority.

"It was Teezle killed the redcoat," muttered Glunt triumphantly.

"Teezle? Who is Teezle? And what redcoat?" asked Slank.

Impatiently, Glunt shifted his weight while scraping wax from his fingernails. "Zeke Teezle is a candlemaker on Milk Street. I heard him say he killed a redcoat."

"Let me write this down," said Slank, with a quill pen scratching.

Watching Slank scribble with his pen, he asked quietly, "I don't suppose there's a reward for reportin' and solvin' a crime, is there?"

Smiling condescendingly, Slank said, "I'm sure there is something for a good citizen such as you. Now where do you live, Master Glunt?"

"I live with the Teezles on Milk Street, just two blocks from here," said Glunt, eagerly. "He's the only candlemaker on the street, and you can see the sign out front of the shop. How big a reward will I get?"

"I'm sure the reward will be more than you can imagine, Master Glunt," said Slank in a soothing tone. "Now, why don't you just get back to that shop and tell no one about this meeting. Do you understand?"

"Yessir!" muttered Glunt. "You mean it's a secret between us?"

"That's correct. A secret between us gentlemen!" exclaimed Slank with a smile. "Now off with you, so I can finish an official report – for the sheriff."

With a broad triumphant grin, Glunt exited the side door, turning left down King Street, passing the sentry without a word. It was still early evening, and the sky was turning a pale yellow, as he made his way to Long Wharf. He paused at the doorway to the Bunch of Grapes to hear the regimental singing. Peering in, he noticed old Sheriff Greenleaf, sitting among a group of redcoats from the Twenty-ninth Regiment.

His chest puffed, Glunt swaggered into the taproom. The pipe smoke was so dense, no one seemed to notice the chubby apprentice candlemaker. Moving close to the sheriff, he tugged his sleeve intrusively. Greenleaf looked askance at the rude young man, grumbling, "This better be good, lad. I've spanked many for much less."

"I thought you should know, sheriff, that I just met with your secretary, and he has the report about the killin'," reported Glunt, smartly.

"Killing? What killing?" growled Greenleaf. The entire table, at the sound of trouble, became silent.

Glunt gazed at everyone, realizing that he was now the center of attention. Clearing his throat, he announced, "It's the killin' of the redcoat."

Standing quickly for a heavy old man, Greenleaf grabbed Glunt by the collar and dragged him to the door, to the collective laughter of the redcoats. Placing him outside, Greenleaf said sternly, "I did that to save your skin, you little whelp. Those redcoats are sensitive about that execution; even though it did happen months ago. Now you mind your mouth, lad."

Glunt place his hands on his hips, "That's not the killin' I was talkin' about."

His eyes widening, Greenleaf leaned forward, resting his hands on his knees. "Another killing? Of another redcoat?"

"That's a fact. I heard it from the killer himself," stated Glunt proudly, wallowing in his self-importance.

At that moment, Big Bessie, wearing a bright yellow satin dress, stepped into the doorway. "Is there a problem, Sheriff?" she asked. "Is this lad bothering you? I won't tolerate intrusions of any sort at the Bunch of Grapes. Now you just – "

Greenleaf rose to his full height. "No bother, Bessie. Just giving the lad a bit of advice." Turning to Glunt, he said, "Now, lad, don't you forget. I expect to see you at the Old State House tomorrow at 10:00 AM. Don't you be late." He winked, in confidence, as he tossed a shilling to him.

Catching the coin, Glunt smiled. "Yessir!" With that, he ran off, leaving Big Bessie in the doorway with a frown on her face.

ΩΩΩ

Thursday, July 27, 1769
9:30 AM

The following morning, the doors and windows of the Snug Harbor Tavern were wide open to air the place out. Amos was again wiping down the bar while Imp was busy with a mop, swabbing the taproom floor. Angus was playfully jousting with every movement of the mop. Imp grumbled, "I don't know why some of these ladies can't do this instead of me. I have work to do at the *Gazette* with Mr. Edes."

Amos, carrying an empty barrel, smiled. "Those ladies have been working all night, my boy. And the work they do takes a bundle of energy. They's tired! I'm sure of it."

Amanda trudged down the stairs, noting that the clock read ten o'clock. "Give me a cup of tea, Amos." She rubbed her eyes as she pulled her shift closer to cover her exposed bosom. "I hate mornings," she said to no one.

Amos gave a deep baritone laugh. "It was busy last night, Ms. Amanda. I expect you would be tired. But don't you worry; me and Imp and Angus got the chores around here handled."

Imp looked up at the sound of his name. Leaning on the mop, he glanced at the clock on the mantle. "I got work at the *Gazette*, Ms. Amanda. The moppin' is finished," he pleaded.

Nodding her head, she said absently, "Go ahead, Imp." As an afterthought, she added, "You tell Mr. Hancock, if you see him, that there is a message for him down here at the tavern. He'll understand."

With that, Imp placed his red feather in his cap and sprinted out the door and down Fish Street. It was half past 10:00 AM.

Meanwhile, Emmet Glunt had just left the Old State House meeting with Sheriff Greenleaf, heading toward Long Wharf.

Imp passed Faneuil Hall, turning right on King Street at Long Wharf. As he started up the street, Big Bessie Clump, wearing her mobcap and red dressing gown, stepped out into the street to purchase vegetables from a huckster's cart. She smiled broadly. "Imp, it is so good to see you this morning. Come over here and let me get you an apple. Now tell me; what's going on down at the Snug Harbor this morning?"

Imp moved closer, saying, "Can't really stop, Ms. Bessie. I gotta get to the *Gazette*."

At that moment, Glunt stopped in his tracks at the doorway to the Bunch of Grapes, as he did the previous night. This time his eyes were riveted on the red feather, fluttering in the July breeze, in Imp's tricorn. Without hesitation, he leaped from the doorway, striking Imp in the back and knocking him into Bessie, who dropped her produce. Imp was sprawled in the street when Glunt kicked him in the ribs, grabbing his tricorn. "You won't be needin' this red feather any longer, Pimp. As of now, you and the Snug Harbor Tavern are out of business." He laughed as he ran off down the street.

Bessie, having recovered from the assault, yelled, "You little bastard. Come back here." By that time, Glunt had turned the corner and was running to the safety of Milk Street. "Are you all right, Imp?" she asked, dusting him off.

With a frown, Imp said, "I'm all right." Shaking his head and staring at his tricorn, he added, "I lost my feather." Turning up the street, he continued, "Gotta be getting to the *Gazette*, Ms. Bessie."

Big Bessie looked in the direction of Glunt's retreat. She mumbled to herself, "Snug Harbor . . . out of business." She immediately turned on her heels and rushed back into the Bunch of Grapes, mumbling, "I'd best get my fat ass down to Amanda. Something is brewing, and it stinks."

ΩΩΩ

Thursday, July 27, 1769
11:00 AM

Sheriff Greenleaf stood at the upstairs window in Governor Bernard's office, gazing down the length of King Street. His eyes seemed to penetrate the back of Emmet Glunt's head, as he made his way toward Long Wharf. Turning back to the room, he asked slowly, "Well, Mr. Hutchinson, what do you think?"

Thomas Hutchinson walked over to the sidebar, slowly pouring himself a glass of Madeira. He looked at Francis Bernard, who had busied himself with a sheaf of documents. "Its not so much what I think but rather what Governor Bernard has decided." The statement seemed to hang in the air. Hubert Slank strode over to the window to stand at Greenleaf's side, sharing the view of King Street.

Bernard leaned back in his seat, holding his fingers in tentlike fashion, obviously deep in thought. Finally, he arose saying, "Hand me one of those glasses of wine, Thomas." Looking at Slank and Greenleaf, he spoke sternly, "Gentlemen, I have news to share with you and, hopefully, a solution to this new development." Accepting a glass from Hutchinson, he wandered across the room to a more comfortable chair.

"What's the news, Governor?" queried Hutchinson in a relaxed tone.

"First, let me address this new situation with this Glunt lad. From what you gentlemen tell me, this boy could prove to be very dangerous. Am I correct?"

"More than dangerous, Governor," said Greenleaf. "If that brat opens his mouth to the wrong people, our whole network could be dissolved. For me personally, it could be implied that I let the murder of a redcoat go unreported to His Majesty's army. We all know that there was absolutely no investigation whatsoever."

Hutchinson grinned. "Not really a factor, Stephen. With all the desertions, the whole town figured this redcoat had departed like all the others. Besides, no body was ever found. As a judge, I would need a dead body to try someone for a murder."

Slank spoke up slowly, "Perhaps it is time for me to share a bit more information, gentlemen. I have it from reliable sources, namely, the fat man and the old sailor, that this situation goes much deeper. Our real situation is with this candlemaker Teezle."

Bernard laughed. "What bearing could an insignificant candlemaker have on us? He was merely a minor spy in our network, wasn't he?"

Slank shook his head, "It pains me to tell you this, Governor, but that insignificant candlemaker proved to be one of the best agents of Omega we ever recruited. The fat man did a premier job with him."

"Go on, Slank. This is getting interesting," prodded Bernard.

"Teezle worked so well with the strumpets that he was able to become a trusted member of not only the Sons of Liberty, but also a trusted comrade to the redcoats at the same time. He was so good that he was present when that lummox of a redcoat killed that poor doxy at the Bunch of Grapes. It seems she was helping the redcoats in his regiment desert." He paused to look at Greenleaf.

As expected, Greenleaf exploded, "You mean to tell me that you knew who killed that doxy, and you left me wavering and looking foolish? That big fat Bessie bitch raked me over the coals, and I suffered a ton of abuse from the rabble out there."

Hutchinson interjected, "It was necessary, Stephen. You were kept ignorant of the facts on my orders. We couldn't afford to let you have any reason to drag the army into an investigation. After all, what's another dead doxy to the town of Boston?"

Clearing his throat, Slank continued, "After that mess at the Bunch of Grapes, this same sergeant major apparently decided to wander down to the Snug Harbor Tavern to kill another strumpet. Only this time, he picked Teezle's main contact for Omega. The candlemaker killed him to protect her."

Bernard stood impatiently, "The solution is simple; we sacrifice this Teezle in the name of justice."

Hutchinson chortled, "As a justice of the superior court, I can guarantee this candlemaker will make no trouble and will be eternally quiet – after a fair trial, of course."

Slank raised his hand, "Not so fast, gentlemen. You see, the surviving doxy and this Teezle have formed a bit of a partnership. And contrary to orders, they have saved certain documents that should have been destroyed. Those documents are instructions with the Omega seal. If they get into the wrong hands, we can all find ourselves in the Tower of London."

"And Sam Adams wins!" growled Bernard. "By god, I will not let that happen."

"I agree," said Hutchinson, calmly. "There is only one other solution. Teezle must be convinced that he is cherished and loved. Meanwhile, our little informant Glunt must be eliminated." He looked sternly at Slank. "It's one or the other, gentlemen."

"I feel the old sailor should have a meeting with the fat man," said Slank. "I have a feeling that our little lad will not see the next sunrise." He marched out the door without another word.

Sheriff Greenleaf muttered, "The least you could do, Governor, is let me – "

Holding his hand up in a silencing motion, Bernard said, "It was and is for the best, Stephen. You'll have to trust our judgment. Or, perhaps I should say, Mr. Hutchinson's judgment."

"What does that mean exactly?" asked the sheriff.

"Actually, that is the other news I was speaking of," said Bernard. He wandered over to his desk, lifting a stack of documents. "This is the latest packet from London. Per my request, I have been summoned to London for consultations about the situation here in the colony of Massachusetts."

Hutchinson stared in astonishment. "When do you plan to leave, Francis? And who will replace you?"

"Actually, I'll be leaving on August 1, a few days from now," said a smiling Bernard. "Let's face it, Thomas. I have done what I could here. At my recommendation, General MacKay has removed the Sixty-fourth and Sixty-fifth regiments back to their original stations. This reduction has forced Sam Adams and his rabble to lessen their rhetoric and resort to merely complaining about the right to tax the citizens. That is something he will always complain about. Now, with me leaving, I feel you, as my temporary replacement, should have a better time of it than I. Perhaps they will work with you, Thomas. You've gone to Harvard College together, and you share the same business interests. I'll do what I can to help you from the halls of Parliament. I understand that there is a peerage in this for me."

"Sheriff Greenleaf and I will certainly do our best in your absence, Governor," said Hutchinson. "We will look forward to your return."

"We'll see about that," murmured Bernard. "We'll see!"

ΩΩΩ

Thursday, July 27, 1769
1:00 PM

"Tell me again, Imp. Exactly, what did he say?" asked Hancock, urgently. Standing by the window, Sam Adams gazed at the foot traffic on Queen Street. To his dismay, a detachment of redcoats passed by the window below.

Imp looked about the room at those gathered at the *Gazette*. Joseph Warren, Ben Church, and Paul Revere stood quietly as Hancock probed for information. "As I said, Emmet Glunt stole my red feather and said that the Snug Harbor Tavern is finished."

"Who is this chap? And who exactly does this Glunt work for?" interrupted Revere.

"He's apprenticed to that candlemaker on Milk Street. I don't know his name," muttered Imp. "I did the best I could, but I didn't see him coming. Otherwise, I would have – "

"Don't worry about it," said Hancock calmly. Turning to the others, he asked, "Do any of you know about this candlemaker on Milk Street?"

"I do," said Revere angrily. "His name's Teezle. And listen to me, gentlemen. I have seen this fellow mingling with Mackintosh and our Sons of Liberty. That tells me that somehow this apprentice has learned a bit too much."

Warren added, "From what we hear, it seems that this Glunt is working for the Tories or maybe the redcoats themselves."

Church chuckled, "He's certainly no friend to our little Imp here."

Sam Adams interrupted. "Enough talk, gentlemen. Paul, I need you to get in touch with Mackintosh. Let's have him talk with Teezle as soon as possible and get this Glunt taken care of. The last thing we need is a mouthy little apprentice messing with our hard work. At last, we have Bernard and his army on the run, and I expect to keep them there."

Revere nodded, "Consider it done, Sam." He rushed out the door.

Sam looked at the others. "I'll stay here at the *Gazette* with Dr. Warren, gentlemen. We have a few columns to write. I suggest you get our minions out on the street to learn what is going on. Since those two regiments left, I've heard very little from the Old State House."

Hancock patted Imp on the head. "You come with me, Imp. I have a new red feather for you at my warehouse down by the Snug Harbor Tavern. Let's get going."

Dr. Church said, "I too have business to take care of on the north side of town. I'll see you gentlemen later."

ΩΩΩ

Thursday, July 27, 1769
2:00 PM

Big Bessie Clump sat heavily in her seat in the taproom of the Snug Harbor Tavern, gasping for air. She had her mobcap pushed back from her sweaty brow as she fanned herself. "Give me another cold tankard of ale, Amos. I'm just dying in this heat. I thought you folks always had a sea breeze down here."

Amanda sat across from her, listening intently. "You were saying something about Imp, Bessie." Hope and Purity had joined them, also agitated about any harm to their boy.

Gulping the cold ale, Bessie stammered, "Listen, girlie. There's something brewing in this town. That fat little kid that assaulted Imp said something about the Snug Harbor Tavern being finished. I figured you should know."

"Who assaulted Imp? What kid said this? And just where is Imp now?" asked Amanda anxiously, raising her voice. Hope and Purity muttered the same question.

"I think you've seen him around. A little fat kid! Sells candles or some such stuff," said Bessie. "As for Imp, he said something about going to the *Gazette*."

Sitting back in thought, Amanda said, "I think I know who this fat little – "

Just then, Imp ran in the front door. Immediately Amanda arose from her chair, relief in her eyes. As she embraced the little boy, her eyes caught the vision of Hancock standing in the doorway.

"Pardon the interruption, Mrs. Griffith. I'm sorry to intrude, but could I have a private word with you?" Hancock asked.

"Excuse me a moment, Bessie," said Amanda. She stepped to the end of the bar, where Hancock joined her.

"What happened with Imp?" muttered Amanda, unconsciously straightening her hair. "Bessie has told me what she saw, but it seems that the lad has spent time with you."

Imp jumped on the bar at Amanda's side. "He's all right," said Hancock.

Imp echoed the sentiment. "Look, Amanda. I have a new feather. As for that Glunt, I – "

Her cold stare stopped him at midsentence. Even Amos stopped his swabbing with a mop behind the bar. Angel seemed frozen in place, holding a dripping mug. The silence was deafening.

Hancock continued, "Don't worry about this, Amanda. We have people who will take care of this kid named Glunt on Milk Street. Apparently, he knows too much because he works for this Teezle chap. It seems that he has taken some of this information to the wrong people. Again, it will be handled tonight. I'll let you know, if I hear anything more. Now I have work to do." He rushed out the door, headed for his warehouses on Hancock's Wharf.

Amanda looked coldly at her bartender. "Amos, I want to be sure this Glunt kid never touches Imp again."

"I understand, Ms. Amanda. I understand," said Amos in a flat tone.

No one noticed that Hope had rushed up the stairs for no apparent reason.

ΩΩΩ

Thursday, July 27, 1769
11:00 PM

Gerty Teezle stumbled down the stairs, a lone candle in her hand to light her way. "What in hell is all the racket down here, Glunt? I'd better not find you with – " She stopped at the doorway of the back workroom on her way to the cramped little storeroom where Glunt had his cot. "EEK! EEK!" she screamed.

Zeke Teezle, in his night shirt, stumbled down the stairs, yelling, "Shut your trap, Gerty. You'll wake the whole town. What's the – " He too stopped at Gerty's side. "Oh my god!" he muttered.

Their eyes beheld a pair of fat chubby legs sticking up from a barrel of tallow. Those legs could belong to only one person, Emmet Glunt. Gerty immediately turned, darting to the front door. Before Zeke could stifle her actions, she had screamed for the night watchman. In no time at all, every denizen of Milk Street had been aroused and had congregated in the street.

It was past midnight when Sheriff Greenleaf arrived. He carefully examined the splayed rigid legs protruding from the barrel of tallow, noting bite marks on the ankles. As he asked questions of Zeke and Gerty, a group of men removed Emmet Glunt's body. "Where do you want the body taken?" asked one man. Without looking up, Greenleaf said, "Take him to Dr. Church. He can take care of it. Tell him that I'll meet with him after daybreak."

Gerty was in tears, as she huddled her head into Zeke Teezle's puny chest. Sheriff Greenleaf stood looking at the disheveled couple. "Since you didn't see anyone, it will be hard to solve this. Are you certain he couldn't have simply slipped and fell into the barrel?"

"Not a chance," said Gerty defiantly. "This was murder, Sheriff. Murder I tell you!"

Turning to the door, Greenleaf said, "Why don't you get some sleep? If I learn anything more, I'll let you know. Sorry about your loss, Mr. Teezle."

As he wandered down the street, he muttered to himself, "I wonder what could have bit the kid on the ankles?"

ΩΩΩ

Friday, July 28, 1769
8:00 AM

Zeke and Gerty were awakened to the sound of pushcarts on Milk Street and vendors howling for business. The morning sun was streaming through the window, promising another hot July day. They rumbled out of bed, slipped into their work clothes, and stumbled down the stairs. Zeke rushed to the front of the shop to open the door, when he noticed a note on the floor at the entrance. His suspicions were confirmed when he saw the "Ω" on the wax seal. Looking at the stairway to see if Gerty was yet on her way down, he hurriedly opened the note.

Teezle,

Good work. Glunt had to go, and you did what was necessary. We owe you and will not forget. You can expect a few golden guineas for taking care of this.

Ω

ΩΩΩ

Meanwhile, Governor Bernard sat in his office, cleaning out his desk and boxing personal items. Hutchinson, Greenleaf, Slank, and the fat man arrived as a group, much to his surprise. Looking up from his tasks, Bernard asked, "Well, gentlemen, did you take care of our problem?"

Hutchinson said, "You tell him, Slank."

Clearing his throat, Slank said quietly, "Governor, the problem has been taken care of."

"Well, that's good. I congratulate you. How did you do it? Without sharing too many gory details, of course," said Bernard.

"That's the point, Governor," said Slank. "We don't know who did it."

Greenleaf interjected, "That's a fact, Governor. Glunt was found drowned in a barrel of tallow."

"But we didn't do it," said the fat man. "The old sailor and I stopped by to take care of it, as planned, and all we found were these legs sticking out from the barrel of tallow. So we left immediately. Our guess is that Teezle took care of the fat little bastard himself."

With a muted laugh, Bernard said, "This Teezle seems to be a real killer. First, he kills a few doxies, then a redcoat, and now a young troublemaker!"

Hutchinson added with a smile, "We will be sure to reward him and keep him as part of Omega."

ΩΩΩ

At noon, Sam Adams sat with his inner circle in the upstairs room of the Green Dragon. "All right, gentlemen, tell me about it. How did we take care of that little rat who threatened Imp?" He looked directly at Paul Revere.

Paul lifted his shoulders in surrender. "We don't know, Sam. When Mackintosh and his men arrived to take care of the situation, Sheriff Greenleaf was talking with Teezle, and I'm told they witnessed the fat little body being carried from the candle shop. It's my guess that Teezle killed the little bastard himself to save us the trouble; at least, that's what Mackintosh thinks. This Teezle must be a real killer."

"How about that, gentlemen?" asked Adams.

Hancock smiled. "Seems he saved us from soiling our hands. I'll find some way to repay the fellow. The least we can do is purchase our candles there from now on."

ΩΩΩ

The heat of the sun was made bearable by the stiff ocean breeze coming through the open windows and doors. The Snug Harbor taproom was cool and fully occupied with shipwrights and dockhands catching a late afternoon meal.

Imp wandered in and leaped on the bar, saying, "Just been to the *Gazette* and got the latest issue; I need you to read this to me."

Amanda took the paper from his hands, reading aloud, MILK STREET APPRENTICE DROWNS IN TALLOW. Amos, that is one nasty headline, isn't it?"

Amos shook his head in disbelief. "I find that the older I get, the stranger I find things in this world. Go figure a kid drowning in tallow. Terrible! Just terrible!" He continued to mumble to himself, as he wandered to the end of the bar, peeling wax from beneath his fingernails. Unconsciously, he tossed a scrap of bread to Angus, happily wagging his stub of a tail.

ΩΩΩ

EPILOGUE

August 1, 1769

T HE SUN WAS beginning to set, creating a warm glow over the harbor. Sam Adams and John Hancock stood before the mansion on Beacon Street, enjoying the vista of Boston, which included the Common, the Neck, and the harbor. When the fireworks lit up the sky and the church bells rang, both men were absorbed in thought.

At last, Hancock thought as he watched the king's frigate make its way out of the harbor, *with Governor Bernard gone, I can get back to business.* On the other hand, Sam Adams wondered aloud, "That's one tyrant down, John. Now we should consider how to handle Hutchinson."

"Will you ever be satisfied, Sam?" muttered Hancock. Adams simply gazed at the harbor.

ΩΩΩ

Thomas Hutchinson stared out the second-story window of Old State House, watching the frigate struggle with a weak wind to make its way from the harbor. He cringed at the incessant bell ringing.

Andrew Oliver, Sheriff Greenleaf, John Mien, Hubert Slank, and the fat man sat around the room, having been summoned earlier. Greenleaf, interrupting Hutchinson's private musings at the window, said, "Mr. Hutchinson, I'm sure I speak for all the others here, when I say that we are certain that under your personal control, the streets of Boston will finally enjoy the peace we have been waiting for."

Turning to the group of men, Hutchinson smiled. "I'm not so sure, gentlemen. Adams and his so-called patriots are men of perpetual discontent. Little do they realize that I am prepared to use the king's army more effectively than our dear friend Francis Bernard." Looking to the rear of the room, he added, "Doctor, let's be sure to keep Omega alert. I want news of Adams's every move, and let's not forget Hancock."

ΩΩΩ

Seated in the back room of the candle shop, Gerty Teezle picked at her teeth as she muttered, "Zeke, where in the world did they come from?"

Teezle, seated next to her, replied in astonishment, "I'm not exactly sure, Gerty. I just found them by that barrel of tallow after making my deliveries." Both leaned forward, as Teezle emptied the two pouches on the table. Their eyes widened into globes, as they beheld twenty gold coins. "I must be doing something right, Gerty. Those clanging bells remind me that we should get to church to thank God for his blessings."

Looking over her shoulder, Gerty pointed to the barrel. "Now you can afford to get rid of that thing. It would be a blessing to see it gone. There's something ghostly about it, Zeke."

ΩΩΩ

Out of her second-story window of the Snug Harbor Tavern, Amanda stared at the departing frigate with the sagging sails. "It's not making much headway, is it?" she asked rhetorically.

Standing at her side, he pulled her closer. "Forget about the governor and all like him, Amanda. Now that he is gone, this Boston rabble has nothing to complain about. And I will have more time to spend with you."

Looking into his eyes and then at the red coat hanging over a chair, she responded, "I hope you're right, Captain." The song from the taproom below, in contrast to the church bells, made them laugh.

> *The governor was filled with dread,*
> *Scared that he soon would be dead,*
> *So he's gone to sea,*
> *He left without me,*
> *I came to the Snug Harbor instead.*

ΩΩΩ

As the sun was beginning to set, Francis Bernard, royal governor of the colony of Massachusetts, gazed at Boston from the ramparts of the HMS *Rippon*. He could clearly make out the spire of the Old North Church, the Old State House, and even Hancock's mansion on Beacon Hill. The ship's captain, resplendent in blue and gold, quietly eased his way next to him at the rail saying, "I'll venture that you are filled with joy to be leaving that den of thieves and rioters, Governor. If only this wind would pick up, we could be free of this harbor." Gazing aloft at the sails, he added, "I'll get the sailing master to add more canvas." Again looking westward, he continued, "Be advised that we have stowed, by the purser's count, 36,563 ounces of Custom House silver in the hold."

Bernard smiled with his gaze fixed on the Boston skyline. His visage reflected the glow of a bonfire that had been set on Fort Hill. Every church bell in the town was ringing. "It seems to me, Captain, that Boston is quite happy to be rid of me as I am to depart."

"Hell with that rabble, Governor. We should make Portsmouth, England, in five weeks with a fair wind and I'll see to it personally that the sailing is safe and comfortable as can be for you. I expect that you will join me shortly in my cabin for dinner, sir. I'm only sorry that your wife and children couldn't make the passage with you."

Bernard turned with a wry smile. "Thank you, Captain. It will be a pleasure and an honor to join you. As for my family, I am confident that they will join me in England in short order. I've been advised that the Crown will honor me with a peerage as a baronet and my wife wouldn't miss that for the world. Eventually, after these radicals come to their senses, I'll return to take care of my properties and establish order."

His thoughts were a tart mixture of anger and relief. Thanks to Adams and Hancock, it was obvious that the citizens of Boston had been convinced that all their problems with increased taxes and the invasion of the king's troops were entirely due to his nefarious activities. Now it was time to bid these colonials a fond farewell, leaving the burden of mob rule in the hands of Thomas Hutchinson. He grumbled to himself, realizing the winds were not favorable, and the *Rippon* merely inched her way slowly from the harbor.

After sunset, the ship began to enjoy the heavy swells of the Atlantic Ocean. By that time, Bernard sat at dinner in the captain's cabin. Despite the fine company of ship's officers, he couldn't rid his mind of Boston's jubilation and celebrations at his departure. Bells rang, fireworks exploded, cannon fire echoed, and flags had waved. The joy of Boston was devastating to Bernard. Little did he realize that he would never return to the American colonies.

Come back for the sequel, *Sowing the Seeds of Love – and War*, where you will find Amanda and Imp mired in the hell of the Boston Massacre and the retribution of the Boston Tea Party. Through it all, the Snug Harbor Tavern somehow prevails, as the patriot leaders Adams, Hancock, Warren, Revere, and the others lead us to the formation of a new country, the United States of America.